POT LUCK

ÉMILE ZOLA was born in Paris in 18.. .e son of a Venetian engineer and his French wife. He grew u. ...-Provence, where he made friends with Paul Cézanne. A... ...ished school career and a brief period of dire pov... ...s. Zol. joined the newly founded publishing firm of H... ...rt in 1866 to live by his pen. He had already pub... ... his first collection of short stories. Other novel... ...ed until in 1871 Zola published the first volume ... .cquart series with the subtitle *Histoire naturelle et socia... ...e sous le Second Empire*, in which he sets out to illustrate the ...uence of heredity and environment on a wide range of characters a..d milieux. However, it was not until 1877 that his novel *L'Assommoir*, a study of alcoholism in the working classes, brought him wealth and fame. The last of the Rougon–Macquart series appeared in 1893 and his subsequent writing was far less successful, although he achieved fame of a different sort in his vigorous and influential intervention in the Dreyfus case. His marriage in 1870 had remained childless but his extremely happy liaison in later life with Jeanne Rozerot, initially one of his domestic servants, gave him a son and a daughter. He died in 1902.

BRIAN NELSON is Professor of French at Monash University, Melbourne. His publications include *Zola and the Bourgeoisie* and, as editor, *Naturalism in the European Novel: New Critical Perspectives* and *Forms of Commitment: Intellectuals in Contemporary France*. He has translated and edited Zola's *The Ladies' Paradise* for Oxford World's Classics, and his current projects include a study of dandies and dandyism from Charles Baudelaire to David Bowie.

OXFORD WORLD'S CLASSICS

*For over 100 years Oxford World's Classics have brought
readers closer to the world's great literature. Now with over 700
titles—from the 4,000-year-old myths of Mesopotamia to the
twentieth century's greatest novels—the series makes available
lesser-known as well as celebrated writing.*

*The pocket-sized hardbacks of the early years contained
introductions by Virginia Woolf, T. S. Eliot, Graham Greene,
and other literary figures which enriched the experience of reading.
Today the series is recognized for its fine scholarship and
reliability in texts that span world literature, drama and poetry,
religion, philosophy and politics. Each edition includes perceptive
commentary and essential background information to meet the
changing needs of readers.*

OXFORD WORLD'S CLASSICS

ÉMILE ZOLA

Pot Luck
(Pot-Bouille)

Translated with an Introduction and Notes by
BRIAN NELSON

OXFORD
UNIVERSITY PRESS

OXFORD
UNIVERSITY PRESS

Great Clarendon Street, Oxford OX2 6DP

Oxford University Press is a department of the University of Oxford.
It furthers the University's objective of excellence in research, scholarship,
and education by publishing worldwide in

Oxford New York

Athens Auckland Bangkok Bogotá Buenos Aires Calcutta
Cape Town Chennai Dar es Salaam Delhi Florence Hong Kong Istanbul
Karachi Kuala Lumpur Madrid Melbourne Mexico City Mumbai
Nairobi Paris São Paulo Singapore Taipei Tokyo Toronto Warsaw

with associated companies in Berlin Ibadan

Oxford is a registered trade mark of Oxford University Press
in the UK and in certain other countries

Published in the United States
by Oxford University Press Inc., New York

British Library Cataloguing in Publication Data

Data available

Library of Congress Cataloging in Publication Data

Zola, Emile, 1840–1902
[Pot-bouille. English]
Pot luck / Emile Zola : translated with an introduction and notes
by Brian Nelson.
I. Nelson, Brian, 1946–   . II. Title.
PQ2514.P6E5 1999 843'.8—dc21 98–19514

ISBN 978-0-19-283179-8

6

Typeset at The Spartan Press Ltd,
Lymington, Hants
Printed in Great Britain by
Clays Ltd, St Ives plc

CONTENTS

INTRODUCTION

Pot Luck is the story of an apartment building and of the juxtaposed lives of its bourgeois tenants and their servants—a simmering, bubbling melting-pot of public and private life, class and gender relations. The novel's French title, *Pot-Bouille*, is virtually untranslatable. 'Restless House', the title chosen for a previous edition of the novel, captures something of the mood of the building's tenants and the metaphoric importance of the building itself, though 'Stew' or 'Stewpot', with their associations with the ordinary meal, household routine, and everyday bourgeois life, are the closest literal equivalents in English. However, there is no term in English which conveys so concisely Zola's idea of a melting-pot of sexual promiscuity, while at the same time incorporating the culinary notion of a stew, as well as a swill of fetid household waste, which is the author's metaphor for the confusions and contradictions of bourgeois society and the messy mishmash of moral and physical corruption concealed beneath the veneer of bourgeois respectability.

Pot Luck is the tenth in Zola's great cycle of twenty novels, *Les Rougon-Macquart*, on which he began work in 1870 at the age of 30, and to which he devoted the next quarter of a century. The subtitle of the cycle, *The Natural and Social History of a Family Under the Second Empire*, suggests the way that at one level Zola gives us a documentary account of French society in the second half of the nineteenth century. It is the result of dedicated first-hand observation and research—in the Halles, the department stores, the mines, the French countryside—combining a novelist's skills with those of the investigative journalist in a way that only Balzac can match. In his representation of various milieux Zola always combined the vision of a painter with that of a sociologist, attentive to the patterns and rituals that govern the daily life of a given community. From the vantage-point of the fortunes of one family, Zola examined the political, moral, and above all, sexual landscape of the late nineteenth century, in a way that scandalized the grossly materialistic and hypocritical bourgeois society of France both before and after the disaster of the Franco–Prussian War.

Zola's basic themes include nature, the body, and the working class. His representation of the natural and material world is often more expressionist than impressionist; he animates it with extraordinary anthropomorphic life, giving it a heightened, hallucinatory quality, so that in *Pot Luck*, for example, the apartment house itself, with its sham façade and filthy inner courtyard, becomes one of the characters of the novel. His symbolic world is deeply marked by patterns of ambivalence, an inversion of signs: the nourishing earth becomes deadly, Eros becomes Thanatos, catastrophe is followed by regeneration. Zola's representation of the body and its affects is similarly ambivalent. Although his vision was puritanical, he broke the mould of Victorian moral cant in his representation of sexual appetites, frustrations, and inhibitions; the most innovative aspect of Zola's Naturalism was its discovery of the body. There is a striking recurrence in his fiction of Oedipal situations and of situations that portray women in ambivalent patterns of attraction/repulsion. In psychoanalytic terms, his fiction describes a painful evolution from an experience of sexuality in terms of nauseous anxiety (reflected in *Pot Luck* in his fascination with 'filth') to the attainment of salvation in the idealized possession, in the later works, of a woman who is simultaneously wife, sister, and servant.[1] Zola's new vision of the body is matched by a new vision of the working class, combining the carnivalesque images of the Rabelais/Molière tradition (reflected in the name-day feast in *L'Assommoir* and the miners' fair in *Germinal*, for instance) with serious analysis of its socio-political condition. For Zola the power of mass working-class movements is a radically new, and frightening, element in human history, whose presence is felt to underlie the cynical but frightened discussions of politics in *Pot Luck*. And yet (especially as described in *Germinal*) the people lose their struggle for self-determination: the motor of revolution, like all machines, real and metaphorical, in *Les Rougon-Macquart*, cannot avoid the laws of entropy.[2]

In *Pot Luck*, as in other novels of the series, Zola reveals his fascination with moral and physical degeneracy within the individual, the family, and society. The novel is the most acerbic expression in the Rougon-Macquart cycle of the themes adumbrated in *The Fortune of the Rougons*: bourgeois hypocrisy and corruption.

[1] See Jean Borie, *Zola et les mythes, ou de la nausée au salut* (Paris: Seuil, 1971).
[2] See Michel Serres, *Feux et signaux de brume: Zola* (Paris: Grasset, 1975).

The Kill had shown the moral corruption behind social glitter, *The Belly of Paris* the brutality behind lower-middle-class respectability, *L'Assommoir* the misery of the working-class slums behind the public splendour of the Empire. *Pot Luck* continues the sexual denunciation of *Nana*, which immediately preceded it in the cycle, but on a different level and in a different register. Sexuality is now viewed in a more sharply satirical framework. While *Nana* had revealed the sexual dissipation of the upper classes through the mythical figure of the prostitute, *Pot Luck* shows that the bourgeoisie are no less squalid in their sexual habits, just more dissimulating. *Pot Luck* was also intended to complement *L'Assommoir*, and bourgeois applause at what it saw as the representation of working-class degeneracy in the latter novel was to become howls of rage at the unflinching portrayal of its own debasement. Adultery is one manifestation of a diseased civilization, frustrated by a moral code so dehumanizing that it is unworkable, all normal biological impulses transformed into tawdry exercises in lust and debauchery. Bourgeois promiscuity has the effect of sterilizing the family and contaminating the environment. This is a society that oozes with the excretions of lust, where unwanted babies are murdered by their mothers, and where those that survive grow up to be pitiable individuals stricken with nervous disorders, mental instability, skin diseases, and other maladies. The bourgeoisie is in danger, Zola suggests, of sinking under the weight of its own corruption, its pretended virtue merely a façade concealing the degradation within.

Tony Tanner observes, in his study of adultery in the novel,[3] that the ability to mark out boundaries for human activity is what distinguishes the human from the pre-human, and is intimately linked to the institution of marriage, just as promiscuity is linked to barbarity. The marriage contract gives form to society and identity to individuals, families, and in turn, nations. The ability to identify one's father and one's offspring is intrinsic to family lineage where property can be bequeathed and inherited, citizenship established, societies and nations founded. In short, marriage has been the catalyst of modern man, and the alternative—which is what adultery signifies—could be envisaged as a return to chaos. The nineteenth-

---

[3] Tony Tanner, *Adultery in the Novel: Contract and Transgression* (Baltimore and London: Johns Hopkins University Press, 1979).

century bourgeoisie accorded the greatest importance to the stability of marriage as an institution, for marriage was what guaranteed the stability and permanence of bourgeois society. By means of the ownership of land, property, and capital, safeguarded and transmitted by means of the family, the bourgeoisie had mastered the lower orders of society; in other words, it had appropriated from the former nobility the customs and laws which regulated society, and through this appropriation it had not only won control of the nation's workers but had also sought to reaffirm its ascendancy over women. Adultery on the part of a wife was denounced because it usurped the laws men used to determine the social role of women—to bring into the world only the offspring of their husbands, thereby ensuring the purity of their husbands' lineage. The infidelities of the bourgeoisie were much more significant than those of the working class because, as transgressors of their own law, the bourgeoisie put at risk an order of civilization structured precisely to sustain their own privileged position. Nineteenth-century novelists were obsessively drawn to the theme of adultery, and the more searchingly and explicitly they investigated it, the more they risked uncovering the arbitrariness and fragility of the whole bourgeois social order: 'If society depends for its existence on certain rules governing what may be combined and what should be kept separate, then adultery, by bringing the wrong things together in the wrong places (or the wrong people in the wrong beds), offers an attack on those rules, revealing them to be arbitrary rather than absolute.'[4] Written at a time when divorce was generally inconceivable as a viable alternative to an unhappy marriage, the nineteenth-century novel of adultery hints at impending doom for bourgeois civilization once marriage has been displaced, throwing into question the stability of other institutions, such as religion and the law, which sustain the marriage contract.

Adultery in the nineteenth century was most likely, of course, to be that of the husband. While husbands cheated on their wives with near impunity, female infidelity was considered a most reprehensible crime, for it jeopardized what was most prized in bourgeois society: legitimacy of descent. The crime of female adultery was considered so grievous that an adulterous woman could be imprisoned for up to

---

[4] Tanner, *Adultery in the Novel*, 13.

two years,[5] or at the very least expelled from the family home. Female sexuality was thus a constant source of concern for the family and for society as a whole. Piety was impressed upon women in general, and the Church and the bourgeois family combined forces to protect the chastity of adolescent girls. In Catholic France the convent took on the role of moral instructor. Convent instruction was infused with a sense of 'forbidden knowledge'—things carnal were equated with sin, an inquisitive mind with disobedience, and ignorance with purity and innocence.

In *Pot Luck*, the container of the stew of sexual decadence, the apartment building in the Rue de Choiseul, itself provides us with clues as to what lies behind the façade. The beginning of the novel, coinciding with the arrival of Octave Mouret, a young salesman from the provinces come to make his fortune in Paris, describes in great detail the physical appearance of the building. Octave is shown round by the architect Campardon, and is initially overawed by the new building and its extravagant decoration—its gilt carvings, red carpet, and heated main staircase, typical in its gaudy splendour of the new bourgeois constructions of the time. The grand main entrance, with its imitation marble panelling and the cast-iron banisters which were meant to look like old silver, suggests falseness and deceptive appearances. This impression is reinforced by the grotesque image of the imitation windows painted on the blank walls of the courtyard. Octave soon learns, indeed, that structurally the building is far from sound. After twelve years there are enormous cracks and the paint is beginning to peel. The house is a symbol of the society and lifestyles of the bourgeois tenants: everything is for show, the keeping up of appearances, while the foundations are weak. What seems to be a place of prosperity and harmony, in accordance with accepted standards and conventions, is in fact home to a population riddled with defects: hypocrisy, snobbery, tacit sexual permissiveness, and other forms of immorality. The result is instability and tension: in architectural terms, major structural problems.

The social relations between the two types of occupants of the building, the bourgeois tenants and the working-class servants, are at first, and outwardly, presented as rigidly separate—in manners, morals, hygiene, language, education, and wealth. Once again, the structure and décor of the building give symbolic expression to this need for distance and separation: the main staircase is red-carpeted and heated, spacious and brightly lit, while the service stairs are dark, narrow, dirty, and freezing cold; the bourgeois tenants live in the heated apartments at the front of the house, while the servants live in cold, partitioned cubicles under the roof and work in the filthy kitchens overlooking the courtyard; and the neat, paved, well-scrubbed outer courtyard, with its fountain, reserved exclusively for the use of the bourgeois tenants, contrasts with the filthy, foul-smelling inner courtyard onto which face the kitchens and the servants' quarters. The inner courtyard acts as a literal and figurative rubbish dump for the building, and is frequently described in the text as a sewer or cesspool. During the guided tour by Campardon, Octave is introduced to the kitchens and finds the servants exchanging raucous gossip from window to window, with the courtyard below: 'It was as if a sewer had brimmed over' (p. 9). The courtyard becomes a symbolic image of the sordid reality of bourgeois domestic life, and the unwholesome smells become the true essence of the house's moral filth: 'from the depths of the dark, narrow courtyard only the stench of drains came up, like the smell of the hidden filth of the various families, stirred up by the servants' rancour' (p. 105). These physical details reinforce on a symbolic level the enormous disparity and the seemingly unbridgeable distance between the two classes. As Janet Beizer puts it: 'Manifest physical segregation of the lower classes becomes increasingly necessary to the bourgeoisie after 1789, as rigid moral barriers are eroded. In a paradoxical sense . . . the imposing presence of material barriers speaks to the disappearance of more effective if less tangible social barriers.'[6] The bourgeois go to extreme lengths to maintain this segregation, insistently portraying the lower classes as dirty, immoral, promiscuous, stupid—at best a lesser type of human, at worst some kind of wild beast. The bourgeois themselves wish to be seen as respectable, honest, law-abiding citizens, with culture and education on their side—in short, a superior class.

However, just as Octave's initial impressions of the grandeur of the building are shown to be false, so the reader, with Octave as

[6] Janet Beizer, *Ventriloquized Bodies: Narratives of Hysteria in Nineteenth-Century France* (Ithaca and London: Cornell University Press, 1994), 195.

guide, shares in his discoveries that the bourgeois tenants are not what they seem. Admittance into the closed circle of bourgeois society reveals behaviour every bit as promiscuous and immoral as that of the filthy, despised working class: indeed it is worse, because it is hypocritical. No institution held to be sacred by bourgeois society is left unscathed by the actions of the bourgeoisie themselves. Money, manners, and power are what really separate them from their servants, a privileged social encoding that forms the thin veneer of respectability that gives them a specious air of legitimacy and protects them from the gaze of the outside world. Marriage, the cornerstone of bourgeois society, is revealed to be a sham, concealing a multitude of adulteries and betrayals by both husband and wife. The true rationale of marriage is seen to be a contract for the attainment of wealth and social standing, and nothing whatever to do with love and affection. Traditional family virtues—order, comfort, security, generosity, happiness, harmony—are all negated: mothers are go-betweens in the endless quest for husbands, fathers are grotesquely ineffectual. The bourgeois family is corrupted by a conflict of interests in its function as mediator between the individual and society. Its duty to shelter its members from a competitive and brutalizing world is subordinated to its role as defender of the rigid, impersonal laws which the bourgeoisie had constructed to maintain its position in the social order. The family, as the vehicle of a corrupt system, is of little comfort to the individual, frequently rendering him neurotic, depraved, and dissolute. The disorder of family life is reflected in the dirt and untidiness of the kitchens, which provide the analogue, at the level of the individual family, of the central sewer image. Even religion, the provider of moral guidance, is only concerned with external appearances. Father Mauduit is presented more as a worldly than a spiritual man, happy to turn a blind eye to the double standards of his bourgeois parishioners.

The working class and the body, the popular and the natural, are closely identified in Zola. Each functions as a metaphor of the other. The social repression of the servants becomes the reverse side of bourgeois sexual repression, sexual exploitation the counterpart of social exploitation. Adèle, exploited by all, takes on the figure of scapegoat. The agony of her confinement, described with Naturalist intimacy of physical detail, is an image of bourgeois indifference: 'So it wasn't enough to be starved to death, and the dirty drudge whom everyone bullied: her masters had to get her pregnant as well!' (p. 361). Jean Borie describes thus the vicious circle of Zola's social vision:

If the workers are identified with the body, it is because they are condemned by the bourgeoisie to remain separate, to remain workers . . . We may thus formulate the following contradiction: the malady both emanates from the workers and is imposed upon them. Zola, in his 'generosity', gives them absolution, but his social vision remains at an impasse, and it will necessarily remain so as long as the body is constrained to be a kind of infernal prisoner.[7]

Thus Zola systematically reduces the difference separating the bourgeois and the servants, exposing the hypocrisy of the dominant class. They are no more able to control their natural instincts than the working class, but are simply more dissimulating. The satirical implication is that morality, though not in itself bourgeois, is appropriated by Zola's bourgeoisie, since they alone are in a position to abide by its standards, in the sense that they are not put to the test of gross material deprivation. Class difference is a matter of money and power, and has a tenuous hold on the raging forces of sexuality and corruption that lie beneath the surface. What we are left with is precisely a melting-pot, a stew, an undifferentiated world where no clear boundaries remain.

This idea is symbolized by the image of the sewer, which encapsulates Zola's attitude to social relations, and in particular to the blurred boundaries between the classes. As its degenerate moral and sexual behaviour is progressively exposed, the bourgeoisie is seen to become contaminated with the filth of the sewer, tainted with the stench of corruption. Berthe's underwear is of doubtful cleanliness beneath her exterior finery; Trublot, searching for his possessions in the cook Julie's room, creates a cloud of dust and dirt as he shakes out her clothes; the filthy and despised Adèle has sexual liaisons with both Trublot and Duveyrier. The texture of the novel is characterized by impressions of staleness and sourness. Images of ordure are linked to images of mud, evoking a sense of sexual revulsion. The implication is that sexual indulgence is circumscribed by nauseous connotations and destructive consequences.

---

[7] Jean Borie, *Zola et les mythes*, 26–7.

The atmosphere of anxiety and recriminations, of desultory sexual anticipation and dissatisfaction, culminates in the description of Octave and Berthe, in the servant-girl Rachel's room, suddenly overhearing the foul-mouthed talk of the servants, at first describing their various filching triumphs and then reaching a crescendo of sexual gossip which includes cutting comments on both of them: 'Their liaison, so carefully concealed, was now being trailed through all the garbage and slops of the kitchen' (p. 263). The fetid inner courtyard is marked out from the beginning as the workers' physical space; and the association of the bourgeois characters with the image of the sewer implies, as Janet Beizer has suggested, that the bourgeoisie has become infected with working-class failings, thus revealing a class bias implicit in Zola's text on a symbolic level, even though he exposes bourgeois hypocrisy—as equivalent to popular degradation—on another, overt level.

The gynecological secrets contained within whispered conversations between men in the parlor are loudly and repeatedly exposed by the maids in the kitchen . . . Rhetorically confluent with streams of dirty dishwater, rotting cooking wastes, and rank female secretions, the servantwomen's gossip serves as a narrative filtering system that works to purify the very pollution it is designed to convey. The text's recurrent return to the scene of the filthy inner courtyard, the contaminated kitchens, and the foul tongues and bodies of the maids as signifiers of bourgeois degradation effectively purges the bourgeoisie by deflecting the image of its impurity.[8]

Gender relations in the novel are no less warped than class relations. The adulteries of the men in the novel, such as Campardon and Duveyrier, are blamed on the mysterious maladies and hysterical natures of their wives: Mme Campardon has a vague female affliction which prevents her from having sexual relations with her husband, while Mme Duveyrier is depicted as cold, even frigid, and disdainful of her husband, preferring music and the company of her drawing-room. Images of sterility, of a repressed and abnormal sexuality, abound: the taboos of Mme Juzeur, the imperious and calculating 'chastity' of the despotic Mme Josserand, the hysteria of Valérie Vabre, the vaginal constriction of Rose Campardon. Rooms and houses in Zola are often symbolic reflections of the bodies of their owners, bearing the firm imprint of their inhabitants. Thus, just as Nana's gaping, engulfing mansion,

---

[8] Beizer, *Ventriloquized Bodies*, 188.

like a vast vagina, becomes an organic image of its owner, so the closed doors and introverted apartments of *Pot Luck* mirror the inviolable bodies of the bourgeois ladies within them. Despite Zola's intended blanket condemnation of the bourgeoisie in *Pot Luck*, the text of the masters' sins is clearly written in the feminine.

Though deeply marked by the mythology of the bourgeois society Zola endeavours to expose, *Pot Luck* is remarkable in its anti-bourgeois ferocity. The indignant and abusive reactions the novel provoked in its first bourgeois readers and critics was clear testimony to that. The novel moves immediately beyond the strict perspectives of sociological analysis to attain a heightened satiric fantasy. It is important to note, however, that despite Zola's stress on bourgeois degeneracy, his portrayal of the bourgeoisie is not wholly black. Compassion is expressed for M. Josserand, who has a clear sense of personal and professional integrity; Mme Hédouin is a model of industry and virtue; and the philandering adventurer Octave Mouret, though utterly opportunistic, is in a sense the least degenerate character in the novel. Octave always retains control over his appetites, using sex to advance his career, and he wins the respect of his employer Mme Hédouin with his energy and his extraordinary business flair. *The Ladies' Paradise*, the novel Zola wrote immediately after *Pot Luck*, describes his spectacular success as a businessman—as the quintessential Conquering Bourgeois who creates the world's first great department store, a vast dream-machine, in the heart of Paris.

TRANSLATOR'S NOTE

This translation is based on the text of *Pot-Bouille* edited by Henri Mitterand and published in volume 3 of his Bibliothèque de la Pléiade edition of *Les Rougon-Macquart* (Paris: Gallimard, 1964) and as a separate volume (Gallimard, Folio, 1982).

The first translations of the novel were those by Henry Vizetelly (*Piping Hot!*, published by Vizetelly & Co., London, in 1886) and Percy Pinkerton (*Pot-Bouille*, published by the Lutetian Society, London, in 1895). Vizetelly's translation was reprinted as *Lesson in Love* by Pyramid Books, New York (1953), and by World Distributors, London (1958). This version is both grossly abridged (the most glaring omission being the description in the final chapter of the maidservant Adèle's agony as she gives birth alone in a dark, freezing attic room, afraid even to cry out in case she is discovered and reported to the police) and timidly euphemistic in its translation of physical references. Pinkerton's translation (reprinted by Boni & Liveright, New York, 1924, and as *Restless House* by Weidenfeld & Nicolson, London, 1953, by Farrar, Straus & Young, New York, 1953, Elek Books, London, 1957, and Grafton Books, London, 1986) is readable, but is rather stiff and prone to antiquated colloquialisms. I have tried in my own translation to capture the directness and robustness of Zola's language and to give a modern colloquial quality and an appropriate idiomatic pitch to the extensive dialogue between masters, mistresses, concierge, and servants. My choice of title aims to echo the original while evoking some of the confusions and contradictions of bourgeois life, as well as the activities of Octave Mouret as he runs up and down the stairs 'trying his luck' with the various bourgeois ladies he encounters.

I am grateful to the Australia Council for a grant that facilitated the completion of this project, and to Marie-Rose Auguste, Janet Beizer, Barbara Caine, David Davatchi, Judith Luna, Jocelyne Mohamudally, and Jeff New for the help they have given me.

SELECT BIBLIOGRAPHY

Pot Luck (*Pot-Bouille*) was serialized in *Le Gaulois* between 23 January and 14 April 1882 and published in book form by the Librairie Charpentier in 1883. It is included in volume 3 of Henri Mitterand's superb scholarly edition of *Les Rougon-Macquart* in the 'Bibliothèque de la Pléiade' (Paris: Gallimard, 1964). Paperback editions exist in the following popular collections: GF-Flammarion, ed. Colette Becker (Paris, 1969); Folio, ed. Henri Mitterand (Paris, 1982); Livre de Poche, ed. Pierre Marotte (Paris, 1984); Presses Pocket, ed. Gérard Gengembre (Paris, 1990).

Biographies in English

Brown, Frederick, *Zola: A Life* (New York: Farrar, Straus & Giroux, 1995; London: Macmillan, 1996).

Hemmings, F. W. J., *The Life and Times of Émile Zola* (London: Elek, 1977).

Schom, Alan, *Émile Zola: A Bourgeois Rebel* (New York: Henry Holt, 1987; London: Queen Anne Press, 1987).

Walker, Philip, *Zola* (London: Routledge & Kegan Paul, 1985).

Studies of Zola and Naturalism in English

Baguley, David, *Naturalist Fiction: The Entropic Vision* (Cambridge: Cambridge University Press, 1990).

—— (ed.), *Critical Essays on Émile Zola* (Boston, Mass.: G. K. Hall, 1986).

Hemmings, F. W. J., *Émile Zola* (2nd edn., Oxford: Clarendon Press, 1966).

King, Graham, *Garden of Zola* (London: Barrie & Jenkins, 1978).

Lethbridge, R. and Keefe, T. (eds.), *Zola and the Craft of Fiction* (Leicester: Leicester University Press, 1990).

Nelson, Brian (ed.), *Naturalism in the European Novel: New Critical Perspectives* (New York/Oxford: Berg, 1992).

Schor, Naomi, *Zola's Crowds* (Baltimore: Johns Hopkins University Press, 1978).

Wilson, Angus, *Émile Zola: An Introductory Study of his Novels* (London: Secker & Warburg, 1953; rev. edn. 1964).

*Articles and chapters of books in English wholly or partly
devoted to* Pot Luck

Alcorn, Clayton R., 'The Domestic Servant in Zola's Novels', *L'Esprit créateur*, 11 (Winter 1971), 21–35.

Beizer, Janet L., 'The Return of the Maids', in *Ventriloquized Bodies: Narratives of Hysteria in Nineteenth-Century France* (Ithaca: Cornell University Press, 1994), 188–200.

Bryant, David, ' "Deux Amours" in *Pot-Bouille* and *L'Ami Patience*', *French Studies Bulletin*, 23 (1987), 14–15.

Cousins, R. F., 'Recasting Zola: Gérard Philippe's Influence on Duvivier's Adaptation of *Pot-Bouille*', *Literature–Film Quarterly*, 17/3 (1989), 142–8.

Gantrel, Martine, 'Homeless Women: Maidservants in Fiction', in Suzanne Nash (ed.), *Home and its Dislocations in Nineteenth-Century France* (Albany: State University of New York Press, 1993), 247–63.

Grant, Elliott M., 'The Political Scene in Zola's *Pot-Bouille*', *French Studies*, 8 (1954), 342–7.

Nelson, Brian, '*Pot-Bouille*: Black Comedy', in *Zola and the Bourgeoisie* (London: Macmillan; Totowa, New Jersey: Barnes & Noble, 1983), 129–57.

Schor, Naomi, 'Mother's Day: Zola's Women', *Diacritics*, 5/4 (1975), 11–17.

Solomon, Philip, 'The Space of Bourgeois Hypocrisy in Zola's *Pot-Bouille*', *Kentucky Romance Quarterly*, 32/3 (1985), 255–64.

Trilling, Lionel, 'In Defense of Zola', in *A Gathering of Fugitives* (London: Secker & Warburg, 1957), 12–19.

White, Nicholas, 'Carnal Knowledge in French Naturalist Fiction', in Nicholas White and Naomi Segal (eds.), *Scarlet Letters: Fictions of Adultery from Antiquity to the 1990s* (London: Macmillan, 1997), 123–33.

Yates, Susan, 'The Maid in the Bourgeois Imagination' and '*Pot-Bouille*', in *Maid and Mistress: Feminine Solidarity and Class Difference in Five Nineteenth-Century French Texts* (New York: Peter Lang, 1991), 65–92 and 92–125.

On adultery and the novel

Armstrong, Judith, *The Novel of Adultery* (London: Macmillan, 1976).

Tanner, Tony, *Adultery in the Novel: Contract and Transgression* (Baltimore: Johns Hopkins University Press, 1979).

White, Nicholas and Segal, Naomi (eds.), *Scarlet Letters: Fictions of Adultery from Antiquity to the 1990s* (London: Macmillan, 1997).

On the social history of women, the family and the bourgeoisie

Branca, Patricia, *Silent Sisterhood: Middle-Class Women in the Victorian Home* (London: Croom Helm, 1975).

Degler, Carl N., 'What Ought to Be and What Was: Women's Sexuality in the Nineteenth Century', *American Historical Review*, 79 (Dec. 1974), 147–91.

Fuchs, Rachel G., *Poor and Pregnant in Paris: Strategies for Survival in the Nineteenth Century* (New Brunswick, New Jersey: Rutgers University Press, 1992).

Gay, Peter, *The Bourgeois Experience: Victoria to Freud*, ii: *The Tender Passion* (New York: Oxford University Press, 1986).

Goody, Jack, *The Development of the Family and Marriage in Europe* (Cambridge: Cambridge University Press, 1983).

Harrison, Fraser, *The Dark Angel: Aspects of Victorian Sexuality* (London: Sheldon Press, 1977).

Hobsbawm, Eric, 'The Bourgeois World', in *The Age of Capital: 1848–1875* (London: Weidenfeld & Nicolson, 1975; Abacus, 1977), 270–93.

Hudson, Derek (ed.), *Munby: Man of Two Worlds* (London: Murray, 1972).

McLaren, Angus, 'Some Secular Attitudes Toward Sexual Behaviour in France: 1760–1860', *French Historical Studies*, 8/4 (Fall 1974), 604–24.

McMillan, James F., *Housewife or Harlot: The Place of Women in French Society, 1870–1940* (Brighton: Harvester Press, 1981).

Marcus, Stephen, *The Other Victorians* (London: Weidenfeld & Nicolson, 1966).

Mason, Michael, *The Making of Victorian Sexuality* (Oxford: Oxford University Press, 1995).

[Anon.], *My Secret Life* (London, *c.*1890).

Newton, Judith L., Ryan, Mary P. and Walkowitz, Judith R. (eds.), *Sex and Class in Women's History* (London/Boston: Routledge & Kegan Paul, 1985).

Palamari, Demetra, 'The Shark Who Swallowed his Epoch: Family, Nature and Society in the Novels of Emile Zola', in Virginia Tufte and Barbara Myerhoff (eds.), *Changing Images of the Family* (New Haven: Yale University Press, 1979), 155–72.

Pearsall, Ronald, *The Worm in the Bud: The World of Victorian Sexuality* (London: Weidenfeld & Nicolson, 1969).

Perrot, Michelle (ed.), *A History of Private Life*, iv: *From the Fires of Revolution to the Great War* (Cambridge, Mass.: Harvard University Press, 1990).

'Sexuality and the Social Body in the Nineteenth Century', Special Issue, *Representations*, 14 (1986).

Shorter, Edward, *The Making of the Modern Family* (New York: Basic Books, 1975).
— *A History of Women's Bodies* (New York: Basic Books, 1982).
Smith, Bonnie, *Ladies of the Leisure Class: The Bourgeoises of Northern France in the Nineteenth Century* (Princeton: Princeton University Press, 1981).
Zeldin, Theodore, *France 1848–1945*, i: *Ambition, Love and Politics* (Oxford: Oxford University Press, 1973).

Further reading in Oxford World's Classics

Zola, Émile, *L'Assommoir*, trans. Margaret Mauldon, ed. Robert Lethbridge.
— *The Attack on the Mill and Other Stories*, trans. and ed. Douglas Parmée.
— *La Bête humaine*, trans. and ed. Roger Pearson.
— *La Débâcle*, trans. Elinor Dorday, ed. Robert Lethbridge.
— *Germinal*, trans. and ed. Peter Collier, with an introduction by Robert Lethbridge.
— *The Ladies' Paradise*, trans. and ed. Brian Nelson.
— *The Masterpiece*, trans. Thomas Walton, ed. Roger Pearson.
—— *Nana*, trans. and ed. Douglas Parmée.
—— *Thérèse Raquin*, trans. and ed. Andrew Rothwell.

A CHRONOLOGY OF ÉMILE ZOLA

1840   (2 April) Born in Paris, the only child of Francesco Zola
        (b. 1795), an Italian engineer, and Émilie, née Aubert (b. 1819),
        the daughter of a glazier. The Naturalist novelist was later proud
        that 'zolla' in Italian means 'clod of earth'

1843   Family moves to Aix-en-Provence

1844   (27 March) Death of father from pneumonia following a chill
        caught while supervising work on his scheme to supply Aix-en-
        Provence with drinking water

1852–   Becomes a boarder at the Collège Bourbon at Aix. Friendship
        with Baptistin Baille and Paul Cézanne. Zola, not Cézanne, wins
        the school prize for drawing.

1858   (February) Leaves Aix to settle in Paris with his mother (who
        had preceded him in December). Offered a place and bursary at
        the Lycée Saint-Louis. (November) Falls ill with 'brain fever'
        (typhoid) and convalescence is slow

1859   Fails his *baccalauréat* twice

1860   (Spring) Is found employment as a copy-clerk but abandons it
        after two months, preferring to eke out an existence as an
        impecunious writer in the Latin Quarter of Paris

1861   Cézanne follows Zola to Paris, where he meets Camille Pissarro,
        fails the entrance examination to the École des Beaux-Arts, and
        returns to Aix in September

1862   (February) Taken on by Hachette, the well-known publishing
        house, at first in the dispatch office and subsequently as head of
        the publicity department. (31 October) Naturalized as a French
        citizen. Cézanne returns to Paris and stays with Zola

1863   (31 January) First literary article published. (1 May) Manet's
        Déjeuner sur l'herbe exhibited at the Salon des Refusés, which
        Zola visits with Cézanne

1864   (October) *Tales for Ninon*

1865   *Claude's Confession*. A *succès de scandale* thanks to its bedroom
        scenes. Meets future wife Alexandrine-Gabrielle Meley
        (b. 1839), the illegitimate daughter of teenage parents who soon
        separated, and whose mother died in September 1849

1866   Forced to resign his position at Hachette (salary: 200 francs a
        month) and becomes a literary critic on the recently launched
        daily *L'Événement* (salary: 500 francs a month). Self-styled
        'humble disciple' of Hippolyte Taine. Writes a series of

provocative articles condemning the official Salon Selection Committee, expressing reservations about Courbet, and praising Manet and Monet. Begins to frequent the Café Guerbois in the Batignolles quarter of Paris, the meeting-place of the future Impressionists. Antoine Guillemet takes Zola to meet Manet. Summer months spent with Cézanne at Bennecourt on the Seine. (15 November) *L'Événement* suppressed by the authorities

1867 (November) *Thérèse Raquin*

1868 (April) Preface to second edition of *Thérèse Raquin*. (May) Manet's portrait of Zola exhibited at the Salon. (December) *Madeleine Férat*. Begins to plan for the Rougon-Macquart series of novels

1868–70 Working as journalist for a number of different newspapers

1870 (31 May) Marries Alexandrine in a registry office. (September) Moves temporarily to Marseilles because of the Franco–Prussian War

1871 Political reporter for *La Cloche* (in Paris) and *Le Sémaphore de Marseille*. (March) Returns to Paris. (October) Publishes *The Fortune of the Rougons*, the first of the twenty novels making up the Rougon-Macquart series

1872 *The Kill*

1873 (April) *The Belly of Paris*

1874 (May) *The Conquest of Plassans*. First independent Impressionist exhibition. (November) *Further Tales for Ninon*

1875 Begins to contribute articles to the Russian newspaper *Vestnik Evropy* (*European Herald*). (April) *The Sin of Father Mouret*

1876 (February) *His Excellency Eugène Rougon*. Second Impressionist exhibition

1877 (February) *L'Assommoir*

1878 Buys a house at Médan on the Seine, 40 kilometres west of Paris. (June) *A Page of Love*

1880 (March) *Nana*. (May) *Les Soirées de Médan* (an anthology of short stories by Zola and some of his Naturalist 'disciples', including Maupassant). (8 May) Death of Flaubert. (September) First of a series of articles for *Le Figaro*. (17 October) Death of his mother. (December) *The Experimental Novel*

1882 (April) *Pot Luck* (*Pot-Bouille*). (3 September) Death of Turgenev

1883 (13 February) Death of Wagner. (March) *The Ladies' Paradise* (*Au Bonheur des Dames*). (30 April) Death of Manet

1884 (March) *La Joie de vivre*. Preface to catalogue of Manet exhibition

1885   (March) *Germinal*. (12 May) Begins writing *The Masterpiece* (*L'Œuvre*). (22 May) Death of Victor Hugo. (23 December) First instalment of *The Masterpiece* appears in *Le Gil Blas*

1886   (27 March) Final instalment of *The Masterpiece*, which is published in book form in April

1887   (18 August) Denounced as an onanistic pornographer in the *Manifesto of the Five* in *Le Figaro*. (November) *Earth*

1888   (October) *The Dream*. Jeanne Rozerot becomes his mistress

1889   (20 September) Birth of Denise, daughter of Zola and Jeanne

1890   (March) *the Beast in Man*.

1891   (March) *Money*. (April) Elected President of the Société des Gens de Lettres. (25 September) Birth of Jacques, son of Zola and Jeanne

1892   (June) *The Débâcle*

1893   (July) *Doctor Pascal*, the last of the Rougon-Macquart novels. Fêted on a visit to London

1894   (August) *Lourdes*, the first novel of the trilogy *Three Cities*. (22 December) Dreyfus found guilty by a court martial

1896   (May) *Rome*

1898   (13 January) 'J'accuse', his article in defence of Dreyfus, published in *L'Aurore*. (21 February) Found guilty of libelling the Minister of War and given the maximum sentence of one year's imprisonment and a fine of 3,000 francs. Appeal for retrial granted on a technicality. (March) *Paris*. (23 May) Retrial delayed. (18 July) Leaves for England instead of attending court.

1899   (4 June) Returns to France. (October) *Fecundity*, the first of his *Four Gospels*

1901   (May) *Toil*, the second 'Gospel'

1902   (29 September) Dies of fumes from his bedroom fire, the chimney having been capped either by accident or anti-Dreyfusard design. Wife survives. (5 October) Public funeral.

1903   (March) *Truth*, the third 'Gospel', published posthumously. *Justice* was to be the fourth

1908   (4 June) Remains transferred to the Panthéon

Pot Luck

In the Rue Neuve-Saint-Augustin, a hold-up in the traffic stopped the cab which was bringing Octave and his three trunks from the Gare de Lyon. The young man lowered one of the windows, although it was already bitterly cold on that dull November afternoon.* He was surprised at how quickly dusk had fallen in this neighbourhood of narrow streets, swarming with people. The drivers' curses as they lashed their snorting horses, the endless jostling along the pavements, the serried row of shops full of assistants and customers bewildered him; for, though he had imagined Paris to be cleaner than this, he had never hoped to find business so brisk, and he felt that it was publicly offering itself to the appetites of any energetic young man.

The driver leaned back towards him. 'It was the Passage Choiseul you wanted, wasn't it?'

'No, the Rue de Choiseul. It's a new house, I think.'

The cab had only to turn the corner, for the house in question, a big, four-storeyed one, was the second in the street. Its stonework was hardly discoloured, in the middle of the dirty stucco façades of the adjoining buildings. Octave, who had got out and was now standing on the pavement, measured it and studied it with a mechanical glance, from the silk shop on the ground floor to the recessed windows on the fourth floor, which opened on to a narrow terrace. On the first floor, carved female heads supported a cast-iron balcony of intricate design. The surroundings of the windows, roughly chiselled in soft stone, were very elaborate; and lower down, over the ornamental doorway, were two Cupids holding a scroll bearing the number, which was lit up at night by a gas-jet from within.

A stout, fair gentleman, who was coming out of the hall, stopped short when he saw Octave.

'What! You're here already!' he exclaimed. 'I wasn't expecting you until tomorrow.'

'Well,' replied the young man, 'I left Plassans* a day earlier than I'd planned. Is the room not ready?'

'Oh, yes! It fell vacant two weeks ago, and I had it furnished straight away just as you said. If you can wait a moment, I'll take you up.'

Despite Octave's entreaties, he went back into the house. The driver had brought in the three trunks. In the concierge's room a dignified-looking man, with a long, clean-shaven face like a diplomat, stood gravely reading the *Moniteur*.* He deigned, however, to show some concern about the luggage that was being deposited at his door, and stepping forward he asked his tenant, the architect from the third floor as he called him:

'Is this the person, Monsieur Campardon?'

'Yes Monsieur Gourd, this is Monsieur Octave Mouret, for whom I took the room on the fourth floor. He'll sleep there and take his meals with us. Monsieur Mouret is a friend of my wife's relations, and I would ask you to show him every attention.'

Octave was examining the entrance with its imitation marble panelling and its vaulted ceiling decorated with roses. The paved and cemented courtyard at the back had a grand air of chilly cleanliness; at the stable-door a solitary groom stood polishing a bit with a wash-leather. No doubt the sun never shone there.

In the meantime, Monsieur Gourd inspected the luggage. He pushed the trunks with his foot and, impressed by their weight, talked of fetching a porter to carry them up the servants' stair-case.

Putting his head round the door of the lodge, he called out to his wife: 'Madame Gourd, I'm going out.'

The lodge was like a little drawing-room, with shining mirrors, a red-flowered carpet, and rosewood furniture; and, through a half-open door, one caught a glimpse of the bedroom and the bed hung with garnet rep. Madame Gourd, a very fat woman with yellow ribbons in her hair, was stretched out in an armchair with her hands clasped, doing nothing.

'Well, let's go up,' said the architect. And seeing the impression made on the young man by Monsieur Gourd's black velvet cap and sky-blue slippers, he added, as he pushed open the mahogany door of the hall:

'You know, he used to be valet to the Duc de Vaugelade.'

'Oh!' said Octave, simply.

'Yes, indeed he was; and married the widow of a little bailiff from Mort-la-Ville. They even own a house there. But they're waiting until they get three thousand francs a year before they go there to live. Oh, they're most respectable people!'

There was a certain gaudy splendour about the hall and staircase. At the foot of the stairs was the gilt figure of a Neapolitan woman with a jar on her head, from which issued three gas-jets in ground-glass globes. The imitation marble panelling, white with pink edges, went right up the staircase at regular intervals, while the cast-iron balustrade, with its mahogany handrail, was in imitation of old silver, with thick clusters of gold leaves. A red carpet with brass rods covered the stairs. But what struck Octave most on entering was the hothouse temperature, a warm breath which seemed puffed by some mouth into his face.

'So the staircase is heated?' he said.

'Of course,' replied Campardon. 'All self-respecting landlords go to that expense nowadays. The house is a very fine one, very fine.'

He looked about him as though testing the solidity of the walls with his architect's eyes.

'My dear fellow, the house, as you will see, is very comfortable, and only lived in by thoroughly respectable people.'

Then, as they slowly climbed the stairs, he mentioned the names of the various tenants. On each floor there were two sets of apartments, one overlooking the street and the other the courtyard, their polished mahogany doors facing each other. He began by saying a word or two about Monsieur Auguste Vabre. He was the landlord's eldest son, and that spring he had taken the silk shop on the ground floor, and also occupied the whole of the entresol. Then, on the first floor, the landlord's other son, Théophile Vabre, and his wife lived in the apartment at the back, and in the one overlooking the street lived the landlord himself, formerly a Versailles notary, but now living with his son-in-law, a judge at the Court of Appeal.

'He isn't yet forty-five,' said Campardon, stopping short. 'That's not bad, is it?'

He climbed two more steps and then suddenly turned round and added:

'Water and gas on every floor.'

On each landing, under a high window whose panes, bordered with fretwork, lit up the staircase with a white light, there was a narrow, velvet-covered bench. Here, as the architect pointed out, elderly people could sit and rest. Then, as he went past the second floor without mentioning the occupants, Octave asked:

'And who lives there?' pointing to the door of the main suite.

'Oh, there!' he said. 'People we never see, whom no one knows. The house could well do without them. But nowhere's perfect, I suppose.'

He sniffed disdainfully.

'The gentleman writes books, I believe.'

But on the third floor his complacent smile returned. The apartment facing the courtyard was divided into two. It was occupied by Madame Juzeur, a little woman who had known great misfortune, and a very distinguished gentleman who had taken a room to which he came on business once a week. While explaining this to Octave, Campardon opened the door of the apartment opposite.

'This is where I live,' he went on. 'Wait a minute, I must get your key. We'll go up to your room first, and then I'll introduce you to my wife.'

In the two minutes he was left alone, Octave felt penetrated by the grave silence of the staircase. He leaned over the banisters in the warm air which came up from the hall below; then he looked up, listening for any noise coming from above. There was a deadly calm, the peace of a bourgeois drawing-room, carefully shut in, admitting no whisper from without. Behind those fine doors of shining mahogany there seemed to lie infinite depths of respectability.

'You'll have excellent neighbours,' said Campardon, reappearing with the key. 'On the street side are the Josserands—quite a family; the father is cashier at the Saint-Joseph glassworks, and he's got two marriageable daughters. Next door to you are the Pichons —he's a clerk; they're not exactly rolling in money, but they're very well-bred. Everything has to be let, hasn't it? Even in a house like this.'

After the third floor the red carpet came to an end, and was replaced by a simple grey covering. Octave's vanity was slightly hurt. Little by little the staircase had filled him with awe; he felt quite flattered at the thought of living in such a fine house, as Campardon had termed it. As he followed the architect along the corridor to his room, through a half-open door he caught sight of a young woman standing beside a cradle. Hearing them pass, she looked up. She was fair, with light, expressionless eyes; and all that Octave retained was this look, for the young woman, blushing, suddenly pushed the door to with the embarrassment of someone taken by surprise.

Campardon, turning round, repeated:

'Water and gas on every floor, my dear fellow.'

Then he pointed out a door opening on to the servants' staircase—their rooms were overhead. Then, coming to a halt at the end of the corridor, he said:

'Here we are at last.'

The room was quite large, square-shaped, and hung with wallpaper with blue flowers on a grey ground. It was simply furnished. Near the alcove there was a washstand, leaving just enough room to wash one's hands. Octave went straight to the window, through which a greenish light entered. Down below was the courtyard, depressingly clean, with its even paving-stones, and its cistern with a shining copper tap. And still not a soul, not a sound; nothing but rows of windows, all the same, without even a birdcage or a flower-pot, displaying the monotony of identical white curtains. To hide the great, bare wall of the house on the left, which shut in the square courtyard, imitation windows had been painted on it, with shutters eternally closed, behind which the walled-in life of the adjoining apartments seemed to continue.

'It will suit me perfectly,' cried Octave, delighted.

'I thought it would,' said Campardon. 'You know, I took as much trouble as if it were for myself, and I carried out all your instructions. So you like the furniture? It's all a young man wants. You can see about getting more things later on.'

As Octave shook him by the hand and thanked him, while apologizing for having given him so much trouble, he added in a more serious tone:

'The only thing, my boy, is that there must be no noise, and above all no women. My word! If you brought a woman here there would be a revolution in the house.'

'Don't worry,' muttered the young man, a little uneasily.

'Because, I can tell you, I'd be the one who'd be compromised. You can see what the house is like. They're all bourgeois people, and so terribly moral. Between ourselves, I think they overdo it. Ah, well! Monsieur Gourd would go straight to Monsieur Vabre and we'd both be in a fine mess. My dear chap, for my own peace of mind, I ask you: respect the house.'

Octave, overcome by so much virtue, swore that he would do so. Then Campardon, looking round warily and lowering his voice as if fearful of being overheard, added, with shining eyes:

'Outside it's nobody's business, eh? Paris is big enough, there's plenty of room. As for me, I'm an artist at heart, and I don't care a damn about such things.'

A porter brought up the trunks. When everything had been sorted out, the architect took a paternal interest in Octave's toilet. Then, standing up, he said:

'Now let's go down and see my wife.'

On the third floor the maidservant, a slim, dark, coquettish-looking girl, said that madame was busy. To put his friend at ease, Campardon showed him round the apartment. First of all, there was the big white-and-gold drawing-room, elaborately decorated with imitation mouldings. This was situated between a little green parlour which had been turned into a study, and the bedroom, which they could not enter but whose narrow shape and mauve wallpaper the architect described. When he took him into the dining-room, all in imitation wood, with its strange mixture of beading and panels, Octave, enchanted, exclaimed: 'It's very handsome!'

There were two great cracks running right through the panelling on the ceiling, and in one corner the paint had peeled off and was showing the plaster.

'Yes, it certainly creates an effect,' said the architect slowly, with his eyes riveted to the ceiling. 'You see, these kinds of houses are built for effect. The walls, though, aren't very solid. The house was only built twelve years ago, and they're already cracking. They build the frontage of very fine stone, with all sorts of sculpture, give the staircase three coats of varnish, and touch up the rooms with gilt and paint; that's what impresses people and inspires respect. But it's still solid enough! It'll last as long as we will.'

He led Octave through the anteroom again, with its ground-glass windows. To the left, overlooking the courtyard, there was a second bedroom where his daughter Angèle slept; it was all in white, which, on this November afternoon, made it seem as sad as a tomb. Then, at the end of the passage, there was the kitchen, which he insisted on showing Octave, saying that he must see everything.

'Come in,' he repeated, as he pushed the door open.

A hideous noise greeted them as they entered. Despite the cold, the window was wide open. Leaning over the rail, the dark maidservant and a fat old cook were looking down into the narrow well of the inner courtyard, which let some light into the kitchens that faced each other on every floor. Bending forward, they were both yelling, while from the bowels of the courtyard rose the sound of crude laughter, mingled with curses. It was as if a sewer had brimmed over. All the domestics in the house were there, letting off steam. Octave thought of the bourgeois majesty of the grand staircase.

As if by instinct, the two women turned round. At the sight of their master with a gentleman they were struck dumb. There was a slight hissing noise, the windows were shut, and all became once more as silent as the grave.

'What's the matter, Lisa?' asked Campardon.

'If you please, sir,' said the maid, greatly excited, 'it's that dirty Adèle again. She's thrown some rabbit's guts out of the window. You should speak to Monsieur Josserand, sir.'

Campardon looked very serious, anxious not to make any promises. He withdrew to the study, saying to Octave:

'You've seen everything now. The rooms are the same on every floor. Mine cost me two thousand five hundred francs; on the third floor, too! Rents are going up every day.* Monsieur Vabre must make about twenty-two thousand francs a year out of his house. And it'll go on increasing, because there's talk of a big thoroughfare from the Place de la Bourse to the new opera house.* And the land the house is built on he got for virtually nothing, about twelve years ago, when there was that big fire started by some chemist's servant.'

As they entered Octave noticed, above a drawing-table, and with the light from the window shining directly upon it, a handsomely framed picture of the Holy Virgin displaying on her breast an enormous flaming heart. He could not conceal his surprise, and looked at Campardon, whom he remembered as being rather a wild fellow in Plassans.

'Oh!' said the latter, blushing a little, 'I forgot to tell you I've been appointed architect to the diocese—at Evreux. It doesn't pay much, barely two thousand francs a year. But there's nothing to do—the occasional trip; in any case, I've got a surveyor down there. And, you see, it's quite an advantage if you can put on your card, "Government Architect". You can't imagine how much work it brings me from society people.'

As he spoke, he gazed at the Virgin with her flaming heart.

'After all,' he added in a sudden fit of candour, 'I don't believe in any of their claptrap.'

But when Octave burst out laughing, the architect became worried. Why confide in this young man? He gave him a sideways glance, assumed an air of contrition, and tried to smooth over what he had said.

'Well, I don't care, and yet I do. That's about it. You'll see, you'll see: when you're a bit older you'll do like everybody else.'

He spoke of his age—forty-two—of the emptiness of existence, and hinted at a melancholy which in no way matched his robust health. Beneath his flowing hair and neatly trimmed beard there was the flat skull and square jaw of a bourgeois man of limited intelligence and animal appetites. When younger, he had been fun-loving to the point of tedium.

Octave's eyes fell on a copy of the *Gazette de France*,* which was lying among some plans. Then Campardon, becoming more and more embarrassed, rang for the maid, to know if madame was now free. Yes, the doctor was just leaving and madame would be there directly.

'Is Madame Campardon not well?' asked the young man.

'No, she's the same as usual,' said the architect, with a touch of annoyance in his voice.

'Oh, what's the matter with her?'

More embarrassed than ever, he answered evasively: 'You know, women have always got something wrong with them. She's been like that for the last thirteen years, ever since her confinement. Otherwise she's very well. You'll even find that she's put on a little weight.'

Octave desisted from further questions. Just then Lisa came back, bringing a card, and the architect, apologizing, hurried into the drawing-room, begging the young man to talk to his wife in the meantime. As the door quickly opened and closed, in the middle of the spacious white-and-gold drawing-room Octave caught sight of the black spot of a cassock.

At the same moment Madame Campardon came in from the anteroom. He did not recognize her. Years before, when as a youngster he knew her in Plassans, at the house of her father Monsieur Domergue, who worked for the local board of works, she had been thin and plain and, for all her twenty years, as puny as a girl who has just reached puberty. Now he found her plump, with a clear complexion, and as placid as a nun; soft-eyed, dimpled, with the air of a fat tabby cat. Though she had not become pretty, she had ripened at about thirty, gaining a sweet savour, a pleasant, fresh odour as of autumn fruit. He noticed, however, that she walked with difficulty, her hips swaying in a long loose dressing-gown of mignonette-coloured silk, which gave her a languid air.

'You're quite a man now,' she said jovially, holding out her hands. 'You've grown since we last saw you!'

She looked him up and down—tall, dark, handsome young man that he was, with his carefully trimmed beard and moustache. When he told her his age, twenty-two, she could hardly believe it, declaring that he looked at least twenty-five. He—whom the very presence of a woman, even of the lowest maidservant, enraptured—laughed a silvery laugh as he returned her gaze with eyes the colour of old gold and soft as velvet.

'Yes,' he repeated gently. 'I've grown, I've grown. Do you remember when your cousin Gasparine used to buy me marbles?'

Then he gave her news of her parents. Monsieur and Madame Domergue were living happily in the house to which they had retired; all they complained of was that they were very lonely, and they bore Campardon a grudge for having taken their little Rose from them when he had come down to Plassans on business. Octave then tried to turn the conversation round to his cousin Gasparine, hoping to satisfy his curiosity about a mystery that for him had never been solved—the architect's sudden passion for Gasparine, a tall, handsome girl who didn't have a penny, and his hasty marriage with skinny Rose, who had a dowry of thirty thousand francs, the tearful scene and the recriminations, followed by the flight of the forsaken one to her dressmaker aunt in Paris. But Madame Campardon, though she blushed slightly, appeared not to understand. He could get no details from her.

'And your parents, how are they?' she enquired in her turn.

'They're very well, thank you,' he replied. 'My mother never leaves her garden now. You'd find the house in the Rue de la Banne just the same as when you left it.'*

Madame Campardon, who seemed unable to stand for any length of time without feeling tired, had sat down in a high easy-chair, her legs stretched out under her dressing-gown; and taking a low chair beside her, he looked up at her when speaking, with his usual air of adoration. Though broad-shouldered, there was nevertheless something feminine about him, something that appealed to women and made them instantly take him to their hearts. Thus, after ten minutes they were both chatting away like two old friends.

'So now I'm your boarder,' he said, stroking his beard with a shapely hand, the nails of which were neatly trimmed. 'We'll get on very well together, you'll see. It was extremely nice of you to think of the little boy from Plassans, and to take all this trouble for me.'

'No, no, don't thank me,' she protested. 'I'm far too lazy, I never do anything. It was Achille who arranged everything. Besides, when my mother told us you wanted to board with a family, that was enough for us to make you welcome. You won't be among strangers, and it'll be company for us.'

Then he told her about himself. After passing his baccalaureate, to please his family, he had spent the last three years in Marseilles, in a big calico print shop which had a factory near Plassans. He had a passion for business, for the new trade in women's luxury goods, in which there was something of the pleasure of seduction, of slow possession by gilded phrases and flattering looks. Laughing victoriously, he told her how he had made the five thousand francs without which he would never have risked coming to Paris, for he had the prudence of a Jew beneath his appearance of carefree good-nature.

'Just think, they had some Pompadour calico, an old design, quite marvellous. Nobody wanted it, it had been gathering dust in the warehouse for two years. So, as I was going on a trip through the Var and the Basses-Alpes, I suddenly thought of buying up the whole stock and selling it on my own account. It was a huge success. The women almost came to blows over the remnants, and today every one of them is wearing some of my calico. I must say, I talked them over quite beautifully! I had them all at my feet, I could have done what I liked with them.'

He laughed, while Madame Campardon, charmed and somewhat troubled by the thought of that Pompadour calico, kept asking him questions. Little bunches of flowers on a light-brown ground, wasn't that the pattern? She had been looking everywhere for something similar, for her summer dressing-gown.

'I was travelling around for two years,' he went on, 'and that's enough. Now there's Paris to conquer. I must look out for something at once.'

'But didn't Achille tell you?' she exclaimed. 'He's found a position for you, and close by, too.'

He thanked her, as astonished as if he were in fairyland, and was asking jokingly if he would find a wife with a hundred thousand francs a year in his room that evening when the door was pushed open by a plain, lanky girl of fourteen with straw-coloured hair, who uttered a slight cry of surprise.

'Come in, don't be shy,' said Madame Campardon. 'This is Monsieur Octave Mouret, whom you've heard us mention.'

Then, turning to Octave, she said:

'My daughter, Angèle. We didn't take her with us on our last trip. She was so delicate. But she's putting on weight now.'

Angèle, with the awkwardness of girls of her age, had planted herself behind her mother and was staring at the smiling young man. Almost immediately Campardon came back, looking excited, and could not resist telling his wife immediately of the good luck he had had. Father Mauduit, vicar of Saint-Roch, had called about some work—just a few repairs, but it might lead to something much bigger. Then, annoyed at having talked like this in front of Octave, but still trembling with excitement, he clapped his hands and said:

'Well, well, what are we going to do?'

'You were going out,' said Octave. 'Don't let me hold you up.'

'Achille,' murmured Madame Campardon, 'that situation, at the Hédouins' . . .'

'Of course,' exclaimed the architect, 'I'd forgotten. My dear fellow, it's the job of head assistant at a large draper's shop. I know somebody there who put in a word for you. They're expecting you. Since it's not yet four o'clock, would you like me to take you there?'

Octave hesitated, and, in his mania for being well-dressed, felt nervous about the bow of his necktie. However, when Madame Campardon assured him that he looked very smart he decided to go. She languidly offered her forehead to her husband, who kissed her with effusive tenderness, repeating:

'Goodbye, my darling; goodbye, my pet.'

'Remember, dinner's at seven,' she said, as she accompanied them across the drawing-room to get their hats.

Angèle awkwardly followed them. Her music-master was waiting for her, and she immediately attacked the instrument with her skinny fingers. Octave, who lingered in the anteroom repeating his thanks, could hardly hear himself speak. As he went down the stairs the sound of the piano seemed to pursue him. In the warm silence other pianos, from Madame Juzeur's, the Vabres', and the Duveyriers', were answering, different tunes sounding from every floor, distant and mystical, behind the chaste solemnity of the mahogany doors.

Outside, Campardon turned into the Rue Neuve-Sante-Augustin. He was silent and preoccupied, like a man waiting to broach something.

'Do you remember Mademoiselle Gasparine?' he asked eventually. 'She's forewoman at the Hédouins'. You'll be seeing her.'

Octave thought this a good opportunity to satisfy his curiosity.

'Oh!' he said, 'does she live with you?'

'No, no!' exclaimed the architect, as if hurt by the suggestion.

Then, as Octave seemed surprised by the sharpness of his reaction, he added, in a gentler tone, and somewhat embarrassed:

'No, she and my wife never see each other now. You know what families are like . . . Well, I bumped into her, and I could hardly refuse to shake hands, could I? Especially as the poor girl's not well off. So now they get news of each other through me. In old quarrels like this only time can heal the wounds.'

Octave was about to ask him about his marriage, when the architect suddenly cut him short by saying:

'Here we are!'

At the corner of the Rue Neuve-Saint-Augustin and the Rue de la Michodière, facing the narrow, three-cornered Place Gaillon, was a linen-draper's shop. Across two windows just above the shop was a signboard, with the words, 'The Ladies' Paradise: Established 1822,' in faded gilt lettering, while the shop-windows bore the name of the firm, in red: 'Deleuze, Hédouin & Co.'

'It's not quite in the modern style, but it's a good, solid business,' explained Campardon rapidly. 'Monsieur Hédouin, who started off as a clerk, married the daughter of the elder Deleuze, who died two years ago, so that the business is now managed by the young couple—old Deleuze and another partner, I think, both keep out of it. You'll meet Madame Hédouin. She's got a good head on her shoulders! Let's go in.'

Monsieur Hédouin happened to be away in Lille, buying linen, so Madame Hédouin received them. She was standing with a pen behind her ear, giving orders to two shopmen who were arranging pieces of stuff on the shelves. Octave thought her so tall and attractive, with her regular features and neatly plaited hair, black dress, turn-down collar, and man's tie, that when she smiled gravely at him he could hardly stammer out a reply, though he was not usually bashful. Everything was settled without any waste of words.

'Well,' she said, in her quiet way and easy professional manner, 'as you're free, perhaps you'd like to look over the shop.'

She called one of the clerks, entrusted Octave to his care, and then, after politely replying to Campardon that Mademoiselle Gasparine was out on an errand, turned her back and went on with her work, giving orders in the same gentle, firm voice.

'Not there, Alexandre. Put the silks up at the top. Be careful! Those aren't the same sort.'

After some hesitation, Campardon said he would come back and fetch Octave for dinner. So for two hours the young man explored the shop. He found it badly lit, small, and cluttered with stock, which, as there was no room for it in the basement, was piled up in corners, leaving only narrow passages between high walls of bales. Several times he ran into Madame Hédouin gliding along the narrowest passages without ever snagging her dress. She seemed to be the life and soul of the place; the assistants responded to the slightest gesture of her white hands. Octave was hurt that she did not take more notice of him. At about a quarter to seven, just as he was coming up from the basement for the last time, he was told that Campardon was on the first floor with Mademoiselle Gasparine. That was the hosiery department, which the young lady looked after. But, at the top of the winding staircase, Octave stopped short behind a pyramid of calico-bales, symmetrically arranged, on hearing the architect talking in the most familiar way to Gasparine.

'I swear I haven't,' he cried, forgetting himself so far as to raise his voice.

There was a pause.

'How is she now?' asked the young woman.

'She's always the same, of course. Sometimes better, sometimes worse. She thinks it's all over now, and that she'll never be right again.'

Then Gasparine, with pity in her voice, continued:

'It's you, my poor friend, who are to be pitied. However, as you've been able to manage in another way, do tell her how sorry I am to hear that she's still unwell . . .'

Campardon, without letting her finish her sentence, had seized her by the shoulders and was kissing her roughly on the lips, in the gas-heated air that grew ever more stuffy under the low ceiling. She returned his kiss, murmuring:

'Tomorrow morning, then, at six, if you can manage it. I'll stay in bed. Knock three times.'

Octave, astonished, but beginning to understand, coughed and then stepped forward. Another surprise awaited him. His cousin Gasparine had become shrivelled, thin and angular, with a prominent jaw and coarse hair. All she had kept of her former beauty were the large, splendid eyes in her cadaverous face. With her anxious brow and intense, stubborn mouth, she distressed him as much as Rose had charmed him by her late development into an indolent blonde.

Gasparine, if not effusive, was polite. She remembered Plassans, and talked to the young man of old times. As Campardon and he took their leave she shook them by the hand. Downstairs Madame Hédouin simply said to Octave:

'Well, then, we'll see you tomorrow.'

When they were in the street, deafened by cabs and jostled by passers-by, Octave could not help observing that she was certainly a very handsome woman, if not particularly affable. The windows of newly painted shops, ablaze with gas,* threw squares of bright light across the black, muddy pavement, while the older shops, with their windows dimly lit by smoking lamps, like distant stars, made the streets more gloomy with their broad patches of shadow. In the Rue Neuve-Saint-Augustin, just before turning into the Rue de Choiseul, Campardon bowed as he passed one of these shops.

A young woman, slim and elegant, wearing a silk cape, was standing in the doorway, holding a little boy of three close to her so that he would not get run over. She was talking in a friendly way to an old, bareheaded woman, evidently the shopkeeper. It was too dark for Octave to distinguish her features in the flickering gaslight, but she seemed to be pretty; he only caught sight of two bright eyes, fixed upon him for a moment like two flames. The shop stretched back behind her, dank and cellar-like, giving off a faint odour of saltpetre.

'That's Madame Valérie, the wife of Monsieur Théophile Vabre, the landlord's younger son; you know—the people on the first floor,' said Campardon after they had gone a little further. 'She's a most charming person. She was born in that very shop, one of the best-paying linen-drapers in the neighbourhood, which her parents, Monsieur and Madame Louhette, still manage, just to have something to do. They've made quite a pile, I can tell you!'

But trade of that sort was beyond Octave's comprehension, in such dingy holes of old Paris, where they used to make do with a single piece of stuff displayed in the window for a shop-sign. He vowed that nothing on earth would ever make him agree to live in the bottom of a cellar like that. You'd die of rheumatism!

Still chatting, they reached the top of the stairs. Madame Campardon was waiting for them. She had put on a grey silk dress, arranged her hair coquettishly, and appeared very neat and elegant. Campardon kissed her on the neck, with all the emotion of a dutiful husband.

'Good evening, my darling; good evening, my pet.'

They went into the drawing-room. The dinner was delightful. At first Madame Campardon talked about the Deleuzes and the Hédouins—families well known and respected throughout the neighbourhood. A cousin of theirs was a stationer in the Rue Gaillon; an uncle kept an umbrella-shop in the Passage Choiseul; while their nephews and nieces were all in business round about. Then the conversation turned to Angèle, who was sitting upright in her chair and eating listlessly. Madame Campardon said that she was being brought up at home because it was safer; and not wishing to say any more, she blinked her eyes in order to suggest that at boarding-schools young girls learnt the most awful things. Meanwhile, the child was slyly trying to balance her plate on her knife. Lisa, who was clearing away, just missed breaking it, and exclaimed:

'That was your fault, mademoiselle!'

Angèle could barely refrain from giggling, while her mother only shook her head. When Lisa had left the room to bring in the dessert, Madame Campardon began to sing her praises—very intelligent, very active, a real Parisienne, never at a loss. They might easily do without Victoire, the cook, who because of her great age was no longer very clean; but she had been in the service of her master's father before Campardon was born. In short, she was a family ruin who commanded their respect. Then, as the maid came back with some baked apples, Madame Campardon continued, in Octave's ear: 'Conduct irreproachable. So far, I've found nothing to complain about. Just one day off a month, when she goes to see an old aunt, who lives a good way off.'

Octave looked at Lisa. Noticing how nervous, flat-chested, and puffy-eyed she was, he thought to himself that she must have a high old time at that aunt's. However, he declared himself fully in agreement with Madame Campardon, who continued to impart to him her views on education: a daughter was such a big responsibility, she had to be shielded from the very breath of the streets. In the meantime, whenever Lisa leaned across near Angèle's chair to change a plate, the child would pinch her thighs in a kind of mad familiarity, though both remained as grave as could be, neither of them batting an eyelid.

'Virtue is its own reward,' said the architect sagely, as if to draw a conclusion from thoughts he had not expressed. 'For my part, I don't care a damn what people think; I'm an artist!'

After dinner, they stayed in the drawing-room until midnight. It was a sort of orgy to celebrate Octave's arrival. Madame Campardon seemed very tired, and gradually subsided on the sofa.

'Are you in pain, my darling?' asked her husband.

'No,' she replied in a faint voice. 'It's the usual thing.'

Then, looking at him, she said softly:

'Did you see her at the Hédouins?'

'Yes! She asked how you were.'

Tears came to Rose's eyes.

'She's always well, she is!'

'There, there,' said Campardon as he lightly kissed her hair, forgetting that they were not alone. 'You'll make yourself worse again. You know I love you all the same, my poor darling!'

Octave, who had discreetly moved to the window under the pretence of looking into the street, came back and scrutinized

Madame Campardon's face, for his curiosity was again aroused, and he wondered if she knew. But she wore her usual expression, a mixture of amiability and dolefulness, as she curled up on the sofa, like a woman who has to find her pleasure in herself as she submits resignedly to her share of caresses.

At length Octave bade them goodnight. Candlestick in hand, he was still on the landing when he heard the rustle of silk dresses brushing the stairs. He politely stood to one side. Evidently these were the ladies who lived on the fourth floor, Madame Josserand and her two daughters, coming home from a party. As they passed, the mother, a stout, haughty-looking woman, stared him full in his face, while the elder of the daughters stepped aside with a petulant air, and her sister looked boldly up at him and smiled in the bright light of the candle. She was very pretty, with tiny features, fair skin, and auburn hair flecked with golden reflections; and there was about her a certain intrepid grace, the carefree charm of a young bride returning from a ball, in an elaborate gown covered with bows and lace such as unmarried girls never wear. Their trains disappeared at the top of the stairs, and a door closed behind them. Octave was greatly amused by the merry twinkle in her eye.

He went slowly upstairs in his turn. Only one gas-jet was alight; the staircase, in this heavy, heated air, seemed fast asleep. It appeared more venerable than ever, with its chaste portals of handsome mahogany that enclosed so many respectable hearths. Not a whisper was audible, it was a silence as of well-mannered people holding their breath. But now he heard a slight noise. Leaning over the banister, he saw Monsieur Gourd, in velvet cap and slippers, turning out the last gas burner. Then the whole house was enveloped in solemn darkness, as if obliterated in the refinement and propriety of its slumbers.

However, Octave found it hard to get to sleep. He tossed about feverishly, his brain filled with all the new faces he had seen. What on earth made the Campardons so friendly towards him? Were they dreaming of marrying their daughter to him later on? Perhaps the husband had taken him in as a boarder to give his wife some company and cheer her up. And what could the strange complaint be from which the poor woman suffered? Then his ideas grew more confused; phantoms passed before him; little Madame Pichon, his neighbour, with her vacuous look; beautiful Madame Hédouin,

serious and correct in her black dress; the fiery eyes of Madame
Valérie, and the merry smile of Mademoiselle Josserand. How many
he had encountered in just a few hours in Paris! It had always been
his dream, ladies who would take him by the hand, and help him on
in business. Their images kept returning and mingling in his mind
with relentless insistence. He did not know which to choose, as he
strove to keep his voice soft and his gestures seductive. Then,
suddenly, exhausted, exasperated, he gave way to his brutal inner
nature, to the ferocious disdain of women that lay behind his air of
amorous devotion.

'Are they ever going to let me go to sleep?' he said out loud,
throwing himself violently on his back. 'I'll take on the first one that
wants it, it's all the same to me; and straight away if they like! Sleep!
Sleep!'

II

WHEN Madame Josserand, preceded by her daughters, left Madame Dambreville's party in the Rue de Rivoli, on the fourth floor at the corner of the Rue de l'Oratoire, she slammed the street door in a sudden outburst of the anger she had been holding back for the last two hours. Her younger daughter Berthe had again just missed getting a husband.

'Well, what are you standing there for?' she angrily asked the girls, who had stopped under the arcade and were watching the cabs go by. 'Walk on! You needn't think we're going to take a cab and waste another two francs!'

And when Hortense, the elder, grumbled:

'Hmm! It's nice walking through all this mud! It'll ruin my shoes.'

'Walk on!' rejoined her mother, quite beside herself. 'When your shoes are gone, you can stay in bed, that's all! A lot of good it is, taking you out!'

With bowed heads, Berthe and Hortense turned into the Rue de l'Oratoire. They held their long skirts as high as they could above their crinolines, their shoulders hunched, shivering in their opera cloaks. Madame Josserand followed, wrapped in an old fur cloak that looked like a shabby cat-skin. None of them wore bonnets, but had enveloped their hair in lace wraps, a headgear that made passers-by look round in surprise as they slipped past the houses, with backs bent and eyes fixed on the puddles. Madame Josserand grew even more exasperated as she thought of many similar homecomings over the last three winters, hampered by their smart gowns, in the black mud of the streets, sniggered at by men. No, she had certainly had enough of it, of carting her daughters all over Paris, without ever daring to enjoy the luxury of a cab for fear of having to remove a dish from the following day's dinner!

'So she's a matchmaker, is she?' she said out loud, as she thought of Madame Dambreville, talking to herself by way of solace, not even addressing her daughters, who had turned down the Rue Saint-Honoré. 'Fine matches she makes! A lot of impertinent hussies who come from goodness knows where! Oh, if only we weren't obliged to go through it all! . . . That was her last success, I suppose—that bride she brought out just to show us she isn't always a failure! A fine example, too! A wretched child that had an unfortunate lapse and had to be sent back to the convent for six months to get another coat of whitewash!'

As the girls crossed the Place du Palais-Royal a shower came on. This was the last straw. Slipping and splashing about, they stopped and again cast glances at the empty cabs that rolled past.

'Walk on!' cried the mother, ruthlessly. 'We're too close to home now; it's not worth forty sous . . . And your brother Léon, who wouldn't leave with us for fear of having to pay for the cab! If he can get what he wants at that woman's, so much the better! But it isn't at all decent. A woman over fifty who only invites young men to her house! An old tart that some eminent person made that idiot Dambreville marry by bribing him with a head-clerkship!'

Hortense and Berthe trudged along in the rain, one in front of the other, without seeming to hear. When their mother let herself go like this, forgetting the strict rules she had laid down for their fine education, it was tacitly agreed that they would act as if they were deaf. But on reaching the dark, deserted Rue de l'Echelle, Berthe rebelled.

'Oh, no!' she cried. 'My heel's coming off! I can't go another step!'

Madame Josserand became utterly furious.

'Just walk on! Do I complain? Do you think it's right for me to be traipsing about the streets at this time of night, and in such weather? It would be different if you had a father like other people. But no, my lord must stay at home and take his ease! I'm the one who has to take you to parties; he can never be bothered! I can tell you I've had just about enough of it. Your father can take you out in future, if he likes; you can think again if you expect me to drag you about any more to places where I only get put out! A man who completely deceived me as to his capabilities, and who has never given me the least pleasure! Oh! If ever I married again, it wouldn't be to a man like that!'*

The girls stopped grumbling. They already knew so well this eternal chapter in the history of their mother's blighted hopes. With their lace mantillas sticking to their faces, and their ball-shoes soaked through, they hurried along the Rue Sainte-Anne. In the Rue de Choiseul, at the door of her own house, Madame Josserand had to undergo a final humiliation, for the Duveyriers' carriage splashed her all over as it drew up.

Exhausted and furious, both mother and girls recovered some of their grace and poise when they had to pass Octave on the stairs. But as soon as their door was shut they rushed headlong through the dark apartment, bumping against the furniture, till they got to the dining-room where Monsieur Josserand was writing by the feeble light of a little lamp.

'Another failure!' cried Madame Josserand, as she sank into a chair.

She roughly tore the lace covering from her head, threw off her fur cloak, and revealed a gaudy red dress, trimmed with black satin and cut very low. She looked enormous, though her shoulders were still shapely, and resembled the shining flanks of a mare. Her square face, with its big nose and flabby cheeks, expressed all the tragic fury of a queen striving to contain her desire to lapse into the language of the gutter.

'Ah!' said Monsieur Josserand simply, bewildered by this violent entrance.

He kept blinking uneasily. His wife positively overwhelmed him when she displayed that mammoth bosom; it seemed as if he could feel its weight crushing the back of his neck. Dressed in a threadbare frock-coat he was wearing out at home, his face haggard and dingy from thirty-five years of office work, he looked at her for a moment with his large, lacklustre eyes. Pushing his grey locks back behind his ears, he was too disconcerted to speak, and attempted to go on writing.

'But you don't seem to understand!' continued Madame Josserand in a shrill voice. 'That's another marriage that hasn't come off—the fourth!'

'Yes, yes, I know—the fourth,' he murmured. 'It's annoying, very annoying.'

To avoid his wife's terrifying nudity he turned towards his daughters with a kindly smile. They also took off their lace wraps and their cloaks; the elder was in blue, the younger in pink, and their dresses, too daring in cut and over-trimmed, were decidedly provocative. Hortense had a sallow complexion; her face was spoilt by a nose, like her mother's, which gave her an air of stubborn disdain. She had just turned twenty-three, but looked twenty-eight.

Berthe, however, who was two years younger, had kept all her childish grace, with the same features, only more delicate, and skin of dazzling whiteness, to be menaced only by the coarse family mask when she reached fifty.

'What's the point of staring at us?' cried Madame Josserand. 'For God's sake put your writing away; it gets on my nerves!'

'But, my dear, I've got these wrappers to do!' he said gently.

'Oh, yes, I know your wrappers—three francs a thousand! Perhaps you think that those three francs will be enough to marry your daughters!'

By the faint light of the little lamp one could see that the table was strewn with large sheets of coarse paper, printed wrappers on which Monsieur Josserand was writing addresses for a well-known publisher who had several periodicals. He could not make ends meet with his cashier's salary, he spent whole nights at this unprofitable sort of work, doing it in secret, afraid that someone might find out how poor they were.

'Three francs are three francs,' he replied in his slow, tired voice. 'With those three francs you'll be able to put ribbons on your dresses, and offer cakes to your guests on Tuesdays.'

He regretted the remark as soon as he had made it, for he felt that with Madame Josserand it had gone straight home, and had wounded her pride in its most sensitive part. Her shoulders grew purple; she seemed about to burst out with some vengeful reply, but, with a majestic effort, she merely stammered:

'Goodness gracious me! Really!' And she looked at her daughters, shrugging her terrible shoulders in magisterial scorn, as if to say: 'There! Did you hear that? What an idiot!'

The girls nodded. Seeing himself vanquished, he regretfully put down his pen and opened a copy of *Le Temps*,* which he brought home every evening from the office.

'Is Saturnin asleep?' asked Madame Josserand curtly, referring to her younger son.

'Yes, ages ago,' he replied. 'And I told Adèle she could go to bed, too . . . Did you see Léon at the Dambrevilles?'

'Of course! He sleeps there!' she exclaimed, unable to contain her spite.

Monsieur Josserand, surprised, ingenuously asked:

'Do you think so?'

Hortense and Berthe had become deaf. They smiled slightly, however, pretending to be busy with their shoes, which were in a pitiful state. By way of a diversion, Madame Josserand tried to pick another quarrel with her husband. She begged him to take away his newspaper every morning, and not to leave it lying about all day, as he had done the day before for instance. That issue happened to contain a report of a scandalous trial, which his daughters might easily have read. It was clear that he was utterly lacking in any moral sense.

'Is it bedtime?' asked Hortense. 'I'm hungry.'

'What about me?' said Berthe. 'I'm starving.'

'What!' cried Madame Josserand, beside herself. 'Hungry? Didn't you have some *brioche* when you were there? What silly things you are! Hungry, indeed! I made sure I had something to eat.'

But the girls persisted in saying that they were dying of hunger, so their mother at last went with them to the kitchen to see if there was anything left. Their father furtively set to work on his wrappers again. He was well aware that without those wrappers all the little luxuries in the home would have disappeared, and that was why, in spite of the scornful remarks and the bickering, he doggedly kept at his secret work until daybreak, quite pleased at the thought that just one more scrap of lace might bring about a wealthy marriage. Though expenditure on food was being cut down, they could still hardly afford to pay for dresses and those Tuesday receptions, and so he was resigned to his martyr-like task, dressed in tatters, while his wife and daughters went out to parties with flowers in their hair.

'What a stench!' cried Madame Josserand as she entered the kitchen. 'I can never get that slut Adèle to leave the window open. She always says it makes the room so cold in the morning.'

She opened the window, and from the narrow courtyard separating the kitchens an icy dampness rose, a stale odour like that of a musty cellar. Berthe's lighted candle threw dancing shadows of huge bare shoulders on the opposite wall.

'And what a state it's in!' continued Madame Josserand, sniffing about everywhere in all the dirty corners. 'She hasn't scrubbed her table for a fortnight. Those are the plates we used two days ago. It's absolutely disgusting! And her sink! Just smell her sink!'

She was getting more and more worked up. She knocked over plates and dishes with her arms all white with rice-powder and laden with gold bracelets. She trailed her red skirts through the filth until they caught in pans shoved under the tables, at the risk of spoiling her elaborate finery with the dirty peelings. Finally, at the sight of a knife with its blade badly notched, she exploded.

'I'll send her packing first thing in the morning!'

'What good will that do?' asked Hortense quietly. 'We can never keep anybody. She's the first one who's stayed three months. The moment they get a little decent and learn how to make a white sauce, off they go.'

Madame Josserand bit her lip. As a matter of fact Adèle, fresh from Brittany, dirty and stupid, had been the only one to stay in this pompous, penny-pinching bourgeois home, where they took advantage of her dirt and ignorance to starve her. Scores of times, when they had found a comb in the bread or some abominable stew had given them stomach-ache, they had talked of getting rid of her; but on reflection they preferred to put up with her rather than face the difficulty of finding another cook, for even pilferers refused to take service in such a hole, where every lump of sugar was counted.

'I can't find anything,' muttered Berthe, poking about in a cupboard.

The shelves had the dismal bareness and sham display of households where poor-quality meat is bought so that there can be a show of flowers on the table. There were just some clean china plates with gold edges, a crumb-brush with some of the plated silver rubbed off its handle, and a cruet-stand in which the oil and vinegar had dried up; but not a single crust, not a scrap of fruit or pastry or cheese. Obviously Adèle's insatiable hunger made her lick the plates clean of any rare drop of gravy or sauce left by her employers, until she nearly rubbed the gilt off.

'She must have eaten all the rabbit!' cried Madame Josserand.

'Yes,' said Hortense, 'there were some leftovers! Ah, here they are! I'd have been surprised if she'd dared to have them. They'll do me. They're cold, but they're better than nothing.'

Berthe kept rummaging about, but without success. At last she caught hold of a bottle in which her mother had diluted the contents of an old pot of jam, so as to manufacture some redcurrant syrup for her evening parties. She poured herself a glass, saying:

'I'll soak some bread in this, since there's nothing else.'

But Madame Josserand, looking very anxious, said cuttingly:

'Oh, don't hold back; fill your tumbler up while you're about it. Tomorrow I'll just offer our guests cold water.'

Luckily, another of Adèle's misdeeds cut her reprimand short. As she was prying about, searching for evidence of the servant's crimes, she caught sight of a book lying on the table, and this provoked a supreme outburst.

'Oh, the slut! She's brought my Lamartine into the kitchen again!'

It was a copy of *Jocelyn*.* Picking it up, she rubbed it, as if to get it clean, and went on saying that she had told her scores of times not to drag it about with her everywhere to write her accounts on. Meanwhile Berthe and Hortense had divided the little piece of bread between them, and carrying their suppers said they would undress first. Their mother cast a parting glance at the ice-cold oven and went back to the dining-room, holding her Lamartine tightly under her fleshy arm.

Monsieur Josserand continued writing. He hoped that his wife would be satisfied with a crushing look of contempt as she went past on her way to bed. But she again sank into a chair and gazed at him without speaking. Her gaze made him so uncomfortable that his pen kept sputtering on the flimsy wrapping-paper.

'So it was you who stopped Adèle from making a custard for tomorrow night,' she said at last.

He looked up in amazement.

'I did, my dear?'

'Oh, you'll deny it, as you always do! So, why hasn't she made it as I told her to? You know very well that uncle Bachelard is coming to dinner before the party tomorrow; it's his saint's day,* unfortunately, on the same day as our party! If there's no custard we must have ice cream, which means throwing away another five francs!'

He did not try to exculpate himself. Afraid to carry on with his work, he began to toy with the penholder. There was a lull.

'Tomorrow morning,' resumed Madame Josserand, 'I'd like you to call on the Campardons and remind them as politely as you can that we're expecting them in the evening. The young man who's staying with them arrived this afternoon. Ask them to bring him along. Remember, I want him to come.'

'What young man?'

'A young man; it would take far too long to explain. I've found out everything about him. I have to try everything, since you leave your daughters entirely to me, like a bundle of rubbish—you don't seem to care in the slightest about getting them married.'

Her anger was rekindled.

'You see, I keep it to myself, but, oh! it's more than I can stand. Don't say anything, sir; don't say anything, or I'll explode!'

He said nothing, and she exploded all the same.

'I won't put up with it any more. I warn you, one of these fine days I'll go off and leave you with your two empty-headed daughters. Do you think I was born to lead such a miserable life as this? Always straining to make ends meet, never even having a decent pair of boots, and never able to entertain my friends properly! And it's all your fault! Don't shake your head, sir; don't make me even more angry! Yes, it's your fault; I repeat, your fault! You deceived me, sir; basely deceived me. One shouldn't marry a woman if one has resolved to let her go without everything. You boasted about your fine future, you claimed you were the friend of your employer's sons, those Bernheim brothers who've made such a fool of you. What! Do you dare to pretend that they didn't make a fool of you? You ought to be their partner by now! It was you who made their business what it is—one of the biggest in Paris, and you're still just their cashier, a subordinate, an underling! Really! You've got no spirit! Hold your tongue!'

'I get eight thousand francs a year,' murmured the hireling. 'It's a very good position.'

'A good position, indeed! After more than thirty years' service. They grind you down, and you're delighted. Do you know what I would have done, if it had been me? I would have made sure that the business filled my pockets twenty times over. It would have been so easy; I saw it when I married you, and I've never stopped urging you to do so ever since. But it needed initiative and intelligence, rather than just going to sleep like a blockhead on the office stool!'

'Come, come,' broke in Monsieur Josserand, 'are you going to reproach me now for being honest?'

She stood up and advanced towards him, brandishing her Lamartine.

'Honest! What do you mean? You can start by being honest towards me; others come second, I hope! And I tell you again, sir, it's not honest to take a girl in by pretending to want to become rich some day, and then to lose your wits looking after someone else's money! It's true, I was absolutely swindled! If only I could turn the clock back! Ah, if I'd only known what your family was like!'

She was pacing up and down the room in a rage. He could not restrain a gesture of impatience, despite his great desire for peace.

'You ought to go to bed, Eléonore,' he said. 'It's past one o'clock, and this work must be finished. My family has done you no harm, so why mention them?'

'And why not, may I ask? Your family is no more sacred than anybody else's, I presume? Everyone at Clermont knows that your father, after selling his solicitor's practice, let himself be ruined by a servant girl. You could have married your daughters off long ago if he hadn't taken up with a tart when he was over seventy. He swindled me, too!'

Monsieur Josserand turned pale, and replied in a trembling voice, which grew louder as he went on:

'Look, don't let us start attacking each other's family again. Your father still hasn't paid me your dowry of thirty thousand francs, as he promised.'

'Eh? What? Thirty thousand francs!'

'That's right; don't pretend to be surprised. If my father was unfortunate, yours has behaved most shamefully towards us. I never got to know what really happened to his will; there were all sorts of funny deals so that your sister's husband would get the school in the Rue des Fossés-Saint-Victor. That no-hoper just ignores us now. We were robbed, as plain as could be!'

Madame Josserand grew livid with suppressed rage at this inconceivable outburst on the part of her husband.

'Don't say a word against papa! For forty years he was a credit to his profession. Mention the Bachelard Academy in the Panthéon quarter, and see what they say! And as for my sister and her husband, they are what they are. They tricked me, I know; but it's not for you to tell me so, and I won't tolerate it, do you hear me? Do I ever talk to you about your sister, who ran off with an army officer? Oh! Your family's perfect, isn't it?'

'But the officer married her, madam. And then there's Bachelard, that immoral brother of yours.'

'Are you going mad, sir? He's rich, he's made a fortune with his commission agency, and he's promised to give Berthe a dowry. Have you no respect for anyone?'

'Ah! yes, give Berthe a dowry! I wouldn't mind betting he won't give her a sou, and that we'll have to put up with his revolting habits for nothing. Every time he comes here I'm quite ashamed of him. A liar, a womanizer, an opportunist who takes advantage of the situation, who for the last fifteen years has got me to spend two hours every Saturday in his office checking his accounts, because he can see us grovelling before his fortune! That saves him five francs, but he hasn't given us a sou yet!'

Madame Josserand, catching her breath, paused for a moment. Then she uttered a final cry:

'And you, sir, have got a nephew in the police!'

There was another pause. The light from the little lamp grew dimmer, as Monsieur Josserand feverishly gesticulated and the wrappers fluttered about in all directions. He looked at his wife full in the face, as she sat there in her low-necked dress; quivering with courage, he was resolved to say everything.

'With eight thousand francs a year one can do a great deal,' he went on. 'You're always complaining. But you shouldn't have tried to make us live beyond our means. It's your mania for entertaining and paying visits, for having your "at homes" with tea and cakes . . .'

She did not let him finish. 'Now we're getting down to it! You'd better shut me up in a box at once. Why don't you scold me for not going about stark naked? And your daughters, sir, how are they to get husbands if we never see anybody? We don't see many people as it is. To think that after all the sacrifices I've made, I'm judged in this despicable way!'

'We must all make sacrifices, madam. Léon had to make way for his sisters, leave the house, and earn his own living. As for Saturnin, the poor boy can't even read. And as for me, I deny myself everything, and spend my nights . . .'

'Then why did you ever have daughters, sir? You're surely not going to grudge them their education? Any other man, in your place, would be proud of Hortense's certificate and Berthe's artistic talents. Everyone tonight adored the dear girl's playing of that waltz, "Aux bords de l'Oise", and I'm sure her last watercolour sketch will delight our guests tomorrow. But you, sir, you're not a real father;

you'd rather have your daughters look after cows than send them to school!'

'Oh! and what about the insurance policy I took out for Berthe? Wasn't it you, madam, who spent the money for the fourth instalment on chair-covers for the drawing-room? Since then you've even got hold of the premiums as well.'

'Of course I did, because you just leave us to die of hunger. It'll be your fault if your daughters become old maids!'

'What! It's you who scare off all the likely men, with your dresses and your ridiculous parties!'

Never had Monsieur Josserand gone so far. His wife, gasping, stammered: '*Me!* Ridiculous!' when the door opened. Hortense and Berthe came back in petticoats and dressing-gowns, with their hair down, and wearing slippers.

'Oh, the cold in our room!' said Berthe, shivering. 'The food freezes in your mouth. At least there's been a fire here this evening.'

They both drew up their chairs and sat close to the stove, which still retained some heat. Hortense held the rabbit bone between her fingertips, and adroitly picked it. Berthe dipped bits of bread in her tumbler of syrup. But their parents were so excited that they hardly noticed them come in, and went on:

'Ridiculous? Did you say ridiculous, sir? Then I won't be ridiculous any more. I'll be hanged if I ever wear out another pair of gloves trying to get them husbands! Now it's your turn! Do try not to be more ridiculous than I've been!'

'That would be difficult, madam, after the way you've trotted them about and compromised them everywhere! I don't care a hang now whether you get them married or not!'

'And I care even less, Monsieur Josserand! So little that if you aggravate me much more I'll throw them into the street. And you can go too, if you like; the door's open. Good Lord! What a good riddance that would be!'

The girls listened quietly. They were used to these arguments. They went on eating, their dressing-gowns unbuttoned and showing their shoulders, gently rubbing their bare skin against the warm earthenware of the stove. They looked charming in this undress, with their youth and healthy appetites, and their eyes heavy with sleep.

'It's silly of you to quarrel like this,' said Hortense at length, with her mouth full. 'Mamma will be in a terrible mood, and papa will be ill at the office again tomorrow. I think we're old enough to get husbands for ourselves.'

This created a diversion. The father, utterly worn out, pretended to carry on with his wrappers; he sat bent over the paper, unable to write, his hands trembling violently. The mother, who had been pacing up and down the room like a lioness on the loose, came and planted herself in front of Hortense.

'If you're talking about yourself,' she cried, 'you're a silly fool! That Verdier of yours will never marry you!'

'That's my lookout,' Hortense bluntly replied.

After disdainfully refusing five or six suitors—a clerk, a tailor's son, and other young men of no prospects, so she thought—she had finally set her sights on a lawyer, over forty, whom she had met at the Dambrevilles'. She thought him very clever, and bound to make a fortune by his talents. Unfortunately, however, for the last fifteen years Verdier had been living with a mistress, who, in their neighbourhood, even passed as his wife. Hortense was aware of this, but did not appear to be much troubled by it.

'My child,' said Monsieur Josserand, looking up from his work, 'I begged you to give up the idea of marrying that man. You know what the situation is.'

She stopped sucking her bone and replied impatiently:

'Well, so what? Verdier's promised to give her up. She's just a fool.'

'You shouldn't talk like that, Hortense. What if he gave you up too, one day, and went back to the woman you made him leave?'

'That's my lookout,' she retorted once more.

Berthe listened in silence; she knew all about the situation, and discussed each new development with her sister every day. Like her father, she was on the side of the poor woman who, after performing all the duties of a wife for fifteen years, was about to be turned into the street. But Madame Josserand intervened:

'Oh, do leave off! Dreadful women like that always end up in the gutter. Verdier, though, will never bring himself to leave her. He's just deceiving you, my dear. If I were you I wouldn't wait another second for him; I'd try and find somebody else.'

Hortense's voice grew harsher still, and two livid spots appeared on her cheeks.

'You know what I'm like, mamma. I want him, and I'll have him. I'll never marry anybody else, even if I have to wait a hundred years!'

Madame Josserand shrugged her shoulders.

'And you call other people fools!'

Hortense stood up, trembling with anger.

'Now, don't start on me!' she cried. 'I've finished my rabbit, and I'd rather go to bed. Since you can't manage to find us husbands, you must let us find them ourselves in whatever way we choose!'

And she went out, slamming the door behind her.

Madame Josserand turned majestically towards her husband and remarked profoundly:

'That, sir, is the result of your upbringing.'

Monsieur Josserand made no reply, but kept inking little dots on his fingernail as he waited to continue his writing. Berthe, who had eaten her bread, was dipping a finger in the glass to finish her syrup. Her back was nice and warm, and she was in no hurry to go back to her room where she would have to put up with her sister's ill-temper.

'Yes, that's how much gratitude you get,' continued Madame Josserand, pacing up and down the dining-room again. 'For twenty years you wear yourself out for these girls, you go without so that they can become refined, and then they won't even give you the satisfaction of making a marriage you approve of. It would be different if they had ever been refused anything. But I've never spent a sou on myself; I've gone without proper clothes in an attempt to dress them as if we had an income of fifty thousand francs a year. No, it's really too much. When the little brats have got the right education, with just enough religion, and the manners of rich young ladies, they turn their backs on you and talk of marrying lawyers, adventurers who lead lives of debauchery.'

She stood in front of Berthe and, wagging her finger, said:

'As for you, if you behave like your sister you'll have me to deal with.'

Then she resumed her pacing, talking now to herself, jumping from one idea to another, contradicting herself with the brazenness of a woman who thinks she is always right.

'I did what I had to do, and if need be I'd do it all over again. In life it's only the faint-hearted who go to the wall. Money's money, and if you haven't got any you might as well give up. For my part, whenever I had twenty sous I always said I had forty, because the great thing is to be envied, not pitied. It's no good having a fine education if you haven't got good clothes to wear, then people only look down on you. It may not be right, but that's how it is. I'd rather wear dirty petticoats than a cotton dress. Eat potatoes if you like, but put a chicken on the table if you have people to dinner. Only fools would deny that!'

She looked hard at her husband, for whom these last remarks were intended, but, utterly exhausted, he refused to be drawn a second time and was cowardly enough to declare:

'Yes, very true! Money's everything nowadays.'

'Do you hear?' resumed Madame Josserand, returning towards her daughter. 'Behave correctly and try to do us credit. How did you manage to let that marriage slip through your fingers?'

Berthe could see that it was her turn now.

'I don't know, mamma,' she said softly.

'An assistant manager,' continued her mother, 'not yet thirty, and with splendid prospects. Money coming in every month—a regular income, there's nothing like it. I'm sure you made some silly blunder, as you have with all the others.'

'No, I'm sure I didn't, mamma. I expect he found out that I haven't got a penny.'

Madame Josserand's voice rose.

'And what about the dowry your uncle's going to give you? Everyone knows about it. No, it must have been something else; he disappeared too abruptly. After dancing with him you went into the parlour, and . . .'

Berthe became confused.

'Yes, mamma, and, as we were alone, he tried to do all sorts of horrid things—he caught me by the waist and kissed me. I was frightened, and pushed him up against a table . . .'

Her mother, once more overcome with rage, interrupted her.

'Pushed him up against a table! Oh, you stupid thing! You pushed him up against a table, did you?'

'Well, mamma, he caught hold of me . . .'

'What of it? Caught hold of you? As if that mattered. A lot of good it is to send simpletons like you to school! Whatever did they teach you there, eh?'

A rush of colour rose to the girl's cheeks and shoulders, while, in her virginal confusion, tears came into her eyes.

'It wasn't my fault. He looked so wicked; I didn't know what to do.'

'Didn't know what to do? She didn't know what to do! Haven't I told you a hundred times not to be so absurdly timid? You've got to live in society. When a man takes liberties it means he's in love with you, and there's always a nice way of keeping him in his place. Just for a kiss behind the door! It's not even worth mentioning! And you go pushing people up against a table and spoiling all your chances of getting married!'

Then, assuming a sage air, she went on:

'I give up; there's nothing to be done with you—you're so silly, my dear. I'd have to coach you in everything, and that would be a bore. Try and understand that, as you've no fortune, you've got to catch a man by some other means. You should be friendly, give tender glances, let your hand go sometimes, and permit a little playfulness without appearing to do so; in short, you should fish for a husband. And it certainly doesn't improve your eyes to cry like a big baby.'

Berthe was sobbing violently.

'You really annoy me—do stop crying! Monsieur Josserand, just tell your daughter not to spoil her face by crying like that. If she lost her looks, that would really be too much.'

'My dear,' said her father, 'be good and listen to your mother's advice. You mustn't spoil your looks, my darling.'

'What irritates me is that she can be pleasant enough when she likes,' continued Madame Josserand. 'Come on, wipe your eyes and look at me as if I was a gentleman courting you. You must smile and drop your fan, so that, as he picks it up, his fingers just touch yours. No, no, not like that! You're holding your head up too stiffly—it makes you look like a sick hen. Lean back more, show your neck; you're still young enough to show it off.'

'Like this, mamma?'

'Yes, that's better. Don't be so stiff; keep your waist supple. Men don't care for girls who look like wooden planks. And, above all, if they go a bit too far don't behave like a simpleton. When a man goes too far, he's cooked, my dear.'

The drawing-room clock struck two and, excited as she was by sitting up so late, and becoming quite frenzied in her desire for an immediate marriage, Madame Josserand began thinking aloud as she twisted her daughter about like a Dutch doll. Berthe, heavy at heart, submitted in a tame, spiritless fashion; fear and confusion half choked her. Suddenly, in the middle of a merry laugh that her mother was forcing her to attempt, she burst into tears and exclaimed:

'No, no, it's no use; I just can't do it!'

For a moment Madame Josserand remained speechless with amazement. Ever since leaving the Dambrevilles' party her hand had been itching; all at once she slapped Berthe with all her might.

'There, take that! You're really so annoying, you great ninny! If you ask me, the men are right!'

This convulsion had made her drop her Lamartine. Picking it up, she wiped it and swept majestically out of the room without another word.

'It was bound to end like that,' muttered Monsieur Josserand, who was afraid to detain his daughter. She also went off to bed, holding her cheek and sobbing louder than ever.

As Berthe felt her way across the anteroom she found that her brother Saturnin, barefooted, was still up, listening. Saturnin was a big, hulking fellow of twenty-five, wild-eyed, who had remained childish after an attack of brain fever. Without being actually insane, he occasionally terrified everybody in the house by fits of blind fury whenever anybody annoyed him. Berthe alone was able to subdue him by a look. When she was still a little girl he had nursed her through a long illness, obedient as a dog to all her little caprices; and ever since he had saved her, he adored her with a deep, passionate devotion.

'Has she been beating you again?' he asked, in a low, tender voice.

Disturbed at meeting him, Berthe tried to send him back to his room.

'Go to bed; it has nothing to do with you.'

'Yes, it has. I won't let her beat you. She woke me up with her shouting. She'd better not do it again, or I'll give her one back.'

She caught hold of his wrists, and talked to him as if he were a disobedient animal. He was subdued at once, and started whimpering like a little boy:

'It hurts terribly, doesn't it? Show me where, so that I can kiss it better.'

When he had found her cheek in the dark, he kissed it, wetting it with his tears, as he repeated:

'Now it's better again; now it's better again.'

Meanwhile Monsieur Josserand, left alone, had put down his pen, too grieved to go on writing. After a few minutes he got up and went quietly to listen at the various doors. Madame Josserand was snoring. No sounds of weeping came from his daughters' room. All was dark and silent. Then, somewhat reassured, he came back. He adjusted the lamp, which was smoking, and mechanically began writing again. He did not feel the two great tears which fell on to the wrappers, in the solemn silence of the sleeping house.

III

As soon as the fish had been served (some dubiously fresh skate in black butter, which the clumsy Adèle had swamped in vinegar), Hortense and Berthe, seated on either side of uncle Bachelard, kept urging him to drink, filling his glass in turns and repeating:

'It's your saint's day, you should drink to it! Here's to your health, uncle!'

They had plotted to make him give them twenty francs. Every year their mother deliberately placed them thus, on either side of her brother, leaving him to their tender mercies. But it was hard work, needing all the cupidity of two girls spurred on by visions of Louis Quinze shoes and five-button gloves. To get him to give them the twenty francs, they had to make him completely drunk. He was ferociously miserly whenever he was with his own family, though elsewhere he would squander in drunken debauchery the eighty thousand francs a year he made from his commission agency. Fortunately, that evening he had arrived half-drunk, having spent the afternoon with a lady in the Faubourg Montmartre, a dyer, who used to get vermouth for him from Marseilles.

'Your health, duckies!' he replied in his thick, husky voice, each time he emptied his glass.

Covered in jewellery, and with a rose in his buttonhole, he sat in the middle of the table—the type of huge, rough, boozing tradesman who had wallowed in all sorts of vice. There was a lurid brilliancy about the false teeth in his furrowed, dissolute face; his great red nose shone like a beacon beneath his snow-white, close-cropped hair; while now and again his eyelids drooped involuntarily over his pale, rheumy eyes. Gueulin, the son of his wife's sister, declared that his uncle had never been sober during the whole ten years that he had been a widower.

'Narcisse, can I give you some skate? It's excellent,' said Madame Josserand, smiling at her brother's drunken condition, though inwardly somewhat disgusted.

She sat opposite him, with little Gueulin on her left, and on her right, Hector Trublot, a young man to whom she was obliged to show some attention. She usually took advantage of this family dinner to pay back certain invitations she had received, and so it was that Madame Juzeur, a lady living in the house, was also present, next to Monsieur Josserand. As the uncle always behaved very badly at table, and it was only the thought of his fortune which helped to temper their disgust, she only asked her intimate acquaintances to meet him, or else such people whom she no longer considered it worth trying to impress. For instance, at one time she had thought of young Trublot as a son-in-law, for he was then in a money-changer's office, waiting for his wealthy father to buy him a share in the business. But as Trublot professed total contempt for marriage she no longer took any trouble over him, even putting him next to Saturnin, who had never learnt how to eat properly. Berthe, who always had to sit next to her brother, was charged with keeping him in order with a look whenever his fingers strayed too often into the gravy.

After the fish came a meat pie, and the young ladies thought the moment had come to begin their attack.

'Have some more wine, uncle dear!' said Hortense. 'It's your saint's day; aren't you going to give us something on your saint's day?'

'Oh! so it is,' added Berthe, innocently. 'People always give something on their saint's day; so you must give us twenty francs.'

As soon as he heard the mention of money, Bachelard pretended to be more tipsy still. It was his usual trick. His eyelids drooped, and he became absolutely drivelling.

'Eh? what?' he stuttered.

'Twenty francs. You know very well what twenty francs are; it's no use pretending you don't,' said Berthe. 'Give us twenty francs; and then we'll love you—oh, ever so much!'

They threw their arms round his neck, called him the sweetest names, and kissed his rubicund face, without showing the slightest disgust at the revolting odour of debauchery he exhaled. Monsieur Josserand, bothered by this smell—a mixture of absinthe, tobacco, and musk—was disturbed to see his daughter's virginal charms in such close contact with this lecherous old rogue.

'Leave him alone!' he cried.

'Why?' asked Madame Josserand, looking daggers at her husband. 'It's just a game. If Narcisse wants to give them twenty francs, that's up to him!'

'Monsieur Bachelard is so good to them,' murmured little Madame Juzeur, complacently.

But Bachelard, still uncooperative, became more drivelling than ever, as he slobbered out:

'It's funny . . . I don't know, really not! I don't know . . .'

Hortense and Berthe exchanged glances and then let him go. No doubt he had not had enough to drink. So they filled his glass once more, laughing like prostitutes about to relieve a man of his wallet. Their bare arms, delightfully plump and fresh, passed backwards and forwards under their uncle's big red nose.

Meanwhile, Trublot, like a quiet fellow who prefers having fun in private, kept looking at Adèle as she clumsily waited on the guests. He was very short-sighted, and thought she looked pretty with her strong Breton features and her hair the colour of dirty hemp. When she brought in the roast, a piece of veal, she stretched right across him, and he, pretending to pick up his napkin, gave her a good pinch on the calf. The girl, not understanding, looked at him as if he had asked her for some bread.

'What's the matter?' said Madame Josserand. 'Did she push against you, sir? Oh, that girl! she's so awkward! But what can you expect? She's quite new to service, you know, she'll be better when she's had some training.'

'Of course; it's quite all right,' replied Trublot, stroking his bushy black beard with the serenity of some young Indian god.

The conversation was becoming more animated in the dining-room, which, icy cold at first, was gradually being warmed by the steam from the dishes. Once more Madame Juzeur was confiding to Monsieur Josserand the sad story of her thirty years of solitude. She raised her eyes to heaven, and contented herself with this discreet allusion to the drama of her life: her husband had left her after ten days of married bliss, and no one ever knew why; more than this she did not say. Now she lived by herself in quiet and very cosy lodgings, which were often visited by priests.

'It's so sad, though, at my age!' she simpered, cutting up her veal in a most delicate manner.

'A very unfortunate little woman,' whispered Madame Josserand in Trublot's ear, with an air of profound sympathy.

But Trublot glanced indifferently at this pious woman, so full of reserve and mystery. She was not his type.

Then they had a sudden scare. Saturnin, whom Berthe, being so busy with her uncle, was no longer watching, had begun playing with his food, cutting up his meat and arranging it into various shapes on his plate. The poor lad was a source of exasperation to his mother, who was both afraid and ashamed of him; she did not know how to rid herself of him, her pride forbidding her to make him a common workman after she had sacrificed him in favour of his sisters by taking him out of a school where his slothful intelligence could hardly be roused. During the years that he had been hanging about the house, helpless and stupid, she had lived in constant fear, especially when she had to let him appear in company. Her pride suffered cruelly.

'Saturnin!' she cried.

But Saturnin began to chuckle, delighted at the nasty mess on his plate. He had no respect for his mother, but openly called her a lying old hag, with the strange clairvoyance of lunatics who think out loud. The situation seemed, indeed, to be turning ugly, and he would have thrown the plate at her if Berthe, reminded of her duty, had not given him a stern look. He tried to resist; then his eyes dulled and he slumped back in his chair, gloomy and depressed, as if in a trance, until dinner was over.

'Gueulin, I hope you've brought your flute?' asked Madame Josserand, trying to dispel the general feeling of unease.

Gueulin was an amateur flautist, but only played in houses where he felt quite at home.

'My flute? Of course I have,' he replied.

His red hair and whiskers seemed more bristly than usual as he looked on, quite absorbed, at the girls' manoeuvres around their uncle. Himself a clerk in an insurance office, he used to meet Bachelard directly after office hours and never left him, following him round all the usual cafés and brothels. Behind the huge, ungainly figure of the one, you were sure to see the small, pale features of the other.

'That's it; keep at it!' he cried, as if he were a spectator at a fight.

Uncle Bachelard was, in fact, getting the worst of it. When, after the vegetables—French beans swimming in water—Adèle brought in a vanilla-and-currant ice, there was great rejoicing round the table; and the young ladies took advantage of the situation to make their uncle drink half the bottle of champagne which Madame Josserand had bought at a grocer's round the corner for three francs. He was getting maudlin, and forgot to keep up the farce of appearing imbecilic.

'Eh? twenty francs! Why twenty francs? Oh, I see! You want me to give you twenty francs? But I haven't got them, really I haven't! Ask Gueulin. Didn't I come away without my wallet, Gueulin, and you had to pay at the café? If I'd got them, my darlings, I'd give them to you for being so sweet!'

Gueulin, in his detached way, was laughing like an ill-greased cartwheel.

'Oh, the old humbug!' he muttered.

Then, suddenly getting carried away, he cried:

'Search him!'

Then, losing all restraint, Hortense and Berthe threw themselves upon their uncle once more. Checked at first by their good breeding, this desire for the twenty francs suddenly got the better of them, and all pretence was now abandoned. The one, with both hands, searched his waistcoat pockets, while the other thrust her fist into the pockets of his frock-coat. Bachelard, however, pinned back in his chair, continued to struggle, but laughter broken by drunken hiccups overcame him.

'I swear, I 'aven't got a penny. Leave off, you're tickling me!'

'Look in his trousers!' cried Gueulin, excited by the whole spectacle.

Berthe determinedly thrust her hand into one of his trouser pockets. They were trembling with excitement as they grew rougher and rougher, and they could almost have slapped their uncle's face. Suddenly Berthe uttered a cry of victory; from the depths of his pocket she drew forth a handful of money, which she scattered on a plate, and there, among the copper and silver, was a gold twenty-franc piece.

'I've got it!' she cried, as, with flushed cheeks, and her hair in disorder, she tossed the coin in the air and caught it again.

All the guests clapped their hands; they thought it terribly funny. There was a hum of excitement, and it was the success of the dinner. Madame Josserand smiled tenderly at her dear daughters. Bachelard, picking up his money, remarked sententiously that if they wanted twenty francs they had to earn them. And the two girls, exhausted but content, sat panting on either side of him, their lips still quivering with the excitement of the fray.

A bell rang. They had been at table for a long time, and guests were now beginning to arrive. Monsieur Josserand, who had decided to laugh, like his wife, at what had occurred, would have liked them to sing a little Béranger,* but she silenced him; that sort of entertainment was too much for her poetic taste. She hurried on the dessert, the more so because Bachelard, annoyed at having to give away the twenty francs, was becoming quarrelsome, complaining that Léon, his nephew, had not even bothered to wish him many happy returns. Léon had only been invited to the soirée. Then, as they rose from table, Adèle said that the architect from downstairs and a young gentleman were in the drawing-room.

'Ah, yes! that young man,' whispered Madame Juzeur, as she took Monsieur Josserand's arm. 'So you invited him? I saw him earlier talking to the concierge. He's very nice-looking.'

Madame Josserand took Trublot's arm, and then Saturnin, left alone at table, and whom all the fuss about the twenty francs had not roused from his torpor, upset his chair in a sudden paroxysm of fury, shouting:

'I won't have it, by God! I won't!'

This was just what his mother always dreaded. She motioned to Monsieur Josserand to go on with Madame Juzeur, while she disengaged her arm from that of Trublot, who understood the situation and disappeared; but he must have made a mistake, for he slipped off towards the kitchen in the wake of Adèle. Bachelard and Gueulin, ignoring the 'maniac', as they called him, stood chuckling and nudging each other in a corner.

'He was very strange all evening; I was afraid something like this might happen,' muttered Madame Josserand, in a state of high anxiety. 'Berthe, quick, quick!'

But Berthe was showing the twenty-franc piece to Hortense. Saturnin had grabbed a knife, and kept repeating: 'My God! I won't have it! I'll rip them open!'

'Berthe!' shrieked Madame Josserand, in despair.

As the girl came rushing up, she only just had time to prevent her brother from going into the drawing-room, knife in hand. She shook him angrily, while he, with his madman's logic, tried to explain.

'Don't try to stop me; they deserve it . . . It's for the best . . . I'm sick of their awful ways. They just want to sell us.'

'Nonsense!' cried Berthe. 'What's the matter with you? What are you shouting about?'

Confused and trembling with fury, he stared at her and stammered out:

'They're trying to get you married. But they never will! I won't let them hurt you!'

His sister could not help laughing. Where had he got the idea that they were going to marry her? He nodded his head, declaring that he knew it, that he was sure of it. When his mother tried to soothe him he gripped the knife so firmly that she shrank back, appalled. It alarmed her to think that they had been overheard, and she hurriedly told Berthe to take Saturnin away and lock him in his room, while he, however, kept raising his voice as he became more and more excited.

'I won't let them marry you. I won't let them hurt you. If they do, I'll rip them open!'

Then Berthe put her hands on his shoulders and looked him straight in the face.

'Listen,' she said, 'be quiet, or I won't love you any more.'

He staggered back; his face took on a gentler, despairing look, and his eyes filled with tears.

'You won't love me any more? You won't love me any more? Don't say that! Oh, please say you'll still love me; say you'll always love me, and never love anybody else!'

She caught him by the wrist and led him out, docile as a child.

In the drawing-room Madame Josserand, with exaggerated cordiality, greeted Campardon as her dear neighbour. Why hadn't Madame Campardon given her the great pleasure of her company? When the architect replied that his wife was still rather poorly, she became even more gushing, and declared that she would have been delighted to receive her in a dressing-gown and slippers. But her smile was directed at Octave, who was talking to Monsieur Josserand; all her gushing amiability was intended to reach him over Campardon's shoulder. When her husband introduced the young man to her, she was so effusive that Octave became quite embarrassed.

Other guests were arriving—stout mothers with skinny daughters; fathers and uncles only just roused from their day of somnolence at the office, driving before them their flocks of marriageable daughters. Two lamps, covered with pink paper shades, threw a subdued light over the room, hiding the shabby yellow velvet of the furniture, the dingy piano, and the three dirty prints of Swiss scenery, which formed black patches against the bare, chilly panels of white and gold. This niggardly brilliance served to cloak the guests' shortcomings, veiling their worn faces and their crude attempts at finery. Madame Josserand wore her flame-coloured gown of the previous evening; but, in order to put people off the scent, she had spent the whole day sewing new sleeves on to the bodice and embellishing it with a lace cape to hide her shoulders, while her daughters sat beside her in their greasy dressing-gowns, stitching away ferociously, putting new trimmings on their only gowns, which ever since the previous winter they had been patching up and altering in this way.

Each time the bell rang there was a sound of whispering in the anteroom. In the gloomy drawing-room people talked in an undertone, while every now and then the forced laugh of some young lady struck a discordant note. Behind little Madame Juzeur, Bachelard and Gueulin kept nudging each other and making smutty remarks; Madame Josserand anxiously watched them, afraid, as ever, that her brother might misbehave. Madame Juzeur could hear everything they said, her lips trembling as she smiled angelically at all the naughty anecdotes. Uncle Bachelard had the reputation of having an eye for the ladies. His nephew, on the other hand, was chaste. However tempting the opportunity, Gueulin refused women's favours on principle; not because he despised them, but because he was fearful as to the consequences of such bliss. 'There's always some bother,' he would say.

At last Berthe reappeared, and went hurriedly up to her mother.

'Well, that wasn't easy,' she whispered. 'He wouldn't go to bed. I double-locked the door, but I'm afraid he'll break everything in his room.'

Madame Josserand tugged violently at her daughter's dress. Octave, close by, had turned his head.

'My daughter Berthe, Monsieur Mouret,' she said, in her most gracious manner, as she introduced her to him. 'Monsieur Octave Mouret, my dear.'

She gave her daughter a look. The latter well knew the significance of that look—it was a call, as it were, to arms, and it reminded her of the lessons of the previous night. She obeyed immediately, with the complacent indifference of a girl who no longer cares to stop and examine a potential suitor. She recited her part quite prettily, with the easy grace of a Parisienne already a little weary of the world, but completely at home with all subjects, speaking enthusiastically of the South, where she had never been. Octave, used to the stiffness of provincial virgins, was quite charmed by all this friendly chatter.

Just then Trublot, who had not been seen since dinner, furtively slipped in from the dining-room, and Berthe, noticing him, asked thoughtlessly where he had been. He did not answer, which embarrassed her somewhat, and to get out of her awkward position she introduced the two young men to each other. Her mother, meanwhile, had not taken her eyes off her, assuming the attitude of a commander-in-chief, and directing the campaign from her armchair. When satisfied that the first engagement had been successful, she recalled her daughter with a sign, and whispered:

'Wait until the Vabres are here before you play. And make sure you play loud enough.'

Octave, left alone with Trublot, began to question him.

'Charming, isn't she?'

'Yes, not bad.'

'The young lady in blue is her elder sister, isn't she? She isn't as pretty.'

'No, she certainly isn't. She's much thinner.'

Trublot, who was short-sighted, could not see her clearly. He had come back very contented, chewing little black things, which Octave, to his surprise, perceived to be coffee-beans.

'Tell me,' he asked bluntly, 'in the South the women are plump, aren't they?'

Octave smiled, and immediately he and Trublot were on the best of terms. They had many ideas in common. They sat down on a sofa in the corner and proceeded to exchange confidences. The one talked of his employer at the Ladies' Paradise—Madame Hédouin, a damned fine woman, but too frigid; the other said that he was employed as correspondent from nine to five at Monsieur Desmarquay's, the money-changer's, where there was a stunning maidservant. Just then the drawing-room door opened, and three people came in.

'Those are the Vabres,' whispered Trublot, leaning over to his new friend. 'Auguste, the tall one, with the face like a sick sheep, is the landlord's eldest son. He's thirty-three, and suffers from continual migraine, which affects his eyesight and at one time prevented him from learning Latin. He's very bad-tempered, and has gone into business. The other, Théophile, that weedy fellow with sandy hair and a straggly beard, that little old man of twenty-eight, forever coughing and wracked by toothache, tried all sorts of trades, and then married the young woman in front of him, Madame Valérie.'

'I've seen her before,' interrupted Octave. 'She's the daughter of a local haberdasher, isn't she? But how deceptive those little veils are. I thought she was pretty, but she's just striking-looking, with that dried-up, leaden complexion.'

'Yes, she's another one who isn't my type at all,' replied Trublot sententiously. 'She's got wonderful eyes; that's enough for some men. But she's as thin as a rake!'

Madame Josserand had risen to shake hands with Valérie.

'What?' she cried. 'Monsieur Vabre hasn't come with you? And Monsieur and Madame Duveyrier haven't done us the honour of coming either, although they promised they would. It really isn't fair of them!'

The young woman made excuses for her father-in-law on account of his age, though he really preferred to stay at home and work in the evening. As for her brother-in-law and sister-in-law, they had asked her to give their apologies, as they had been invited to an official reception they were obliged to attend. Madame Josserand bit her lips. She had never missed one of the Saturdays of those stuck-up people on the first floor, who thought it beneath them to come up to the fourth floor for her Tuesdays. No doubt her modest tea-parties weren't the same as their grand orchestral concerts. But when her daughters were both married, and she had got two sons-in-law and their relatives to fill her drawing-room, she would have choral entertainments too.

'Get ready,' she whispered in Berthe's ear.

There were about thirty guests, packed in rather tightly as they had not thrown open the little drawing-room, which was being used as a cloakroom for the ladies. The newcomers shook hands all round. Valérie sat next to Madame Juzeur, while Bachelard and Gueulin made fond remarks about Théophile Vabre, whom they thought it funny to describe as 'useless'. Monsieur Josserand, invisible in his own drawing-room, blotted out as completely as if he were a guest for whom everyone was looking, although he stood right in front of them, was listening in horror to a story told by one of his old friends: Bonnaud—he knew Bonnaud, didn't he?—the chief accountant of the Northern Railways, whose daughter had got married last spring? Well, Bonnaud, it seemed, had just discovered that his son-in-law, to all appearances a most respectable person, had once been a clown, and for ten years had been kept by a female circus-rider!

'Ssh, ssh!' murmured several obliging voices. Berthe had opened the piano.

'Oh,' explained Madame Josserand, 'it's an unpretentious little piece—a simple reverie. I'm sure you like music, Monsieur Mouret. Come closer to the piano. My daughter plays this rather well—just an amateur, you know; but she plays with feeling, a great deal of feeling.'

'Watch out!' said Trublot, under his breath. 'That's the sonata trick.'

Octave was obliged to go and stand near the piano. To see the attentions which Madame Josserand showered upon him, one would have thought that she was making Berthe play solely for him.

' "The Banks of the Oise",' she went on. 'It's really very pretty. Now, my love, begin; and don't be nervous. I'm sure Monsieur Octave will make allowances.'

The girl attacked the piece without the least sign of nervousness; but her mother never took her eyes off her, with the air of a sergeant ready to punish with a slap the least technical blunder. What mortified her was that the instrument, cracked and wheezy after fifteen years of daily scale-playing, did not have the sonorous quality of tone possessed by the Duveyriers' grand piano. Moreover, she felt that her daughter never played loud enough.

After the tenth bar Octave, looking quite enraptured, and keeping time with his head to the more flamboyant passages, no longer listened. He watched the audience, noting the polite efforts on the part of the men to pay attention, and the affected delight of the women. He examined them now that they were left to themselves, and saw how their daily cares were once more reflected in their tired faces. The mothers were visibly dreaming of marrying their daughters, as they stood there with open mouths and ferocious teeth, unconsciously letting themselves go. It was the strange madness that pervaded this drawing-room—a ravenous appetite for sons-in-law—that consumed these bourgeois women as they listened to the asthmatic sounds of the piano. The girls, quite exhausted, were dozing off; their heads drooped, and they forgot to hold themselves upright. Octave, who despised innocent young ladies, was more interested in Valérie. Plain she certainly was, in that extraordinary yellow silk dress, trimmed with black satin; but he found her attractive, his gaze kept returning uneasily to her, while she, unnerved by the shrill music, had a vague look in her eyes, and wore a sickly, neurotic smile.

At this moment a catastrophe occurred. The bell rang, and a gentleman entered the room without paying the slightest attention to the music.

'Oh, doctor!' said Madame Josserand in annoyance.

Doctor Juillerat made a gesture of apology, and stood stock-still. At this moment Berthe dwelt lingeringly on a certain tender phrase, which her listeners greeted with murmurs of approval. 'Charming!' 'Delightful!' Madame Juzeur seemed to be swooning, as if someone were tickling her. Hortense stood beside her sister, turning over the pages, oblivious to the surging torrent of notes, straining her ear to catch the sound of the doorbell; and when the doctor came in, her gesture of disappointment was so marked that she tore one of the pages. Then suddenly the piano trembled beneath Berthe's frail fingers, which beat upon it like hammers. The dream had come to an end in a deafening crash of furious harmonies.

There was a moment's hesitation. The audience began to wake up. Had it finished? Then came a shower of compliments. 'Absolutely lovely!' 'What talent!'

'Mademoiselle is a really wonderful musician,' said Octave, interrupted in his observations. 'No one has ever given me such pleasure.'

'Really?' exclaimed Madame Josserand in delight. 'She plays rather well, I must admit. You know, we've never refused her anything; she's our treasure! She has every talent she ever wished for. Ah! if you only knew her, sir.'

Once more a confused sound of voices filled the room. Berthe coolly accepted all the praise bestowed upon her performance, and did not leave the piano, waiting for her mother to relieve her from her duty. The latter was just telling Octave of the remarkable way her daughter played 'The Reapers', a brilliant tour-de-force, when a dull, far-off sound of knocking created a stir among the guests. The noise grew louder and more violent, as if someone were trying to break open a door. The guests stopped talking, and exchanged questioning glances.

'What's that noise?' Valérie ventured to ask. 'I heard it just now, when the music was ending.'

Madame Josserand had turned quite pale. She had recognized Saturnin's blows. The wretched lunatic! She imagined him leaping into the room and scattering her guests. If he went on thumping like that, there would be another marriage down the drain!

'It's the kitchen-door that keeps banging,' she said with a forced smile. 'Adèle never shuts it. Go and see to it, Berthe.'

Her daughter had also understood. She rose and disappeared. The knocking ceased at once, but she did not return immediately. Uncle Bachelard, who had scandalously disturbed the performance of 'The Banks of the Oise' with his loud remarks, succeeded in disconcerting his sister by shouting out to Gueulin that he was bored to death and was going to get some grog. They both returned to the dining-room, slamming the door after them.

'Dear old Narcisse—he's so eccentric!' Madame Josserand said to Valérie and Madame Juzeur, as she sat down between them. 'He works so hard at his business! You know, he made nearly a hundred thousand francs this year!'

Free at last, Octave had rejoined Trublot, who was half asleep on the sofa. Near them a group surrounded Doctor Juillerat, the old neighbourhood physician, a man of little talent, but who, by degrees, had built up a good practice, having attended all the mothers in their confinements and prescribed remedies for all their daughters' ills. He had made a speciality of women's ailments, so that in the evenings he was besieged by husbands eager to obtain free advice in some corner of the room. Théophile was just telling him that Valérie had had another attack the day before; she was always short of breath and complaining of a lump in her throat;* and he himself was not very well, but his symptoms were not the same. Then he talked of nothing but himself, and of his bad luck. He had begun to study law, had dabbled in industry at an iron foundry, tried administrative work in the pawnshop offices. Then he had taken up photography, and believed he had discovered a patent for automatic cabs; and at the same time he had got a commission on the sale of piano-flutes, invented by one of his friends. He eventually returned to the subject of his wife; it was her fault if things never went right for them; she was killing him with her perpetual nervous attacks.

'Do give her something, doctor,' he pleaded, his eyes gleaming with hatred, as he coughed and moaned in all the mad exasperation of impotence.

Trublot watched him, full of disdain, laughing inwardly as he glanced at Octave. Doctor Juillerat, meanwhile, uttered vague and soothing words: doubtless something could be found to help the dear lady. At the age of fourteen she used to have similar attacks at the shop in the Rue Neuve-Saint-Augustin; he had treated her for dizzy spells, which had always ended with nosebleeds. And as Théophile recollected in despair her languid apathy as a girl, while now she was a source of torture to him—capricious, her mood changing a score of times every day—the doctor simply nodded his head. Marriage did not agree with all women.

'No, it certainly doesn't!' murmured Trublot. 'A father who's turned himself into a vegetable by spending thirty years of his life selling needles and thread, and a mother whose face has always been a mass of pimples, and living in that stuffy hole of a shop—how can you expect such people to produce normal daughters?'

Octave was surprised. He had begun to lose some of his respect for this drawing-room, which he had entered with all the awe of a provincial. His curiosity was reawakened when he saw Campardon consulting the doctor in his turn, but whispering, like a serious person who does not want anyone to know about his domestic misfortunes.

'By the way,' said Octave to Trublot, 'as you seem to know everything, tell me what's the matter with Madame Campardon. Whenever her ill-health is mentioned I see everyone put on a very sad face.'

'Well, my dear fellow,' replied the young man, 'she's got . . .'

And he whispered in Octave's ear. At first his listener smiled, then his face became very serious with a look of deep astonishment.

'Is it possible?' he said.

Trublot gave his solemn word that it was so. He knew another lady who had the same thing.

'Besides,' he added, 'after a confinement it sometimes happens that . . .'

And he began to whisper again. Octave, convinced, felt quite sad. For a moment he had imagined all sorts of things—romance, the architect occupied elsewhere and urging him to provide amusement for his wife! At any rate he knew now that her honour was safe. The young men pressed closer against each other in the excitement of disclosing all these feminine secrets, forgetful that they might be overheard.

Just then Madame Juzeur was imparting to Madame Josserand her impressions of Octave. She certainly thought him most agreeable, but she preferred Monsieur Auguste Vabre. This gentleman stood, mute and insignificant, in a corner of the room, with his usual evening headache.

'What surprises me, my dear, is that you haven't thought of him for your daughter Berthe. A young man established in business and extremely steady. He wants a wife, too. I know he's interested in getting married.'

Madame Josserand listened in surprise. She would never have thought of the haberdasher. Madame Juzeur, however, insisted, for, unfortunate herself, it was her passion to work for the happiness of other women, so that she took an interest in all the romantic affairs of the house. She declared that Auguste had never taken his eyes off Berthe. In short, she invoked her own experience of men: Monsieur Mouret would never let himself be caught, whereas a match with that nice Monsieur Vabre would be very easy and very advantageous. But Madame Josserand, weighing up the latter with a glance, felt quite sure that a son-in-law like that would never be of much use in filling her drawing-room.

'My daughter hates him,' she said, 'and I'll never go against her feelings.'

A gawky young lady had just played a fantasia on the *Dame Blanche*.* As uncle Bachelard had fallen asleep in the dining-room, Gueulin reappeared with his flute and gave imitations of the nightingale. Nobody listened, however, for the story about Bonnaud had spread. It had quite upset Monsieur Josserand; fathers held up their hands in horror, while mothers gasped for breath. What! Bonnaud's son-in-law was a clown! Whom, then, could they trust? The parents, in their lust for marriage, were as distressed as if they had had nightmares about distinguished-looking convicts in evening-dress. As a matter of fact, Bonnaud had been so delighted to get rid of his daughter that he had hardly bothered with references, despite his rigid prudence as a fussy chief accountant.

'Mamma, tea's ready,' said Berthe, as she and Adèle opened the folding doors.

Then, as people passed slowly into the dining-room, she went up to her mother and whispered:

'I've had about enough of it! He wants me to stay and tell him stories, or else he says he'll smash everything.'

On a grey cloth, too small for the table, one of those laboriously served teas was spread, with a *brioche* bought at a neighbouring baker's and flanked by sandwiches and little cakes. At either end of the table were flowers in profusion; magnificent and expensive roses prevented anyone from noticing the stale biscuits and rancid butter. There were more cries of admiration and more heart-burnings; those Josserands were clearly ruining themselves in their attempt to marry off their daughters. The guests, casting sidelong glances at the flowers, gorged themselves with weak tea and threw themselves upon the stale buns and badly baked *brioche*, for they had dined frugally, and their one thought was to go to bed with their bellies full. For those who did not like tea, Adèle handed round redcurrant syrup in glasses. This was pronounced excellent.

Meanwhile the uncle slumbered in a corner. They did not wake him; they even politely pretended not to see him. One lady spoke of the fatigues of business. Berthe was very busy, offering sandwiches, carrying cups of tea, asking the men if they would like more sugar. But she could not attend to everybody, and Madame Josserand kept looking for Hortense, whom she suddenly caught sight of in the middle of the empty drawing-room talking to a gentleman whose back alone was visible.

'Yes, yes!' she blurted out, in a sudden fit of wrath, 'he's come at last!'

The guests began to whisper. It was that Verdier, who had been living with a woman for fifteen years while waiting to marry Hortense. Everybody knew the story, and the young ladies exchanged meaningful glances; but for propriety's sake they forbore to speak of it, and merely bit their lips. When Octave had been enlightened, he watched the gentleman's back with interest. Trublot knew the mistress, a good-hearted woman—a reformed prostitute, who was better now, he said, than the best of wives, looking after her man and keeping all his shirts in order. He was full of brotherly sympathy for her. While they were being watched from the dining-room, Hortense was scolding Verdier for being so late, rebuking him with the peevishness of an embittered virgin.

'I say! Redcurrant syrup!' said Trublot, seeing Adèle standing before him, tray in hand. Sniffing at it, he declined. But as Adèle turned round she was pushed against him by a stout lady's elbow, and he squeezed her waist hard. She smiled, and came back with the tray.

'No, thanks,' he said. 'A little later, perhaps.'

The ladies were now sitting round the table, while the men stood, eating, behind them. Enthusiastic exclamations were heard, which subsided as mouths became full. The gentlemen were asked for their opinions.

Madame Josserand exclaimed:

'True; I was forgetting. Come and look, Monsieur Mouret—you're fond of art.'

'Be careful! That's the watercolour trick,' murmured Trublot, who knew all the ways of the house. It was better than a watercolour. As if by chance, there was a porcelain bowl on the table, on the bottom of which, in a mount of freshly varnished bronze, was a miniature copy of Greuze's 'Girl with a Broken Pitcher',* painted in washy tints varying from lilac to pale blue. At the chorus of praise Berthe smiled.

'Mademoiselle is very talented,' said Octave, in his most urbane manner. 'The colours are so well blended! And such a wonderful copy!'

'The drawing certainly is!' said Madame Josserand, exultant. 'There's not a hair too many or too few. Berthe copied it at home from an engraving. At the Louvre there are so many nude subjects, and such strange people, too.'

As she made this last remark she lowered her voice, anxious to assure the young man that, although her daughter was an artist, this did not mean that she was unable to keep within the bounds of propriety. However, she clearly thought that Octave seemed indifferent; she felt that the bowl had not made its mark, and she watched him uneasily, while Valérie and Madame Juzeur, who had got to their fourth cup of tea, were uttering faint cries of admiration as they examined Berthe's masterpiece.

'You're looking at her again,' said Trublot to Octave, who was staring at Valérie.

'So I am,' he replied, somewhat confused. 'It's funny, but just now she looks quite pretty. A hot-blooded woman, obviously. I say, do you think one might risk it?'

Trublot puffed out his cheeks.

'Hot-blooded? You can never be sure. Strange you should fancy her. Anyway, it's better than marrying that little girl.'

'What little girl?' cried Octave, forgetting himself. 'What? Do you think I'm going to let myself be caught? Never! We don't go in for marriage in Marseilles.'

Madame Josserand, who was standing close by, overheard the last phrase. It was like a stab-wound to the heart. Another fruitless campaign, another wasted soirée. The blow was such that she had to lean against a chair as she despairingly surveyed the table, now cleared of all refreshment, on which there only remained the burnt top of the *brioche*. She no longer counted her defeats; but this, she resolved, would be the last. Never again, she swore, would she feed folk who simply came to stuff themselves. In her exasperation, she looked round the room to see at which man she could hurl her daughter, when she spied Auguste leaning listlessly against the wall, having had nothing to eat.

Just then Berthe, all smiles, was moving towards Octave with a cup of tea in her hand. She was carrying on the campaign in obedience to her mother's instructions. But the latter seized her by the arm and called her a silly fool under her breath. Then she said out loud, in her most gracious manner:

'Take that cup of tea to Monsieur Vabre; he's been waiting a whole hour.'

Then, whispering again in her daughter's ear, and giving her another warlike look, she added: 'Be nice, or you'll have me to deal with!'

Berthe was disconcerted for a moment, but quickly recovered. Such changes in the line of attack occurred as often as three times in an evening. She took the cup of tea to Auguste, together with the smile she had begun to wear for Octave. She made herself most agreeable, talked about Lyons silks, and gave herself the airs of an engaging young lady who would look charming behind a counter. Auguste's hands trembled a little, and he was very red, since that evening his headache was worse than usual.

Out of politeness, some of the guests went and sat down again for a moment in the drawing-room. They had eaten well, and now it was time to go. When they looked for Verdier he had already left, and the girls in their merriment could only take away with them the blurred impression of his back. Without waiting for Octave, Campardon went away with the doctor, whom he stopped on the landing to ask if there was really no hope. During tea one of the lamps had gone out, leaving a smell of rancid oil; the other lamp, with its burnt wick, gave such a lugubrious light that the Vabres rose of their own accord, despite the profuse attentions with which Madame Josserand overwhelmed them. Octave had preceded them into the anteroom, where he had a surprise. Trublot, who was looking for his hat, had disappeared. He could only have made his exit by the passage leading to the kitchen.

'Wherever has he got to? Does he use the servants' staircase?' murmured the young man.

However, he thought no more about the matter. Valérie was there, looking for her crêpe scarf. The two brothers, Théophile and Auguste, were going downstairs, without taking any notice of her. Octave, finding the scarf, handed it to her with the air of rapt attention with which he served pretty customers at the Ladies' Paradise. She looked at him, and he felt certain that her eyes, as they met his, shot forth amorous flames.

'You're too kind, sir,' she said, simply.

Madame Juzeur, who was the last to leave, gave them both a smile, at once tender and discreet. And when Octave, greatly excited, had got back to his cold bedroom, he glanced at himself in the mirror and determined that he would have a try for it!

Meanwhile, Madame Josserand was pacing up and down the deserted apartment, not saying a word, as if swept along by a whirlwind. She shut the piano with a bang, put out the last lamp, and then, going into the dining-room, began to blow out the candles with such force that the sockets shook. The sight of the devastated table, covered with dirty plates and empty cups, enraged her even more, and as she walked round she cast terrible glances at her daughter Hortense, who sat calmly crunching the burnt top of the *brioche*.

'You're getting yourself into a state again, mamma,' said the latter. 'Did it go wrong again? I'm quite happy, though: he's going to buy her some chemises so as to get rid of her.'

Madame Josserand shrugged her shoulders.

'Ah!' continued Hortense, 'you'll say that that proves nothing. All right, but steer your ship as well as I steer mine. Well, this really is a vile *brioche*. They must be desperate if they can eat this filth.'

Monsieur Josserand, who always found his wife's parties exhausting, was leaning back in his chair; but, dreading another confrontation—that Madame Josserand might sweep him aside in her fury—he joined Bachelard and Gueulin, who were sitting at the table opposite Hortense. Bachelard, on waking, had found a flask of rum. As he emptied it, he returned to the bitter subject of the twenty francs.

'It's not the money I mind,' he kept repeating to his nephew, 'it's the way they did it. You know how I am with women; I'd give them the shirt off my back, but I don't like them to ask like that. As soon as they begin asking it annoys me, and I wouldn't give them a penny.'

Then his sister began reminding him of his promises:

'Hold your tongue, Eléonore!' he barked. 'I know what I ought to do for the child! But when a woman asks like that, it's more than I can stand. I've never been able to keep friends with one, have I, Gueulin? And besides, I'm given such little respect! Léon hasn't even bothered to wish me many happy returns of the day!'

With clenched fists, Madame Josserand resumed her pacing. It was true; Léon had promised to come, but, like the others, had let her down. A man who wouldn't give up an evening even to get one of his sisters married! She had just found a little cake which had fallen behind one of the vases, and was locking it up in a drawer, when Berthe entered the room with Saturnin, whom she had gone to release. She was trying to soothe him as, haggard and with a look of mistrust in his eyes, he hunted feverishly about in the corners of the room like a dog that has been shut up for a long time.

'How silly he is!' said Berthe; 'he thinks I've just got married, and he's looking for the husband! My dear boy, you can look as long as you like! I told you it had all come to nothing. You know very well that it never does come to anything!'

Then Madame Josserand exploded:

'Ah, but it won't come to nothing this time, that I swear! Even if I have to hook him on to you myself! He'll pay for all the others. Yes, yes, Monsieur Josserand, you can stare, as if you didn't understand. The wedding will come off; and, if you don't like it, you can stay away. So, Berthe, you've only got to pick him up, do you hear?'

Saturnin apparently did not understand. He was looking under the table. The girl pointed to him, but Madame Josserand gestured as if to say that he would be got out of the way. And Berthe murmured:

'So it's settled then, it's to be Monsieur Vabre? It's all the same to me. But I do think you could have saved me a sandwich!'

IV

THE next day Octave began to focus his attention on Valérie. He studied her habits, and worked out the times when he was likely to meet her on the stairs, managing to go up frequently to his room, either when lunching at the Campardons' or when he got away under some pretext from the Ladies' Paradise. He soon noticed that every day, at about two o'clock, when taking her child to the Tuileries gardens, the young woman went down the Rue Gaillon. Accordingly, he would stand at the door and wait for her, then greet her with one of his charming shopman's smiles. Every time they met Valérie nodded politely, but never stopped, though he noticed that her dark glance was full of the fire of passion, and he found encouragement in her ravaged complexion and the supple undulation of her hips.

He had already made his plan—the bold one of a seducer used to the easy conquest of shop-girl virtue. It was simply a question of luring Valérie into his room on the fourth floor; the staircase was always silent and deserted, and up there nobody would ever discover them. He laughed to himself at the thought of the architect's moral advice; for having a woman who lived in the house was not the same as bringing one into it.

There was one thing, however, that made him uneasy. The Pichons' kitchen was separated from their dining-room by the passage, and this constantly obliged them to leave their door open. At nine in the morning Pichon went off to his office, and did not return until five o'clock. On alternate evenings he went out after dinner, from eight to twelve, to do some bookkeeping. Moreover, as soon as she heard Octave's step, the young woman, who was very shy, would push the door to, and he would only get a back view of her as she fled, with her light hair tied up in a small bun. He had thus only caught discreet glimpses of part of the room: the furniture, sad-looking and clean; the linen, of a dull whiteness in the grey light of an unseen window; the corner of a cot, at the back of the small bedroom—in fact, all the monotonous solitude of a woman who busies herself from morning till night with the petty cares of a clerk's household. But not a sound was heard there; the child seemed as silent and apathetic as its mother. At times Marie could be heard humming some tune for hours in a feeble voice. Octave, however, was furious with the stuck-up bitch, as he called her. Perhaps she was spying on him. In any case, Valérie could never come up to his room if the Pichons' door was always being opened in this way.

He was just beginning to think that things were going well. One Sunday, in the husband's absence, he had managed to be on the first-floor landing just as Valérie, in her dressing-gown, was leaving her sister-in-law's to return to her own apartment. She was obliged to speak to him, and they had stood for several minutes exchanging polite remarks. He hoped that next time she would ask him in. With a woman of her temperament the rest would follow as a matter of course.

That evening Valérie was the subject of conversation during dinner at the Campardons', as Octave tried to draw them out. But as Angèle was listening, and casting sly glances at Lisa, who was gravely handing round the roast mutton, the parents at first did nothing but sing her praises. Besides, the architect was forever extolling the respectability of the house, with the conceited assurance of a tenant who appeared to derive from this confirmation of his own moral probity.

'Most respectable people, my dear boy! You met them at the Josserands'. The husband is no fool—he's full of ideas; some day he'll make some great discovery. As for his wife, she's got a certain style, as we artists say.'

Then Madame Campardon, rather worse than the day before and half recumbent, though her illness did not prevent her from eating large slices of meat, languidly murmured:

'Poor Monsieur Théophile! He's like me; he just drags along. There's a lot to be said for Valérie—it's not easy to be tied to a man who's forever shaking with fever, and whose ailments make him irritable and unreasonable.'

During dessert Octave, seated between the architect and his wife, got to know more than he had asked. They forgot Angèle's presence, and talked with hints and winks that underlined the double meaning of their words; and if these failed them, they leaned over and whispered crudely in his ear. In short, Théophile was both stupid and impotent, and deserved to be what his wife had made him. As for Valérie, she was not worth much; she would have behaved just as badly even if her husband had been able to satisfy her, being so carried away by her natural impulses. Moreover, everybody knew that, two months after her marriage, in despair at finding that she could never have a child by her husband, and fearing that she would lose her share of old Vabre's fortune if Théophile happened to die, she had conceived her little Camille with the help of a brawny young butcher's assistant in the Rue Saint-Anne.

Finally, Campardon whispered:

'In short, my dear fellow, a hysterical woman!'

And he put into the words all the lascivious indecency of the bourgeoisie, together with the loose-lipped grin of the father of a family, whose imagination, suddenly let loose, creates images of wild orgies. Angèle looked down at her plate, afraid that she would burst out laughing if she caught Lisa's eye. The conversation then took another turn: they spoke about the Pichons, lavishing upon them words of praise.

'Oh, such respectable people!' repeated Madame Campardon. 'Sometimes, when Marie takes her little Lilitte out for a walk, I let Angèle go with her. And I can assure you, Monsieur Mouret, that I wouldn't entrust my daughter to everybody; I must be absolutely certain that their morals are unquestionable. You're very fond of Marie, aren't you, Angèle?'

'Yes, mamma,' replied the little girl.

Then came other details. It would be impossible to find a woman better brought up than she, or who had stricter principles. And how happy her husband was! Their little home was so neat, so pretty; each adored the other, and they never exchanged a single cross word!

'Besides, if they misbehaved, they wouldn't be allowed to stay in the house,' said the architect gravely, forgetting his disclosures about Valérie. 'We only want decent folk here. My word! I'd give notice the day my daughter ran the risk of meeting disreputable women on the stairs.'

He had secretly arranged to take Gasparine, that very evening, to the Opéra-Comique. So he at once went to fetch his hat, saying something about a business engagement which might detain him until very late. However, Rose must have known something about the arrangement, for Octave heard her murmur, in her resigned, motherly way, as Campardon kissed her with his usual effusive tenderness:

'Enjoy yourself—and don't catch cold coming out.'

The following morning Octave had an idea. It was to make Madame Pichon's acquaintance by doing her a few neighbourly favours; in this way, if she ever caught Valérie she would say nothing. That very day an opportunity presented itself. Madame Pichon used to take out her little Lilitte, aged eighteen months, in a wicker pram; this always annoyed Monsieur Gourd, who would never allow the vehicle to be taken up by the main staircase, so that Madame Pichon had to pull it up by the servants' stairway. Moreover, as the door of her apartment was too narrow, she had to take the wheels off every time, which was quite a job. It so happened that on this particular day, as Octave returned home, he found Marie struggling with her gloves on to unscrew the wheels. When she felt him standing behind her, waiting until the way was clear, her hands trembled and she quite lost her head.

'Why do you take all that trouble, madam?' he asked after a while. 'It would be much simpler to put the pram at the end of the passage, behind my door.'

She did not reply but remained in a squatting position, her excessive timidity preventing her from rising, and under the flaps of her bonnet he noticed that her neck and ears were suffused by a hot blush. Then he insisted:

'I assure you, madam, it won't bother me in the least.'

Without waiting for an answer, he lifted the pram and carried it off in his easy, confident way. She had to follow him, but felt so confused, so disturbed at this startling adventure in her humdrum everyday existence, that she simply looked on, unable to do more than stammer out a few disjointed phrases:

'Dear me, sir, it's too much trouble. I don't think . . . It'll be so inconvenient for you . . . My husband will be very pleased . . .'

She went in, this time tightly fastening the door after her, feeling somehow ashamed. Octave thought she must be stupid. The pram was very much in his way, for it prevented him from opening his door, and he had to slip into his room sideways. But he seemed to have won her over, the more so because Monsieur Gourd, thanks to Campardon's influence, had graciously consented to sanction this obstruction at the end of this out-of-the-way passage.

Every Sunday Marie's parents, Monsieur and Madame Vuillaume, came to spend the day with her. The following Sunday, as

Octave was going out, he saw the whole family just about to have their coffee, and was discreetly hurrying past when Marie quickly whispered something to her husband. The latter at once rose, saying:

'Excuse me, sir. I'm always out, and I haven't yet had the opportunity to thank you; I really wanted to tell you how pleased I was . . .'

Octave, protesting, was at last obliged to go in and, though he had already had some coffee, was persuaded to accept another cup. He was given the place of honour between Monsieur and Madame Vuillaume. Marie, facing him on the other side of the round table, had one of her sudden blushing fits, which for no apparent reason sent all the blood from her heart to her face. He observed her for a while, noting how she never seemed at her ease. But, as Trublot would say, she wasn't his type; she looked puny and washed-out, with her flat face and thin hair, though her features were delicate, even pretty. When she had somewhat regained her composure, she began laughing as she described the pram incident, a topic she never tired of.

'Jules, if you could only have seen the way Monsieur Mouret picked it up! It didn't take a second!'

Pichon reiterated his thanks. He was tall and thin, with a mournful air, already bowed beneath the dull routine of office life, and his eyes had a look of weary resignation, like those of an old cab-horse.

'Please, it was really no trouble,' Octave said at last. 'It isn't worth mentioning. Your coffee, madam, is delicious; I've never tasted any quite like it.'

She blushed again, so violently this time that even her hands turned bright pink.

'Don't spoil her, sir,' said Monsieur Vuillaume gravely. 'Her coffee's good, but there's better than that to be got. You see how proud she's become all of a sudden.'

'Pride comes before a fall,' declared Madame Vuillaume. 'We've always taught her to be modest.'

They were both little, shrivelled, grey-faced old people—she squeezed into a black dress, and he into an undersized frock-coat, with a large red ribbon in his button-hole.

'Yes, sir,' he said, 'I was decorated when I was sixty, the day I got my pension, after thirty-nine years as clerk at the Ministry of Public

Instruction. Well, sir, that day I dined just as usual, without letting pride interfere with my ordinary habits. The cross was my due, I knew that. I simply felt profoundly grateful.'

His record was impeccable, and he wanted everybody to know it. After twenty-five years' service his salary had been raised to four thousand francs. His pension therefore amounted to two thousand. But he had been obliged to re-enter the service as a copying clerk, with a salary of fifteen hundred, as little Marie had been born to them late in life, when Madame Vuillaume had given up all hope of having either a girl or a boy. Now that the child had a home of her own they lived on the pension-money, saving everything they could, in the Rue Durantin in Montmartre, where it was less expensive.

'And I'm seventy-six,' he said, in conclusion. 'So there, my dear son-in-law, just think of that.'

Pichon, tired and silent, looked at him, his eyes fixed on the decoration in his buttonhole. Yes, if fortune smiled on him he would be able to tell the same story. He was the youngest son of a greengrocer's widow, who had spent everything earned at the shop in enabling him to take the baccalaureate, because all her neighbours pronounced him to be such an intelligent lad; and she had died insolvent a week after his triumph at the Sorbonne. After three years of bullying at an uncle's, he had had the good luck to get a government appointment, which ought to lead him on to great things, and on the strength of which he had married.

'We do our duty, and so does the government,' he murmured, reckoning that he would have another thirty-six years to wait before he could be decorated and obtain a pension of two thousand francs.

Then, turning to Octave, he said:

'Children, you know, are such a burden.'

'Indeed they are,' remarked Madame Vuillaume. 'If we'd had another one we would never have been able to make ends meet. So remember, Jules, what I made you promise when I gave you our Marie: one child and no more, or else we'll fall out. It's only the working classes that have children as hens lay eggs, regardless of what it'll cost them. It's true, they turn them loose into the street like so many flocks of sheep. I must say it makes me quite sick.'

Octave looked at Marie, for he thought that so delicate a subject would have made her blush once more. But her face was pale as, serenely ingenuous, she nodded in agreement. He was bored to death, and did not know how to escape. These people would spend the whole afternoon in this chilly little dining-room, making a few mild remarks every now and then, as they talked of nothing but their affairs. Even dominoes would be too disturbing for them.

Madame Vuillaume now began to expound her views. After a long silence, which caused them no embarrassment, as if they had felt the need to collect their thoughts, she began:

'You have no child, sir? That'll come later. Oh, it's a great responsibility, especially for a mother! When my little girl over there was born I was forty-nine, an age when, fortunately, one knows how to behave. A boy can cope for himself, but a girl! However, I've got the consolation of knowing I did my duty by her!'

Then she briefly explained her method of education. Propriety first of all. No playing on the stairs, the child always kept at home and closely watched, for children were always up to mischief. Doors and windows tightly shut; no draughts which bring with them all sorts of nasty things from the street. Out of doors, never let go of the child's hand, and teach it always to cast its eyes downwards so as to avoid seeing anything improper. Religion should not be overdone, but simply used as a moral safeguard. Then, as she grows up, governesses must be engaged for the girl, who should never be sent to a boarding-school, where innocent children are corrupted; and one should be present at her lessons, to see that she is kept in ignorance of certain things; all newspapers should be hidden, of course, and the bookcase locked.

'A girl always knows too much,' declared the old lady, in conclusion.

As her mother was holding forth, Marie gazed vacantly into space. In imagination she again saw the claustral little lodging, those stuffy rooms in the Rue Durantin where she was not even allowed to look out of the window. She had had a long-drawn-out childhood: all sorts of prohibitions she could not understand; lines in fashion journals which her mother had inked over—black bars that made her blush; pieces cut out of her lessons which embarrassed the governesses themselves when she asked about them. There had been a sweetness about her childhood, a soft tepid growth as in a greenhouse, a waking dream in which the words and deeds of each day assumed a distorted, foolish significance. And even now, as, with a far-off look in her eyes, all these memories came back to her, the smile on her lips was the smile of a child, as ignorant after marriage as she had been before.

'You may not believe me,' said Monsieur Vuillaume, 'but my daughter had not read a single novel until she was over eighteen. Isn't that true, Marie?'

'Yes, papa.'

'I have a very nicely bound edition of George Sand,' he continued, 'and, despite her mother's fears, I decided, a few months before her marriage, to let her read *André*, a perfectly harmless work, full of imagination, and very uplifting.* I'm all for a liberal education, you know. There's certainly a place for literature. Well, the book had a most extraordinary effect on her. She cried at night in her sleep—proof that there is nothing like having a pure, innocent imagination to understand genius.'

'It's such a beautiful book,' murmured Marie, her eyes sparkling.

But, Pichon having expounded his theory of no novels before marriage and as many as one likes after marriage, Madame Vuillaume shook her head. She never read at all, and was none the worse for it. Then, Marie gently alluded to her loneliness. 'You know, I sometimes get a book to read. Jules chooses one for me from the lending library in the Passage Choiseul. I'd really like to play the piano too.'

For some time Octave had wanted to put in a word.

'Why, madam! Don't you play the piano?'

There was an awkward silence, and then the parents made a long excuse about unfortunate circumstances, not wishing to admit that they had been afraid of the expense. However, Madame Vuillaume declared that Marie had sung beautifully ever since she was born, and as a little girl had known all sorts of pretty songs by heart. She had only to hear a tune once to remember it; and her mother gave as an example a song about Spain, which told of a captive who mourned for his lady-love, a song the child sang with such expression that she drew tears from the hardest of hearts. Marie, however, remained disconsolate. Pointing to the bedroom, where her little child lay asleep, she cried:

'Ah, I swear that Lilitte will learn to play the piano, even if I have to make the greatest sacrifices!'*

'Think first of bringing her up as we brought you up,' said

Madame Vuillaume severely. 'Of course, I'm not condemning music; it develops one's feelings. But, above all, watch over your daughter; keep every foul breath from her; and do all you can to ensure that she remains ignorant.'

Then she began all over again, giving further stress to religion, stating the appropriate number of confessions each month, naming the masses it was essential to attend, and making all these pronouncements from the standpoint of propriety. Octave could bear it no longer, and mentioned an appointment which obliged him to leave. His ears buzzed from sheer boredom; it was plain that they would go on talking like this until the evening. So he escaped, leaving the Vuillaumes and the Pichons to their tedious chit-chat over their coffee-cups, which they slowly emptied, as they did every Sunday. As he made his final bow, Marie, for no reason whatever, suddenly blushed violently.

After this encounter, on Sundays Octave would always hurry past the Pichons' door, especially if he heard the clipped tones of the Vuillaumes. Besides, he was wholly bent on the conquest of Valérie. Despite the burning glances, of which he believed himself the object, she maintained an unaccountable reserve; this was a form of coquetry, he thought. One day he met her by chance in the Tuileries gardens, and she began to talk calmly about a storm the previous night; this was enough to convince him that she had a devilish amount of nerve. He was constantly on the staircase, watching for an opportunity to pay her a visit, determined to make an immediate assault.

Now, every time he passed, Marie smiled and blushed. They nodded to each other in neighbourly fashion. One morning, at lunchtime, as he was bringing her a letter that Monsieur Gourd had entrusted to him so as to avoid the climb up to the fourth floor, he found her in an agitated state. She had just put Lilitte on the round table in her chemise, and was trying to dress her.

'What's the matter?' asked the young man.

'Oh, it's this child!' she replied. 'I was silly enough to take her things off, because she was complaining, and now I don't know how to get them back on!'

He looked at her in astonishment. She kept turning the child's petticoat over and over, trying to find the hooks and eyes. Then she added:

'You see, her father always helps me to dress her in the morning before he leaves. I never have to do it on my own. It's such a bother, it quite upsets me!'

The little girl, tired of being in her chemise, and frightened at seeing Octave, struggled and turned over on the table.

'Be careful,' he cried, 'or she'll fall off.'

It was dreadful. Marie looked as though she dared not touch her child's naked limbs. She gazed at her, as if with the innocence of a virgin, amazed at having been able to produce such a thing. Besides the fear of hurting the child, there was in her awkwardness a certain vague repugnance at its bodily presence. However, helped by Octave, who managed to calm the little girl, she was able to dress her again.

'How will you manage when you've got a dozen?' he asked, laughingly.

'But we'll never have any more!' she replied, in a frightened tone.

Then he teased her a little, telling her it was a mistake to be so sure; it was so easy to make a little baby!

'No, no,' she repeated obstinately. 'You heard what mamma said the other day. She told Jules she wouldn't allow it. You don't know what she's like; there would be endless quarrels if another baby came along.'

Octave was amused at the serious way in which she discussed this question. Though he kept drawing her out, he could not succeed in embarrassing her. Moreover, she just did as her husband wished. She was fond of children, of course, and if he wanted any more she would not say no; and under all her complacent submission to her mother's orders, one could note the indifference of a woman whose maternal instinct had not yet been roused. Lilitte had to be cared for in the same way that her home had to be looked after—a duty that must be done. When she had washed the dishes and taken the child for a walk, she continued to live her former life as a girl—a somnolent, empty existence, lulled by vague expectations of a joy that never came. When Octave remarked that she must find it very dull to be always alone, she seemed surprised. Oh, no, it was never dull, the days passed without her knowing, when she went to bed, how she had spent her time. Then, on Sundays, she sometimes went out with her husband, or her parents called, or she read a book. If reading did not give her headaches, she would have read from morning till night, now that she was allowed to read every sort of book.

'The annoying thing is', she continued, 'that they haven't got anything at the lending library in the Passage Choiseul. For instance, I wanted to read *André* again, because it made me cry so much when I read it the first time. Well, their copy has been stolen, and my father won't lend me his copy because Lilitte might tear the pictures.'

'Well, my friend Campardon has got George Sand's complete works,' said Octave. 'I'll ask him to lend me *André* for you.'

She blushed again, and her eyes sparkled. It was really too kind of him! And when he left her she stood there, in front of Lilitte, her arms hanging loosely by her sides, without an idea in her head, in the position she often remained in for whole afternoons at a stretch. She hated sewing, but used to do crochet; always the same little scrap of wool, which was left lying about the room.

The following day, which was a Sunday, Octave brought her the book. Pichon had been obliged to go out, to leave a card with one of his superiors. Finding her dressed for outdoors, as she had just come back from an errand in the neighbourhood, Octave asked her out of curiosity if she had been to mass, thinking that she was religious. She said no. Before her marriage her mother used to take her to church regularly, and for six months after her marriage she used to go from sheer force of habit, always afraid of arriving late. Then, without really knowing why, after missing two or three times she stopped going altogether. Her husband could not bear priests, and her mother now never mentioned the subject. Octave's question, however, disturbed her, as if it had awakened within her emotions long since buried beneath the apathy of her existence.

'I must go to Saint-Roch one of these days,' she said. 'When you stop doing something you've been used to, you always miss it.'

And over the pallid features of this girl born of elderly parents there appeared an expression of sickly regret, of longing for some other existence, dreamed of in her imagination. She could hide nothing; everything was revealed in her face, with her skin as tender and delicate as that of some chlorotic* patient. Suddenly she seemed moved, and caught hold of Octave's hand.

'Oh, I'm so grateful that you brought me the book! Call in

tomorrow, after lunch. I'll give it back to you, and tell you what effect it's had on me. That'll be interesting, won't it?'

There was something funny about her, thought Octave, as he came away. She was beginning to interest him, and he thought of speaking to Pichon, so as to get him to wake her up a bit, for there was no doubt that this was what she wanted. It so happened that he met Pichon the very next day as he was going out, and he walked some part of the way with him, at the risk of being a quarter of an hour late at the Ladies' Paradise. Pichon, however, appeared to be even less wide-awake than his wife, full of incipient manias, and entirely concerned not to dirty his boots, as it was going to rain. He walked along on tiptoe, talking incessantly about his boss's deputy. As Octave's motive in this matter was a purely brotherly one, he left him at last in the Rue Saint-Honoré, after advising him to take Marie as often as possible to the theatre.

'Whatever for?' asked Pichon in amazement.

'Because it does women good. It makes them nicer.'

'Do you really think so?'

He promised to think about it, and crossed the street, looking about in terror lest the cabs should splash him, this being his one and only torment in life.

At lunchtime Octave knocked at the Pichons' door to fetch the book. Marie was reading, her elbows on the table, her hands buried in her dishevelled hair. She had just eaten an egg out of a tin pan, which now lay on the untidy table on which she had not bothered to put a cloth. Lilitte, forgotten, was asleep on the floor, her nose touching the fragments of a plate which she had no doubt smashed.

'Well?' said Octave, quizzically.

Marie did not reply at once. She was still in her dressing-gown, which, having lost its buttons, left her neck and shoulders bare, in all the disorder of a woman who has just got out of bed.

'I've only read about a hundred pages,' she said at last. 'My parents were here yesterday.'

Her voice was hard as she said this, her mouth twisted. When she was younger she had longed to live in the depths of a forest, and was forever dreaming that she would meet a huntsman there sounding his horn. He would come and kneel down before her. The scene took place in a distant coppice, where roses bloomed as in a park. Then, all at once, they were married, and lived on there, wandering about together eternally. She, in her perfect happiness, desired nothing more; while he, tender and submissive as a slave, remained forever at her feet.

'I had a chat with your husband this morning,' said Octave. 'You don't go out enough, and I've persuaded him to take you to the theatre.'

But she shook her head, pale and trembling. There was a silence. The chilly, narrow dining-room reappeared before her, and the dull, decorous figure of Jules suddenly blotted out the huntsman of her romance, the distant sound of whose horn still rang in her ears. At times she would listen; perhaps he was coming. Her husband had never taken her feet in his hands and kissed them, nor had he ever knelt down to tell her he adored her. And yet, she was very fond of him; but she was surprised that love did not possess more sweetness.

'What moves me most in novels', she said, coming back to the book, 'are the parts where lovers tell each other of their love.'

Octave sat down at last. He wanted to treat the whole thing as a joke, caring little for such sentimental stuff.

'I hate speechifying,' he said. 'If two people adore each other, the best thing is for them to prove it straight away.'

But she did not seem to understand, as she looked at him with shining eyes. Stretching out his hand, he lightly touched hers, and leant close to her to look at a passage in the book, so closely that his breath warmed her bare shoulder. But she gave no reaction. Then he got up to go, full of contempt touched with pity. As he was leaving, she said:

'I read very slowly; I won't finish it until tomorrow. That's when it'll be interesting! So do drop in in the evening.'

Octave certainly had no designs on the woman; and yet he felt angry with her. He had formed a curious attachment to this young couple, who exasperated him, however, because they were content to lead such a dull life. He resolved to do them a good turn, in spite of themselves. He would take them out to dinner, make them drunk, and then amuse himself by pushing them into each other's arms. When such fits of kindness came over him, he, who was loath to lend anyone ten francs, delighted in spending his money in bringing lovers together and giving them joy.

However, the coldness of little Madame Pichon reminded Octave of the ardent Valérie, who would surely not need her neck to be breathed upon twice. He had made advances in her favour. One day, as she was going upstairs in front of him, he had ventured to compliment her on her legs without her showing any signs of displeasure.

At length the long-awaited opportunity came. It was the evening that Marie had made him promise to call in to talk about the novel, as they would be alone, for her husband was not coming home until very late. Octave would have preferred to go out, since the mere thought of this literary treat appalled him. However, at about ten o'clock he thought he would try it when, on the first-floor landing, he bumped into Valérie's maid, who said, with a scared look:

'Madame is in hysterics, master is out, and everyone opposite has gone to the theatre. Please come in, I'm all alone and I don't know what to do.'

Valérie was in her bedroom, stretched out in an armchair, her limbs rigid. The maid had unlaced her stays, freeing her breasts from her corset. The attack was over almost at once. She opened her eyes, seemed surprised to see Octave standing there, and behaved just as if he were the doctor.

'I do beg your pardon, sir,' she murmured, in a choking voice. 'The girl only arrived yesterday, and she lost her head.'

Her perfect composure in taking off her stays and buttoning up her dress disconcerted Octave. He remained standing, resolved not to go yet not daring to sit down. She had sent away the maid, the sight of whom seemed to irritate her, and went to the window to breathe in the cool night air, which she gulped in with her mouth wide open. After a pause they began to talk. She had starting having these attacks when she was fourteen, and Doctor Juillerat was tired of prescribing for her; sometimes she had them in her arms, and sometimes in her back. However, she was getting used to them; she might as well suffer from them as from anything else, for nobody had perfect health, of course. As she talked, her limbs languidly stretched out, the sight of her began to excite him and he thought her tempting in all her disorder, with her leaden complexion and her features drawn, as if she were exhausted by a night of lovemaking. Behind the dark mass of her hair, which fell over her shoulders, he fancied he beheld the small, beardless face of her husband. Then, stretching out his arms, he caught her round the waist, as he would have grabbed some tart.

'What are you doing?' she asked, in surprise.

Now, in her turn, she looked at him, her eyes so cold, her body so impassive that he felt frozen and let his hands fall awkwardly by his side. The absurdity of his gesture did not escape him. Then, stifling a last nervous yawn, she slowly murmured:

'Ah, my dear sir, if you only knew!'

She shrugged her shoulders, showing no sign of anger, but merely of overwhelming contempt and weariness of men. Octave thought she was about to have him turned out when he saw her move towards the bell-pull, trailing her petticoats as she went. But she only wanted some tea, and this she ordered to be very weak and very hot. Utterly nonplussed, he muttered some excuse and made for the door, while she lay back in her armchair, as if she were feeling chilly and in desperate need of sleep.

As he went upstairs, Octave stopped on each landing. So she did not care for that, then? He had just seen how indifferent she was, without desire and without resentment, as disobliging as his employer, Madame Hédouin. Why, then, did Campardon say she was hysterical? It was stupid to have deceived him with such a nonsensical tale! But for the architect's lie he would never have risked such an adventure. The whole episode quite bewildered him, and his ideas as to hysteria became confused as he thought of the various stories that circulated about Valérie. He remembered Trublot's remark that you never knew what to expect from this sort of crazy woman with eyes like burning coals.

On reaching his own floor Octave, now feeling thoroughly exasperated with women, walked as softly as he could. But the Pichons' door opened and he was obliged to resign himself to his fate. Marie stood waiting for him in the little, dimly lit room. She had pulled the cot close to the table, and Lilitte lay asleep in the yellow circle of light made by the lamp. The dishes which had been used at lunchtime must have been kept on the table for dinner, for the closed book lay close to a dirty plate full of radish ends.

'Have you finished it?' asked Octave, surprised at the young woman's silence.

She looked like someone who was drunk, her cheeks were puffy as if she had just awakened from a heavy sleep.

'Yes, yes!' she exclaimed with difficulty. 'I've spent the whole day reading it! When you lose yourself in a book like that you hardly know where you are. Oh, my neck aches!'

She was so exhausted that she was unable to say anything more about the novel; the emotions, the confused reveries it had aroused in her, seemed to have overwhelmed her. Her ears were still ringing with the clarion call of her ideal huntsman, whom she could see in the blue haze of her dreams. Then, without reason, she said that she had been to the nine o'clock mass at Saint-Roch. She had wept a great deal; religion replaced everything.

'Oh, I feel better now!' she said, sighing deeply and standing still in front of Octave.

There was a pause. She smiled at him innocently. Never had she seemed to him so useless, with her short hair and drawn features. Then, as she continued to gaze at him, she became very pale and almost fell, so that he had to hold out his hands to save her.

'My God! My God!' she sobbed.

He continued to hold her, feeling embarrassed.

'You should have a cup of tea. You've clearly been reading too much.'

'Yes, I was upset when I closed the book and found myself alone. You're very kind, Monsieur Mouret! If it hadn't been for you I might have hurt myself.'

Octave looked round for a chair on which to sit her down.

'Would you like me to light a fire?'

'No, thank you; it would make your hands dirty. I've noticed that you always wear gloves.'

The idea brought back the choking sensation in her throat and, half swooning, she clumsily launched a kiss into the air, as if in her dream. It just touched Octave's ear.

The kiss amazed him. Her lips were as cold as ice. Then, as she fell forward on his breast, yielding up her whole body, he was seized with a sudden desire and was going to pick her up and carry her into the bedroom. But this abrupt advance roused Marie from her swoon; her womanly instincts revolted. Struggling, she called out for her mother, forgetting her husband who would soon be home, and her daughter who was asleep at her side.

'No, no, not that! It's wrong.'

But he kept repeating, in his excitement:

'Nobody will know; I'll never tell.'

'No, no, Monsieur Octave! Please don't spoil the happiness I have in knowing you. It won't do us any good, and I had such wonderful dreams!'

Then, without another word, he felt that he must have his revenge upon womankind and said crudely to himself: 'you're going to get it now!' As she would not go into the bedroom with him he roughly pushed her backwards across the table. She gave in, and he took her there, midway between the dirty plate and the novel, which, when the table shook, fell on to the floor. The door had not even been shut; the solemn silence of the staircase pervaded all. Lilitte lay sleeping peacefully in her cot.

When Marie and Octave got up, she with her rumpled petticoats, they had nothing to say to each other. Mechanically she went and looked at her daughter, picked up the plate, and then put it down again. He remained silent, feeling equally ill at ease, for it had happened so unexpectedly. He recalled how he had formed the brotherly plan of making husband and wife fall into each other's arms. In order to break the awful silence, he muttered at length:

'So you didn't shut the door!'

She looked out on to the landing, and stammered:

'That's true, it was open.'

She seemed to walk with difficulty, and on her face there was a look of disgust. Octave began to think that there was nothing particularly exciting in an adventure of this sort with a helpless, lonely, empty-headed woman. She had not even had any pleasure from it.

'Oh, dear! The book has fallen on the floor!' she continued, as she picked the volume up.

One of the corners of the cover was bent. This brought them together again; it was a relief. They began to talk again. Marie appeared distressed.

'It wasn't my fault. I put a paper cover on it, so it wouldn't get dirty. We must have knocked it off the table by accident.'

'It was there, then?' asked Octave. 'I didn't notice it. It doesn't bother me, but Campardon thinks such a lot of his books.'

They kept handing the book to each other, trying to put the corner straight. Their fingers touched, yet neither felt a thrill. As they thought of the consequences, they were both dismayed at the accident which had befallen the beautiful volume of George Sand.

'It was bound to end badly,' said Marie, with tears in her eyes.

Octave felt obliged to console her. He would invent some story or other. Campardon wouldn't eat him. And as they were about to separate, their feeling of uneasiness returned. They would have liked to say something pleasant to each other, but somehow the words stuck in their throats. Fortunately, at that moment they heard a step on the stairs; it was Monsieur Pichon coming home. Silently Octave took her in his arms again, and kissed her on the mouth. Again she complacently submitted, her lips icy cold as before. When he had noiselessly got back to his room, he thought to himself, as he took off his coat, that apparently she didn't like that either. So whatever was it that she wanted? And why did she go tumbling into men's arms? Women were certainly very strange.

The next day, after lunch at the Campardons', as Octave was explaining once more how he had clumsily knocked the book on to the floor, Marie came in. She was going to take Lilitte to the Tuileries gardens, and had called to ask if they would let Angèle go with her. She smiled at Octave with perfect self-possession, and glanced innocently at the book lying on a chair.

'Of course,' said Madame Campardon, 'I'd be delighted. Angèle, go and put your hat on. I know she's quite safe with you.'

Looking like modesty personified in her simple dark woollen dress, Marie talked about her husband, who had come home with a cold the night before; and she also mentioned the price of meat, which was becoming so expensive that soon people would not be able to afford any at all. Then, after she had left, taking Angèle with her, they all leant out of the window to see them go off. Marie gently pushed Lilitte's pram along with her gloved hands, while Angèle, who knew they were watching, walked beside her with downcast eyes.

'Doesn't she look nice!' exclaimed Madame Campardon. 'So ladylike, so respectable!'

Then, slapping Octave on the back, her husband said:

'In a family, education is everything, my dear boy—everything!'

V

At the Duveyriers' that evening there was a reception and a concert. Octave had been invited for the first time, and at about ten o'clock he was just finishing dressing. He was in a sombre mood, and felt quite annoyed with himself. How had he failed to bring off his affair with Valérie—a woman so well connected? And Berthe Josserand, ought he not to have thought more carefully before refusing her? As he was tying his white tie, the thought of Marie Pichon became positively unbearable to him. Five months in Paris, and only that pathetic little adventure to show for it! He almost felt ashamed, for he was well aware of the uselessness of such a connection. As he pulled on his gloves he vowed that he would no longer waste his time in such a way. Now that he had at last entered society he was resolved to act, for opportunities were certainly not lacking.

Marie was looking out for him at the end of the corridor. As Pichon was not there, he had to go in for a moment.

'You're so smart!' she whispered.

They had never been invited to the Duveyriers', and she was quite in awe of them. But she was jealous of no one; for this she had neither the strength nor the will.

'I'll wait for you,' she said, looking up at him. 'Don't stay too late; and you must tell me afterwards what it was like.'

Octave was obliged to kiss her hair. Though a relationship had been established between them which depended on his inclination, it was not really an intimate one. At last he went downstairs, and she, leaning over the banisters, watched him until he disappeared.

At the same moment quite a drama was being enacted at the Josserands'. According to Madame Josserand, the party at the Duveyriers' would decide the match between her daughter Berthe and Auguste Vabre. Despite a number of vigorous onslaughts during the past fortnight, the latter was still hesitating, evidently exercised by doubts as to the dowry. So Madame Josserand, in order to strike a decisive blow, had written to her brother announcing the projected marriage, and reminding him of his promises, hoping that his reply would give her something she could use to her advantage. And, as the whole family stood round the

dining-room stove, dressed up and ready to go downstairs at nine
o'clock, Monsieur Gourd brought up a letter from uncle Bachelard
which had been left lying under Madame Gourd's snuffbox since
the last delivery.

'Ah, at last!' cried Madame Josserand, tearing open the envelope.

The girls and their father anxiously watched her as she read.
Adèle, who had been obliged to dress the ladies, was moving about
in her clumsy fashion as she cleared away the dinner-service.
Madame Josserand turned very pale.

'Not a word!' she stuttered, 'not a single clear sentence! He says
he'll see later on, when they get married. And he sends his love to
everybody! The rotten old humbug!'

Monsieur Josserand, in evening clothes, had sunk into a chair.
Hortense and Berthe, whose legs ached, sat down as well; the one in
blue, the other in pink, in those eternal frocks of theirs which they
had refurbished once again.

'Bachelard can't be relied upon; I've always said so,' murmured
Monsieur Josserand. 'He'll never give us a penny.'

Standing there in her flaming red dress, Madame Josserand read
the letter again. Then she burst forth:

'Oh, men! men! Just look at him, for example. You'd think he was
an idiot, to judge by the life he leads. But, no, not a bit of it! He may
look like one, but he perks up as soon as you mention money. Oh,
men!'

Then she turned towards her daughters, to whom this lesson was
addressed.

'You know, I'm really beginning to wonder why you girls are so
obsessed with getting married! Ah, if you'd been worried to death by
it, as I have! No one who loves you for yourself, or brings you a
fortune without haggling over it! A millionaire uncle who lives on
you for twenty years and then refuses even to give his niece a dowry!
And a husband who's useless—oh yes, sir, useless!'

Monsieur Josserand bowed his head.

Adèle, not even listening, finished clearing the table. Madame
Josserand suddenly turned on her.

'What are you doing, spying on us? Go back to the kitchen at
once!'

Then came her peroration.

'Those beasts have everything and we get nothing—not even a

crust if we're starving! The only thing they're fit for is to be taken in! Just mark my words!'

Hortense and Berthe nodded, as though profoundly impressed by the wisdom of their mother's pronouncements. She had long since convinced them of the absolute inferiority of men, whose sole function in life was to marry and to pay. There was a long silence in the smoky dining-room, pervaded now by the smell of the food which Adèle had been obliged to leave. Sitting about in their finery, the Josserands forgot the Duveyriers' concert as they reflected on life's perpetual disappointments. From the adjoining room came the sound of Saturnin, whom they had sent to bed early, snoring.

At last, Berthe spoke.

'So that's the end of that! Shall we go and take our things off?'

At this, Madame Josserand's energy came flooding back. What! Take their things off! And why, pray? Were they not respectable people? Was an alliance with their family not as good as with any other? The marriage should come off all the same; she would rather die. And she quickly gave each of them their parts. The girls were told to be particularly nice to Auguste, and not to let go of him until he had taken the plunge. Monsieur Josserand was entrusted with the task of gaining the sympathies of old Vabre and Duveyrier, by always agreeing with everything they said—assuming that this would not place too great a strain on his intellect. As for herself, she would take care of the women; she wished to leave nothing to chance, and knew well how to win them all over. Then, collecting her thoughts and casting a last glance round the dining-room, as if to make sure that no weapon had been forgotten, she assumed the terrible mien of a warrior leading forth his daughters to be massacred, as in a loud voice she cried:

'Let's go down!'

And down they went. In the solemn atmosphere of the staircase, Monsieur Josserand felt very uneasy. He foresaw many things, all too unpleasant for such a strait-laced, decent man as himself.

The Duveyriers' apartment was already crowded as they entered. The enormous grand piano filled one side of the panelled drawing-room; the ladies were seated before it in rows, as if at the theatre, against a dense black background of men in evening dress, which extended through the door of the dining-room to the parlour beyond. The chandelier and the candelabra and the six bracket-lamps standing on side-tables lit up in a quite dazzling fashion the white and gold apartment, exhibiting in all their crudeness the red silk hangings and furniture. It was extremely hot; and the regular movement of fans dispersed the pungent aroma of bodices and bare shoulders.

Just at that moment Madame Duveyrier was about to sit down at the piano. With a gesture, Madame Josserand smilingly bade her hostess not to trouble herself. Leaving her daughters among the men, she took a chair between Valérie and Madame Juzeur. Monsieur Josserand had found his way to the parlour, where Monsieur Vabre, the landlord, was asleep in his customary corner of the sofa. Here too, in a group, were Campardon, Théophile and Auguste Vabre, Doctor Juillerat, and Father Mauduit; while Trublot and Octave had just fled together from the music to the far corner of the dining-room. Near them, behind the sea of black coats, stood Duveyrier, tall and thin, watching his wife at the piano and waiting for silence. In his buttonhole, in a neat little rosette, he wore the ribbon of the Legion of Honour.

'Hush! hush! Quiet!' murmured various sympathetic voices.

Then Clotilde Duveyrier attacked one of Chopin's most difficult nocturnes. Tall and good-looking, with splendid auburn hair, she had a long face, pale and cold as snow. In her grey eyes the music had ignited a flame—an exaggerated passion on which she lived without any other need, either of the flesh or the spirit. Duveyrier continued looking at her; then, after the first few bars, his lips began to twitch nervously and he withdrew to the far end of the dining-room. On his clean-shaven face, with its pointed chin and crooked eyes, large red blotches showed the unhealthy state of his blood—a festering mass of scrofula just beneath the skin.

Trublot, examining him, quietly observed:

'He doesn't like music.'

'Nor do I,' replied Octave.

'Ah! but it's not as unpleasant for you as it is for him. He was always lucky, you know. He's no cleverer than anyone else, but he was helped along by everybody. He comes from an old bourgeois family; his father's an ex-chief justice. He was called to the bar as soon as he passed his exams; got appointed assistant judge at Reims; then transferred to Paris, to the High Court of Appeal; and was decorated and made a judge by the age of forty-five. Pretty impressive, isn't it? But he doesn't like music; that piano has been the bane of his life. Well, you can't have everything!'

Meanwhile, Clotilde was rattling off the most difficult passages with tremendous sang-froid. She handled her piano as a circus-rider would her horse. Octave was interested only in the furious working of her hands.

'Just look at her fingers,' he said; 'it's amazing! It must really hurt after a quarter of an hour of that sort of playing!'

Then they both began talking about women, without paying any further attention to her performance. On seeing Valérie, Octave felt rather embarrassed. How should he behave? Speak to her, or pretend not to see her? Trublot put on an air of great disdain; there was not a single woman there that took his fancy; and, when his companion protested that there was surely somebody to suit his taste, he sagely remarked:

'Well, take your pick, and you'll soon see what they're really like, eh? Not that one at the back there, with feathers; or the blonde one in the mauve dress; or that old one, although at least she's nice and plump. I tell you, it's absurd to look for anything good in society. Lots of airs and graces, but no fun!'

Octave smiled. He had to make his way in the world; he could not afford simply to follow his taste like Trublot, whose father was so rich. The long rows of women set him thinking, and he asked himself which of them he would choose for his fortune or his pleasure if he could take one of them away. Suddenly, as he was casting his eye over them, he exclaimed in surprise:

'Hullo! There's my employer's wife! Does she come here?'

'Yes; didn't you know that?' said Trublot. 'In spite of the difference in their ages, Madame Hédouin and Madame Duveyrier are old school-friends. They were quite inseparable, and used to be called "the polar bears", because they were always twenty degrees below zero. Another pair of figureheads! I'd be sorry for Duveyrier if that's the only hot-water bottle he's got for the winter!'

Octave, however, had become quite serious. It was the first time he had seen Madame Hédouin in an evening dress; it was low-cut, showing her neck and arms; her dark hair was plaited across her forehead, and in the heat and glare of the drawing-room she seemed the realization of his desires. A superb woman—vibrantly healthy and quite beautiful, who would be an advantage to any man. A host of different schemes were already forming in his mind, when the loud noise of clapping awoke him from his dream.

'Thank God! It's over!' said Trublot.

Everyone was congratulating Clotilde. Rushing forward, Madame Josserand seized her by both hands, as the men went on talking and the women plied their fans with greater vigour. Duveyrier then ventured to retreat to the parlour, and Trublot and Octave followed him. Surrounded by petticoats, the former whispered:

'Look over there, on your right! The hooking business has begun.'

Madame Josserand was setting Berthe on young Vabre, who had imprudently gone up to the ladies to pay his respects. That evening his headache was better, and he only felt a slight ache in his left eye; but he dreaded the end of the party as there was going to be singing—the worst thing for him.

'Berthe, tell Monsieur Auguste about the remedy you copied for him out of that book—a wonderful cure for headaches!'

Having started them off, Madame Josserand left them standing near the window.

'Good heavens! They're going in for chemistry now!' murmured Trublot.

In the parlour Monsieur Josserand, anxious to please his wife, was sitting in a state of great embarrassment before Monsieur Vabre, for the old fellow was asleep and he did not like to disturb him. But when the music stopped Monsieur Vabre opened his eyes. He was a short, stout man, quite bald, with two tufts of white hair on his ears, a red face, flabby lips, and goggle eyes. After a polite enquiry as to his health, Monsieur Josserand started the conversation. The ex-notary, whose four or five ideas were always expressed in the same order, began by mentioning Versailles, where, for forty years, he had had a practice. Then he spoke of his sons, and once more lamented their incapacity to carry on the business, so that he had decided to sell it and live in Paris. Then came the whole history of his house, the building of which had been the romance of his life.

'I sank three hundred thousand francs in it, sir. A magnificent speculative opportunity, so my architect said. But it'll be hard work getting my money back, especially as all my children have come to live here for nothing, without the slightest intention of paying me. In fact, I'd never get a quarter's rent if I didn't ask for it myself on the fifteenth. I enjoy my work, though, I'm glad to say.'

'Do you still need to work a lot?' asked Monsieur Josserand.

'Absolutely!' replied the old man, with desperate energy. 'Work, to me, is life.'

Then he proceeded to explain the huge amount of work he did. Every year, for the last ten years, he had gone through the official catalogue of the Salon* writing on a slip beside the name of every painter the pictures he exhibited. He alluded to this wearily, distressfully; a year was not long enough for such arduous work; sometimes it proved too much for him. For instance, when a female artist got married and exhibited under her husband's name, how could he possibly know this?

'My work will never be finished; that's what's killing me,' he murmured.

'I suppose you take a great interest in art, don't you?' said Monsieur Josserand, trying to flatter him.

The old man stared at him in astonishment.

'Oh, no! There's no need for me to see the pictures, it's just a matter of statistics. Well, well! I'd better get to bed, so that my head will be clearer in the morning. Goodnight, sir.'

He leant on a stick, which he used even indoors, and hobbled off, evidently suffering from partial paralysis of the spine. Monsieur Josserand was perplexed; he felt he hadn't quite grasped what the old man had said, and was afraid that he had not reacted with sufficient enthusiasm to the mention of catalogue-slips.

Just then there was a faint murmur in the drawing-room, which brought Trublot and Octave back to the door. They saw a lady of about fifty coming in. She was powerfully built, still good-looking, and accompanied by a serious, carefully dressed young man.

'What! They've come together!' murmured Trublot. 'Well I never!'

The newcomers were Madame Dambreville and Léon Josserand. She had agreed to find him a wife, but in the meantime had kept him for her own personal use, and now, with their romance in full swing, they advertised their affair in every bourgeois drawing-room. There was much whispering among mothers with marriageable daughters. Madame Duveyrier, however, hastened to welcome Madame Dambreville, who was useful in finding her young men to sing in her choruses. Then Madame Josserand, in turn, showered her with polite conversation, thinking that some day she might make use of her son's friend. Léon drily exchanged a few words with his mother, who was beginning to believe that he might be able to do something for himself, after all.

'Berthe hasn't noticed you,' she said to Madame Dambreville. 'She's just telling Monsieur Auguste about a cure for his headaches.'

'But of course. They really shouldn't be disturbed,' said Madame Dambreville, understanding at a glance.

With maternal solicitude, they both watched Berthe. She had contrived to push Auguste into the window-recess, and had hemmed him in there with her pretty gestures. He was becoming quite animated and running the risk of a migraine.

Meanwhile, in the parlour, several of the men were gravely talking politics. The day before there had been a stormy sitting of the Senate, when the Roman question had come up for debate. Doctor Juillerat, an atheist and a revolutionary, was in favour of giving Rome up to the King of Italy, while Father Mauduit, one of the heads of the Ultramontane party, prophesied the direst catastrophes if France did not shed the last drop of her blood in support of the temporal power of the Pope.*

'Perhaps some *modus vivendi* acceptable to both parties can be found,' said Léon Josserand, who had joined the group.

He was acting then as secretary to a famous barrister, one of the deputies of the Left. For the last two years, expecting nothing from his parents, whose mediocrity exasperated him, he had posed in the Latin Quarter as a red-hot Radical. But since he had got to know the Dambrevilles his radicalism had become blunted, he had grown calmer and was gradually becoming a doctrinaire Republican.

'No,' said the priest, 'no agreement is possible. The Church can't compromise.'

'Then it will disappear,' cried the doctor.

Though great friends, having met at the bedsides of all those who had died in the Saint-Roch district, they now seemed irreconcilable—the doctor thin and nervous, the priest portly and affable. The latter smiled politely even when making the most absolute statements, like a man of the world who tolerates the ills of life, but also like a good Catholic who has no intention of abandoning his beliefs.

'The Church disappear? Nonsense!' said Campardon, with a show of anger, for he wanted to ingratiate himself with the priest from whom he expected to get work.

Moreover, all those present shared his opinion: the Church could never disappear. Théophile Vabre, as he coughed and spat and shivered, dreamed of universal happiness achieved by the formation of a humanitarian republic, and was the only one to say that the Church would have to change.

Then, in his gentle voice, the priest continued:

'The Empire is committing suicide. Wait and see what happens next year, at the elections.'

'Oh! As far as the Empire's concerned, you can get rid of that,' said the doctor, bluntly. 'You'd be doing us a great favour.'

Whereupon Duveyrier, who appeared to be profoundly interested in the discussion, shook his head. He belonged to an Orleanist* family; but he owed everything to the Empire and thought himself bound to defend it.

'Believe me,' he said at last, severely, 'it won't do to shake the foundations of society, or everything will collapse. We're the ones who suffer from every disaster.'

'That's very true,' remarked Monsieur Josserand, who had no opinion of his own, but remembered his wife's instructions.

Then everybody spoke at once. None of them was in favour of the Empire. Doctor Juillerat condemned the Mexican Expedition,* Father Mauduit spoke against the recognition of the Kingdom of Italy. Yet Théophile Vabre, and even Léon, felt anxious when Duveyrier threatened them with another '93. What was the use of these perpetual revolutions? Hadn't liberty been achieved? Hatred of new ideas, fear of the people claiming their share, tempered the liberalism of these self-satisfied bourgeois. However, they all declared that they would vote against the Emperor. He had to be taught a lesson.

'Oh, dear! How boring they are,' said Trublot, who had been trying to understand for some minutes past.

Octave persuaded him to return to the ladies. In the window recess Berthe was deafening Auguste with her laughter. The big, sickly fellow was forgetting his fear of women, and had become quite flushed before the attacks of his bewitching companion, whose warm breath touched his face. Madame Josserand, however, appeared to feel that the campaign was flagging, for she looked meaningfully at Hortense who, obedient to the signal, went to her sister's aid.

'I hope you've fully recovered, madam,' Octave ventured to say to Valérie.

'Yes, thank you,' she coolly replied, as if she remembered nothing.

Madame Juzeur asked the young man about some old lace she wanted to show him and get his opinion on, and he had to promise to drop in on her the next day. Then, as Father Mauduit came back to the drawing-room, she called him and made him sit beside her, as she assumed an air of rapture.

The conversation continued. The ladies were discussing their servants.

'Well, yes,' said Madame Duveyrier, 'I'm quite satisfied with Clémence; she's a very clean, active girl.'

'And Hippolyte?' asked Madame Josserand. 'Weren't you thinking of dismissing him?'

Just then Hippolyte, the manservant, was handing round ices. He was tall and strong, with a ruddy complexion, and when he had withdrawn Clotilde replied, with some embarrassment:

'We've decided to keep him; changing is so difficult. Servants get used to each other, you see, and I couldn't part with Clémence.'

Madame Josserand was quick to agree, feeling they were on delicate ground. They hoped to arrange a marriage between them some day; and Father Mauduit, whom the Duveyriers had consulted about the matter, gently shook his head, as if to hide a scandal which everyone in the house knew about, but which no one ever mentioned. However, the ladies unburdened themselves in other ways. That very morning Valérie had sent away another maid—the third within a week; Madame Juzeur had decided to get a little girl of fifteen from the Foundling Hospital and train her herself; as for Madame Josserand, she never tired of abusing Adèle, whom she called a slut and a good-for-nothing, and whose terrible habits she described at length. Sitting languidly amid the glare of the candles and the perfume of the flowers, they wallowed in all this below-stairs gossip, as they eagerly discussed badly kept accounts, a coachman's insolence, or the surliness of a parlourmaid.

'Have you seen Julie?' Trublot suddenly asked Octave, in a mysterious voice.

As Octave looked at him in amazement, he added:

'My dear fellow, she's stunning. Go and have a look at her. Just pretend you want to leave the room for a moment and slip into the kitchen. She's simply stunning.'

He was talking about the Duveyriers' cook. Meanwhile, the ladies' conversation had taken another turn. Madame Josserand, in the most gushing manner, was praising the very modest estate the Duveyriers owned near Villeneuve-Saint-Georges, and which she had noticed once from the train when going to Fontainebleau. But Clotilde did not like the country; she lived there as little as possible, only during the holidays of her son Gustave, who was in the top class at the Lycée Bonaparte.

'Caroline is quite right not to want any children,' she declared, turning to Madame Hédouin, who was sitting two chairs away. 'They interfere so much with all one's habits.'

Madame Hédouin said she liked children very much. But she was far too busy for babies; her husband was constantly travelling, and she had the business to look after.

Octave, standing behind her, noticed the little black curls on the nape of her neck and the snowy whiteness of her bosom, which disappeared in a mass of delicate lace on her low-cut dress. She began to disconcert him as she sat there so calmly, saying little, and with her beautiful smile. He had never met anyone so fascinating, not even in Marseilles. It was certainly worth trying for, even if it took a long time.

'Having children spoils a woman's looks,' he whispered in her ear, anxious to say something to her yet not knowing what other remark to make.

She slowly raised her large eyes and said simply, just as if she were giving him an order at the shop:

'Oh, no! Monsieur Octave, with me that's not the reason. I need the time, that's all.'

Madame Duveyrier interrupted them. She had merely greeted Octave with a slight nod when Campardon had introduced him to her. Now she watched him and listened to his conversation with sudden, undisguised interest. As she heard him talking to her friend, she could not resist enquiring:

'I'm sorry to interrupt, but—what sort of voice do you have?'

At first he hardly understood what she meant, but ended by saying that he had a tenor voice. Clotilde became quite enthusiastic. A tenor voice—really! What a piece of luck—tenor voices were

becoming so rare! For the 'Benediction of the Poniards',* which they
were going to sing directly, she had never been able to find more
than three tenors among all her acquaintances, though at least five
were needed. And, her eyes sparkling with sudden excitement, she
could hardly refrain from going straight to the piano to try his voice.
He had to promise to call in on her one evening and let her do so.
Trublot kept nudging him from behind, enjoying himself enor-
mously in his impassive way.

'So you're in for it too, are you?' he murmured, when she had
moved away. 'She thought I was a baritone at first. Then, when that
didn't do, she tried me as a tenor, which was worse still. So she's
decided to use me tonight as a bass. I'm one of the monks.'

Just then he was called away by Madame Duveyrier. They were
going to sing the chorus from the *Huguenots*, the great event of the
evening. There was a great commotion as fifteen men, all amateurs
recruited from among the guests, tried to squeeze past the ladies and
reach their positions near the piano. They kept stopping and begging
to be excused, their voices drowned by the buzz of conversation,
while fans moved more rapidly as the heat increased. Madame
Duveyrier counted them at last: they were all there, and she began to
distribute the parts which she herself had copied out. Campardon
took the role of Saint-Bris; a young auditor employed by the Council
of State had been entrusted with De Nevers' few bars; and there
were eight nobles, four provosts, and three monks, represented by
barristers, clerks, and simple householders. Madame Duveyrier
accompanied, having, moreover, reserved the part of Valentina for
herself, uttering passionate shrieks as she struck crashing chords.
She was resolved to have no lady among all the gentlemen, whom, in
a resigned troop, she led with all the rigour of an orchestra
conductor.

Meanwhile the talking went on, the noise in the parlour, where
obviously the political discussion had grown more heated, becoming
quite intolerable. So, taking a key from her pocket, Clotilde tapped
gently on the piano with it. There was a murmur throughout the
room, a hush of voices, two streams of black evening coats again
surged towards the doors, and above the rows of heads for an instant
Duveyrier's blotchy face was seen, wearing a look of anguish. Octave
had remained standing behind Madame Hédouin, looking down at
the shadows around her bosom swathed in lace. But just as silence

had been established there was a burst of laughter, and he looked up. It was Berthe, amused by a joke of Auguste's. She had heated up his poor blood to such a pitch that he was becoming quite rakish. Everyone looked at them; mothers became grave, and relatives exchanged meaningful glances.

'She's so highly strung!' murmured Madame Josserand fondly, loud enough to be heard.

Hortense, with a complacent air of self-sacrifice, stood close to her sister in order to help, echoing her laughter and pushing her up against the young man, while a breeze from the open window behind them gently stirred the large red-silk curtains.

Suddenly a sepulchral voice was heard, and all heads turned towards the piano. With mouth agape and beard waving in a gust of lyrical fervour, Campardon declaimed the opening stave:

Aye, by the Queen's command we are gathered here.

Clotilde immediately ran up the scale and down again; then, with her eyes fixed on the ceiling, and a look of terror on her face, she screamed:

I tremble!

And then the whole thing began, as the eight lawyers, house-holders, and clerks, their noses glued to the score and looking like schoolboys mumbling a page of Greek, swore that, one and all, they were ready to deliver France. This beginning created some surprise, as the voices were deadened by the low ceiling, so that one could only hear a rumbling like the noise of carts full of pavingstones, which make the window-panes rattle as they pass. But when Saint-Bris's melodious phrase, 'For this cause so holy,' developed the leading theme, some of the ladies recognized it and nodded to show how clever they were. They were warming to the work, and the nobles shouted out at random:

We swear! We will follow you!

Every time it was like an explosion, a blow that struck each guest full in the face.

'They're singing too loud,' murmured Octave in Madame Hédouin's ear.

She did not move. Then, bored by the vocal explanations of De

Nevers and Valentina, the more so because the auditor attached to the Council of State was not a baritone at all, he made signs to Trublot, who was waiting for the monks' entrance, and winked significantly at the window-recess, where Berthe still kept Auguste imprisoned. The two were now alone, breathing in the cool outdoor air, while Hortense was keeping a lookout, leaning against the curtain and mechanically twisting its loop. No one was looking at them now; even Madame Josserand and Madame Dambreville had given up watching them, after exchanging significant glances.

Meanwhile, with her fingers on the keys, Clotilde, who in her excitement dared not gesticulate, could only stretch out her neck as she addressed to the music-stand the following vow, intended for De Nevers:

Ah, from this day forth my blood shall all be yours!

The aldermen had now entered, as well as a substitute, two solicitors, and a notary. The quartet was doing its utmost with the phrase, 'For this cause so holy,' which was repeated in broader style, half the chorus taking it up as the whole theme gradually expanded. Campardon, whose mouth grew ever wider, gave the order to attack with a tremendous volley of syllables. Then all at once the monks' chant broke forth; Trublot's psalm-singing came from his stomach, so as to get at the low notes.

Octave, who had watched him singing with some curiosity, was greatly surprised when he looked once more at the curtained window. As if carried away by the singing, Hortense had unhooked the loop by a movement which might have been unintentional, and the curtain had completely hidden Auguste and Berthe. They were there behind it, leaning against the window-bar; not a single movement betrayed their presence. Octave had lost all interest in Trublot, who just then was blessing the poniards:

Ye holy poniards, now by us be blessed.

What could they be doing behind that curtain? The fugue was beginning as, to the monks' deep tones, the chorus replied: 'Death! death! death!' And still the couple behind the curtain did not move. Perhaps, overcome by the heat, they were simply looking out at the passing cabs. Saint-Bris's melodious phrase again came back; all the singers gradually uttered it at the top of their voices, progressively, in a final outburst of amazing force. It was like a sudden gust of wind that swept through the narrow room, making the candles flare and the guests grow pale as the blood rushed to their ears. Clotilde furiously thumped the piano, galvanizing the chorus by her very glance; then the voices sank to a whisper:

At midnight, not a sound!

Then she went on by herself, using the soft pedal as she imitated the regular footfall of the patrol dying away in the distance.

All at once, as the music slowly expired, providing a pleasant lull after the storm, a voice was heard to exclaim:

'Don't! You're hurting me!'

Everyone looked round again towards the window. Madame Dambreville, anxious to make herself useful, was kind enough to pull the curtain aside. And the whole room beheld Auguste looking very confused, and Berthe very red, still leaning against the window-bar.

'What is it, my precious?' asked Madame Josserand earnestly.

'Nothing, mamma. Monsieur Auguste knocked my arm with the window. I was so hot.'

And she blushed deeper still. There were some suppressed smiles and scandalized pouts among the audience. Madame Duveyrier, who for a month had been trying to keep her brother out of Berthe's way, turned pale, especially as the incident had completely spoilt the effect of her chorus. However, after the initial surprise there was a burst of applause. Congratulations were showered upon her, as well as compliments for the vocalists. How well they had sung! What pains she must have taken to make them sing with such precision! It was as well done as at any theatre! But under all this noisy praise she could not help hearing the whispering that went round: the girl had been too greatly compromised, an engagement was inevitable.

'Well! He's hooked!' said Trublot as he rejoined Octave. 'What a fool! Couldn't he have squeezed her while we were all bellowing! I thought he would have taken that opportunity. You know, at parties where there's singing you can pinch a lady, and if she cries out it doesn't matter, because nobody can hear!'

Berthe, who had regained her composure, was laughing again, while Hortense was looking at Auguste with a sullen air, and, in their triumph, one could detect the mother's tuition, her lessons regarding undisguised contempt for men. All the male guests had now invaded the drawing-room, mingling with the ladies and talking in loud voices. Monsieur Josserand, greatly agitated by the episode involving Berthe, had drawn nearer to his wife. He listened uneasily as she thanked Madame Dambreville for all her kindness to Léon, in whom she had undoubtedly wrought a most beneficial change. But his uneasiness increased when he heard her refer again to her daughters. She pretended to talk in a low voice to Madame Juzeur, while intending Valérie and Clotilde, who were standing close by, to overhear her.

'Yes! Her uncle wrote to me today; Berthe is to have fifty thousand francs. It's not much, of course, but it's a lump sum, in hard cash you know!'

This lie absolutely disgusted her husband. He could not help lightly touching her on the shoulder. She looked up at him; the expression on her face was so resolute that he lowered his eyes. Then, as Madame Duveyrier turned around, she smiled and asked with an air of concern about her dear father.

'Oh! papa must have gone up to bed,' replied Clotilde, quite won over. 'He works so hard!'

Monsieur Josserand said that Monsieur Vabre had indeed retired, so that his mind would be perfectly clear in the morning. And he mumbled a few words about 'a most remarkable intellect, extraordinary faculties,' while wondering at the same time where on earth the dowry would come from, and what sort of figure he would cut on the day the marriage contract had to be signed.

A great noise of chairs being pushed back filled the drawing-room. The ladies trooped into the dining-room, where tea was served. Madame Josserand sailed in victoriously, surrounded by her daughters and the Vabre family. Soon, amid the disordered array of chairs, only the group of grave debaters remained. Campardon had got hold of Father Mauduit. The Calvary of Saint-Roch, it seemed, needed certain repairs. The architect declared that he was perfectly ready to undertake them, as the Évreux diocese gave him very little to do. He had only to construct a pulpit there and put in heating apparatus, as well as new ovens in the Bishop's kitchen; besides, these were all things his surveyor could attend to. The priest accordingly promised to submit the matter for consideration at the next meeting of the directors. Then they both joined the others, who were complimenting Duveyrier on the drawing up of a judgment of which he confessed himself the author. The presiding judge, who was his friend, got him certain jobs, at once easy and showy, which would help to enhance his reputation.

'Have you read this new novel?' asked Léon, as he turned over the pages of a copy of the *Revue des Deux Mondes*,* which lay on the table. 'It's well written, but it's another adultery story; they really are going too far!'

They began to talk about morality. Some women, said Campardon, were perfectly blameless. Everybody agreed with him. Moreover, the architect observed, married life was easy enough if you knew how to give and take. Théophile Vabre remarked that that depended on the woman, without explaining himself further. They were anxious to have Doctor Juillerat's opinion, but he simply smiled and declined to express one; he thought that virtue was a question of health. Duveyrier, meanwhile, had remained silent, lost in thought.

'Dear me!' he murmured at last, 'those novelists do exaggerate; adultery is very rare among the well-educated classes. A woman from a good family has in her soul a flower . . .'

He spoke of noble feelings, and uttered the word 'ideal' with such fervour that his eyes were dimmed. He applauded Father Mauduit when the latter spoke of the necessity of religious beliefs for wives and mothers. The conversation was thus brought back to religion and politics, to the point where these gentlemen had left it. Never would the Church disappear, because it was the foundation of family life as well as the natural support of governments.

'As a kind of police, it is,' muttered the doctor.

Duveyrier did not like politics being discussed in his house, and contented himself by remarking, as he glanced across at the dining-room where Berthe and Hortense were stuffing Auguste with sandwiches:

'Gentlemen, one thing is certain: religion makes marriage moral.'

At the same moment Trublot, seated on a sofa, was leaning over and whispering to Octave.

'By the way,' he asked, 'would you like me to get you invited to a lady's at whose house you can have a good time?'

As his companion wanted to know what kind of lady, he added, pointing to Duveyrier:

'His mistress.'

'Surely not!' exclaimed Octave in amazement.

Trublot slowly opened and shut his eyes. It was so. When you married a woman who was disobliging, who appeared disgusted by all your little needs, and who thumped on the piano to the point of making all the dogs in the neighbourhood quite ill, you had to go elsewhere to get a little fun.

'Let us make marriage moral, gentlemen; let us make it moral,' repeated Duveyrier, stiffly, with his inflamed face, in which Octave now thought he could detect the traces of disordered blood, the result of secret vices.

The gentlemen were called away to the dining-room, and Father Mauduit, who remained alone for a moment in the middle of the empty drawing-room, watched the crush of guests from a distance. His fat, sensitive face wore a sad expression. As confessor to these ladies and their daughters, he knew them all intimately, like Doctor Juillerat, and he had finally been obliged to concern himself with outward appearances only, as a sort of master of ceremonies covering this corrupt bourgeoisie with the cloak of religion, trembling at the certain prospect of a final collapse, whenever the canker should be exposed to the light of day. Feelings of revulsion sometimes troubled him, for his faith as priest was ardent and sincere. But his smile soon returned, as he took the cup of tea brought to him by Berthe and chatted to her for a moment, so as to cover by his priestly office the scandal of the window incident. Thus he again became a man of the world, content merely to exact decorous behaviour from his penitent flock, the members of which had strayed far from the fold, and who would have compromised the Deity himself.

'Well, these are fine goings-on!' murmured Octave whose respect for the house had received another shock.

Then, seeing that Madame Hédouin was going to fetch her cloak from the anteroom, and wishing to get there before her, he followed Trublot, who was also about to leave. He thought he might see her home. She declined his offer, as it was barely midnight and she lived so close by. Then, as a rose fell from the bouquet on her breast, he picked it up with an injured air and made a show of keeping it as a souvenir. For a moment her beautiful eyebrows contracted. Then she said, in her calm, self-possessed way:

'Please open the door for me, Monsieur Octave. Thank you.'

When she had gone downstairs, Octave, in his embarrassment, looked about for Trublot. But, as he had done at the Josserands', Trublot had just disappeared. He must have slipped away again by the servants' staircase.

So, somewhat put out, Octave went up to bed still holding the rose. Upstairs, he saw Marie leaning over the banisters, just where he had left her; she had been waiting to hear his step, and had run to see him coming up. She invited him in, saying:

'Jules hasn't come home yet. Did you enjoy yourself? Were there any pretty dresses?'

But she did not let him answer. She had just noticed the rose and, with childish gaiety, exclaimed:

'Is that flower for me? You thought of me, then. How very kind of you!'

Her eyes filled with tears, and she blushed deeply. Moved by a sudden impulse, Octave kissed her tenderly.

At about one o'clock the Josserands, in their turn, returned home. On a chair in the hall Adèle had placed a candlestick and some matches. None of them spoke as they came upstairs, but on entering the dining-room, from which they had departed in such despair, they yielded to a sudden burst of mad merriment, wildly seizing each other's hands and dancing a sort of savage dance round the table. Even Monsieur Josserand was caught up in the frenzy; the mother cut capers, and the girls uttered little inarticulate cries, while the candle on the table flung their huge dancing shadows on to the walls.

'At last, it's settled!' exclaimed Madame Josserand, sinking breathlessly into a chair.

But in a sudden fit of maternal tenderness, she immediately jumped up again, ran over to Berthe, and planted a kiss on both cheeks.

'I'm very, very pleased with you, my darling. You've rewarded me for all my efforts. My sweet child! It really is true this time.'

Her voice broke with genuine emotion, as, in her flame-coloured dress, she collapsed at the very moment of victory, finally overwhelmed by the fatigues of her terrible campaign which had lasted for three winters. Berthe was obliged to protest that she was not feeling unwell, for her mother thought that she was looking pale, and paid her all sorts of little attentions. She even insisted on making her a cup of lime-blossom tea. When Berthe had gone to bed, her mother, barefoot, went to tuck her in, as if she were a little girl again.

Meanwhile, with his head on the pillow, Monsieur Josserand awaited his wife's return. She blew out the candle and stepped over him to lie down on her side, nearest the wall. He was again troubled by uneasy thoughts, his conscience disturbed by the promise of a dowry of fifty thousand francs. And he ventured to express his scruples out loud. Why make a promise if you don't know if you can keep it? It was not honourable.

'Not honourable, indeed!' cried Madame Josserand in the darkness, her voice taking on again its usual ferocity of tone. 'It isn't honourable, sir, to let your daughters turn into old maids; yes, old maids—that was probably what you wanted! Good heavens! We've got lots of time to sort things out; we must talk it over, and get her uncle to make up his mind. In any case, *my* family, I would have you know, sir, has always acted honourably.'

VI

THE next day, which was a Sunday, Octave lay for an extra hour in the warm sheets of his bed. He had awoken in the mood of lazy good-humour that accompanies the mental clearness that morning brings. Why should he be in any hurry? He was completely at home at the Ladies' Paradise, he was losing his provincial ways, and he was absolutely certain that one day Madame Hédouin would become his and would make his fortune; but it would require prudence, a long series of gallant tactics, the anticipation of which appealed greatly to his voluptuous feeling for women. As he dropped off to sleep again, making plans and giving himself six months in which to succeed, the vision of Marie Pichon served to soothe his impatience. A woman of that sort was very handy; he had only to stretch out his arm if he wanted her, and she did not cost him a penny. While waiting for the other one, surely no better arrangement than this was possible. As he reflected on her cheapness and utility, he became quite tender-hearted towards her; her good nature began to seem quite charming to him, and he resolved to treat her henceforth with greater kindness.

'Good heavens! It's nine o'clock!' he said, as the clock, striking, made him wide-awake. 'I really must get up.'

A fine rain was falling, so he decided not to go out all day. He would accept an invitation to dine with the Pichons, an invitation he had been refusing for some time, dreading another encounter with the Vuillaumes. That would please Marie; and he would find an opportunity to kiss her behind the door. As she liked books, he even thought of taking her a whole parcel-full as a surprise—some that he had left in one of his trunks in the attic. When he had dressed he went downstairs to Monsieur Gourd to get the key to the attic, which was used by the different tenants for storing superfluous and cumbersome articles.

Down below, on such a damp morning as this, it was stifling on the heated staircase, where vapour dimmed the imitation marble walls, long mirrors, and mahogany doors. Under the porch, a poorly clad woman, Mother Pérou, whom the Gourds paid four sous an hour for doing the heavy work of the house, was scrubbing the pavement as the icy blast from the courtyard blew straight at her.

'Now then, old girl, make sure you scrub that properly; I want to find it absolutely clean!' cried Monsieur Gourd, who, warmly wrapped up, was standing at the door of his lodge.

As Octave arrived, he spoke to him about Mother Pérou in that brutally domineering way which shows the mad longing for revenge which ex-servants have when they, in their turn, are waited upon.

'She's a lazy old thing! I can't do anything with her! I'd like to have seen her at the duke's! They never stood any nonsense there! I'll kick her out if she doesn't give me my money's worth; that's all I'm concerned about! But what was it you wanted, Monsieur Mouret?'

Octave asked for the key. Then the porter, without hurrying, went on explaining that he and Madame Gourd, if they had wanted to, could have lived in their own house at Mort-la-Ville, but Madame Gourd adored Paris, in spite of her swollen legs which prevented her from even getting as far as the pavement. They were just waiting until they had a decent income, forever longing for the time when they would be able to retire on the little fortune they were slowly accumulating.

'I don't need to knock myself out working, you know,' he said, drawing up his majestic figure to its full height. 'I don't need to work any longer for my daily bread. The key to the attic, I think you said, Monsieur Mouret? Where did we put the key to the attic, my dear?'

Madame Gourd, cosily ensconced in an armchair, was drinking her coffee out of a silver cup before a wood fire, which brightened the whole room with its blaze. She had no idea where the key was—in one of the drawers, perhaps. And, while dipping her toast in the coffee, she did not take her eyes off the door of the servants' staircase at the other end of the courtyard, which looked bleaker and gloomier than ever in the rain.

'Look! There she is!' she said suddenly, as a woman appeared in the doorway.

Monsieur Gourd immediately stood in front of his lodge to block the woman's path. She slackened her pace, looking uneasy.

'We've been looking out for her all morning, Monsieur Mouret,' continued Gourd, under his breath. 'We saw her go by last night. She's come from that carpenter upstairs—the only working-man in

the house, thank God! If the landlord only listened to me, he'd keep
the room empty—it's just a servant's room, after all. For a hundred
and thirty francs a year, it's really not worth having filthy goings-on
in your house . . .'

Interrupting himself, he asked the woman roughly:

'Where have you come from?'

'From upstairs, of course!' she replied without stopping.

Then he burst out:

'We won't have any women here, you know! The man who brings
you here has been told that already. If you stay the night here again
I'll fetch the police, and we'll soon see if you carry on with your dirty
games in a decent house.'

'Don't be stupid!' said the woman. 'It's my home, and I'll come
back when I like.'

And she went off, pursued by the righteous wrath of Monsieur
Gourd, who talked of going upstairs to fetch the landlord. Did you
ever hear of such a thing? A creature like that among respectable
folk, in a house where not the faintest suspicion of immorality would
be tolerated! It seemed as if the carpenter's garret was the cesspool,
so to speak, of the house, a den of iniquity, the surveillance of which
offended all his delicate instincts and prevented him from sleeping at
night.

'And the key, where is it?' Octave ventured to repeat.

But the porter, furious that a lodger should have seen his
authority questioned in this way, set on poor Mother Pérou again, in
his desire to show how he could command obedience. Did she take
him for a fool? She had just splashed his door again with her broom.
If he paid her out of his own pocket it was because he did not want to
soil his hands, and yet he always had to clean up after her! He'd be
damned if he would ever give her another job just for charity's sake.
She could starve first. Worn out by her work, which was too hard for
her, the old woman, without answering, went on scrubbing with her
skinny arms, struggling to keep back her tears, so great was the
respect and fear which this large gentleman in smoking-cap and
slippers inspired in her.

'Now I remember, my dear,' cried Madame Gourd from the
armchair in which she spent her days, warming her fat body. 'I hid
the key under some shirts so that the servants wouldn't always be
going up there. Do give it to Monsieur Mouret.'

'A fine lot, too, those servants!' muttered Monsieur Gourd, whose many years in service had left him with a hatred for menials. 'Here's the key, sir, but please let me have it back, because you can't leave anywhere unlocked or the maids get in and misbehave.'

Not wishing to cross the wet courtyard Octave went up the front stairs, and only took the back stairs when he got to the fourth floor, as the communicating door was close to his room. At the top was a long passage, with two turnings at right angles; it was painted in light yellow, with a darker dado of ochre, and, as in hospital corridors, the doors of the servants' rooms, also painted in yellow, were positioned at regular intervals. It was as cold as ice under the zinc roofing, bare and clean, with the stale smell of paupers' lodging-houses.

The attic overlooked the courtyard at the far end of the right wing. But Octave, who had not been up there since the day of his arrival, was going along the left-hand passage when suddenly a sight which met his eyes through one of the half-open doors caused him to stop short in amazement. A gentleman in shirtsleeves was standing before a small looking-glass, tying his white cravat.

'What! You here?' he exclaimed.

It was Trublot. At first he seemed petrified. No one ever came up at that hour. Octave, who had stepped into the room, looked first at Trublot and then at the narrow iron bedstead and washstand, where a little ball of woman's hair was floating on the soapy water in the basin. Seeing a black dress-coat still hanging up among some aprons, he could not help exclaiming:

'So you sleep with the cook?'

'Of course not!' replied Trublot, looking startled.

Then, realizing the stupidity of telling such a lie, he began to laugh complacently.

'Well, she's really good fun, my dear chap; and very chic, too.'

Whenever he dined out he used to slip out of the drawing-room and go and pinch the cooks over their ovens, and when one of them let him have her key he would leave before midnight and wait patiently in her room, sitting on her trunk in his evening clothes and white cravat. The next morning, at about ten o'clock, he would leave by the front stairs and walk past the concierge's lodge as if he had been calling on one of the tenants at an early hour. As long as he kept office hours his father was satisfied. Besides, he had to be at the

Bourse now every day from twelve to three. On Sundays he sometimes spent the whole day in some servant's bed, quite happy, with his nose buried under her pillow.

'You as well, who are going to be so rich some day!' said Octave, with a look of disgust.

Then Trublot learnedly declared:

'My dear boy, you don't know what she's like, so you can't judge.'

And he began to sing the praises of Julie, a tall Burgundian woman of forty, her big face all pockmarked, but whose body was superbly built. You could strip all the other women in the house; they were all sticks, not one of them would come up to her knee. Moreover, she was a well-to-do girl; and to prove this he opened some drawers and showed Octave a bonnet, some jewellery, and some lace-trimmed skirts, all of which had doubtless been stolen from Madame Duveyrier. Octave, in fact, now noticed a certain coquettishness about the room—some gilt cardboard boxes on the drawers, a chintz curtain hanging over the petticoats, and other things which suggested that the cook was trying to play the fine lady.

'With this one,' said Trublot, 'I don't mind owning up. If only the rest were like her!'

Just then there was a noise on the back stairs; it was Adèle coming up to wash her ears, for Madame Josserand, furious, had forbidden her to touch the meat until she had cleaned them with soap and water. Trublot peeped out and recognized her.

'Shut the door, quick,' he said anxiously. 'Hush! Not a word.'

Listening attentively, he followed Adèle's footstep along the passage.

'So you sleep with her too, then?' asked Octave, surprised to see him turn so pale, and guessing that he was afraid of a scene.

This time, however, Trublot's cowardice got the better of him:

'Of course not—not with that slut! My dear fellow, what do you take me for?'

He was sitting on the edge of the bed waiting to finish dressing, and begged Octave not to move. So they both remained perfectly still while Adèle scrubbed her ears, an operation which lasted a good ten minutes. They heard the water slopping about in the basin.

'There's a room, though, between this one and hers,' Trublot explained, in a whisper. 'It's let to a workman, a carpenter, who stinks the place out with his onion soup. This morning again it

almost made me sick. And, you know, these days they make the
partitions in the servants' rooms as thin as paper. I don't know what
the landlords think they're doing, but I don't call it decent; you can
hardly turn round in your bed. Most inconvenient, I think!'

When Adèle had gone downstairs again, his bold air returned as
he finished dressing with the help of Julie's combs and pomade.
When Octave mentioned the attic he insisted on showing him where
it was, as he knew the top floor intimately. And as they passed the
doors of the servants' rooms he familiarly mentioned their names: at
this end of the passage, after Adèle, came Lisa, the Campardons'
maid, a wench who got what she wanted outside; then there was
Victoire, their cook, a pathetic old whale of seventy, but the only one
for whom he had any respect. Then came Françoise, who, the day
before, had entered Madame Valérie's service, and whose trunk
would perhaps remain only twenty-four hours behind the squalid
bed in which so many maids had slept that you always had to make
sure that it was empty before going there to wait between the warm
sheets. Then there was a quiet couple in the service of people on the
second floor; then came their coachman, a strapping fellow, of whom
he spoke jealously, as one handsome man might speak of another,
suspecting him of going from door to door, silently enjoying each
maid in turn. At the other end of the passage there was Clémence,
the Duveyriers' maid, whom her neighbour, Hippolyte the butler,
visited conjugally every night; and finally there was little Louise, the
orphan whom Madame Juzeur had engaged on trial, a mere girl of
fifteen, who must hear some strange things at night if she were a
light sleeper.

'Don't lock the door again, there's a good fellow,' said Trublot,
when he had helped Octave to get out the books. 'You see, when the
attic's left open you can hide there and wait.'

Having consented to deceive Monsieur Gourd, Octave returned
with Trublot to Julie's room, where the latter had left his overcoat.
Then he could not find his gloves; he shook the petticoats, turned
the bedclothes inside out, raising such a cloud of dust and such a
fusty smell of dirty linen that Octave, half-choking, opened the
window. It looked on to the narrow inner courtyard, from which all
the kitchens in the house got whatever light they had. He was
leaning over this damp well, from which there rose the fetid odours
of dirty sinks, when a sound of voices made him hastily withdraw.

'That's their little morning gossip,' said Trublot, who was on all fours, still looking under the bed. 'Just listen to it.'

It was Lisa, who was leaning out of the Campardons' kitchen to talk to Julie, two floors below.

'So it's come off this time, has it?'

'Seems so,' replied Julie, looking up. 'You know, she did everything but pull his trousers down in her efforts to catch him. Hippolyte came back from the drawing-room so disgusted that he was nearly sick.'

'If we were only to do a quarter as much!' said Lisa.

For a moment she disappeared to drink some broth that Victoire had brought her. They got on well together, pandering to each other's vices, the maid hiding the cook's drunkenness, and the cook helping the maid to have those outings from which she came back quite worn out, her back aching and her eyelids blue.

'Ah, my children,' said Victoire, leaning out in her turn, her elbows touching Lisa's, 'you're young! Wait until you've seen what I've seen! At old Campardon's there was his niece, a girl who had been well brought up, who used to look at men through the keyhole.'

'Fine goings-on!' muttered Julie, with the scandalized air of a lady. 'If I'd been the little girl on the fourth floor, I'd have given Monsieur Auguste such a smack on the face if he'd pinched me in the drawing-room. A nice fellow, indeed!'

At these words a shrill laugh came from Madame Juzeur's kitchen. Lisa, who was opposite, looked quickly round the room and spotted Louise, who in her precocity delighted in listening to the servants.

'That brat keeps spying on us from morning till night,' she said. 'It's a real nuisance having a child like that hanging around! We won't be able to talk at all soon!'

She did not finish, for the noise of a window opening suddenly made them all vanish. There was a profound silence; then they ventured to look out again. What was it, after all? They thought it was Madame Valérie or Madame Josserand.

'It's all right,' said Lisa. 'They're all soaking their faces in their basins. Too concerned about their complexions to think about bothering us! It's the only time in the day that we can breathe!'

'So things are still the same at your place, are they?' enquired Julie, as she peeled a carrot.

'Still the same!' replied Victoire. 'She's completely stopped up now.'

The other two sniggered gleefully, titillated by this crude reference to Madame Campardon.

'What does that idiot of an architect do, then?'

'He just has her cousin instead, of course!'

They laughed louder still, until Françoise, Madame Valérie's new maid, looked out. It was she who had caused the alarm by opening the window. At first there was an exchange of civilities.

'Oh, it's you, mademoiselle!'

'Yes, indeed, mademoiselle! I'm trying to straighten up this kitchen, but it's so filthy!'

Then came certain nauseous details.

'You'll have to have the patience of Jove to stop there. The last one had her arms all scratched by the child, and madame made her work so hard that we could hear her crying from here.'

'Well, that won't suit me very long!' said Françoise. 'Thanks, though, for telling me.'

'Where is she, your missus?' asked Victoire inquisitively.

'She's just gone out to have lunch with a lady friend.'

Leaning out, Lisa and Julie exchanged glances. They knew her well, that lady. A funny sort of lunch, too, with her head down and her legs in the air! How could people dare to tell such shocking lies! They did not pity the husband, who deserved all he got; but all the same, it was a disgrace to humanity when a woman could not behave better.

'There's Dish–cloth!' cried Lisa, as she spied the Josserands' maid above her.

Then a volley of vulgar abuse was bawled out from this hole, as dark and stinking as a sewer. All of them, looking up at Adèle, yelled violently at her; she was their scapegoat—the dirty, clumsy creature on whom all those in the building vented their spite.

'Oh, look! She's washed herself, that's obvious!'

'Just you throw your offal into the yard again, and I'll come and rub your face in it!'

'Well you can go and stick God in *your* gob! The dirty cow, she chews it over like the cud from one Sunday to the next.'

Adèle, bewildered, looked down at them, her body half out of the window. At last she said:

'Leave me alone, or you'll get a bucketful!'

But the shouts and laughter increased.

'You got your young mistress married last night, did you? Perhaps it's you who taught her how to catch men!'

'Oh, the spineless thing! She stays in a place where they don't give you enough to eat! That's what really annoys me about her! What a fool you are! Why don't you tell them all to go to hell?'

Adèle's eyes filled with tears.

'Stop talking nonsense,' she stammered. 'It's not my fault if I don't get enough to eat.'

The voices grew louder, as harsh words were exchanged between Lisa and the new servant, Françoise, who sided with Adèle; but suddenly the latter, forgetting how they had abused her, and yielding to her instinctive *esprit de corps*, cried:

'Look out! Here's madame!'

The courtyard became as silent as the grave. They all plunged back into their kitchens; and from the dark bowels of the narrow courtyard only the stench of drains came up, like the smell of the hidden filth of the various families, stirred up by the servants' rancour. This was the sewer of the house, draining off the house's shames, while the masters lounged about in their slippers and the front staircase displayed all its solemn majesty amid the stuffy silence of the hot-air stove. Octave remembered the sudden explosion that had greeted him from the courtyard on entering the Campardons' kitchen, the day of his arrival.

'How charming,' he said simply.

Leaning out in his turn, he looked at the walls as if annoyed that he had not seen through the whole sham at once, covered up as it was by imitation marble and gilt stucco.

'Where the devil has she put them?' said Trublot, who had been looking everywhere for his white gloves.

He finally discovered them at the bottom of the bed; they were flattened out and quite warm. He gave a last glance at the mirror, and then hid the bedroom key in the place agreed upon, at the end of the passage, under an old sideboard left behind by some lodger. Then he led the way downstairs, accompanied by Octave. On the front stairs, having got past the Josserands' door, all his assurance returned as he buttoned his overcoat up to his neck to hide his evening clothes and white tie.

'Goodbye, old chap,' he said, raising his voice. 'I was rather worried, so I just called to see how the ladies were. They slept very well, it seems. Goodbye!'

Octave, smiling, watched him as he went downstairs. Then, as it was almost lunchtime, he decided to return the key to the loft later on. During lunch, at the Campardons', he watched Lisa with particular interest as she waited at table. She looked pleasant and neat as usual, though her foul words still echoed in his mind. His flair for women had not deceived him with regard to this flat-chested wench. Madame Campardon continued to be delighted with her, and was pleasantly surprised that she did not steal anything. That was true enough, for her vice was of another kind. Moreover, she appeared to be very kind to Angèle, and the mother trusted her completely.

That very morning, as it happened, Angèle disappeared at dessert, and they heard her laughing in the kitchen. Octave ventured to remark:

'Perhaps it's not very wise to let her be so familiar with the servants.'

'Oh, there's no great harm in that!' replied Madame Campardon, in her languid way. 'Victoire saw my husband born, and I have every confidence in Lisa. And, you know, the child gives me headaches. I'd go mad if she was dancing round me all day.'

The architect sat gravely chewing the end of his cigar.

'I'm the one', he said, 'who makes Angèle spend two hours in the kitchen every afternoon. I want her to learn housekeeping, and that's the best way to teach her. She never goes out, my dear boy; she's always under our wing. You'll see what a treasure we'll make of her!'

Octave said no more. Sometimes Campardon seemed to him to be absolutely stupid; and when the architect urged him to come to Saint-Roch and hear a famous preacher, he refused, obstinately persisting in remaining at home. Having told Madame Campardon that he would not dine there that evening, he was on his way to his room when he felt the key to the attic in his pocket. He thought he had better return it at once.

On the landing an unexpected sight attracted his attention. The door of the room let to the distinguished gentleman whose name nobody knew was open. This was quite an event, for it was always shut, as if barred by the silence of the tomb. His surprise increased when, on looking for the gentleman's writing-table, he saw in its place the corner of a large bedstead, and perceived a slim lady coming out of the room. She was dressed in black, and wore a thick veil which concealed her features. The door closed noiselessly behind her.

His curiosity roused, he followed the lady downstairs to see if she was pretty. But she tripped along with nervous little steps, her tiny boots barely touching the stair-carpet, and leaving no trace behind her but a faint perfume of verbena. As he reached the hall she disappeared, and he only saw Monsieur Gourd standing in the doorway, cap in hand, making a low bow to her.

As Octave returned the key, he tried to make the doorkeeper talk.

'She looks very ladylike,' he said. 'Who is she?'

'A lady,' replied Monsieur Gourd.

And he would not add anything further. But he was more communicative regarding the gentleman on the third floor. A man, you know, who belonged to the best society; he had taken the room to come and work there quietly one night a week.

'Oh, he works, does he? I wonder what at?' asked Octave.

'He was good enough to ask me to look after his room,' continued Monsieur Gourd, pretending not to have heard, 'and, you know, he pays cash on the nail. Ah, sir! when you wait on people, you soon find out if they're all right or not. He's a real gentleman, he is; you can tell that from his clothes.'

He was obliged to stand on one side, and Octave even had to step back for a moment into the concierge's lodge, so as to let the carriage of the second-floor people go by on their way to the Bois de Boulogne. The horses, reined in by the coachman, pawed the ground; and as the large closed landau rolled along under the vaulted roof, two handsome children were seen through the windows, their smiling faces almost hiding the indistinct profiles of their father and mother. Monsieur Gourd stood to attention, polite but cold.

'Those people don't make much noise in the house,' said Octave.

'Nobody makes any noise,' replied the concierge, drily. 'Each one lives as he thinks best, that's all. Some people know how to live, and some don't.'

The people on the second floor were not well regarded, because they associated with no one. They appeared to be rich, however. The husband wrote books, but Monsieur Gourd's curled lip showed that he put little faith in that sort of thing, especially as nobody knew what went on in the household, which never seemed to want anybody, but which always appeared to be perfectly happy. That was not natural, so he thought.

Octave was opening the hall door when Valérie came back. He politely stood aside to let her pass.

'Are you well, madam?'

'Yes, thank you, sir.'

She was out of breath, and as she went upstairs he looked at her muddy boots, and thought about the lunch alluded to by the servants. No doubt she had walked home, not having been able to get a cab. A warm, stale smell came from her damp petticoats. Fatigue, utter physical weariness, made her catch hold of the banisters every now and then.

'What an awful day, madam, isn't it?'

'Awful, and so close, too!'

On reaching the first floor, they parted. At a glance Octave saw how haggard her face was, how heavy with sleep her eyelids were, and how her unkempt hair showed underneath her hastily tied bonnet. As he proceeded upstairs, his thoughts troubled and angered him. Why would she not do it with him? He was not more stupid or ugly than anybody else.

On passing the door to Madame Juzeur's apartment on the third floor, he remembered his promise of the previous evening. He felt quite curious about that discreet little woman with eyes like periwinkles. He rang. It was Madame Juzeur herself who answered the door.

'Oh, my dear sir, how good of you! Do come in!'

There was a certain stuffiness about the apartment. There were carpets and curtains everywhere, chairs as soft as eiderdown, and the atmosphere as warm and heavy as that of a chest lined with old rainbow-coloured satin. In the drawing-room, which with its double curtains had the solemn stillness of a sacristy, Octave was asked to take a seat on a broad, low sofa.

'This is the lace,' said Madame Juzeur, as she came back with a sandalwood box full of pieces of stuff. 'I want to make a present of it to somebody, and I'm curious to know its value.'

It was a piece of very fine old *point d'Angleterre*. Octave examined it with his professional eye, and declared that it was worth three hundred francs. Then, without waiting further, as they were both handling the lace, he bent down and kissed her fingers, which were as small and delicate as those of a little girl.

'Oh, Monsieur Octave, at my age! You can't think what you're doing!' exclaimed Madame Juzeur, with a pretty air of surprise, though not at all annoyed.

She was thirty-two, and gave out that she was quite an old woman. As usual, she spoke of her troubles: goodness gracious! Ten days after their marriage the cruel man had disappeared one morning and had never returned—nobody knew why.

'You can understand', she said, gazing up at the ceiling, 'that after a shock like that, it's all over for any woman.'

Octave had kept hold of her warm little hand, which seemed to melt into his, and he kept lightly kissing it on the fingertips. She looked at him vaguely, tenderly, and then, in a maternal way, she exclaimed:

'Child!'

Thinking himself encouraged, he tried to put his arm round her waist and pull her on to the sofa, but she gently freed herself from his grasp, laughing, as if she thought he was just playing.

'No, leave me alone, and don't touch me if you want us to remain good friends.'

'Then you don't want to?' he asked in a low voice.

'Want what? I don't know what you mean. Oh! you can hold my hand as long as you like.'

He caught hold of her hand again. But this time he opened it, and began kissing the palm. With half-shut eyes, she treated the process as a joke, opening her fingers as a cat puts out its claws to be tickled inside its paw. She would not let him go further than the wrist. The first day a sacred line was drawn there beyond which impropriety began.

'Father Mauduit is coming upstairs,' said Louise, suddenly returning from an errand.

The orphan had the sallow complexion and insignificant features of a foundling. She giggled idiotically when she caught sight of the gentleman nibbling at her mistress's hand. But at a glance from Madame Juzeur she disappeared.

'I fear I'll never be able to do anything with her,' said Madame Juzeur. 'But, all the same, one ought to try and put one of those poor creatures on the right path. Would you come this way, Monsieur Mouret?'

She took him into the dining-room, so as to leave the other room for the priest, whom Louise showed in. As she said goodbye, she expressed the hope that Octave would come again and have a chat. It would be a little company for her; she was always so lonely and depressed. Happily, in religion she had her consolation.

That evening, at about five o'clock, Octave felt positively relieved as he made himself at home at the Pichons' while waiting for dinner. The house and its inmates bewildered him somewhat. After feeling all the provincial's awe for the grave splendour of its staircase, he was gradually becoming filled with supreme contempt for all that he imagined took place behind those big mahogany doors. He did not know what to think; these bourgeois women, whose virtue had frozen him at first, seemed now as if they would surrender at a mere sign, and when one of them resisted it filled him with surprise and vexation.

Marie blushed with pleasure when she saw him put down the parcel of books he had fetched for her that morning.

'How good of you, Monsieur Octave!' she kept repeating. 'Thank you so much. How nice of you to come so early. Will you have a glass of sugar and water, with some cognac in it? It's very good for the appetite.'

Just to please her, he accepted. Everything about the evening seemed very pleasant to him, even Pichon and the Vuillaumes, who slowly rehearsed their usual Sunday conversation. Every now and then Marie ran to the kitchen where she was cooking a shoulder of mutton, and Octave jokingly followed her, and catching her round the waist, in front of the oven, kissed the back of her neck. Without a cry, without a start, she turned round and kissed him on the mouth with her icy lips. To the young man their coldness seemed delicious.

'Well, what do you think of your new minister?' he asked Pichon, on coming back to the drawing-room.

The clerk gave a start. What! there was going to be a new minister of public instruction? He had heard nothing about it; in the sort of office he worked in they never took any interest in that sort of thing.

'The weather is so awful,' he said abruptly. 'It's quite impossible to keep one's trousers clean!'

Madame Vuillaume was talking about a girl at Batignolles who had gone to the bad.

'You'll hardly believe me, sir,' she said. 'The girl was extremely well brought up, but she was so bored at having to live with her parents that she twice tried to jump out of the window. It's beyond belief!'

'They should put bars over the windows,' remarked Monsieur Vuillaume simply.

The dinner was delightful. The same sort of conversation went on all the while, as they sat round the frugal board, which was lighted by a little lamp. Pichon and Monsieur Vuillaume, having got on to the subject of government officials, talked interminably about directors and sub-directors. The father-in-law obstinately upheld those of his day, and then remembered that they were dead, while Pichon, for his part, went on talking about the new ones, amid an endless muddle of names. On one point, however, the two men, as well as Madame Vuillaume, were agreed: fat old Chavignat, whose wife was so ugly, had had far too many children. With an income such as his it was quite absurd. Octave, feeling happy and at ease, smiled; he had not spent such a pleasant evening for a long time. After a while he, too, roundly condemned Chavignat. Marie soothed him with her innocent, docile look; she was quite untroubled to see him sitting next to her husband, and helped them both to what they liked best, in her languidly obedient way.

At ten o'clock exactly the Vuillaumes rose to go. Pichon put on his hat. Every Sunday he went with them as far as their omnibus. It was a habit which, out of deference, he had observed ever since his marriage, and the Vuillaumes would have been very hurt if he had now tried to discontinue it. They all three set out for the Rue de Richelieu, and walked slowly up it, scrutinizing the Batignolles omnibuses, which were always full. Pichon thus was often obliged to go as far as Montmartre, for it would never have done for him to leave the Vuillaumes before putting them on their bus. As they walked very slowly, it took him nearly two hours to go there and back.

There was much friendly shaking of hands on the landing. As Octave went back with Marie to the sitting-room, he said:

'It's raining. Jules won't get back before midnight.'

As Lilitte had been put to bed early, he at once made Marie sit on his knee, drinking the remainder of the coffee with her out of the same cup, like a husband who is glad that his guests have gone and that he is left all to himself after the excitement of a little family gathering, and able to kiss his wife at his ease, with the doors closed. A drowsy warmth pervaded the little room, in which a dish of frosted eggs had left a faint odour of vanilla. As he was lightly kissing the young woman under the chin, someone knocked at the door. Marie did not even give a start. It was the half-witted Josserand boy. Whenever he could escape from the apartment opposite he would come across and chat to her, as her gentleness attracted him; they both got on very well together, sitting in silence for ten minutes at a time, occasionally dropping the odd disconnected remark.

Octave, very put out, stayed silent.

'They've got some people there tonight,' stammered Saturnin. 'I don't care a damn if they won't let me sit with them. I took the lock off and got away. Serves 'em right!'

'They'll wonder what's happened to you. You ought to go back,' said Marie, who had noticed Octave's impatience.

But the idiot simply laughed with delight, and falteringly told her all that had happened at home. Each visit seemed to be in order to relieve his memory.

'Papa has been working all night again, and mamma gave Berthe a slap. Tell me, when people get married, does it hurt?'

Then, as Marie did not answer, he excitedly continued:

'I won't go to the country, I won't! If they touch her, I'll strangle them; it's easy enough, at night, while they're asleep. The palm of her hand is as smooth as notepaper; but the other is a beast of a girl . . .'

Then he began again, and got more muddled, as he could not express what he had come to say. Marie finally persuaded him to go back to his parents, without his even having noticed Octave's presence.

Fearing another interruption, Octave wanted to take the young woman across to his own room but, blushing violently, she refused. Not understanding such bashfulness, he continued to assure her that they would be certain to hear Jules coming upstairs, and she would have plenty of time to get back to her room; and as he began to pull on her arm she became quite angry, as indignant as a woman threatened by violence.

'No, not in your room; never! That would be too awful. Let's stay here.' She ran to the back of the apartment. Octave was still on the landing, surprised at such unexpected resistance, when the sound of a violent quarrel arose from the courtyard. Everything seemed to be going wrong for him; he should simply have gone off to bed. A noise of this sort was so unusual at that hour that at last he opened a window so as to listen. Monsieur Gourd was shouting out:

'I tell you, you shall not pass! The landlord has been sent for. He'll come down and kick you out himself!'

'Kick me out? What for?' said a gruff voice. 'Don't I pay my rent? Go on, Amélie, and if the gentleman touches you, he'll know about it!'

It was the carpenter from upstairs, who was returning with the woman they had chased away that morning. Octave leaned out of the window, but in the black courtyard he only saw great moving shadows thrown by the dim gaslight in the hall.

'Monsieur Vabre! Monsieur Vabre!' cried the porter, as the carpenter pushed him aside. 'Quick, quick! she's coming in!'

Despite her bad legs Madame Gourd had gone to fetch the landlord, who just then was at work on his great task. He was coming down. Octave heard him furiously repeating:

'It's scandalous, disgraceful! I won't allow such a thing in my house!'

Then, addressing the workman, who at first seemed somewhat abashed, he said: 'Send that woman away at once! At once, do you hear? We don't want any women brought in here.'

'But she's my wife!' replied the carpenter, with a scared look. 'She's in service—she only comes once a month, when her people let her have a day off. What a fuss! It's not your place to prevent me from sleeping with my wife, is it?'

Then both porter and landlord lost their heads.

'I'm giving you notice to quit,' stuttered Monsieur Vabre, 'and, meanwhile, I forbid you to turn my premises into a brothel! Gourd, turn that creature into the street. No, sir, I don't like bad jokes. If a man is married he should say so. Hold your tongue, I'll have no more of your insolence!'

The carpenter, good-natured fellow as he was, and who, no doubt, had had a little too much wine, burst out laughing.

'It's a damned funny thing, all the same. Well, Amélie, as the

gentleman objects, you'd better go back to your employer's. We'll
make our baby some other time. We wanted to make a baby, that's
all we wanted. I'll accept your notice with pleasure! I don't want to
stay in this hole. There are some nice goings-on here. He won't have
women brought into the house—oh, no! But he tolerates well-
dressed hussies on every floor, who lead filthy lives behind closed
doors. You bloody toffs!'

Amélie had made herself scarce, so as not to cause her husband
any more bother, while he continued his good-humoured banter. In
the meantime Gourd covered Monsieur Vabre's retreat while
venturing to make certain remarks out loud. What a filthy lot the
lower orders were! One workman in the house was quite enough to
infect it.

Octave closed the window. Then, just as he was returning to
Marie, someone lightly brushed past him in the passage.

'What! you again?' he said, recognizing Trublot.

For a moment the latter was speechless; then he sought to explain
his presence.

'Yes; I've been dining with the Josserands, and I was just going up
to . . .'

Octave felt disgusted.

'To that slut Adèle, I suppose? And you swore you didn't sleep
with her!'

Then, resuming his swagger, Trublot said with a satisfied air:

'I assure you, my dear fellow, she's rather wonderful! Her skin
is . . . you can't imagine!'

Then he abused the workman, who, with his dirty stories about
women, had almost caused him to be caught coming up the back
stairs. He had been obliged to come round by the front staircase.
Then, as he made off, he added:

'Remember next Thursday—I'm taking you to see Duveyrier's
mistress. We'll dine together first.'

The house regained its holy calm, lapsing into the religious silence
that seemed to issue from each chaste bedchamber. Octave had
rejoined Marie in her bedroom, sitting beside her on the conjugal
bed while she arranged the pillows. Upstairs, as the only chair had a
basin on it and an old pair of slippers, Trublot had sat down on
Adèle's narrow bed and was waiting for her in his dinner suit and
white tie. When he recognized Julie's step as she came up to bed he

held his breath, for he was in constant dread of women's quarrels. At last Adèle appeared. She was angry and, seizing his arm, said:

'You could treat me better when I'm waiting at table!'

'What do you mean?'

'Well, you don't even look at me, and you never say "please" when you want some bread. This evening, when I was handing the veal round, you looked as if you'd never seen me before in your life. I've had enough of it. They're always getting at me, and it's just too much if you side with them!'

She undressed in a fury, and, flinging herself down on the old mattress, which cracked again, she turned her back on him.

Meanwhile in the next room, the carpenter, still full of wine, was talking to himself at the top of his voice, so that the whole corridor could hear him.

'Well, it's a queer business when you can't sleep with your own wife! So you won't have any women in the house, will you, you silly old bugger? Just go and have a look under all the bedclothes, and you'll soon see!'

VII

In order to get uncle Bachelard to give Berthe a dowry, for the past two weeks the Josserands had been asking him to dinner almost every evening, in spite of his revolting habits.

When they told him about the marriage all he did was pat his niece on the cheek and say:

'What! So you're going to get married? That's very nice, isn't it, my little girl!'

He turned a deaf ear to all hints, exaggerating his behaviour as a bibulous old rake, becoming suddenly drunk whenever the subject of money was mentioned.

Madame Josserand thought of asking him to meet Auguste, the bridegroom-elect, feeling that the sight of the young man might induce him to hand over the money. This stratagem was quite heroic, for the family did not like exhibiting their uncle for fear that it might create a false impression. However, he behaved fairly well; there was only a large syrup stain on his waistcoat, no doubt acquired at some café. Yet when, after Auguste's departure, his sister questioned him and asked what he thought of the bridegroom, he merely said, without compromising himself:

'Charming, quite charming.'

The thing must be settled somehow, for time was running out. Madame Josserand determined to put matters plainly before him.

'As we're now by ourselves,' she continued, 'let's make the most of it. Could you please leave us alone, my dears; we must have a talk with your uncle. Berthe, please keep an eye on Saturnin, and see that he doesn't take the lock off the door again.'

Ever since they had become busy with his sister's marriage, keeping it a secret, Saturnin wandered about the house with wild eyes, feeling that something was going on; he imagined all sorts of terrible things, to the consternation of his family.

'I've made enquiries,' said Madame Josserand, when she had shut herself in with Bachelard and her husband. 'This is the Vabres' position.'

Then she went into long details about figures. Old Vabre had brought half-a-million with him from Versailles. If the house had cost him three hundred thousand francs, he would have two hundred thousand left, which in the last twelve years had been producing interest. Besides, every year his rents brought him in twenty-two thousand francs, and, as he lived with the Duveyriers and hardly spent anything at all, he must be worth five or six hundred thousand francs, not counting the house. Thus there were handsome expectations on that side.

'He doesn't have any vices, then?' asked Bachelard. 'I thought he speculated on the Bourse.'

Madame Josserand loudly protested at this. Such a quiet old man, absorbed in such important work! He, at least, had shown that he could make a fortune! She smiled bitterly as she glanced at her husband, who lowered his head.

As for Vabre's three children, Auguste, Clotilde, and Théophile, they had each had a hundred thousand francs on their mother's death. Théophile, after certain ruinous enterprises, was living as best he could on the remains of this inheritance. Clotilde, whose only passion was her piano, had probably invested her share. Auguste had just bought the business on the ground floor, and had started in the silk trade with his hundred thousand francs, which he had long been keeping in reserve.

'Of course, the old boy won't give his children anything when they marry,' remarked Bachelard.

Well, he wasn't very keen on giving; that was very clear. When Clotilde married he had undertaken to give her a dowry of eighty thousand francs; but Duveyrier had never received more than ten thousand. He had never asked for the balance, but even gave his father-in-law free board and lodging—flattering his avarice, no doubt in the hope of one day acquiring his whole fortune. In the same way, after promising Théophile fifty thousand francs when he married Valérie, at first he had merely paid the interest, and since then had not parted with a single penny, even going so far as to demand rent from the young couple, which they paid for fear of being struck out of his will. Thus it was not possible to count too much on the fifty thousand francs Auguste was to receive when the marriage contract was signed; he would be lucky enough if his father let him have the ground-floor shop rent free for a few years.

'Well,' declared Bachelard, 'it's always hard on the parents, you know. Dowries are never really paid.'

'Let's go back to Auguste,' continued Madame Josserand. 'I've told you what his expectations are; the only possible danger is from the Duveyriers, and Berthe will do well to keep a close eye on them when she becomes one of the family. As things stand, Auguste, having bought the business for sixty thousand francs, has started with the other forty thousand. But that isn't really enough; besides which, he's single and wants a wife, so he means to marry. Berthe's pretty, and he can see already how nice she would look in his counting-house; and as for her dowry, fifty thousand francs is a respectable sum, and that's helped him to make up his mind.'

Uncle Bachelard did not bat an eyelid. At last he said, with a tender air, that he had dreamed of something better. And he began to criticize the future son-in-law. A charming fellow, certainly, but too old, much too old, over thirty-three in fact; and he was always ill, with constant migraines, a sorry sight, certainly not lively enough to be a tradesman.

'Have you got anybody else?' asked Madame Josserand, whose patience was running out. 'I hunted all over Paris before I found him.'

However, she had no illusions about him; and in her turn she too picked him to pieces.

'Oh, he's nothing special, its true; in fact, I think he's rather stupid. And I always distrust men who've never had their fling when young, and have to reflect for years before taking the slightest risky step in life. When he left school, after his headaches put a stop to his studies, he stayed a clerk for fifteen years before daring to touch his hundred thousand francs, while his father, so it seems, cheated him out of the interest on it. No, he's not brilliant.'

So far, Monsieur Josserand had remained silent. He now ventured to remark:

'But, my dear, why insist on this marriage if the young man is in such bad health . . .?'

'Oh,' interjected Bachelard, 'bad health is no reason against it. Berthe would find it easy enough to marry again.'

'But suppose he's impotent,' said Monsieur Josserand. 'Suppose he makes our daughter unhappy?'

'Unhappy!' cried Madame Josserand. 'Why don't you say at once that I've thrown my girl into the arms of the first-comer? Among ourselves, surely, we can discuss him, and say he's this, or he's that—not young, not good-looking, not clever. It's only natural that we should talk the matter over like this, isn't it? But he's not too bad, we won't find anybody better! And, let me tell you, it's a most unexpected match for Berthe. I was going to give it all up as a bad job, I really was!'

She rose; and Monsieur Josserand, reduced to silence, pushed back his chair.

'I'm only afraid of one thing,' she continued, resolutely planting herself in front of her brother, 'and it's that he may break it off if the dowry isn't forthcoming on the day the contract is to be signed. That's understandable; he's short of money, you know.'

Just then she heard the sound of heavy breathing close behind her, and turned round. It was Saturnin, who had stuck his head round the door and was glaring at her with wolfish eyes. They were all panic-stricken, for he had stolen a spit from the kitchen, to spit the geese, so he said. Uncle Bachelard, who was feeling very uncomfortable at the turn the conversation was taking, took advantage of the general alarm.

'Don't disturb yourselves,' he called out from the anteroom. 'I'm off; I've got a midnight appointment with one of my clients, who's come over specially from Brazil.'

When they had managed to put Saturnin to bed, Madame Josserand, in her exasperation, declared that it was impossible to keep him any longer. He would do someone an injury if he was not shut up in an asylum. It was intolerable to have to keep him out of the way all the time. His sisters would never get married as long as he was there to disgust and terrify everybody.

'Let's wait a bit longer,' muttered Monsieur Josserand, whose heart bled at the thought of this separation.

'No, no,' declared his wife. 'I don't want to end up being spitted. I'd just got my brother cornered, and was going to get him to make a commitment. Never mind. We'll go with Berthe tomorrow, and have it out with him at his place, and then we'll see if he's got the cheek not to keep his promises. Besides, Berthe owes her godfather a visit. It's only proper.'

The following day all three—mother, father, and daughter—paid an official visit to the uncle's premises, which occupied the basement and the ground floor of an enormous house in the Rue d'Enghien. The entrance was blocked by large vans. In the covered courtyard a gang of packers was nailing up cases, and through open doorways they caught sight of piles of goods, dried vegetables, remnants of silk, stationery, and tallow, all accumulated in executing the thousands of commissions given by customers, and by buying in advance when prices were low. Bachelard was there, with his big red nose, his eyes still inflamed by the previous night's drinking, but with his head clear, as his business acumen returned the moment he sat down to his account-books.

'Hullo! What are you doing here?' he said, annoyed to see them. He took them into a little office, from which he could keep an eye on his men from a window.

'I've brought Berthe to see you,' explained Madame Josserand. 'She knows how much she owes you.'

Then, when Berthe, responding to a glance from her mother, had kissed her uncle and gone off to look at the goods in the courtyard, Madame Josserand resolutely broached the subject of the dowry.

'Listen, Narcisse, this is the situation we're in. Relying on your kind-heartedness and your promises, I've committed us to a dowry of fifty thousand francs. If I don't produce it, the marriage will be broken off. Now that things have gone so far, that would be a disgrace. You simply can't leave us in such an awkward position.'

Bachelard's eyes had glazed over, and he stammered out, as if quite drunk:

'Eh? What? You promised? You should never make promises; bad thing to promise.'

Then he pleaded poverty. For instance, he had bought a whole lot of horsehair, thinking that the price would go up. Not a bit of it; the price had fallen, and he had been obliged to get rid of it at a loss. Rushing to his books, he opened his ledger and insisted on showing them the invoices. An absolute disaster.

'Rubbish!' exclaimed Monsieur Josserand at last, losing all patience. 'I know all about your business, and that you're making plenty of money. You'd be rolling in it, if you didn't squander it as you do. Mind, I'm not asking you for anything myself. It was Eléonore's idea to come here like this. But allow me to tell you, Bachelard, that you've been fooling us. Every Saturday, for the last fifteen years, when I went through your books for you, you always promised that . . .'

The uncle interrupted him, violently slapping his chest.

'Promised? Quite impossible! No, no! Leave me alone, and we'll see later on. I don't like to be asked; it annoys me and upsets me. We'll see later on.'

Even Madame Josserand could extract nothing further from him. Shaking them by the hand, he brushed away a tear, spoke of his kind-heartedness and of his affection for the family, and begged them to pester him no more, as, by God! they would never have cause to regret it. He knew his duty, and would do it to the uttermost. Later on Berthe would find out how much her uncle was attached to her.

'And what about the dotal insurance?' he asked, resuming his natural tone of voice. 'The fifty thousand francs for which you insured the girl's life?'

Madame Josserand shrugged her shoulders.

'That was killed off fourteen years ago. We've told you a hundred times that when the fourth premium fell due we couldn't pay the two thousand francs.'

'That doesn't matter,' he murmured with a wink. 'The important thing is to talk about the insurance to the family, and take your time paying the dowry money. You should never pay a dowry.'

Monsieur Josserand rose in disgust.

'So that's all you have to say to us, is it?'

Pretending not to understand, the uncle insisted that never paying a dowry was normal.

'You should never pay, I tell you. You pay something on account, and then the interest. Look at Monsieur Vabre! Did my father ever pay for Eléonore's dowry? Of course not! People just don't want to part with their money.'

'So you're advising me to do something really abominable!' cried Monsieur Josserand. 'It would be a lie! I would be committing forgery if I produced the life policy of that insurance . . .'

Madame Josserand cut him short. On hearing her brother's suggestion she had become very serious. She was wondering why she had never thought of this before.

'Dear me! You're very touchy, my dear! Narcisse never told you to forge anything!'

'Of course not,' muttered Bachelard. 'There's no need to show any papers.'

'The point is to gain time,' she continued. 'Promise the dowry, we'll manage to give it later on.'

Then the worthy man spoke out. No! He refused; never again would he venture to approach such a precipice. They were always taking advantage of his easygoing nature, getting him gradually to consent to things which afterwards made him quite ill, so much did he take them to heart. Since he had no dowry to give, it was impossible for him to promise one.

Bachelard was drumming on the windowpane and whistling a tune, as if to show his utter contempt for such scruples. While Madame Josserand had been listening to her husband, her face had grown livid with pent-up fury that suddenly burst forth:

'Very well, sir, since that's so, the marriage shall take place. It's my daughter's last chance. I'd rather cut off my right hand than lose it. So much the worse for the others! When you're pushed far enough, you're capable of anything.'

'So I presume, madam, you would commit murder to get your daughter married?'

She drew herself up to her full height.

'Yes!' she said furiously.

Then she smiled. Bachelard was obliged to quell the storm. What was the use of wrangling? It was far better to come to some amicable arrangement. Thus, worn out and trembling from the effects of the quarrel, Monsieur Josserand agreed to talk matters over with Duveyrier, on whom, according to Madame Josserand, everything depended. In order to get hold of the magistrate when he was in good humour, Bachelard offered to arrange for his brother-in-law to meet him at a house where he could refuse nothing.

'It's just an interview,' said Josserand, still protesting. 'I swear I won't make any commitments.'

'Of course not, of course not,' said Bachelard. 'Eléonore doesn't want you to do anything dishonourable.'

Then Berthe came back. She had spotted some tins of preserved fruits and tried to coax her uncle into giving her one. But he again became afflicted by his stammer. He couldn't possibly give her one; they were all counted, and had to be sent off to St Petersburg that very night. He gradually got them out into the street, while his sister, at the sight of these huge warehouses packed to the roof with every sort of merchandise imaginable, lingered behind, mortified to think that such a fortune should have been made by a man totally devoid of principle, comparing it bitterly with her husband's impotent honesty.

'Well, tomorrow night then, about nine o'clock, at the Café de Mulhouse,' said Bachelard, as he shook Monsieur Josserand's hand when they got into the street.

It so happened that the next day Octave and Trublot, who had dined together before going to see Clarisse, Duveyrier's mistress, went into the Café de Mulhouse so as not to call too early, though she lived a good way off, in the Rue de la Cerisaie. It was hardly eight o'clock. On entering, they heard a loud noise of quarrelling at the far end of the room. There they saw Bachelard already drunk, with flaming cheeks and seeming enormous, having a row with a little, pale-faced, testy gentleman.

'You've been spitting in my beer again,' he thundered. 'I won't stand for it, sir!'

'Leave me alone, or I'll give you something to think about!' said the little man, standing on tiptoe.

Then Bachelard raised his voice to an exasperating pitch, without yielding an inch. 'Just you dare, sir! Just you dare!'

When the other man knocked his hat off, which he always wore cocked on one side of his head, even in cafés, he repeated, with fresh energy:

'Just you dare, sir! Just you dare!'

Then, picking up his hat, he sat down majestically, and called out to the waiter:

'Alfred, change this beer!'

Octave and Trublot, greatly astonished, had noticed Gueulin sitting next to his uncle, with his back to the wall, smoking away with utter indifference. They asked him what the quarrel was about.

'Don't know,' he replied, watching the cigar-smoke curling upwards. 'There's always some row or other. A rare one for getting his head punched! He never gives in!'

Bachelard shook hands with the newcomers. He adored young people. He was delighted to hear that they were going to see Clarisse, for so was he, with Gueulin; only he had to keep an appointment first with Monsieur Josserand, his brother-in-law. And the little room resounded with his voice as he ordered every conceivable sort of drink for his young friends, with the wild prodigality of a man who, when out for a spree, pays no attention to the cost. Uncouth, with glittering false teeth, and his nose aflame below his snowy, close-cropped hair, he chatted away familiarly with the waiters and ran them off their legs, while he became so unbearable to his neighbours that the proprietor twice asked him to leave if he could not be quiet. The night before he had been thrown out of the Café de Madrid.

Just then a girl came in, and went out again after walking round the room with a tired look in her eyes. This set Octave talking about women. Bachelard, spitting sideways, hit Trublot, but he did not even apologize. Women had cost him too much money; he flattered himself that he had had the best to be got in all Paris. In his line of work one never bargained about such things; you had to show yourself independent of your business. But he was giving all that up; he wanted to be loved for his own sake. And as Octave watched Bachelard throwing banknotes about, he thought with surprise of the uncle who exaggerated his drunken stutter to escape family extortion.

'Stop bragging, uncle,' said Gueulin. 'We can all have more women than we want.'

'Then why don't you ever have any, you silly fool?' retorted Bachelard.

Gueulin shrugged his shoulders with a look of profound disdain.

'Why not? Well, only yesterday I dined with a friend and his mistress. She began kicking me under the table straight away. I had a chance there, didn't I? Well, when she asked me to see her home I took off, and I haven't been near her since. Oh! I don't deny that it would have been very pleasant for a little while. But afterwards, uncle, afterwards! She might have been one of those women you just can't get rid of! No, I'm not such a fool!'

Trublot nodded approvingly, for he too had given up society women, through fear of the problems that always came afterwards. Then Gueulin, throwing off his phlegmatic manner, proceeded to cite examples. One day, in the train, a splendid brunette whom he did not know went to sleep on his shoulder; but then he thought about what he would have done with her when he got to the station. Another time, after a wedding, he found a neighbour's wife in his bed. A bit much, wasn't it? And he would certainly have done something foolish, had he not been haunted by the idea that she would certainly ask him to buy her some boots.

'Talk about opportunities, uncle!' he said, in conclusion, 'nobody has had such opportunities as I have! But I restrained myself. In fact, everyone does, being far too afraid of what might happen afterwards. If it weren't for that, it would be very pleasant. Day and night, you'd see nothing but that going on in the streets!'

But Bachelard, dreaming, was no longer listening to him. His bluster had subsided; there was a mist before his eyes.

'If you're very good,' he said suddenly, 'I'll let you see something.'

And, after paying, he led them out.

Octave reminded him of his appointment with Monsieur Josserand. That did not matter; they would come back for him. Before leaving the room Bachelard looked round furtively, and then stole the lumps of sugar left by a customer at an adjoining table.

'Follow me,' he said, when they got out. 'It's close by.'

He walked along, grave and thoughtful, without saying a word, and stopped before a door in the Rue Saint-Marc. The three young men were about to follow him, when suddenly he seemed to hesitate.

'No, let's go back. I don't think I will.'

But they cried out at this. Why was he trying to make fools of them?

'Well, Gueulin mustn't come up, or you either, Monsieur Trublot. You don't behave nicely; you'd only laugh and jeer. Come on, Monsieur Octave, you're a serious sort of fellow.'

He made Octave walk up in front of him, while the other two laughed and called up to him from the pavement to be kindly remembered to the ladies. On reaching the fourth floor he knocked, and an old woman opened the door.

'Oh, it's you is it, Monsieur Narcisse? Fifi didn't expect you this evening.'

She was fat, and her face was as white and calm as that of a nun. In the narrow dining-room into which they were ushered, a tall, fair girl, pretty and simple-looking, was embroidering an altar-cloth.

'Good-day, uncle,' she said, rising to offer her forehead to Bachelard's thick, tremulous lips.

As the latter introduced Monsieur Octave Mouret, a distinguished young friend of his, the two women dropped him an old-fashioned curtsey, and then they all sat down at the table, which was lighted by a paraffin lamp. It was like some calm provincial interior; two regular lives lost to the outside world, supported by next to nothing. As the room looked onto an inner courtyard, even the sound of traffic was inaudible.

While Bachelard paternally questioned the girl about what she had been doing and thinking since the previous evening, her aunt, Mademoiselle Menu, confided their whole history to Octave, with the directness and simplicity of an honest woman who feels she has nothing to conceal.

'Yes, sir, I come from Villeneuve, near Lille. I'm well known at Mardienne Brothers', in the Rue Saint-Sulpice, where I worked as an embroideress for thirty years. Then, when a cousin of mine left me a house in Villeneuve, I was lucky enough to let it for life, at a thousand francs a year, to some people who thought they would bury me the next day, and who have been nicely punished for their wicked thought, because I'm still alive, in spite of my seventy-five years.'

She laughed, showing teeth as white as a young girl's.

'I couldn't work,' she went on, 'because my eyesight was gone, when my niece Fanny needed looking after. Her father, Captain Menu, died without leaving a penny, and not a single relative to help her, sir. So I had to take the girl away from school, and taught her embroidery—it's not a very good trade, it's true, but it was either that or nothing; it's always the women who have to starve to death. Luckily, she met Monsieur Narcisse, so now I can die happy.'

And with hands across her stomach, like some old seamstress who has sworn never to touch a needle again, she enveloped Bachelard and Fifi with a tearful glance. Just then the old man was saying to the child:

'Did you really think about me? What did you think, then?'

Fifi raised her limpid eyes, without ceasing her embroidery.

'That you were a good friend, and that I loved you very much.'

She had hardly looked at Octave, as though indifferent to the charm of such a handsome young man. However, he smiled at her, struck by her grace and not knowing quite what to think; while the spinster aunt, staled by a chastity that had cost her nothing, continued in an undertone:

'I could have married her to somebody, eh? A workman would

beat her; a clerk would only make her have a lot of children. It's better that she should be nice to Monsieur Narcisse, who seems such a kind gentleman.'

Then, raising her voice, she said:

'Well, Monsieur Narcisse, it isn't my fault if you're not satisfied with her. I'm always telling her: "Be pleasant—show your gratitude." It's only natural that I should be glad to know she's well looked after. When you haven't got any relatives, it's so difficult to find a home for a young girl.'

Then Octave gave himself up to the simple pleasures of this little home. The heavy air of the apartment was filled with an odour of ripe fruit. Only Fifi's needle, as it pricked the silk, made a slight noise at regular intervals, like the ticking of a cuckoo-clock, which might have regulated Bachelard's cosy domestic amours. The old spinster, however, was probity personified; she lived on her income of a thousand francs and never touched a penny of Fifi's money, letting her spend it as she pleased. The only things she allowed her to pay for occasionally were roast chestnuts and white wine, when she emptied the moneybox in which she collected the pennies given her as good-conduct medals by her kind friend.

'My little duckie,' said Bachelard, rising to go, 'we've got some business to attend to. I'll look in tomorrow. Be a good girl.'

He kissed her on the forehead. Then, looking affectionately at her, he said to Octave:

'You can give her a kiss too, she's just a child.'

The young man's lips touched her cool skin. She smiled; she was so modest. It seemed as if he were one of the family; he had never met worthier people. Bachelard was walking off, when he suddenly came back and exclaimed:

'I forgot! Here's a little present for you!'

Emptying his pocket, he gave Fifi the sugar he had just stolen at the café. She thanked him profusely, and blushed with pleasure as she crunched one of the lumps. Then, growing bolder, she said:

'You haven't got any four-sou pieces, have you?'

Bachelard searched his pockets, but in vain. Octave happened to have one, which the girl accepted as a souvenir. She did not go to the door with them, no doubt for propriety's sake; and they could hear the click of her needle as she at once sat down to her altar-cloth, while Mademoiselle Menu showed them out in her good-natured, old-fashioned way.

'Well, that's worth seeing, eh?' said Bachelard, stopping on the stairs. 'You know, it costs me less than five louis a month. I've had enough of those bitches that just take your money. I wanted something with a bit of feeling.'

Then, as Octave laughed, he became mistrustful.

'You're a decent chap, you won't take advantage of me, will you? Not a word to Gueulin; swear it on your honour! I'm waiting till he's worthy of being shown such an angelic creature. Say what you like, virtue is a good thing; it refreshes one. I've always believed in the ideal!'

His old drunkard's voice trembled, tears swelled his flabby eyelids. When they were downstairs Trublot began chaffing him, and pretended he would take the number of the house, while Gueulin shrugged his shoulders and asked Octave, to his astonishment, what he thought of the little thing. Whenever he was made maudlin by drink, Bachelard could not resist taking people to see these ladies, caught between his vanity at displaying his treasure and his fear of having it stolen from him. Then, the next day, he would forget all about it, and go back to the Rue Saint-Marc with a secretive air.

'Everybody knows Fifi,' said Gueulin, quietly.

Bachelard, meanwhile, was looking for a cab, when Octave exclaimed:

'What about Josserand? He's waiting for you at the café.'

The other two had forgotten all about him. Furious at wasting his evening like this, Monsieur Josserand stood impatiently at the door of the café, not going inside, as he never took any refreshment out-of-doors. At last they set off for the Rue de la Cerisaie. But they were obliged to take two cabs, the commission agent and the cashier going in one and the three young men in the other.

Gueulin, whose voice was drowned by the rattling of the cab, began talking about the insurance company where he worked. Trublot took the opportunity to declare that insurance companies were as great a bore as stocks and shares. Then the conversation turned to Duveyrier. Wasn't it a pity that a rich man like that—a judge, too—should let himself be fleeced by women in that way! He always wanted them in out-of-the-way neighbourhoods, right at the end of omnibus routes—modest little ladies who had their own apartments, and played the part of widows; so-called milliners, who kept shops which never had any customers; girls picked out of the gutter, whom he clothed and set up somewhere, visiting them regularly once a week, just as a clerk goes to his office. Trublot defended him, however, saying that, to begin with, he behaved as he did because of his temperament, and also, not everybody had a wife like his. People said that she had loathed him ever since their wedding-night, his red blotches filling her with disgust. And so she willingly let him have mistresses, whose favours rid her of him; although occasionally she herself put up with the awful task, with the resignation of a virtuous wife who fulfils all her duties.

'So she's a virtuous woman, is she?' asked Octave, becoming interested.

'Oh, yes! Totally, my dear boy. All the virtues, in fact—pretty, serious, well-bred, clever, lots of taste, chaste, and quite unbearable!'

At the bottom of the Rue Montmartre a traffic jam stopped the cab. The young men, having let down the windows, could hear Bachelard abusing the drivers in a furious voice. Then, as they moved on again, Gueulin gave his listeners certain details about Clarisse. Her name was Clarisse Bocquet, the daughter of a man who once kept a small toyshop but now went about to fairs with his wife and a troop of brats dressed in rags. One evening, when it was thawing, Duveyrier had met her just as one of her lovers had kicked her out. Probably this buxom wench corresponded to the long-sought ideal, for the very next day he was hooked, weeping as he kissed her on the eyelids, overcome by a tender yearning to cultivate just one little blue flower of romance, apart from all his grosser sexual desires. Clarisse had consented to live in the Rue de la Cerisaie, so as not to expose him; but she led him a fine dance, had made him buy her twenty-five thousand francs' worth of furniture, gobbling up his money to her heart's content, together with several artists from the Montmartre Theatre.

'I don't care a damn,' said Trublot, 'as long as she gives us a good time. At least she doesn't make us sing, and she isn't always banging away at her piano, like that other woman. Oh, that piano! I must say, if you're deafened at home because you're unlucky enough to have as a wife a player-piano that drives everybody away, you'd be a fool not to set up some nice little nest for yourself where you can receive your friends quite informally.'

'Last Sunday,' said Gueulin, 'Clarisse wanted me to have lunch with her alone. I said no. After lunches of that sort you're likely to do something foolish, and I was afraid she might come and land on me if she left Duveyrier. She hates him, you know. She's so disgusted with him that it almost makes her ill. She doesn't care for pimples, either, it seems, poor girl! But she can't send him elsewhere, as his wife does; otherwise, if she could hand him over to her maid I'm sure she'd get rid of him in a flash.'

The cab stopped. They alighted in front of a dark, silent house in the Rue de la Cerisaie. But they had to wait a good ten minutes for the other cab, Bachelard having taken his driver to have some grog after their quarrel in the Rue Montmartre. On the stairs, assuming his serious and respectable air, Bachelard, when questioned once more by Josserand as to this friend of Duveyrier's, merely said:

'A woman of the world, a very nice girl. She won't eat you.'

The door was opened by a little maid with a rosy complexion who, smiling in a friendly, indulgent way, helped the men off with their coats. Trublot stopped behind in the anteroom with her for a moment, whispering something in her ear which set her giggling as if she were being tickled. Bachelard had already pushed open the drawing-room door, and he at once introduced Monsieur Josserand. The latter felt momentarily ill at ease, for he found Clarisse quite plain and could not imagine why Duveyrier preferred her to his wife, one of the most beautiful women in society; she was rather girlish, very dark and thin, and with a fluffy head like a poodle's. However, she had charm. She chattered like a true Parisienne, with her superficial, borrowed wit and her droll manner, acquired by constant contact with men; but she could put on the airs of a grand lady when it suited her.

'Sir, I'm delighted to meet you. All of Alphonse's friends are mine too. Please make yourself at home.'

Duveyrier, warned by a note from Bachelard, greeted Monsieur Josserand most cordially. Octave was surprised at his youthful appearance. He was no longer the severe, ill-at-ease individual of the Rue de Choiseul, who never seemed at home in his own drawing-room. The red blotches on his face had taken on a rosy hue, and his squinting eyes shone with childish delight as Clarisse told a group of guests that he sometimes paid her a flying visit during a short adjournment of the Court, having just enough time to leap into a cab, kiss her, and drive back again. Then he complained of being overworked—four sittings a week, from eleven to five; always the same tangled mass of disputes to sort out; it really destroyed all feeling in one's heart.

He was not wearing his red ribbon,* however, which he always took off when visiting his mistress. This was a last scruple, a delicate distinction which, from a sense of decency, he obstinately observed. Though she would not tell him so, it greatly offended Clarisse.

Octave, who had at once shaken her by the hand like an old friend, listened and looked about him. The room, with its floral carpet and red-satin furniture and hangings, was very much like the drawing-room in the Rue de Choiseul, and, as if to complete the resemblance, several of the judge's friends whom Octave had seen on the night of the concert were also there, in the same groups. But here they were smoking and talking loudly; everybody seemed bright and merry in the brilliant candlelight. Two gentlemen, with outstretched legs, took up the whole of a divan; another, seated cross-wise on a chair, was warming his back in front of the fire. There was a pleasant, relaxed atmosphere—a sense of freedom, which, however, did not go any further. Clarisse never invited other women to these parties—for propriety's sake, she said. When her guests complained that ladies were missing from her drawing-room, she would laughingly rejoin:

'Well, and what about me? Don't you think I'm enough?'

She had made a decent home for Alphonse; it was thoroughly bourgeois, for she had a passion for what was respectable and proper, despite the ups and downs of her existence. When she received guests she declined to be addressed in the familiar 'tu' form; but when her guests had gone and the doors were closed, all of Alphonse's friends—not to mention her own: clean-shaven actors, painters with bushy beards—enjoyed her favours in succession. It was an ingrained habit, the need to enjoy herself a little behind her keeper's back. Only two out of all her friends had not been willing to comply—Gueulin, who dreaded the consequences, and Trublot, whose heart lay elsewhere.

The little maid was just then handing round some glasses of

punch in her pleasant way. Octave took one, and whispered in Trublot's ear:

'The maid is better-looking than the mistress.'

'Of course! She always is!' replied Trublot, shrugging his shoulders with an air of disdainful conviction.

Clarisse came up and talked to them for a moment. She was constantly circulating from one group to another, joking, laughing, gesticulating. As each newcomer lit a cigar, the room soon became filled with smoke.

'Oh, you horrid men!' she playfully exclaimed, as she went to open a window.

Bachelard lost no time in making Monsieur Josserand take a seat in the window-recess, so that, as he said, they might get a breath of air. Then, by a masterly manoeuvre, he installed Duveyrier there and at once started talking about the marriage. The two families were about to be united by a close tie; he felt highly honoured. Then he asked what day had been fixed for signing the contract, and this gave him the chance to broach the crucial subject.

'We had meant to call on you tomorrow, Josserand and I, to settle everything, because we're well aware that Monsieur Auguste can do nothing without you. It's about the payment of the dowry, and really, as we seem so comfortable here . . .'

Seized by fresh qualms of conscience, Monsieur Josserand looked out into the gloomy depths of the Rue de la Cerisaie, with its deserted pavements and sombre façades. He was sorry that he had come. They were again going to take advantage of his weakness to involve him in some disgraceful affair which he would live to regret. A sudden feeling of revolt made him interrupt Bachelard.

'Some other time; this is hardly the place.'

'Why not?' exclaimed Duveyrier, most courteously. 'We're more comfortable here than anywhere else. You were saying, sir, that . . .'

'We're going to give Berthe fifty thousand francs. But these fifty thousand francs are represented by a twenty-year dotal insurance, which Josserand took out for his daughter when she was four. So she won't be able to draw the money for another three years.'

'Allow me!' interrupted Josserand, amazed.

'No, just let me finish; Monsieur Duveyrier understands perfectly. We don't want the young couple to wait three years for money they may need at once, and so we're prepared to pay the dowry in instalments of ten thousand francs every six months, on condition that we repay ourselves later with the insurance money.'

There was a silence. Monsieur Josserand, chilled and confused, looked out again into the dark street. The magistrate seemed to be thinking the matter over for a moment. Perhaps he scented something fishy about it, and felt delighted at letting the Vabres be tricked, for he hated them in the person of his wife.

'It all seems very reasonable to me,' he said eventually. 'We ought to thank you. A dowry is rarely paid in full.'

'Indeed not!' affirmed Bachelard, energetically. 'Such a thing is never done!'

The three shook hands, after arranging to meet at the notary's the following Thursday. When Monsieur Josserand came back into the light, he looked so pale that they asked him if he felt unwell. This was, in fact, the case, and he withdrew, not caring to wait for Bachelard, who had just gone into the dining-room where the traditional tea had been replaced by champagne.

Meanwhile Gueulin, sprawling on a sofa near the window, muttered:

'What a crook!'

He had overheard a phrase about the insurance money, and chuckled as he told Octave and Trublot the actual truth of the matter. The policy had been taken out at his office; there was not a penny due; the Vabres had been completely taken in. Then, as the other two laughed heartily at this splendid joke, he added, for further comic effect:

'I want a hundred francs. If uncle doesn't give me a hundred francs, I'll split!'

The voices were becoming louder, as the champagne gradually upset the decorum upon which Clarisse liked to insist. Her parties always became rather rowdy before they ended. She herself had occasional lapses. Trublot drew Octave's attention to her. She was standing behind a door with her arms round the neck of a strapping young fellow with the build of a peasant, a stone-cutter just arrived from the South, whom his native town wanted to turn into an artist. But Duveyrier pushed back the door, whereupon she quickly removed her arms and introduced the young man to him—Monsieur Payan, a sculptor of the most refined talent. Duveyrier was delighted, and promised to find him some work.

'Work, indeed!' muttered Gueulin, under his breath, 'he's got as much work as he wants here, the idiot!'

At about two o'clock, when the three young men left the Rue de la Cerisaie with Bachelard, the latter was completely drunk. They would have liked to pack him into a cab, but the whole neighbourhood was asleep, wrapped in solemn silence—not a sound of a wheel, nor even of some belated footstep. So they decided to help him home. The moon had risen clear and bright, whitening the pavements. In the deserted streets their voices assumed a grave sonority.

'For God's sake hold up, uncle! You'll break our arms!'

Choking back his tears, he was now in a tender moralizing mood.

'Go away, Gueulin! Go away!' he spluttered. 'I don't want you to see your uncle in such a state! No, my boy, it's not right. Go away!'

And when his nephew called him an old swindler, he said:

'Swindler? That doesn't mean anything. One must command respect. I certainly respect women—virtuous women, that is; and if there's no feeling, it disgusts me. Go away, Gueulin, you're making your uncle blush. These gentlemen are sufficient help.'

'Very well, then,' said Gueulin, 'you must give me a hundred francs. I really must have them to pay my rent; otherwise I'll be turned out.'

At this unexpected demand Bachelard's drunkenness increased to such an extent that he had to be propped up against the shutters of a shop. He stuttered:

'Eh? What? A hundred francs? It's no good looking in my pockets—I've only got a few pence. So you can squander the money in some brothel? No, I won't encourage you in your vices! Your mother, on her deathbed, made me promise to look after you! If you look in my pockets I'll call for help!'

And he kept on muttering, condemning the dissolute ways of young men, and insisting on the need for virtue.

'Look,' cried Gueulin, 'I haven't got to the point of swindling whole families! You know what I mean! If I split on you you'd soon give me my hundred francs!'

His uncle had suddenly become stone-deaf, as he went stumbling and grunting along. In the narrow street where they were, behind the church of Saint Gervais, a single white lamp glimmered like a night-light, showing a huge number painted on the frosted glass. A sort of muffled noise could be heard inside the house; a few thin rays of light came through the closed shutters.

'I've had enough of this!' exclaimed Gueulin abruptly. 'Excuse me, uncle, I left my umbrella upstairs.'

So saying, he went into the house. Bachelard, indignant and full of disgust, declared that one ought at least to have a little respect for women. Immorality of that sort would be the ruin of France. On reaching the Place de l'Hôtel-de-Ville, Octave and Trublot eventually found a cab into which they bundled him.

'Rue d'Enghien,' they told the driver. 'You'll have to pay yourself. Look in his pockets.'

On Thursday the marriage contract was signed before the notary, Maître Renaudin, in the Rue de Grammont. Just as they were starting there had been another furious row at the Josserands', with the father, in a moment of supreme revolt, telling his wife that she was responsible for the lie they wanted him to endorse; and once again they dragged each other's families through the mud. Where did they think he was going to get ten thousand francs every six months? The very idea was driving him mad. Uncle Bachelard, who was there, kept slapping his chest and pouring out fresh promises, now that he had arranged things in such a way that he would not have to part with a penny, tenderly declaring that he would never leave his dear little Berthe in a fix. But Josserand, exasperated, only shrugged his shoulders, and asked him if he really thought he was such a fool.

However, at the notary's the reading of the contract, drawn up from notes provided by Duveyrier, calmed Monsieur Josserand somewhat. There was no mention of the insurance; moreover, the first instalment of ten thousand francs was to fall due six months after the marriage. They would thus have a breathing-space. Auguste, who listened very attentively, showed some signs of impatience. He looked at the smiling Berthe, at the Josserands, at Duveyrier, and at last ventured to speak of the insurance, a guarantee which he thought it only reasonable to mention. They all appeared very surprised. What was the good of that? There was surely no need to mention the insurance; and they quickly signed the paper, while Maître Renaudin, a very obliging young man, said nothing but simply handed the ladies a pen. It was not until they were outside that Madame Duveyrier ventured to express her surprise. Not a word had been said about any insurance. The dowry, so they understood, was to have been paid by uncle Bachelard. But Madame Josserand naively remarked that her brother's name had never been mentioned by her in connection with so paltry a sum. He would eventually leave his whole fortune to Berthe.

That same evening a cab came to fetch Saturnin. His mother had declared that it was too dangerous to let him be present at the ceremony. It would hardly do, at a wedding, to turn a lunatic who talked of splitting people's heads open loose among the guests; Monsieur Josserand, broken-hearted, had been obliged to get the poor lad admitted to the Moulineaux Asylum, kept by Doctor Chassagne. The cab was brought up to the porch at dusk. Saturnin came down, holding Berthe's hand, thinking he was going into the country with her. But when he had got into the cab he struggled furiously, breaking the windows and shaking his bloodstained fists through them. Monsieur Josserand went upstairs in tears, overcome by this departure in the dark, his ears still ringing with the wretched boy's shrieks, mingled with the cracking of the whip and the galloping of the horse.

During dinner, as tears again rose to his eyes at the sight of Saturnin's empty place, his wife, not understanding, impatiently exclaimed:

'That's enough, isn't it, sir? Are you going to your daughter's wedding with that miserable face? Listen! By all that I hold most sacred, by my father's grave, I swear that her uncle will pay the first ten thousand francs. He solemnly swore that he would, as we were leaving the notary's!'

Monsieur Josserand did not even answer. He spent the night addressing wrappers. By the chill daybreak he had finished his second thousand, and had earned six francs. Several times he had raised his head, listening, as usual, to know whether Saturnin was moving in his room. Then, at the thought of Berthe, he worked with fresh ardour. Poor child! She would have liked a wedding-dress of white moiré. However, six francs would enable her to have more flowers in her bridal bouquet.

VIII

THE civil marriage had taken place on the Thursday. On the Saturday morning, as early as a quarter-past ten, some of the lady guests were already waiting in the Josserands' drawing-room, the religious ceremony having been fixed for half-past eleven at Saint-Roch. Madame Juzeur was there, in black silk as usual; Madame Dambreville, squeezed into a dress the colour of dead leaves; and Madame Duveyrier, dressed very simply in pale blue. All three were talking in low voices among the rows of empty chairs, while Madame Josserand, in the next room, was putting the finishing touches to Berthe's toilet, assisted by the servant and the two bridesmaids, Hortense and Angèle Campardon.

'Oh, it's not that!' murmured Madame Duveyrier. 'The family is quite honourable. But I must admit that, for Auguste's sake, I'm rather afraid of the mother's domineering temperament. One can't be too careful, you know!'

'No, indeed!' said Madame Juzeur. 'Very often one marries not only the daughter but the mother as well; and it's so disagreeable when she interferes in household matters.'

At this moment the door of the next room opened, and Angèle ran out, exclaiming:

'A hook, at the bottom of the left-hand drawer! Wait a minute!'

She rushed across the drawing-room and then ran back again; her white frock, tied at the waist by a broad blue sash, floating behind her like foam in the wake of a ship.

'I think you're mistaken,' resumed Madame Dambreville. 'The mother's only too glad to get her daughter off her hands. The only thing she cares about is her Tuesday at-homes. And she's still after another victim.'

Valérie now came in, wearing a provocative red dress. She had hurried up the stairs, afraid she would be late.

'Théophile will never be ready,' she said to her sister-in-law. 'I dismissed Françoise this morning, and he's looking everywhere for his tie. I left him in such a mess!'

'The question of health is also very important,' continued Madame Dambreville.

'It is indeed,' replied Madame Duveyrier. 'We had a discreet word with Doctor Juillerat. It seems that the girl has an excellent constitution. The mother's, as you know, is astonishing; and it was that which, to some extent, helped us to make a decision, because nothing's more annoying than looking after sickly relatives. It's always best to have good, healthy relatives.'

'Especially if they haven't got anything to leave,' said Madame Juzeur, in her soft voice.

Valérie had taken a seat, but not having grasped the subject of their conversation, and still out of breath, she asked:

'What? Who are you talking about?'

The door was again suddenly opened, and they could hear the sounds of quarrelling going on in the other room.

'I tell you the box isn't on the table.'

'It's not true; I saw it there just a second ago.'

'Oh, you are obstinate! Go and see for yourself.'

Hortense, also in white, with a large blue sash, passed through the drawing-room. The pale folds of the muslin made her look older, giving a hardness to her features and a yellowness to her complexion. She returned, furious, with the bridal bouquet, for which they had been hunting for the last five minutes in every corner of the disordered apartment.

'Well, you see,' said Madame Dambreville, by way of conclusion, 'marriages never happen just as one would like. The wisest thing is to come to the best possible arrangement afterwards.'

Angèle and Hortense now opened the folding-doors so that the bride's veil would not catch on anything, and Berthe appeared in a white silk dress, with white flowers on a white ground, a white wreath, a white bouquet, and a spray of white flowers across her skirt, which vanished near the train in a shower of little white buds. Amidst all this whiteness she looked charming, with her fresh complexion, golden hair, laughing eyes and ingenuous-looking mouth.

'She looks lovely!' cried all the ladies.

They all embraced her, in ecstasies. The Josserands had been at their wits' end to know how to find the two thousand francs which the wedding would cost—five hundred francs for the dress, and another fifteen hundred for their share of the dinner and dance expenses. So they had been obliged to send Berthe to Doctor

Chassagne's asylum to see Saturnin, to whom an aunt had just left three thousand francs; Berthe, having obtained permission to take her brother out for a drive, smothered him with caresses in the carriage until he became quite dazed, and then took him for a moment to see the lawyer, who, not knowing the poor lad's condition, had everything ready for him to sign. Thus it was that the silk dress and the profusion of flowers came as a surprise to all these ladies, who were estimating the cost while exclaiming in admiration: 'Exquisite! So tasteful!'

Madame Josserand came in, radiant in a garish mauve dress which made her look bigger and rounder than ever—a sort of majestic tower. She fumed at Monsieur Josserand, called to Hortense to bring her her shawl, and vehemently forbade Berthe to sit down.

'Mind, or you'll crush your flowers!'

'Don't worry,' said Clotilde, in her calm voice. 'We've got plenty of time. Auguste has to come and fetch us.'

While they were all waiting in the drawing-room, Théophile suddenly burst in, without a hat, his coat buttoned up the wrong way, and his white tie tied so tightly that it looked like a piece of cord. His face, with its wispy moustache and discoloured teeth, was livid; he was trembling all over with rage, like a feverish child.

'What's the matter with you?' asked his sister in amazement.

'It's . . . It's that . . .'

A fit of coughing cut his sentence short, and he stood there for a minute, choking and spitting in his handkerchief, beside himself at being unable to give vent to his anger. Valérie, disconcerted, watched him, as if some instinct told her the cause of this outburst. At length he shook his fist at her, oblivious to the presence of the bride and the other ladies.

'Yes; as I was hunting everywhere for my tie I found a letter in front of the wardrobe.'

He nervously crumpled a piece of paper between his fingers. His wife turned pale. She saw the situation at a glance and, to avoid the scandal of a public argument, she went into the room Berthe had just left.

'Oh! well,' she said simply. 'I'd rather not stay here if he's going to behave like a lunatic.'

'Leave me alone!' exclaimed Théophile, as Madame Duveyrier tried to pacify him. 'I want to have it out with her. This time I've got proof, absolute proof. I won't just let it pass, because I know the fellow . . .'

His sister, seizing his arm, shook it vigorously.

'Be quiet! Don't you know where you are? This isn't the right time—do you understand?'

But he began again.

'Yes, it *is* the right time! I don't care about the others. Too bad that it's happened today. It'll be a lesson to everybody.'

He lowered his voice, however, and sank exhausted into a chair, almost bursting into tears. Everyone in the drawing-room felt thoroughly uncomfortable. Madame Dambreville and Madame Juzeur politely moved away, affecting not to understand. Madame Josserand, feeling greatly annoyed that an incident of this sort should throw a pall over the wedding, went into the adjoining room to comfort Valérie. As for Berthe, she kept looking at her wreath in the mirror, and pretended not to hear, while questioning Hortense in a low voice. They whispered together, and the elder sister, pointing out Théophile, explained the situation while pretending to be busy arranging the folds of the veil.

'Oh, that's it!' said the bride, with an air of innocent amusement, as she gazed at Théophile, perfectly self-possessed beneath her halo of white flowers.

Clotilde was questioning her brother in an undertone. Madame Josserand came back, exchanged a few words with her, and then returned to the next room. It was an exchange of diplomatic notes. The husband accused Octave, that counter-jumper, whose head he would punch in church if he dared to come there. He swore that he had seen him the day before on the steps of Saint-Roch with his wife. At first he had had his doubts, but now he was sure: everything tallied—his height, his walk. Yes, madame invented stories about luncheons with her lady friends, or else went into Saint-Roch with Camille, by the main entrance, as if to pray; then she would leave the child with the chair-keeper, and go off with her gentleman by the old, dirty passage, where nobody would have thought of looking for her. However, when Octave's name was mentioned Valérie smiled. She hadn't been with him, she swore to Madame Josserand—in fact, she hadn't been with anyone at all, she added, but certainly not with him. Feeling strong in the knowledge that truth was on her side, she in turn talked of confounding her husband by proving that the letter was not in Octave's handwriting, any more than he was the mysterious gentleman of Saint-Roch. Madame Josserand listened and watched her knowingly, merely anxious to find some way for Valérie to deceive her husband. And she gave her the best advice she could.

'Leave it all to me. Since he will have it that it's Monsieur Mouret, very well then, it's Monsieur Mouret! There's no harm, is there, in being seen on the steps of a church with Monsieur Mouret? But the letter is rather compromising. It will be a triumph for you when our young friend shows him a couple of lines in his own handwriting. Be really careful that you say exactly what I say. I can't let him spoil a day like this.'

When she returned to the drawing-room with Valérie, who seemed greatly upset, Théophile was saying to his sister in a choking voice:

'For your sake I won't make a scene here, because it wouldn't be right, on account of the wedding. But I won't be responsible for what might happen at the church. If that counter-jumper dares to show up at the church, in front of my whole family, I'll do for both of them.'

Auguste, looking very smart in his evening coat, his left eye half closed by the migraine he had been dreading for the last three days, now arrived to take his fiancée to church. He was accompanied by his father and brother-in-law, both looking very solemn. There was a little jostling, as they had ended up being late. Two of the ladies, Madame Duveyrier and Madame Dambreville, were obliged to help Madame Josserand to put on her shawl—a sort of huge tapestry shawl with a yellow ground, which she always brought out on special occasions, though the fashion for such things had long gone. It enveloped her in folds so ample and so brilliant that she caused a sensation in the streets. They had still to wait for Monsieur Josserand, who was looking under the furniture for a cufflink which had been swept into the dustbin the day before. At last he made his appearance, stammering excuses, looking bewildered yet happy, as he led the way downstairs, tightly holding Berthe's arm in his. Auguste and Madame Josserand followed, and the others came after, in no particular order, their chatter disturbing the dignified silence of the hall. Théophile had got hold of Duveyrier, whose dignity he upset with his story; pouring all his woes into his ear, he begged for advice, while Valérie, who had recovered her self-possession, walked modestly in front, Madame Juzeur comforting her tenderly. She appeared not to notice the terrible glances of her husband.

'Oh, your prayer-book!' cried Madame Josserand suddenly, in a tone of despair.

They had already got into the carriages. Angèle was obliged to go back and fetch the prayer-book bound in white velvet. At last they started. The whole household was there to see them off, including the maids and the concierges. Marie Pichon had come down with Lilitte, dressed as if about to go for a walk; the sight of the bride, looking so pretty in her wedding dress, touched her to tears. Monsieur Gourd remarked that the people on the second floor were the only ones who had not budged—a queer set of lodgers, who always behaved differently from other people!

At Saint-Roch both big doors had been thrown open, and a red carpet extended as far as the pavement. It was raining, and the air was very chilly on this May morning.

'Thirteen steps,' whispered Madame Juzeur to Valérie, as they entered. 'That's a bad sign.'

As soon as the procession moved up the aisle between the row of chairs towards the altar, on which the candles burned like stars, the organ overhead burst into a paean of joy. It was a comfortable, pleasant-looking church, with its large white windows edged with yellow and pale blue, its dadoes of red marble on the walls and the pillars, its gilded pulpit supported by the four Evangelists, and its side chapels glittering with gold plate. The roof was enlivened by paintings of operatic scenes; crystal chandeliers hung from it, suspended by long cords. As the ladies passed over the broad gratings of the heating apparatus a warm breath penetrated their skirts.

'Are you sure you've got the ring?' Madame Josserand asked Auguste, who was taking his seat with Berthe before the altar.

He was most anxious, afraid that he had forgotten it, but then felt it in his waistcoat pocket. However, she had not waited for an answer. From the moment she had entered she had been standing on tiptoe, scrutinizing the congregation: Trublot and Gueulin, the best men; uncle Bachelard and Campardon, the bride's witnesses; Duveyrier and Doctor Juillerat, witnesses for the bridegroom; and the great crowd of acquaintances of whom she felt so proud. She had just caught sight of Octave, who was doing his utmost to make room for Madame Hédouin to pass. She drew him aside behind a pillar, and hastily whispered something to him. The young man, a look of bewilderment on his face, did not appear to understand. He bowed, however, with an air of polite compliance.

'It's settled,' whispered Madame Josserand in Valérie's ear, and she returned and took a seat behind Berthe and Auguste in one of the chairs reserved for the family. Monsieur Josserand, the Vabres, and the Duveyriers were there too. The organ now showered forth pearly little notes, interrupted by a great deal of wheezing. The crush grew greater, as all the seats in the chancel were filled up and some of the men were obliged to stand in the aisles. Father Mauduit had reserved for himself the joy of pronouncing a blessing upon the nuptials of one of his fair penitents. When he appeared in his surplice, he exchanged a friendly smile with the congregation, whose every face he knew. The choir now struck up the *Veni Creator*, as the organ resumed its song of triumph; and it was just at this moment that Théophile spied Octave, to the left of the chancel, standing before the Chapel of Saint Joseph.

Clotilde tried to restrain him.

'No,' he stammered. 'I won't put up with this!' And he made Duveyrier follow him, as the family's representative. The *Veni Creator* continued. A few people looked round.

Théophile, who had talked about head-punching, became so agitated on going up to Octave that at first he could not say a word, vexed to feel that he was so short, and standing on tiptoe.

'Sir,' he said at last, 'I saw you yesterday with my wife.'

The *Veni Creator* was coming to an end, and the sound of his own voice alarmed him. Duveyrier, much annoyed at what was taking place, tried to make him understand that the church was hardly the best place for such a discussion. The ceremony had now begun before the altar. After a touching address to the happy couple, the priest took the wedding-ring and blessed it:

'*Benedic, Domine Deus noster, annulum nuptialem hunc, quem nos in tuo nomine benedicimus . . .*'*

Then Théophile plucked up courage, and repeated in a low voice:

'Sir, you were in this church yesterday with my wife.'

Octave, still bewildered by Madame Josserand's injunctions,

which he had not really understood, nevertheless told his story in a relaxed tone.

'Yes, that's quite true. I met Madame Vabre and we went and looked at the repairs of the Calvary, which my friend Campardon is supervising.'

'You admit it!' stammered Théophile, again overcome by fury. 'You admit it!'

Duveyrier felt obliged to tap him on the shoulder to calm him. A boy's voice now rang out with a piercing *Amen*.

'You no doubt recognize this letter!' continued Théophile, showing Octave a piece of paper.

'Come on, not here,' whispered Duveyrier, completely scandalized. 'You must be losing your mind, my dear fellow.'

Octave unfolded the letter. This attracted more attention from the congregation. There were whisperings, nudgings, and glances over the tops of prayer-books. No one was paying the least attention to the ceremony. Only the bridal couple remained, grave and stiff, before the priest. Then even Berthe herself looked round, and saw Théophile, white with rage, talking to Octave. From that moment her attention was diverted from the ceremony, and she kept throwing piercing glances towards the Chapel of Saint Joseph.

Meanwhile Octave, in an undertone, read the note:

'"Darling, what a wonderful time we had yesterday. Next Tuesday, at the Chapel of the Holy Angels, in the confessional."'

Having obtained from the bridegroom the 'I do' of a serious man, who signs nothing until he has read it, the priest addressed the bride.

'Do you promise and swear to be faithful to Monsieur Auguste Vabre in all things, as a dutiful wife, and in accordance with God's holy commandment?'

Berthe, having caught sight of the letter, was eagerly awaiting an exchange of blows, and paid no attention, as she kept glancing at the two men from under her veil. There was an embarrassing silence. At last, becoming aware that they were waiting for her, she hastily replied, 'I do! I do!' in an indifferent tone of voice.

The priest, surprised, looked in the same direction, and guessed that something unusual was taking place in one of the side aisles; he, in his turn, became quite distracted. The story by this time had spread throughout the congregation; everybody knew about it. The ladies, pale and grave, never took their eyes off Octave. The men smiled in a discreetly rakish way. And as Madame Josserand, by slight shoulder-shrugs, sought to reassure Madame Duveyrier, Valérie alone seemed to take any interest in the ceremony, for which she was all eyes, as if overwhelmed by emotion.

'"Darling, what a wonderful time we had yesterday."' Octave read the note again, affecting utter bewilderment.

Then, handing the note back to Théophile, he said:

'I don't understand, sir. That's not my handwriting. You can see for yourself.'

And taking from his pocket a notebook, in which, like the careful fellow he was, he had always put down his expenses, he showed it to Théophile.

'What! Not your writing!' stammered the latter. 'You're fooling me; it must be your writing.'

The priest was about to make the sign of the cross on Berthe's left hand. As his eyes were elsewhere, he made it on her right one, by mistake.

'*In nomine Patris, et Filii, et Spiritus Sancti.*'

'Amen!' responded the choir-boy, who also stood up on tiptoe to see.

At any rate, a scandal had been avoided, Duveyrier having convinced the bewildered Théophile that the letter could not have been written by Monsieur Mouret. It was almost a disappointment for the congregation. There were sighs, and hasty words were exchanged. Then, as everyone, still in a state of high excitement, turned round again towards the altar, it was to find that Auguste and Berthe had become man and wife, she apparently unaware of what was taking place, while he had not missed a single word uttered by the priest but had given his whole attention to the subject, distracted only by his migraine, which had closed his left eye.

'Dear children!' murmured Monsieur Josserand, in a trembling voice, to Monsieur Vabre, who ever since the beginning of the ceremony had been counting the lighted candles, always making a mistake and beginning all over again.

The organ again pealed forth from the nave; Father Mauduit had reappeared in his chasuble; the choir had begun the mass, a choral one of a most grandiose kind. Uncle Bachelard was wandering from chapel to chapel reading the Latin epitaphs, which he did not understand. He was particularly interested in the Duc de Créquy's.

Trublot and Gueulin, eager for details, had joined Octave, and all three were laughing together behind the pulpit. There were sudden bursts of song, like gusts of wind in a storm; choirboys swung their censers; and then, when a bell tinkled, there were periods of silence, during which the priest could be heard mumbling at the altar. Théophile could not stay put; he kept following Duveyrier, whom he overwhelmed with his incoherent talk, completely at a loss to comprehend how the gentleman of the assignation was not the gentleman of the letter. The whole congregation continued to observe his every gesture; the entire church, with its procession of priests, its Latin, its music, its incense, excitedly discussed the incident. When, after the *Pater*, the priest came down to give the married couple his final blessing, he looked askance at this commotion among his faithful flock, noticing the women's excited expressions and the sly merriment of the men, amid the bright light that streamed down upon them from the windows, gilding the rich appointments of the side chapels and the nave.

'Don't admit anything,' whispered Madame Josserand to Valérie, as they moved towards the vestry after the mass.

In the vestry the married couple and their witnesses had, first of all, to sign the register. They were kept waiting, however, by Campardon, who had taken some ladies to see the newly restored Calvary at the end of the choir, behind a wooden hoarding. At last he arrived, full of apologies, and signed his name in the register with a huge flourish. Father Mauduit wished to pay both families a compliment by handing round the pen himself and pointing with his finger to the place where each one had to sign; and he smiled with his air of worldly tolerance as he stood in the centre of the solemn room, the woodwork of which was impregnated with the odour of incense.

'Well, mademoiselle,' said Campardon to Hortense, 'don't you feel tempted too?'

Then he regretted his lack of tact. Hortense, who was the elder sister, bit her lip. That evening, at the dance, she was expecting to have a definite answer from Verdier; she had been urging him to choose between herself and that creature. So she replied curtly:

'There's plenty of time . . . When it suits me.'

And, turning her back on the architect, she flew at her brother Léon, who had only just arrived, late as usual.

'How nice! Papa and mamma were very upset! You couldn't even be here in time for your sister's wedding! We thought you might at least have come with Madame Dambreville.'

'Madame Dambreville does what she likes; I do what I can,' replied Léon drily.

Their relationship had cooled. Léon considered that she was keeping him too long for her own use, and was tired of a liaison the boredom of which he had consented to put up with in the sole hope of its leading to some desirable match; and for the last fortnight he had been importuning her to keep her promises. Madame Dambreville, passionately in love, had even complained to Madame Josserand about these fads on the part of her son. His mother was thus all too ready to scold him, reproaching him with his lack of family affection and regard, since he did not scruple to absent himself from the most solemn ceremonies. Then, in his supercilious voice, the young democrat offered various explanations—some unexpected work he had had to do for the deputy whose secretary he was, a lecture he had to prepare, and various other tasks, as well as some important visits he had had to pay.

'It's so easy to get married!' observed Madame Dambreville, without thinking what she was saying, as she looked beggingly at him in order to soften him.

'Not always,' he coldly replied.

Then he went up to kiss Berthe and shake hands with his new brother-in-law, while Madame Dambreville grew pale and, drawing herself up to her full height in her dead-leaf-coloured dress, she smiled vaguely at everybody coming in.

It was one long procession of friends, of mere acquaintances, and guests who had thronged the church and now filed into the vestry. The newly married couple stood shaking hands continually, both looking delighted yet embarrassed. The Josserands and the Duveyriers found it impossible to introduce everyone. Now and again they exchanged glances of surprise, for Bachelard had brought along people whom nobody knew, and who talked much too loudly. The general confusion gradually increased. There was a crush of bodies, arms held up in the air, young girls squeezed between portly gentlemen with huge bellies, leaving the imprint of their white skirts on the legs of these respectable family men who all had some vice which they indulged regularly in some distant part of the city. Indeed Gueulin and Trublot, standing at a distance from the others,

were recounting in front of Octave how, the day before, Clarisse had
nearly been caught by Duveyrier and, to allay his suspicions, had
been obliged to make love to him for hours.

'Oh, look!' whispered Gueulin, 'he's kissing the bride! How nice it
must smell!'

The crowd finally dispersed. Only the family and a few intimate
friends remained. The story of Théophile's misfortune had
continued to spread during all the handshaking and congratulations;
in fact nobody talked of anything else, while exchanging the usual
stereotyped phrases. Madame Hédouin, who had just heard the
story, looked at Valérie with the amazement of a woman for whom
virtue is as natural as breathing. Doubtless Father Mauduit must
have learned about the matter too, for his curiosity seemed satisfied,
and his manner became even more unctuous than usual, amid the
secret frailties of his flock. Here was another terrible sore which had
suddenly begun to bleed, and over which he had to throw the mantle
of religion! He took Théophile aside for a moment, and talked to him
discreetly about the necessity of forgiving injuries and of God's
myterious ways, seeking above all to stifle the scandal, embracing
everyone present in a single gesture of pity and despair, as if to hide
their shame from Heaven itself.

'He's funny, that parson,' murmured Théophile, quite dazed by
the homily. 'He doesn't know what it's like.'

Valérie, clinging to Madame Juzeur for appearance's sake,
listened with emotion to the conciliatory words which Father
Mauduit also deemed it his duty to address to her. Then, as they
were leaving the church, she stopped in front of the two fathers, to
let Berthe go by on her husband's arm.

'You must feel pleased,' she said to Monsieur Josserand, to show
how unconcerned she was. 'My congratulations.'

'Yes, yes,' said Monsieur Vabre in his guttural voice, 'it's a great
responsibility off our minds.'

And while Trublot and Gueulin rushed about, seeing all the ladies
to their carriages, Madame Josserand, whose shawl almost caused a
traffic jam, obstinately remained on the pavement to the last, as if to
make a public display of her triumph as a mother.

That evening the dinner which took place at the Grand Hôtel du
Louvre was also marred by the unfortunate affair of Théophile and
the letter. It became an obsession; people had talked about it the

whole afternoon as they drove in the Bois de Boulogne, all the ladies being of the opinion that the husband ought certainly to have waited until the following day before finding the letter. At the dinner, however, only intimate friends were present. The one merry episode was a toast proposed by uncle Bachelard, whom the Josserands had not been able to avoid inviting, in spite of their terror. He was drunk by the time they got to the toast, and raising his glass, he embarked upon a sentence beginning 'I am happy in the pleasure I feel'. This he repeated over and over again, unable to get any further, while the other guests smiled indulgently. Auguste and Berthe, already quite worn out, exchanged occasional glances, surprised to find themselves sitting opposite each other; then, remembering the reason for this, they looked down, embarrassed, at their plates.

Nearly two hundred invitations had been issued for the ball. The guests began to arrive as early as half-past nine. The large red drawing-room was lit by three chandeliers, chairs had been placed all along the walls, and a chamber orchestra had been installed at one end, in front of the fireplace. There was also a buffet in an adjoining room, another room having been reserved for the two families to retire to when they wished.

Just as Madame Duveyrier and Madame Josserand were receiving the first guests, poor Théophile, whom they had been watching since the morning, once again lost control of himself. Campardon had asked Valérie for the pleasure of the first waltz. She laughed, and her husband saw this as a provocation.

'You laugh! You laugh!' he stammered. 'Tell me who sent the letter! Somebody must have sent it!'

It had taken him the whole afternoon to disengage that one idea from the state of confusion into which Octave's reply had plunged him. Now, he was utterly insistent about it: if it was not from Monsieur Mouret it was from somebody else, and he must have that person's name. As Valérie began to walk away without answering him, he caught hold of her arm and twisted it viciously, like an infuriated child, saying:

'I'll break it if you don't tell me who sent that letter.'

Valérie, frightened, and stifling a cry of pain, turned quite white. Campardon felt her lean on his shoulder in one of those nervous attacks which would torture her for hours at a time. He scarcely had time to take her into the next room, where he laid her on the sofa.

Madame Juzeur and Madame Dambreville followed him and proceeded to unlace her, while he discreetly withdrew.

Meanwhile, in the ballroom, only a few people had noticed this brief dramatic scene. Madame Duveyrier and Madame Josserand continued to receive the guests, who streamed in, gradually filling the vast room with bright dresses and black coats. There was a growing murmur of polite conversation as smiling faces revolved round the bride—the fat faces of fathers and mothers, the angular profiles of their daughters, and the delicate, sympathetic countenances of young women. At the far end of the room a violinist was tuning his A string. It gave out little plaintive cries.

'Sir, I must apologize,' said Théophile, accosting Octave, whose eyes had met his when he was twisting Valérie's arm. 'Anyone in my place would have suspected you, would he not? But I want to shake hands with you, to show you that I recognize my mistake.'

Shaking him by the hand, he took him aside, tortured by the need to pour out his woes, to find some confidant to whom he could unburden himself.

'Ah! sir, if I were to tell you . . .'

And he began to talk at length about his wife. As a girl she was delicate, and people said jokingly that marriage would set her right. She could not get fresh air in her parents' shop, where for three months he visited her every evening, and she had seemed so nice, so obedient, somewhat melancholy in temperament, but quite charming.

'Well, sir, marriage did not set her right—far from it! After a few weeks she was quite dreadful; we could never agree about anything. Quarrels about nothing at all; changes of mood every minute; laughing, crying, without my having the least idea why. Absurd sentimentality, extravagant ideas, an eternal mania for driving people mad. In short, sir, my home has been turned into a perfect hell on earth!'

'It's very odd,' murmured Octave, who felt obliged to say something.

Then the husband, pale with excitement, straightened his short legs to avoid looking ridiculous, and broached the subject of what he termed his wretched wife's misconduct. Twice he had had his suspicions; but he was too decent to think it might be true. This time, however, he was obliged to recognize the evidence. There was no doubt whatever, was there? And, his hands trembling, he felt about in his waistcoat pocket for the letter.

'If she did it for money I could understand it,' he added, 'but they don't give her any, I'm sure of that, because I'd know. Then what is it that drives her to do such a thing? I'm always very nice to her. She's got everything she wants at home. I can't understand it. If you can understand it, sir, please tell me.'

'It's very odd, very odd,' repeated Octave, who found all these confidences embarrassing, and was wondering how to make his escape.

But the husband would not let him go, in his feverish anxiety to get at the truth. At this moment Madame Juzeur came back and whispered something to Madame Josserand, who was just curtseying to a wealthy jeweller of the Palais Royal, and who, quite upset, hastened to follow her.

'I think your wife's having a very bad attack,' Octave said to Théophile.

'Never mind about her!' exclaimed the latter, furious at not being taken ill too, so that they might look after him. 'She's only too glad to have an attack; it always makes everyone sympathize with her. My health is no better than hers, but I've never been unfaithful to her.'

Madame Josserand did not return. Among intimate friends the rumour got about that Valérie was in the throes of the most frightful convulsions. It would take several men to hold her down; but, as they had been obliged partially to undress her, Trublot's and Gueulin's offers to help were declined. Meanwhile the orchestra was playing a quadrille; Berthe was about to open the ball with Duveyrier, in his official capacity, as her partner, while Auguste, unable to find Madame Josserand, took Hortense to form their *vis-à-vis*. The news of Valérie's attack was kept a secret from the bridal pair, for fear that it might upset them. The dance grew lively, and there was a sound of laughter under the gleaming chandeliers. A polka, whose rhythm was vigorously marked by the violins, set all the couples whirling round the room, with trains flowing behind them.

'Doctor Juillerat! Where's Doctor Juillerat?' cried Madame Josserand, rushing back into the room.

The doctor had been invited, but no one had yet noticed his arrival. By now she could no longer contain the rage she had been bottling up since the morning. She was happy to speak quite plainly in front of Octave and Campardon.

'I've had just about enough of it. It's not very nice for my daughter, this endless business about adultery!'

She looked round for Hortense, and at last noticed her talking to a gentleman of whom she could only see the back but whom she recognized by his broad shoulders. It was Verdier. This increased her ill-humour. She sharply called her daughter over to her, and told her in a whisper that it would be better if she remained at her mother's disposal on an occasion such as this. Hortense ignored the rebuke. She was triumphant, for Verdier had just fixed their marriage for June—in two months' time.

'Hold your tongue!' said her mother.

'I assure you he has, mamma. He sleeps out three times a week, to get that other woman used to it, and in a fortnight he's going to stay away altogether. Then it'll all be over, and he'll be mine.'

'Hold your tongue! I've had more than enough of your romance! Just be good enough to wait at the door until Doctor Juillerat comes, and send him to me the moment he does. And don't mention a word of this to your sister!'

Then she went back into the next room, while Hortense muttered something about not wanting anybody, thank goodness, to approve of her conduct, and that they would all be left gaping one day when they discovered that she had made a better match than the rest. She went over to the door, however, to look out for Doctor Juillerat.

The orchestra was now playing a waltz. Berthe was dancing with one of her husband's cousins, so as to get rid of her relations in turn. Madame Duveyrier had not been able to refuse uncle Bachelard, who made her most uncomfortable by breathing in her face. The heat increased; the buffet was crowded with gentlemen mopping their brows. Some little girls hopped about together in a corner, while the mothers, sitting apart, dreamt about the weddings of their own daughters that somehow never took place. Congratulations were showered upon the two fathers, Monsieur Vabre and Monsieur Josserand, who never left each other's side during the whole evening, neither uttering a word. Everyone appeared to be enjoying themselves, and declared that it was a splendid ball. Its gaiety, as Campardon observed, was of the right sort.

Though the architect gallantly professed great concern at

Valérie's condition, he managed not to miss a single dance. He had the idea of sending his daughter Angèle, in his name, to ask for news. The girl, whose childish curiosity had been aroused that morning by this lady about whom everyone was talking, was delighted at being able to go into the next room; but, as she did not return Campardon took the liberty of putting his head round the door. He saw his daughter standing by the couch staring in fascination at Valérie, whose breasts, shaken by spasms, had broken loose from her unhooked bodice. There were loud cries of protest from the ladies, who said that he must not come in; so he withdrew, declaring that he only wanted to know how she was getting on.

'She's no better, no better!' he said mournfully to those who were standing near the door. 'There are four of them holding her down. She must be very strong, to throw herself about like that without hurting herself!'

There was now quite a group of sympathizers. The slightest phases of the attack were discussed in an undertone. Ladies, hearing what had happened, ran up, full of concern, in the pauses of a quadrille, entered the little room, brought back details to the men, and then went on dancing. It became a sort of mysterious corner for the exchange of whispers and glances in the midst of the ever-increasing din of the dance. Théophile, meanwhile, forsaken and alone, paced up and down in front of the door, tortured by the idea that he was being made a fool of and that he ought not to tolerate it.

Doctor Juillerat now swiftly crossed the ballroom, accompanied by Hortense, who was explaining things to him. They were followed by Madame Duveyrier. Some of the guests seemed surprised; fresh rumours began to circulate. No sooner had the doctor arrived than Madame Josserand came out of the room with Madame Dambreville. Her fury was increasing. She had just emptied two bottles of water over Valérie's head; never before had she seen hysterics reach such a pitch. Now she had decided to go round the ballroom to put an end to all the gossip by her presence. However, so terrible was her step and so sour her smile that, as she passed, everyone guessed her secret.

Madame Dambreville remained by her side. Ever since the morning she had been talking to her about Léon, vaguely complaining, trying to persuade her to intercede with him on her behalf, and so patch up their relationship. She pointed him out, as he was escorting a tall, gaunt girl to her seat and pretending to pay her great attention.

'He's avoiding us, can't you see?' she said with a nervous laugh, trembling with suppressed emotion. 'You should scold him for not even looking at us.'

'Léon!' cried Madame Josserand. When he came over she said bluntly, being in no mood to mince her words: 'Why are you angry with Madame Dambreville? She bears you no ill-will. Go and make it up with her. There's no point in sulking.'

And she left them looking at each other in embarrassment. Madame Dambreville took Léon's arm, and they both retired to a window-recess, where they talked for a while, and then left the ballroom together arm-in-arm. She had solemnly sworn to arrange a marriage for him in the autumn.

Meanwhile Madame Josserand was still dispensing smiles, and when she came to Berthe, breathless with dancing, looking quite rosy in her white dress, she was suddenly overcome by emotion. She clasped her in her arms, overwhelmed by a vague association of ideas, as she remembered Valérie lying in the next room with her face convulsed and distorted.

'My poor darling, my poor darling!' she murmured, giving her two big kisses.

'How is she?' asked Berthe, coolly.

Madame Josserand's sour look returned at once. What? Berthe knew about it then? But of course she did; everybody knew about it. It was only her husband over there—whom she pointed out taking an old lady to the buffet—who was still ignorant of what had happened. She had even intended to get someone to tell him all about it, for it made him look so silly afterwards always to be the last to know anything.

'To think that I've been struggling to keep it all quiet!' cried Madame Josserand, beside herself. 'Well, well, I won't bother any more, but it must be put a stop to. I won't let them make you look a fool.'

Everyone did indeed know, but the affair was not talked about so as not to cast any gloom over the ball. The first expressions of sympathy had been drowned by the orchestra, and now, as the dancing became less inhibited, they began to laugh about it. The heat had become intense, and it was growing late. Servants handed round refreshments. On a sofa, overcome by fatigue, two little girls had fallen asleep in each other's arms, cheek touching cheek. Near the orchestra, to the grunting of a cello, Monsieur Vabre had decided to entertain Monsieur Josserand with the details of his great work, dwelling on a doubt which had been bothering him for a fortnight, regarding the real works of two painters of the same name. Close by, Duveyrier, in the middle of a group, was bitterly censuring the Emperor for having allowed the production, at the Comédie Française, of a play which attacked modern society.* But whenever the orchestra struck up a waltz or a polka the men had to move, as couple after couple joined the dance, while skirts swept over the polished floor, filling the heated air with fine dust and a vague odour of musk.

'She's better,' said Campardon, running up after another peep round the door. 'We can go in now.'

Some of the men ventured to enter. Valérie was still lying at full length, but the hysteria had subsided and, for decency's sake, her breasts had been covered by a napkin found lying on a sideboard. At the window Madame Juzeur and Madame Duveyrier stood listening to Doctor Juillerat, who was explaining that attacks of this kind were sometimes relieved by the application of hot-water compresses to the neck. Then, as the patient noticed Octave coming in with Campardon, she beckoned to him and addressed a few incoherent words to him, as if still in a dream. He was obliged to sit down beside her, at the doctor's special request, for the latter was especially anxious to avoid annoying her; and so the young man listened to her disclosures, just as, earlier in the evening, he had listened to those of her husband. Trembling with fright, she took him for her lover and implored him to hide her. Then she recognized him and burst into tears, thanking him for his lie at mass that morning. Like a greedy schoolboy, Octave thought of that other fit of hysterics which he had tried to turn to advantage. He was now her friend, and she would tell him everything; perhaps it was better this way.

At this moment Théophile, who had been striding up and down outside the door, tried to enter. Other men had gone in, so why not he? This, however, created quite a panic. At the mere sound of his voice Valérie's trembling fits came back. Everybody feared that she would have another attack. Begging to be let in, he was pushed back by the ladies, and kept doggedly repeating:

'I only want to ask her his name. Let her tell me the man's name.'

Then Madame Josserand arrived and gave vent to her wrath. Pulling Théophile aside into the little room, to avoid a scene, she said to him furiously:

'Look here, are you going to hold your tongue, sir? You've been driving us mad with all this nonsense ever since this morning. You've no tact, sir, no tact whatever. You shouldn't keep harping about this sort of thing on someone's wedding-day!'

'Excuse me, madam,' he murmured, 'but the matter concerns me. It has nothing to do with you.'

'Oh, really! I'm a member of your family now, sir, and do you suppose I find your affair amusing because of my daughter? A nice wedding she's had, thanks to you! Not another word, sir; you have no tact whatever!'

He looked about him, bewildered, as if to find someone to take his side. But the ladies all showed by their coldness that they judged him just as severely. He had no tact, that was precisely the problem; for there were times when one ought really to control one's temper. Even his own sister sided against him. When he again protested, he created a general revolt. No, no, there was no question about it, his behaviour was utterly unacceptable.

This chorus of opposition silenced him. He looked so scared, so puny, with his slender limbs and his face like an old spinster's, that the women began to smile. When one could not give a woman pleasure, one ought not to marry. Hortense gave him a disdainful glance; little Angèle, whom they had forgotten, hovered about him with her sly air, as if she were looking for something, and he retreated in blushing embarrassment before all these tall, well-built women, who surrounded him with their huge hips. They felt, however, that the matter must be resolved in some way or another. Valérie had started to sob again, while the doctor kept bathing her temples. Understanding one another at a glance, the women were drawn together by a common feeling of defence. They racked their brains in an attempt to explain the letter to Théophile.

'Hmm!' muttered Trublot, who had just joined Octave. 'It's easy enough; they should simply say it was addressed to the maid.'

Madame Josserand overheard him and turned round, her eyes sparkling with admiration. Then, turning back to Théophile, she said:

'Do you really think that an innocent woman would stoop so low as to offer an explanation when accused in the brutal way in which you have accused her? I'm free to speak, however. The letter was dropped by Françoise, the maid your wife was obliged to discharge because of her bad conduct. Does that satisfy you? Aren't you ashamed to look us in the face?'

At first Théophile shrugged his shoulders in disbelief. But they all looked so serious, and met his objections with irresistible logic. He was already quite stunned when, to complete his discomfiture, Madame Duveyrier angrily denounced his behaviour as abominable, and declared that she would have nothing more to do with him. Then, vanquished, yearning for someone to embrace him, he threw his arms round Valérie's neck and begged her forgiveness. It was most touching. Even Madame Josserand seemed moved.

'It's always best to come to an understanding,' she observed with relief. 'The day won't end so badly after all.'

When they had dressed Valérie, and she appeared in the ballroom on Théophile's arm, the gaiety of the guests seemed to become even greater. It was nearly three o'clock; people had begun to leave, and still the orchestra played quadrille after quadrille with feverish energy. Men exchanged smiles behind the backs of the reconciled pair. A medical remark of Campardon's about poor Théophile delighted Madame Juzeur. Girls crowded round to stare at Valérie, and then looked sheepish as their mothers, scandalized, glared at them. Berthe, who at last was dancing with her husband, must have whispered something in his ear, for he turned his head on hearing the story about Théophile and, without getting out of step, watched his brother with astonishment and the superiority of a man to whom things of that sort could never happen. There was a final galop, when everybody lost all restraint in the stifling heat and the reddish light of the candles, whose flickering flames made their sockets flash.

'Are you a close friend of hers?' asked Madame Hédouin, as she whirled round on Octave's arm, having accepted his invitation to dance.

The young man fancied that he felt a slight quiver run through her straight, calm figure.

'Not at all,' he replied. 'They got me involved in the affair, which was very annoying. The poor devil swallowed everything.'

'It's very bad,' she said, in her grave way.

Octave must have been mistaken, for when he withdrew his arm from her waist Madame Hédouin was not even out of breath, her eyes were clear, her hair as neat and straight as ever. But before the ball ended there was another scandalous incident. Uncle Bachelard, who at the buffet had become monstrously drunk, had launched into a piece of merriment. He was suddenly seen dancing a grossly indecent dance in front of Gueulin. He stuffed some napkins into the front of his coat, giving him the appearance of a well endowed wet-nurse; two large oranges, attached to the napkins, stuck out prominently. This time there was a general protest. It was all very well to earn lots of money, but really there were limits which no decent-minded man should ever overstep, especially when young people were present. In shame and despair, Monsieur Josserand got his brother-in-law to withdraw, while Duveyrier did not conceal his intense disgust.

At four o'clock the bridal couple returned to the Rue de Choiseul. They brought Théophile and Valérie back in their carriage. As they went up to the second floor, where an apartment had been prepared for them, they came upon Octave, who was also going upstairs to bed. The young man politely stood aside, but Berthe made a similar movement and they bumped into each other.

'Oh, I beg your pardon, mademoiselle!' he said.

The word 'mademoiselle' amused them greatly. She looked at him, and he remembered the first time their eyes had met on that very staircase, her bold, carefree glance, which again he found charmingly inviting. Perhaps they understood each other. She blushed, and he carried on upstairs to his room, amid the deathly silence of the upper floors.

Auguste, his left eye closed, and half mad with the migraine he had had since the morning, was already in the apartment, where other members of the family now assembled. Then, just as she was leaving Berthe, Valérie, in a sudden fit of emotion, embraced her, crumpling her white dress as she kissed her and saying in a low voice:

'Ah, my dear, I wish you better luck than I've had.'

IX

Two days later, at about seven o'clock, as Octave arrived at the Campardons' for dinner, he found Rose by herself, dressed in a cream-coloured silk dressing-gown trimmed with white lace.

'Are you expecting someone?' he asked.

'Oh, no!' she replied, somewhat embarrassed. 'We'll have dinner as soon as Achille comes.'

Recently the architect had lost his punctual habits and never came back for meals at the proper time, but eventually he would appear, red in the face, flustered, and cursing business. And every night he went off somewhere, making all sorts of excuses: appointments at cafés, distant meetings, and the like. Thus Octave often kept Rose company until eleven o'clock, for he had begun to see that her husband, in taking him as a boarder, only wanted him as a companion for his wife. She would gently complain and tell him her fears: oh yes, she let Achille do just as he liked, but she always began to worry if he was not home by midnight!

'Don't you think he's been looking rather sad lately?' she asked, in her gentle, timorous way.

No, Octave had not noticed. 'He may be rather preoccupied,' he said. 'The restorations at Saint-Roch are probably giving him a lot of trouble.'

But she shook her head, and did not reply. Then she showed her interest in Octave by asking him how he had spent his day, affectionately, as if she were his mother or sister. During the nine months that he had been their boarder she had treated him as if he were one of the family.

At last Campardon appeared.

'Good evening, my pet! Good evening, my darling!' he said, kissing her affectionately like a good husband. 'Another idiot kept me talking a whole hour in the street!'

Octave had moved away, but heard them exchange a few words under their breath.

'Is she coming?'

'No; what's the point? But you really shouldn't worry about it.'

'You said she'd come!'

'All right then, she is coming! Are you pleased? I only asked her to come for your sake.'

Then they sat down for dinner. Throughout the whole meal they talked of nothing but the English language, which little Angèle had been learning for two weeks. Campardon had suddenly insisted on the necessity for a young lady to know English and, as Lisa had come to them from an actress who had just returned from London, every meal was devoted to discussing the English names for the dishes that were brought in. That evening, after long and ineffectual attempts to pronounce the word 'rump-steak', they had to send the meat back, for Victoire had left it too long over the fire and it was as tough as boot-leather.

During dessert, a ring at the bell made Madame Campardon start.

'It's madame's cousin,' said Lisa on returning, in the injured tone of a servant who has been excluded from some family secret.

It was, in fact, Gasparine. She looked quite plain in her black woollen dress, with her thin face and tired, shop-girl air. Snug in her cream-coloured silk dressing-gown Rose, looking plump and fresh, stood up to greet her with tears in her eyes.

'Oh, my dear,' she murmured, 'how nice of you! We'll let bygones be bygones, won't we?'

Putting her arms round her, she kissed her twice. Octave was about to withdraw discreetly, but they insisted that he should stay; he was one of the family. So he amused himself by watching the whole scene. Campardon, at first greatly embarrassed, avoided looking at the women but fussed about in search of a cigar, while Lisa, as she roughly cleared the table, exchanged glances with the astonished Angèle.

At length the architect addressed his daughter: 'This is your cousin. You've heard us talk about her. Come and give her a kiss.'

Angèle kissed her in her sulky way, feeling uncomfortable under the scrutiny of Gasparine's governess eyes as she answered her questions about how old she was and what she was learning at school. Then, as they went into the drawing-room, she preferred to follow Lisa, who slammed the door and remarked, without any concern about being overheard:

'Well, things are getting very interesting!'

In the drawing-room Campardon uneasily began to make excuses.

'Of course, it wasn't my idea, it was Rose's; she wanted to make it up. Every day, for more than a week, she kept saying, "Go and fetch her". So in the end I did as she said.'

Then, as if he felt the need to convince Octave, he led him to the window.

'Well, women will be women. I was fed up with the whole thing, because I dread scenes myself. With one on the right and the other on the left, no squabbling was possible. But I had to give in. Rose says we'll all be much happier. Well, we'll try it. It depends on those two if my life is comfortable or not.'

Meanwhile Rose and Gasparine sat on the sofa side by side. They talked of old times, of days spent with good papa Domergue, at Plassans. Rose at that time had a complexion the colour of lead, and the puny limbs of a child that has been ailing since birth; while Gasparine, already a woman at fifteen, was tall and attractive-looking, with beautiful eyes. Now they hardly recognized each other—the one cool and plump in her enforced chastity, the other dried up by the nervous passion that was consuming her. For a moment Gasparine was dismayed because, with her sallow face and shabby dress, she formed such a contrast to Rose, arranged as she was in silk, and with her soft, white neck swathed in delicate lace. But she overcame this twinge of jealousy, at once accepting her position as poor relation grovelling before her cousin's grace and elegance.

'How's your health?' she asked softly. 'Achille spoke to me about it. Is it no better?'

'No, no better,' replied Rose, mournfully. 'You see, I can eat, and I look perfectly well. But it doesn't get any better; it never will get any better.'

She began to cry, and Gasparine, in her turn, took her in her arms and pressed her against her flat, burning bosom, while Campardon hastened to console them.

'Why are you crying?' she asked, with maternal concern. 'The main thing is that you're not in pain. What does it matter, if you always have people around you who love you?'

Rose, calmer now, smiled through her tears. Then, carried away by his feelings, Campardon clasped them both in one embrace and, kissing them, murmured:

'Yes, yes, we'll all love one another, and love you too, my poor darling. You'll see how well everything will go now that we're united.'

Then, turning to Octave, he added:

'You can say what you like, my boy, there's nothing like family life.'

The evening ended delightfully. Campardon, who, if he stayed at home, usually fell asleep immediately after dinner, rediscovered some of the gaiety of his artist days as he rehearsed the old jokes and bawdy songs of the École des Beaux Arts. When Gasparine got ready to leave, at about eleven o'clock, Rose insisted on accompanying her to the door, in spite of the difficulty which, that day, she found in walking. Leaning over the banisters, in the solemn silence of the staircase, she called after her cousin:

'Come and see us whenever you like!'

The next day, feeling curious, Octave tried to question Gasparine at the Ladies' Paradise, as they were sorting a consignment of linen goods. But she gave him curt answers, and he felt that she was hostile, annoyed that he had been a witness the previous evening. In any case she did not like him, and even in their dealings at work she showed a kind of spite towards him. She had long since seen through the game he was playing with regard to the mistress, and for his assiduous courtship she had only black looks and a contemptuous curl of the lip, which at times made him quite uneasy. As long as this lanky devil of a girl thrust her skinny hands between them, he had the clear impression that Madame Hédouin would never be his.

Octave, however, had given himself six months. Although four had scarcely elapsed, he was growing impatient. Every month he asked himself whether he should not hasten matters somewhat, seeing what little progress he had made in the affections of this woman, always so icy and so calm. However, she had come to show considerable respect for him, taken by his grand ideas, his dreams of huge modern emporiums, unloading millions of francs' worth of merchandise in the streets of Paris.* Often, when her husband was not there, as she and the young man opened the letters in the morning, she kept him talking and asked for his advice. Thus a kind of commercial intimacy was established between the two. Their hands met amid piles of invoices; as they counted rows of figures, they felt each other's warm breath on their cheeks in moments of excitement over the cashbox after unusually large receipts. He even sought to take advantage of such moments, his plan now being to reach her heart through her tradeswoman's instincts, and to conquer her on a day of weakness, in the midst of the excitement of some unexpected sale. So he kept waiting for some surprising stroke of luck which would deliver her up to him. However, whenever he did not keep her talking business, she at once resumed her quiet tone of authority, politely giving him instructions just as she would with the other shopmen. She superintended the operations of the whole shop in her cool way, looking like an ancient statue with a man's little necktie round her neck, and a sober, tight-fitting bodice of eternal black.

About this time Monsieur Hédouin fell ill and went to take a course of the waters at Vichy. Octave was frankly delighted. Though as cold as marble, Madame Hédouin, during this time of widowhood, would, so he thought, relent. But it was in vain that he watched for a single shiver, a single languorous symptom of desire. Never had she seemed so active, her head so clear, her eyes so bright. Rising at daybreak, she herself received the deliveries of goods in the basement, looking as busy as a clerk with her pen behind her ear. She was everywhere—upstairs, downstairs, in the silk department, in the linen department, superintending the window-dressers and the saleswomen, gliding past the huge piles without getting so much as a speck of dust on her. When he met her in some narrow passage between a wall of woollens and a pile of napkins, Octave would stand awkwardly to one side, so that for a second she would be pressed against his chest. But she was so busy that he hardly felt her dress brush past him. Moreover, he was much embarrassed by Mademoiselle Gasparine's cold gaze, which he always found fixed upon them at such moments as these.

However, Octave did not despair. At times he thought he had reached his goal, and was already mapping out his life for the day, so close at hand, when he would be the lover of his employer's wife. He had maintained his contact with Marie merely to sustain his patience; nevertheless, though she was obliging and cost him nothing, she might eventually prove troublesome with her dog-like fidelity. So, while still visiting her on nights when he was bored, he began to think of how to break off their intimacy. To drop her abruptly seemed inexpedient. One holiday morning, as he was on his way to join her in bed while her husband was taking an early constitutional, he conceived the idea of giving her back to Jules and of letting them fall amorously into each other's arms, so that, his conscience clear, he could withdraw. It would be a kind action, after all, so touching, in fact, that it would leave him free of all remorse in the matter. Nevertheless he waited, not wishing to be bereft of all female company.

At the Campardons' another complication gave Octave further food for thought. He felt that the time was coming when he would have to take his meals elsewhere. For three weeks Gasparine had been making herself thoroughly at home there, her authority increasing by the day. At first she had come every evening, then she had appeared at lunch, and, in spite of her work at the shop, she began to take charge of everything, whether it was Angèle's education or the household shopping. Rose never stopped saying to Campardon:

'Oh, if only Gasparine lived with us!'

But every time the architect, conscientiously scrupulous, blushed and, tormented with shame, replied:

'No, no; that would never do! Besides, where would she sleep?'

And he explained that he would have to give Gasparine his study as a bedroom, while he would have to move his table and plans into the drawing-room. Certainly it would not inconvenience him at all, and one day, perhaps, he would agree to the alteration, for he did not need a drawing-room, and his study was becoming too small for all the work he now had in hand. Yet Gasparine had better stay where she was. It was no good living on top of each other.

'When things are working well,' he would say to Octave, 'it would be a mistake to change them.'

About that time he was obliged to go to Evreux for a couple of days. The work for the archbishop worried him. He had acceded to the wishes of Monseigneur, though no credit had been opened for the purpose, to construct new kitchens and heating apparatus; the cost of this seemed likely to be very heavy, far too heavy to include in the cost of repairs. In addition to this, the pulpit, for which there was a grant of three thousand francs, would cost ten at least. To keep things under control, he wanted to come to some arrangement with the archbishop.

Rose did not expect him home before Sunday evening. He arrived, however, in the middle of lunch, and his sudden appearance gave them quite a scare. Gasparine was at table, sitting between Octave and Angèle. They pretended to be totally at ease, but there was clearly something mysterious in the air. Lisa had just closed the drawing-room door, in response to a despairing gesture of her mistress, while Gasparine kicked out of sight some pieces of paper which were lying about. When he talked of changing his things, they stopped him.

'Wait a moment. Have some coffee, if you lunched at Evreux.'

At last, as he could see how embarrassed Rose was, she threw her arms round his neck.

'You mustn't scold me, dear. If you hadn't come until this evening you would have found everything straight.'

She tremblingly opened the doors and took him into the drawing-room and the study. A mahogany bedstead, brought in that morning from a furniture dealer's, stood in the place of his drawing-table, which had been moved into the middle of the next room. But nothing had been put straight yet; portfolios were mixed up with some of Gasparine's clothes, while the Virgin of the Bleeding Heart was leaning against the wall, propped up by a new washstand.

'It was going to be a surprise!' murmured Madame Campardon as, with swelling heart, she hid her face in the folds of her husband's waistcoat.

Deeply moved, he looked about him. He said nothing, and avoided Octave's gaze. Then Gasparine, in her dry voice, asked:

'Does it bother you, cousin? Rose pestered me to agree to it. But if you think I'd be in the way I can still leave.'

'My dear cousin!' cried the architect at last; 'whatever Rose does is right.'

Then, as his wife burst out sobbing on his breast, he added:

'There, there, darling, it's silly to cry. I'm very pleased. You want to have your cousin with you—very well, so you shall! It doesn't bother me in the least. Now, don't cry any more! See, I'll kiss you as I love you—such a lot!'

He devoured her with kisses. Rose, who would dissolve into tears at a word but smile again immediately afterwards, took comfort while she wept. She, in her turn, kissed him on his beard, saying gently:

'You were rather hard on her. Give her a kiss, too.'

Campardon kissed Gasparine. They called Angèle, who had been looking on from the dining-room, her mouth open, her eyes wide;

she too had to kiss Gasparine. Octave had stood back, having come to the conclusion that in this family they were getting far too affectionate. He had noticed with surprise Lisa's respectful manner and smiling attentiveness towards Gasparine. An intelligent girl, evidently, that hussy with the blue eyelids!

Meanwhile the architect had taken off his coat, whistling and singing like a merry schoolboy, and spent the whole afternoon arranging the cousin's room. She helped him to push the furniture into place, unpack the bed-linen, and shake out the clothes, while Rose, who did not leave her armchair for fear of tiring herself, made various suggestions for putting the washstand here or the bed there, so that everyone might find it convenient. It was then that Octave became aware that he was inhibiting their general enthusiasm; he felt out of place in such a close-knit household, and so he told them that he was going to dine out that evening. He was determined, moreover, that the next day he would thank Madame Campardon for her hospitality and invent some story to explain why he had no further need to abuse it.

At about five o'clock, regretting that he did not know where to find Trublot, he suddenly thought he would invite himself to dinner at the Pichons', so as not to spend the evening by himself. No sooner had he entered their apartment, however, than he found himself in the middle of a deplorable family scene. The Vuillaumes were there, trembling with rage and indignation.

'It's disgraceful, sir!' the mother was saying, standing erect as she wagged her finger at her son-in-law, who was sitting crushed on a chair. 'You gave me your word of honour.'

'And you,' added the father, making his daughter retreat in terror to the sideboard, 'don't make excuses for him, you're just as much to blame. You both want to starve, do you?'

Madame Vuillaume had put on her bonnet and shawl again, saying solemnly:

'Goodbye! At least we won't encourage your dissolute behaviour by our presence. Since you no longer pay the least attention to our wishes, we have no reason to stay here. Goodbye!'

As Jules, from force of habit, rose to accompany them, she added:

'Don't trouble yourself, we're quite able to catch the bus without you. Come on, Monsieur Vuillaume. Let them eat their dinner, and much good may it do them, because they won't always have one!'

Octave, quite bewildered, stood aside to let them pass. When they had gone he looked at Jules, still prostrate in his chair, and at Marie, standing by the sideboard as pale as a ghost. Both were speechless.

'What's the matter?' he asked.

Without answering him, Marie dolefully began to scold her husband.

'I told you what would happen. You should've waited until you could've broken it to them gently. There was no hurry, it doesn't show yet.'

'What's the matter?' Octave asked again.

Then, not even looking away, she blurted out in her emotion, 'I'm pregnant.'

'I've had enough of them!' cried Jules indignantly, rising from his chair. 'I thought it right to tell them straight away about this little problem. Do they think it amuses me? It concerns me much more than it does them, especially as it's through no fault of mine. We can't think how it's happened, can we, Marie?'

'No, we can't!' said the young woman.

Octave made a calculation. She was five months gone—from the end of December to the end of May. His calculation was correct; it shook him. Then he preferred to doubt; but, as his emotion persisted, he felt a longing to do the Pichons a good turn of some sort. Jules went on grumbling. They would look after the child, of course; but, all the same, it would have been far better if the pregnancy had never occurred. Marie, usually so quiet, became quite excited too, siding with her mother, who never forgave disobedience. A quarrel was developing, each blaming the other for the baby's appearance, when Octave gaily interposed:

'There's no point in quarrelling, now that it's on the way. I suggest that we dine out; it's too dismal here. I'll take you both to a restaurant. Will you come?'

Marie blushed. Dining at a restaurant was her delight. But she mentioned her little girl, who always prevented her from enjoying herself. However, they agreed that this time Lilitte should come too. They had a most pleasant evening. Octave took them to the Boeuf à la Mode, where they had a private room, to be more at their ease, as he said. Here he plied them with all sorts of food, never thinking about the bill, but only gratified at seeing them eat.

When dessert came, and they laid Lilitte down on two sofa-cushions, he even called for champagne, and they sat there dreaming, their elbows on the table and their eyes moist, sentimentally drowsy in the suffocating warmth of the dining-room. Finally, at eleven o'clock, they talked of going home; their cheeks were flushed and the cool night air seemed intoxicating. Then, as Lilitte, exhausted for want of sleep, refused to walk, Octave, wishing to end the evening with a flourish, insisted on taking a cab, though the Rue de Choiseul was close by. In the cab he scrupulously avoided squeezing Marie's legs between his own. But upstairs, while Jules was tucking Lilitte up in bed, he kissed the young woman's forehead; it was like the parting kiss of a father surrendering his daughter to her husband. Then, as he saw them looking at each other lovingly, in a drunken sort of way, he sent them to bed, wishing them through the door a very good night and lots of pleasant dreams.

'Well,' he thought, as he slipped between the sheets, 'it's cost me fifty francs, but I owed them at least as much as that. My only wish, after all, is that her husband will make her happy, poor little woman!'

And quite overcome by his own benevolence, before falling asleep he resolved to make his grand attempt the following morning.

Every Monday, after dinner, Octave helped Madame Hédouin to check the orders of the week. For this purpose they both withdrew to a little parlour at the back, a narrow room which only contained a safe, a desk, two chairs, and a sofa. It so happened that on this particular Monday the Duveyriers were going to take Madame Hédouin to the Opéra-Comique. Accordingly, she sent for the young man at about three o'clock. In spite of the bright sunshine they had to burn the gas, as the room was only faintly lit by windows overlooking the dismal inner courtyard. He bolted the door, and noticing her surprised look he said gently:

'Now nobody can come and disturb us.'

She nodded, and they set to work. The new summer goods were going splendidly; business was constantly increasing. That week, in particular, the sale of little woollen goods had looked so promising that she heaved a sigh.

'Ah, if we only had enough room!'

'But you know,' he said, beginning the attack, 'that depends on you. For some time I've had an idea, and I'd like to talk to you about it.'

It was a bold stroke of this kind that he had been waiting for. His idea was to buy the adjoining shop, in the Rue Neuve-Saint-Augustin, give the umbrella-maker and the toyshop man notice to quit, and then enlarge the shop, to which several extensive departments could be added. He talked enthusiastically about it all, full of disdain for the old way of doing business in the depths of damp, dark shops, with no display in their window-fronts. With a grand gesture he spoke of creating an entirely new type of commerce, providing every kind of luxury for women in huge palaces of crystal, amassing millions in broad daylight, and at nighttime being brilliantly illuminated as if for some princely festival.

'You'll crush all the other drapers in the Saint-Roch area,' he said, 'and you'll win over all the small customers. For instance, Monsieur Vabre's silk shop does you quite a lot of harm at present, but if you enlarge your shopfront and have a special department for silks, you'll bankrupt him in less than five years. And there's still talk of opening the Rue du Dix-Décembre from the new opera house to the Bourse. My friend Campardon talks about it from time to time. It would increase business in the neighbourhood tenfold.'

Madame Hédouin listened to him, her elbow on a ledger, her beautiful, grave face resting on her hand. She had been born at the Ladies' Paradise, founded by her father and her uncle. She loved the shop and imagined it expanding, swallowing up the neighbouring shops, and displaying a magnificent frontage. It was a dream that suited her keen intelligence, her strong will, her woman's intuition of the Paris of the future.

'Uncle Deleuze would never consent to such a thing,' she murmured. 'Besides, my husband is too unwell.'

Seeing that she was wavering, Octave assumed his seductive voice—the voice of an actor, soft and musical. At the same time he looked ardently at her with his eyes the colour of old gold, which some women said were irresistible. But, though the flaring gas-jet was close to the back of her neck, she remained as cool as ever, falling into a reverie, half dazed by the young man's eloquence. He had even worked out the figures, calculating the probable cost with the passionate air of a page making a declaration of long-hidden love.

Emerging suddenly from her reverie, she found herself in his arms. He thrust her on to the sofa, believing that now at last she would succumb.

'Dear, dear! So that was what it was all about!' she said sadly, shaking him off as if he were some tiresome child.

'Well, yes, I'm in love with you!' he exclaimed. 'Don't repulse me. With you, I could do great things . . .'

And so he went on to the end of his grand speech, which somehow rang false. She did not interrupt him, but stood turning over the leaves of the ledger. Then, when he had finished, she replied:

'I know all that; I've heard it all before. But I thought that you, Monsieur Octave, had more sense than the others. I'm really very sorry, for I had counted on you. However, all young men are foolish. A shop like this needs a great deal of order, and you're starting off by wanting things that would unsettle us from morning to night. I'm not a woman here; there's far too much for me to do. How is it that, with all your intelligence, you couldn't see that it's impossible: first, because it's stupid; secondly, because it's useless; and thirdly, because, luckily for me, I'm not in the least interested!'

He would have preferred to see her full of wrath and indignation, overflowing with exalted sentiments. Her calm voice, her quiet way of reasoning like a practical, self-possessed woman, disconcerted him. He felt that he was becoming ridiculous.

'Have pity, madam,' he stammered. 'You can see how miserable I am!'

'Nonsense! You're not miserable at all. Anyway, you'll soon get over it. Listen! There's somebody knocking; you'd better open the door.'

He was thus obliged to draw the bolt. It was Mademoiselle Gasparine, who wanted to know if they were expecting some lace-trimmed chemises. She had been surprised to find the door bolted. But she knew Madame Hédouin too well, and when she saw her standing with her glacial air before Octave, who looked thoroughly ill at ease, there was something in her smile that seemed to mock him. It exasperated him and made him feel that she was responsible for his failure.

'Madam,' he declared suddenly, when Gasparine had gone, 'I will leave your employ this evening.'

Madame Hédouin looked at him in surprise.

'But why? I haven't dismissed you. Oh, it won't make any difference! I'm not afraid.'

These words infuriated him. He would leave at once; he could not endure his martyrdom a moment longer.

'Very well, Monsieur Octave,' she continued, in her calm way. 'I'll settle with you directly. All the same, the firm will be sorry to lose you—you were a good assistant.'

Once in the street, Octave realized that he had acted like a fool. It was striking four, and the bright May sunshine lit up a whole corner of the Place Gaillon. Furious with himself, he walked blindly along the Rue Saint-Roch, debating how he should have acted. First of all, why had he not pinched that Gasparine's bottom? Probably that was what she wanted but, unlike Campardon, he did not care for hips as scrawny as that. Perhaps, though, he might be mistaken, for she looked like one of those women who are strictly virtuous with Sunday gentlemen when they have a weekday friend to lay them on their backs from Monday to Saturday. Then again, what a stupid idea to try to become his employer's lover! Could he not have earned his money in the firm, without demanding at one and the same time both bread and bed? He was so upset that for a moment he was on the point of returning to the Ladies' Paradise and admitting his error. But the thought of Madame Hédouin, so proud and calm, aroused his wounded vanity, and he walked on in the direction of Saint-Roch. Too bad! It was done now. He would go and see if Campardon was in the church, and take him to the café and have a glass of Madeira. It would take his mind off things. He went in by the vestibule into which the vestry door opened. It was a dark, dirty passage, like that of a brothel.

'Perhaps you're looking for Monsieur Campardon?' said a voice beside him as he stood hesitating, gazing intently along the nave.

It was Father Mauduit, who had just recognized him. Since the architect was away, he insisted on showing Octave the Calvary restorations himself; he was most enthusiastic about them. He took him behind the choir, first showing him the Chapel of the Holy Virgin, with its walls of white marble and its altar surmounted by the manger group, a rococo representation of Jesus between Saint Joseph and the Virgin Mary. Then, further back still, he took him through the Chapel of Perpetual Adoration, with its seven golden lamps, gold candelabra, and gold altar shining in the dim light that came through the gold-coloured windows. There, to left and right, wooden boards fenced off the rear section of the apse; and amid the silence, above the black kneeling shadows mumbling prayers, resounded the blows of pickaxes, the voices of workmen, all the deafening noise of a building-site.

'Come in,' said Father Mauduit, lifting up his cassock. 'I'll explain it all to you.'

On the other side of the boards plaster kept falling from a corner of the church open to the outside air; it was white with lime, and damp with water that had been spilt in various places. To the left the Tenth Station could still be seen, with Jesus nailed to the Cross, while on the right there was the Twelfth, showing the women grouped round Christ. But in between, the Eleventh Station, the group with Jesus on the Cross, had been removed and placed against a wall; it was here that the men were at work.

'Here it is,' continued the priest. 'It was my idea to light up the central group of the Calvary by making an opening in the cupola. You see the effect I wanted to get?'

'Yes, yes,' murmured Octave, who had forgotten his troubles during his tour of the restorations.

Talking at the top of his voice, the priest seemed like a stage-carpenter, directing the artistic arrangement of some gorgeous set.

'It must look absolutely bare, of course; nothing but stone walls, no paint at all, and not a trace of gold. We must imagine that we're in a crypt, in some desolate underground chamber. The great effect will be the Christ on the Cross, with the Virgin Mary and Mary Magdalene at His feet. I'll place the group on a rock, with the white statues standing out against a grey background; and the light from the cupola, like some invisible ray, will illuminate them so brilliantly that they'll seem to be breathing with the breath of supernatural life! Ah, you'll see, you'll see!'

Then he turned round and called out to a workman:

'Move the Virgin! You'll smash her thigh if you're not careful.'

The workman called one of his mates. Between them they held the Virgin by the hips and carried her to one side, as if she were a tall white girl, stiff and prostrate because of some nervous seizure.

'Mind what you're doing!' repeated the priest, following them amid all the rubbish. 'Her robe's cracked already. Wait a second!'

He gave them a hand, seized the Virgin Mary round the waist, and then, white with plaster, relinquished his embrace. Turning to Octave, he said:

'Now, just imagine that the two bays of the nave there, in front of us, are open, and go and stand in the Chapel of the Holy Virgin. Above the altar, through the Chapel of Perpetual Adoration, right at the back, you'll see the Calvary. You can imagine what an effect that'll make, those three great figures, the bare simple drama in the dim tabernacle, beyond the mysterious twilight from the painted windows, with the lamps and the gold candelabra. Ah, I think it will be irresistible!'

He was waxing eloquent and laughed with pleasure, very proud of this idea of his.

'The most unbelieving will surely be moved,' said Octave, just to please him.

'Indeed they will,' he exclaimed. 'I'm anxious to see it all finished.'

On coming back to the nave he forgot to lower his voice, as he swaggered about like some successful entrepreneur, alluding to Campardon in terms of high praise as a fellow who, in the Middle Ages, would have had very remarkable religious feeling.

He led Octave out through the small doorway at the back, keeping him for a moment longer in the courtyard of the vicarage, from which one could see the main body of the church buried amid the surrounding buildings. This was where he lived, on the second floor of a tall house, the façade of which was all decayed. All the clergy of Saint-Roch lived in it. An odour as of discreet clerics and the hushed whisperings of the confessional seemed to come from the vestibule, adorned by an image of the Holy Virgin, and from the high windows, veiled by thick curtains.

'I'll come and see Monsieur Campardon this evening,' said Father Mauduit. 'Please ask him to wait for me. I need to talk to him about some further restorations without being disturbed.'

He bowed with the easy grace of a man of the world. Octave was calmer now; Saint-Roch, with its cool vaulted aisles, had soothed his nerves. He looked with curiosity at this entrance to a church through a private house, at this porter's lodge, where at night the latch had to be lifted to let the Almighty pass, at all this convent corner lost in the black, seething neighbourhood. On reaching the pavement he looked up once more at the bare frontage of the house with its barred, curtainless windows. The windowsills on the fourth floor, however, were bright with flowers, while on the ground floor were little shops which the clergy found handy—a cobbler's, a watchmaker's, an embroiderer's, and even a wineshop where undertakers used to meet whenever there was a funeral. Octave, still smarting from his treatment by Madame Hédouin, felt in a mood to renounce the world, and thought regretfully of the peaceful existence which the priest's servants must lead up there in those rooms bedecked with verbena and sweet-peas.

That evening at half-past six, as he entered the Campardons' apartment without ringing, he surprised the architect and Gasparine kissing in the anteroom. She had only just arrived home from the shop, and had not even given herself time to shut the door. They both looked very confused. 'My wife's combing her hair,' stammered the architect, simply for the sake of saying something. 'Do go in and see her.'

Octave, feeling as embarrassed as they were, knocked immediately at the door of Rose's room, which he usually entered as if he were a relative. He certainly could not continue to board there any longer, now that he caught them kissing behind doors.

'Come in!' cried Rose. 'Oh! it's you, Octave? That's all right.'

She had not yet put on her dressing-gown, and her soft, milk-white arms and shoulders were bare. Studying herself in the mirror, she was twisting her golden hair into tiny curls. Every day she sat for hours, absorbed in minute details of her toilet, thinking of nothing but the pores of her skin, of improving her beauty. Finally, she would recline on a chaise longue, luxurious and lovely, like some sexless idol.

'You're making yourself look very beautiful again tonight, I see,' said Octave, smiling.

'Well it's my only amusement!' she replied. 'It's something to do. I never liked housekeeping, you know; and now that Gasparine is here . . . These little curls suit me, don't you think? It's a sort of consolation to be nicely dressed and to feel I look pretty.'

As dinner was not ready, he told her how he had left the Ladies' Paradise. He invented a story about some other situation he had long been waiting for, and this gave him a pretext for explaining his intention to take his meals elsewhere. She was surprised at his leaving a job with such good prospects. But she was far too busy at her mirror to listen carefully.

'Look at that red spot behind my ear! Is it a pimple?'

He was obliged to examine her neck, which she held out to him with the composure of a woman whose chastity is sacred.

'It's nothing,' he said. 'You probably rubbed yourself too hard.'

Then, after he had helped her to put on her dressing-gown of blue satin and silver, they went into the dining-room. Before the soup was finished the conversation turned to Octave's departure from the Ladies' Paradise. Campardon expressed his surprise, while Gasparine smiled her usual faint smile. Both seemed to be thoroughly at their ease. Octave even felt touched by the tender attentions they lavished on Rose. Campardon poured her wine, while Gasparine chose the best pieces from the dish for her. Did she like the bread? If not, they would go to another baker. Would she like a cushion for her back? Rose, full of gratitude, begged them not to put themselves out in this way. She ate a great deal, throned there between them, with her soft, white neck and queenly dressing-gown, having on the right her husband, always short of breath and apparently losing weight, while on her left sat her thin, desiccated cousin, her shrunken shoulders covered by a black dress, her flesh dissolved by the fires of passion.

At dessert Gasparine scolded Lisa, who had answered rudely when her mistress had enquired about a piece of cheese that was missing. The maid became very humble. Gasparine had already taken the household arrangements in hand and kept the servants in their place; a word from her was enough to set even Victoire shaking among her saucepans. Rose looked at her gratefully with moist eyes; they respected her now that Gasparine was there, and her great desire was that her cousin would leave the Ladies' Paradise as well, and take charge of Angèle's education.

'Come now,' she murmured coaxingly, 'there's quite enough for you to do here. Angèle, ask your cousin to come; tell her how pleased you would be.'

The child entreated her cousin to come, while Lisa nodded approvingly. But Campardon and Gasparine were unmoved; no, no, it was better to wait, one ought not to take a leap of that sort without having something to hold on to.

Evenings in the drawing-room had become delightful. The

architect never went out now. That evening, as it happened, he
was going to hang up some engravings in Gasparine's bedroom.
They had just come back from the framer; one was of Mignon
yearning for Heaven,* another offered a view of the Fountain of
Vaucluse,* and there were several others. His portly figure shook
with merriment, his blond beard was dishevelled, and his cheeks
were flushed from excess of food; he was truly in excellent
humour, now that he could gratify all his appetites. He called
Gasparine to give him a light, and they heard him hammering in
the nails as he stood on a chair. Octave, finding himself alone with
Rose, proceeded to explain that, at the end of the month, he
would be obliged to board elsewhere. She seemed surprised but
her head was full of other things, and she began to talk about her
husband and Gasparine, who were laughing together in the other
room.

'They're having a good time, hanging those pictures! Well,
Achille never stays out now; he hasn't left me alone for a single
evening during the last fortnight. No more going to the café, no
more business meetings, no more appointments! You remember
how worried I used to be if he wasn't home by midnight. Oh! it's
such a relief! At least I've got him near me now!'

'Of course, of course,' muttered Octave.

Then she began to talk about the economy of the new
arrangement. Everything in the house worked much better; they
were all as happy as the day was long.

'When I see Achille happy,' she continued, 'I'm happy too.'

Then, suddenly reverting to the young man's affairs, she added:

'So you're really going to leave us? You really ought to stay, now
that we're all going to be so happy together.'

He began once more to explain. She understood at last, and
looked down; the young fellow, after all, would interfere with their
tender outbursts of domestic affection. She herself was quite
relieved that he was going, since she no longer needed him to keep
her company in the evenings. He had to promise that he would come
and see her often.

'There's your "Mignon" for you!' cried Campardon, gaily. 'Wait
a minute, cousin, and I'll help you down.'

They heard him take her in his arms and deposit her somewhere.
Then there was a silence, followed by a suppressed laugh. Suddenly

the architect reappeared in the drawing-room, and held out his flushed cheek to his wife.

'We've finished, my sweetheart. Give your old darling a kiss for working so hard.'

Gasparine came in with some embroidery and sat down near the lamp. Campardon, laughing, began cutting out a gilt cross of the Legion of Honour, which he had found on some label. He blushed deeply when Rose tried to pin this paper decoration on his coat. Someone had promised him the cross, but there was a great mystery about it. On the other side of the lamp Angèle, learning her Scripture history, kept looking across with a puzzled air, like a well-brought-up young lady taught to be seen but not heard, and whose real thoughts are unrevealed. It was a peaceful evening indeed, in this homely, patriarchal nook.

But suddenly, Campardon's sense of propriety was violently offended. He noticed that, instead of studying her Scripture history, the child was reading the *Gazette de France*, which was lying on the table.

'Angèle!' he said sternly. 'What are you doing? This morning I crossed out that article with red pencil. You know very well that you're not to read what's crossed out.'

'I was reading the piece next to it, papa,' said the girl.

However, he took the newspaper away, complaining in low tones to Octave of how corrupting the press was becoming. That very day there had been another report of some abominable crime. If the *Gazette de France* could no longer be allowed into respectable family homes, then what paper could they take? As he was raising his eyes heavenwards, Lisa announced Father Mauduit.

'Ah! yes,' said Octave. 'He asked me to tell you he was coming.'

The priest came in smiling. As Campardon had forgotten to take off the paper cross, the cleric's smile confused him. Father Mauduit, as it happened, was the very person whose name had to be kept secret, for it was he who had recommended Campardon for the decoration.

'The ladies did it, silly things!' muttered Campardon, beginning to take off the cross.

'No, no! Keep it on,' replied the priest very amiably. 'It's in the right place where it is; we'll find a much better one later on.'

He enquired after Rose's health, and warmly approved of

Gasparine having made her home among relatives; young unmarried
ladies living alone ran such risks in a city like Paris. He said all this in
his unctuous, priestly way, though he was perfectly aware of how
things really stood. Then he spoke of the restorations, and suggested
an important alteration. It seemed as if he had come to bless the
sweet unity of this family, and thus regulate a somewhat delicate
situation which might easily give rise to local gossip. The architect of
the Saint-Roch Calvary must surely command the respect of all
righteous persons.

When the priest appeared Octave had wished the Campardons
good evening. As he crossed the anteroom he heard Angèle's voice in
the darkened dining-room, for she, too, had managed to slip away.

'Was she shouting like that because of the butter?' she asked.

'Yes, of course,' replied another voice, which Octave recognized
as Lisa's. 'She's like poison. You saw how she went on at me during
dinner. I don't care, though! You've got to pretend to obey with
someone like that; it doesn't stop us having our little jokes, does it?'

Then Angèle must have flung her arms round Lisa's neck, for her
voice sounded muffled, as if by the maid's bosom.

'I don't care what happens, it's you, you, I love!'

Octave was about to go upstairs to bed when a desire to get some
fresh air led him out into the street. It was barely ten o'clock; he
would take a stroll as far as the Palais Royal. Now he was single
again, with no woman whatever in tow. Neither Valérie nor Madame
Hédouin had responded to his overtures, and he had been in too
great a hurry to return Marie to Jules—she was his only conquest,
and he had not even gone out of his way to win her. He tried to laugh
at it all, but at heart he felt sad, bitterly recollecting his successes in
Marseilles. In the failure of his attempts at seduction he saw an evil
omen, an actual blow to his good fortune. The atmosphere seemed
so chilly with no petticoats near him. Even Madame Campardon had
let him go without a tear. This was a terrible revenge. Was Paris
going to deny him her favours, after all?

No sooner had he stepped into the street than he heard a woman's
voice calling him. He recognized Berthe, standing at the door of the
silk shop. A man was just putting up the shutters.

'Monsieur Mouret!' she asked, 'is it true that you've left the
Ladies' Paradise?'

He was surprised that people already knew about it in the

neighbourhood. Berthe had called her husband. As he had meant to
have a talk the following day to Monsieur Mouret, he might just as
well do so at once. And there and then Auguste, in his sour way,
offered Octave a position in his employ. Taken by surprise, Octave
hesitated, and was on the point of refusing, thinking of the
insignificance of Auguste's business. But when he saw Berthe's
pretty face and welcoming smile, the same bright glance that twice
had met his, once on the day of his arrival and again on her wedding-
day, he said resolutely:

'All right. I accept.'

X

OCTAVE now found himself brought into closer contact with the Duveyriers. When Madame Duveyrier came through the shop on her way home she would stop and talk to Berthe for a moment; and the first time she saw the young man behind one of the counters, she good-humouredly scolded him for not keeping his promise to come and see her one evening and try his voice. She wanted to put on another performance of the 'Benediction of the Poniards' at one of her Saturday receptions of the winter, but with two more tenors this time—an absolutely full cast.

'If it's not inconvenient,' said Berthe one day to Octave, 'could you go upstairs to my sister-in-law after dinner? She's expecting you.'

She maintained towards him the attitude of a mistress who wishes to be studiously polite.

'Well, the fact is,' he said, 'I was planning to put these shelves in order this evening.'

'Never mind about them,' she rejoined, 'there are plenty of people who do that. You can have the evening off.'

At about nine o'clock Octave found Madame Duveyrier waiting for him in her large white-and-gold drawing-room. Everything was ready, the piano open, the candles lit. A lamp, placed on a small table near the instrument, cast a poor light, leaving half of the room in shadow. Seeing that she was alone, Octave thought it proper to ask after Monsieur Duveyrier. He was extremely well, she said; his colleagues had entrusted him with the drawing up of a report concerning a most serious matter, and he had just gone out to obtain some information for it.

'You know, the affair of the Rue de Provence,' she said naively.

'Oh! he has to deal with that, has he?' exclaimed Octave. It was a scandal that had become the talk of Paris—a story of clandestine prostitution, fourteen-year-old girls procured for people in high places. Clotilde continued:

'Yes, it keeps him very busy. For the past two weeks all his evenings have been taken up with it.'

He looked at her, knowing from Trublot that Bachelard had

invited Duveyrier to dinner that evening, and that they were going to go to Clarisse's afterwards. She seemed quite serious, however, and talked gravely about her husband, relating, in her eminently respectable way, various remarkable stories to explain why the judge was perpetually absent from the conjugal hearth.

'He's responsible for so many souls,' said Octave, somewhat perturbed by her frank gaze.

She seemed to him very beautiful, seated there alone in the empty room. Her reddish hair heightened the pallor of her rather long face, which wore an expression of dogged resignation, the placid look of a woman absorbed in her duties. Dressed in grey silk, her waist and bosom tightly encased in a whalebone corset, she treated him with cold civility, as if separated from him by a triple coat of mail.

'Well, sir, shall we begin?' she went on. 'You will excuse my importunity, won't you? Let yourself go, sing as loud as you like, for Monsieur Duveyrier is not here. You may have heard him boast that he doesn't like music.'

She pronounced this last sentence with such contempt that Octave ventured a gentle laugh. It was, in fact, the only sarcasm levelled at her husband which sometimes escaped her before strangers, when exasperated by his endless jokes about her piano, although she had enough force of character to hide the hatred and the physical repulsion he inspired in her.

'How is it possible not to like music?' said Octave with a passionate air, wishing to make himself agreeable.

Then she sat down at the piano. A collection of old airs lay open before her. She chose the one from Grétry's *Zémire et Azor*.* As Octave could barely read his notes, she made him hum it at first. Then she played the prelude, and he began to sing:

> *When love lights up the heart,*
> *Life becomes so sweet!*

'Perfect!' she cried with delight. 'A tenor, not a doubt about it—a tenor! Please go on, sir!'

Octave, feeling very flattered, sang the next two lines:

> *And I, who feel his dart,*
> *Lie swooning at your feet!*

She beamed with pleasure. For the last three years she had been

looking for a tenor! And she recounted all her disappointments—
Monsieur Trublot, for instance. It would be worth studying the
causes which led to such a dearth of tenors among young men about
town; no doubt, smoking had a lot to do with it.

'Are you ready?' she continued. 'We need more expression: put
everything into it.'

Her cold face assumed a languorous expression as her eyes turned
towards him with a wistful look. Thinking that she was growing
excited, his animation increased, and she seemed to him full of
charm. Not a sound could be heard in the adjoining rooms; the
strange gloom of the large drawing-room seemed to envelop them in
a drowsy voluptuousness. Bending over her to see the music, his
chest touched her chignon, and he seemed to sigh with passion as he
sang the lines:

> *And I, who feel his dart,*
> *Lie swooning at your feet!*

But having delivered this melodious phrase, she dropped her
passionate expression as if it were a mask. The frigid woman lay
beneath. He shrank back in alarm, not wishing for a repetition of his
experience with Madame Hédouin.

'You'll soon handle it very nicely,' she said. 'But you must mark
the time more—like this.'

And she sang the line for him, twenty times over, bringing out
each note with the rigour of a woman who is a stranger to sin, whose
passion for music is shallow—a delight in pure form. Slowly her
voice grew louder, and filled the room with shrill cries, until they
suddenly heard someone shouting out behind them:

'Madam! Madam!'

Starting up, she saw Clémence, her maid.

'Yes, what is it?'

'Oh, madam, Monsieur Vabre has fallen forward on his writing-
desk, and he's not moving! We're all so frightened!'

Then, without exactly grasping the maid's meaning, she rose from
the piano in astonishment and went out with Clémence. Octave, who
did not venture to follow her, paced up and down the room. Then,
after a few minutes of awkward hesitation, as he heard the sound of
hurrying footsteps and anxious voices he decided to see what was
happening. Crossing the next room, which was quite dark, he found

himself in Monsieur Vabre's bedroom. All the servants had hurried there—Julie, in her apron; Clémence and Hippolyte, their minds still full of a game of dominoes they had just left. They all stood in bewilderment round the old man, while Clotilde, bending down, shouted in his ear and implored him to speak. But still he did not move, his face buried in his catalogue-tickets. His forehead had struck the ink-stand. Over his left eye there was a splash of ink, which was trickling slowly down towards his lips.

'He's in a fit,' said Octave. 'He can't be left there. We must get him on to the bed.'

Madame Duveyrier, however, was losing her head. Emotion was gradually rising in her cold nature. She kept repeating:

'Do you think so? Do you think so? Good heavens! Oh, my poor father!'

Hippolyte was in no hurry to move. He was uneasy, visibly repelled at the thought of touching the old man, who perhaps might pass away while he was holding him. Octave was obliged to shout at him for help. Between them, they laid him down on the bed.

'Bring some warm water,' said the young man to Julie. 'Wipe his face.'

Clotilde now became angry at her husband's absence. Was it necessary for him to be away? What would become of her if anything happened? It was as if he'd done it on purpose; he was never at home when he was wanted, and heaven knows that was not very often! Octave, interrupting, advised her to send for Doctor Juillerat. No one had thought of that. Hippolyte started off at once, glad to get away.

'Leaving me alone like this!' Clotilde went on. 'I don't know, but there must be all sorts of things to settle. Oh, my poor father!'

'Would you like me to tell the other members of the family?' said Octave. 'I can fetch your brothers. It might be wise.'

She did not answer. Two large tears filled her eyes, while Julie and Clémence tried to undress the old man. But she stopped Octave; her brother Auguste was out, having an appointment that evening, and as for Théophile, it was better that he should not come up, for the mere sight of him would be enough to kill the old man. Then she described how her father had gone personally to Théophile to get rent from him which was overdue, but they had both given him a most brutal reception, especially Valérie, refusing to pay and claiming the sum which he had promised to let them have at the time of their marriage. This seizure was doubtless the result of that scene, for he had come back in a terrible state.

'Madame,' said Clémence, 'he's already quite cold on one side.'

This merely increased Madame Duveyrier's indignation. She was afraid to say anything more in front of the servants. Her husband obviously could not care less about their interests! If she only had some knowledge of the law! She could not keep still, but walked up and down in front of the bed. Octave, distracted by the sight of the catalogue slips, gazed at the vast preparations that covered the table. There, in a large oak box, was a whole series of cardboard tickets, meticulously classified, a whole lifetime of idiotic labour. Just as he was reading on one of those tickets the inscription: 'Isidore Charbotel: Salon 1857, *Atalanta*; Salon 1859, *Androcles and the Lion*; Salon 1861, *Portrait of Monsieur P**** ', Clotilde stepped forward and said resolutely, in an undertone:

'Go and fetch him.'

As he seemed surprised, she, as it were, shrugged off the tale about drawing up a report on the Rue de Provence affair—one of those eternal fictions with which she supplied the outside world. In her emotion, she kept nothing back.

'You know, Rue de la Cerisaie. All our friends know where he is.'

He began to protest. 'I assure you, madam, that . . .'

'Don't defend him,' she went on. 'I'm only too glad; he can stay there if he likes. Oh, good heavens! If it weren't for my poor father!'

Octave nodded. Julie was wiping Monsieur Vabre's eye with the corner of a towel; but the ink was drying, the splash-mark sinking into the skin, stained with dark blotches. Madame Duveyrier advised her not to rub so hard, and then turned back to Octave, who was moving towards the door.

'Not a word to anyone,' she murmured. 'There's no point in upsetting the whole house. Take a cab, knock at the door, and make sure you bring him back with you.'

When Octave had gone she sank on to a chair near the old man's pillow. He was still unconscious; his slow, painful breathing was all that broke the mournful silence of the bedroom. Then, as the doctor did not come, and seeing herself alone with the two terrified maidservants, she burst into tears, sobbing violently in a paroxysm of grief.

Bachelard had invited Monsieur Duveyrier to dinner at the Café Anglais, though one hardly knew why. Perhaps it was for the pleasure of having an eminent judge as his guest, and of showing him that tradespeople knew how to spend their money. He had invited Trublot and Gueulin as well—four men and no women, for women, he felt, didn't know how to enjoy a good dinner. They prevented one from enjoying the truffles, and ruined one's digestion. Bachelard, in fact, was well known all along the boulevards for his sumptuous dinners whenever some customer of his turned up from India or Brazil—dinners at three hundred francs a head, by which he nobly upheld the prestige of French commission agencies. He had an absolute mania for spending money; he insisted on having the most expensive dishes, gastronomical rarities that were at times uneatable: sterlets from the Volga, eels from the Tiber, grouse from Scotland, bustards from Sweden, bears' feet from the Black Forest, bison-humps from America, turnips from Teltow, gourds from Greece. And he insisted on having things that were not in season, such as peaches in December, or partridges in July, and demanded, too, flowers in profusion, silver plate, cut-glass, and such constant waiting-upon that the whole restaurant was driven half-mad. Then there were the wines, for which the cellar had to be ransacked; he always required unknown vintages, nothing being old or rare enough for him, for he was forever dreaming of unique bottles of wine at two louis a glass.

That evening, as it was summertime, a season when everything is in abundance, he had found it quite difficult to run up a bill. The menu, which had been arranged the day before, was, however, outstanding—cream of asparagus soup, with tiny timbales *à la Pompadour*, two *relevés*, trout *à la genevoise*, and Chateaubriand fillet of beef; two entrées, ortolans *à la Lucullus*, and a crayfish salad; then a haunch of venison, with artichokes *à la jardinière*, followed by a chocolate soufflé and assorted fruits. It was simple in its grandeur, and was made even more remarkable by a princely choice of wines—old Madeira with the soup, Château-Filhot '58 with the hors-d'oeuvre, Johannisberger and Pichon-Longueville with the *relevés*, Château-Lafite '48 with the entrées; sparkling Moselle with the roast, and iced Roederer with the dessert. He was most distressed at the loss of a bottle of Johannisberger, a hundred and five years old, which had been sold just three days before to a Turk for ten louis.

'Drink away, sir, drink away!' he kept telling Duveyrier; 'when wine is good it never goes to your head. It's like food, which never does you any harm if it's of the finest quality.'

He was on his best behaviour, posing as a fine gentleman, with a rose in his buttonhole and carefully groomed, refraining from smashing the dishes as was his wont. Trublot and Gueulin ate of everything. The uncle's theory appeared to be the correct one, for Duveyrier, whose digestion was not of the best, drank great quantities of wine and then had another helping of crayfish salad without feeling any ill effects; the red blotches on his face merely turned purple.

At nine o'clock the dinner was still in full swing. The candles, which flared in the breeze from an open window, made the silver plate and the glass sparkle, while amid the wreckage of the feast stood four large baskets filled with exquisite, fast-fading flowers. Besides the two *maîtres d'hôtel*, each guest had a waiter behind his chair, whose special business it was to supply him with wine and bread and change his plates. Despite the cool breeze from the boulevard, it was very warm. A sense of repletion became general, amid the spicy aroma of the dishes and the vanilla-like perfumes of the fine wines.

Then, when coffee had been served, with liqueurs and cigars, and all the waiters had withdrawn, uncle Bachelard, throwing himself back in his chair, heaved a great sigh of satisfaction.

'Ah, that was really good!' he declared.

Trublot and Gueulin, stretching themselves, leant back in their chairs as well.

'I'm absolutely full!' said the one.

'Up to the eyes!' added the other.

Duveyrier, puffing, gave a nod of assent and murmured:

'Oh, those crayfish!'

All four looked at each other and chuckled. Their bellies distended to bursting-point, they slowly, selfishly proceeded to digest, like four worthy bourgeois citizens who had just enjoyed stuffing themselves away from family worries. It had cost a fortune; no one else was there to partake of it with them; no girl was there to take advantage of their relaxed mood; so they were able to unbutton

and, as it were, lay their paunches on the table. With half-closed
eyes, they at first refrained from speaking, each absorbed in his own
personal bliss. Then, feeling completely free, and glad that no
women were there, they placed their elbows on the table, put their
red faces close together and talked endlessly about women.

'I'm thoroughly disillusioned!' declared uncle Bachelard. 'It's
much better to be virtuous, after all.' Duveyrier nodded in approval.
'So I've turned my back on that sort of thing. At one time I used to
do nothing else, I must confess. You know, in the Rue Godot-de-
Mauroy I know them all—blondes, brunettes, redheads. Some of
them are pretty shapely, but not many. Then there are those dirty
holes in Montmartre—furnished lodgings, you know; and those
filthy alleyways in my part of the world, where you can pick up the
most amazing creatures, very ugly, and with extraordinary bodies.'

'Tarts!' broke in Trublot, in his contemptuous way. 'What a waste
of time! I never touch them—you never get your money's worth.'

This smutty talk tickled Duveyrier's fancy. He drank his kummel
in sips, his stiff features twitching now and again with little sensual
thrills.

'For my part,' he said, 'I can't stand vice; it disgusts me. To love a
woman, you must respect her, mustn't you? I simply couldn't have
anything to do with one of those unfortunate creatures, unless, of
course, she showed some repentance and one was rescuing her from
her terrible life with a view to making an honest woman of her. Love
could not have a nobler mission than that. A respectable mistress,
you understand! In that case I'm not sure I could resist.'

'But I've had no end of respectable mistresses,' cried Bachelard.
'They're even worse than the others, and such sluts too! Bitches
that, behind your back, lead a life fit to give you every sort of disease!
Take the last one I had—a very respectable-looking little lady I met
at a church door. I set her up with a milliner's shop at Ternes, just to
give her a position, you know. She never had a single customer
though. And—would you believe it?—she had the whole street
sleeping with her!'

Gueulin chuckled, his red hair looking even more spiky than
usual, while the heat of the candles brought beads of perspiration to
his brow. Sucking his cigar, he mumbled:

'And the other one, the tall one from Passy, who had a sweetmeat-
shop? And the other one who had a room over there, with her outfits

for orphans? And the captain's widow—you remember, the one who liked to show off the scar on her belly from a sword-cut. All of them, every one, made a fool of you, uncle! I can tell you that now, can't I? You know, one evening I had to fend her off, the one with the sword-mark on her belly. She wanted to . . . but I wasn't such a fool! There's no telling where women like that might lead you.'

Bachelard seemed annoyed. He recovered his good humour however and, screwing up his great eyelids and winking hideously, he said:

'My boy, you can have 'em all if you like. I've got something much better.'

And he refused to explain himself, delighted to have aroused the others' curiosity. Yet he was dying to be indiscreet, to let them guess what his treasure was.

'A young girl,' he said at last; 'but the real thing, I can assure you!'

'Impossible!' cried Trublot. 'You can't find that sort of thing any more.'

'Of good family?' asked Duveyrier.

'Most respectable as regards family,' affirmed Bachelard. 'Imagine something stupidly chaste . . . Purely by chance . . . I just had her like that. I'm absolutely sure she thinks nothing has happened!'

Gueulin listened in astonishment. Then, with a sceptical gesture, he muttered:

'Ah, yes! I know.'

'What do you mean, you know!' said Bachelard angrily. 'You know nothing at all, my boy; nor does any one else. She belongs to yours truly; she isn't to be looked at or touched—she's private property!'

Then, turning to Duveyrier, he said:

'You, sir, being kind-hearted, can understand my feelings. It's quite touching to go and see her; it almost makes me feel young again. Anyhow, there I've got a quiet little nook where I can rest after all that whoring. And if you knew how sweet and clean she is, such soft white skin, and a nice little figure—not undeveloped at all, but round and firm as a peach!'

The judge's red blotches glowed again as the blood rushed to his face. Trublot and Gueulin looked at Bachelard, feeling almost like hitting him as he sat there, with his row of glittering false teeth and saliva dribbling down from both sides of his mouth. What! this wreck of an uncle, this worn-out debauchee, whose big flaming nose alone kept its place between his blubbery cheeks, had got stored up somewhere some flower of innocence, some soft budding body, whose young flesh he was tainting with his filthy middle-aged vices which he concealed under his air of drunken benevolence!

Meanwhile, becoming quite sentimental, he carried on talking as he licked the edge of his liqueur glass:

'After all, my one dream is to make the child happy! But, you know, her belly has begun to swell; I'll soon be a papa! I swear that if I could find some steady young chap, I'd give her to him—in marriage, of course.'

'That would make two people happy,' murmured Duveyrier, becoming sentimental too.

The atmosphere in the little room had become stifling. A glass of chartreuse had been upset, making the tablecloth, blackened by cigar-ash, very sticky. These gentlemen were clearly in need of some fresh air.

'Would you like to have a look at her?' Bachelard suddenly asked, rising from his seat.

They looked at each other. Oh, yes! they would like to very much, if it gave him pleasure; and in their feigned indifference there lurked a sort of epicurean satisfaction at the idea of finishing their dessert by inspecting the old fellow's little girl. Duveyrier merely observed that Clarisse was expecting them. Bachelard, pale and agitated since he had made the proposal, declared that they would not even stop to sit down. They would merely have a look at her and then go off at once. They left the table and stood outside for a few minutes on the boulevard, while their host paid the bill.

When he reappeared, Gueulin pretended not to know where the young lady in question resided.

'So let's go, uncle! Which way is it?'

Bachelard became quite grave, tortured by the vanity that drove him to exhibit Fifi, and the dread that she might thus be stolen from him. He cast an anxious glance to left and right, and then blurted out:

'Well, no, we won't go after all.'

And he obstinately refused, untouched by Trublot's teasing, not even deigning to invent an excuse for his sudden change of mind. They were thus obliged to go to Clarisse's, and since it was a lovely evening they decided to walk, as it would help their digestion. So they set off along the Rue de Richelieu, fairly steady on their legs, but so full that the pavement hardly seemed wide enough.

Gueulin and Trublot went in front. Behind them came Bachelard and Duveyrier, deeply involved in an exchange of fraternal confidences. The former earnestly assured the latter that it was not he whom he distrusted; he would have shown her to him, for he knew how discreet he was; but it was always unwise to expect too much from young people, was it not? Duveyrier agreed with him, admitting that he had had similar fears with regard to Clarisse. At first he had kept all his friends away, but then it had pleased him to invite them and turn the place into a charming little retreat for himself after she had given him singular proofs of her fidelity. Oh, she was an intelligent woman, very discreet, good-hearted, and with very healthy ideas! Of course, there were certain little things in her past with which she could be reproached, things due to lack of guidance. Since loving him, however, she had turned to the path of honour. The judge talked on in this vein all along the Rue de Rivoli, while Bachelard, annoyed at not being able to put in another word or two about his own little girl, only just managed not to inform Duveyrier that his wonderful Clarisse slept with everybody.

'Yes, yes, I'm sure!' he murmured. 'Really, there's nothing like virtue.'

The house in the Rue de la Cerisaie seemed fast asleep amid the emptiness and silence of the street. Duveyrier was surprised at not seeing any lights in the third-floor windows. Trublot gravely observed that no doubt Clarisse had gone to bed to wait for them. Or perhaps, Gueulin added, she was playing a game of bezique in the kitchen with her maid. They knocked. The gas on the stairs was burning with the straight, motionless flame of a lamp in some chapel. Not a sound, not a whisper. But as the four men were about to mount the stairs, the concierge rushed out of his room, saying:

'Sir, sir, the key!'

Duveyrier stopped short on the first step.

'Is madame not at home, then?' he asked.

'No, sir. Wait a moment; you'll need to take a candle.'

As he handed him the candlestick, the concierge, despite the look of exaggerated respect on his pallid face, could not repress a crude chuckle. Neither the uncle nor the two young men said a word. So, in hunched silence, they filed up the stairs, the endless sound of their footsteps echoing along the gloomy corridors. Duveyrier, trying to understand, led the way, lifting his feet mechanically like a sleepwalker, while the candle he held in his trembling hand threw the four shadows of this weird group on the wall, like a procession of broken puppets.

On the third floor he suddenly grew faint and was quite unable to find the keyhole. So Trublot opened the door for him. The key, as it turned in the lock, made a hollow, reverberating sound, as if beneath the vaulted roof of a cathedral.

'I say!' he muttered, 'it doesn't seem as if anybody lives here!'

'Sounds pretty empty,' said Bachelard.

'Like a family vault,' added Gueulin.

They entered. Duveyrier went first, holding the candle aloft.

The anteroom was empty; even the hat-pegs had vanished. The drawing-room was empty; so, too, was the parlour; not a single piece of furniture, not a curtain at any of the windows; not even a curtain-rail. Petrified, Duveyrier glanced down at his feet and then looked up at the ceiling, and then went round examining the walls as if to discover the hole through which everything had disappeared.

'A clean sweep!' said Trublot, despite himself.

'Perhaps the place is going to be done up,' remarked Gueulin gravely. 'Let's look in the bedroom, the furniture might have been moved in there.'

But the bedroom was equally bare, hideous and stark in its nudity, like plaster walls from which the paper has been stripped. Where the bed had stood, the iron supports of the canopy, also removed, had left gaping holes; one of the windows was half open, and the air from the street gave the room the damp, stale smell of a public square.

'My God! My God!' stammered Duveyrier, finally breaking into tears, overcome by the sight of the place where the mattresses had rubbed the paper off the wall.

Bachelard became quite paternal, as he repeated:

'Courage, sir! The same thing happened to me, and I'm still alive. Damn it all, your honour is safe!'

Duveyrier shook his head and moved on to the dressing-room, and then to the kitchen. Yet more disastrous revelations! The oilcloth in the dressing-room had been removed, as well as all the hooks in the kitchen.

'No, really, that's too much!' said Gueulin. 'How awful! She might have left the hooks!'

Tired out by the dinner and the walk, Trublot began to find this desolation far from amusing. But Duveyrier, still clutching his candle, walked round and round, as if determined to sink into the uttermost depths of his abandonment. The others were forced to follow him. He went once more through every room, wishing to reinspect drawing-room, parlour, and bedroom, looking carefully into each corner, light in hand, while his companions trailed behind him, their huge shadows dancing fantastically on the barren walls. In this melancholy atmosphere their footsteps echoed grimly on the wooden floorboards, and, to put the finishing touch to the general desolation, the whole apartment was scrupulously clean, without a single scrap of paper or straw lying about, as spotless as a well-scrubbed bowl, for the concierge had been cruel enough to sweep the whole place thoroughly.

'I can't stand any more of this,' exclaimed Trublot at last, as they were inspecting the drawing-room for the third time. 'I'd give ten sous for a chair to sit in—I really would!'

All four of them stood still.

'When did you see her last?' asked Bachelard.

'Yesterday, sir!' exclaimed Duveyrier.

Gueulin shook his head. Well, it hadn't taken her long; she'd made a neat job of it. Trublot suddenly uttered a cry. He had just spotted on the mantelpiece a dirty collar and a damaged cigar.

'You mustn't complain,' he said, laughing, 'she's left you a keepsake. That's something.'

Duveyrier, suddenly touched, looked at the collar. Then he murmured:

'Twenty-five thousand francs' worth of furniture; there was twenty-five thousand francs' worth! Oh, well, it's not that that I regret—no, not that!'

'Won't you have the cigar?' asked Trublot, interrupting. 'I will, then, if you don't mind. It's got a hole in it, but I can stick some cigarette-paper round it.'

He lit it with the candle Duveyrier was still holding; then, sliding into a sitting posture against the wall, he said:

'I've just got to sit on the floor for a bit; I'm ready to drop!'

'Well,' asked Duveyrier, 'can any of you tell me where she might have gone?'

Bachelard and Gueulin looked at each other. It was a delicate matter. However, the uncle manfully decided to tell the poor fellow everything—all about Clarisse's goings-on, her endless affairs, and the lovers that at every one of their parties she used to pick up behind his back. No doubt she had gone off with her latest, that big fellow, Payan the mason, whom his townsfolk in the South wanted to turn into an artist. Duveyrier listened to these abominable revelations with a look of horror on his face. At last he exclaimed in despair:

'There's no honesty left in this world!'

Then, opening his heart, he told them everything he had done for her. He spoke of his kind-heartedness, accused her of having shaken his belief in all that was best in human life, ingenuously hiding beneath these sentimental protestations all the disorder of his carnal appetites. Clarisse had become a necessity to him. But he would find her again, just to make her blush at her treachery, so he said, and to see if her heart was devoid of all noble feeling.

'Don't bother!' cried Bachelard, secretly delighted at the judge's misfortune; 'she'll only make a fool of you again. There's nothing like virtue, you know. Get yourself some little girl who wouldn't dream of playing tricks, and innocent as a newborn child; then there's no danger, you can sleep in peace.'

Trublot, meanwhile, went on smoking with his back against the wall and his legs stretched out, gravely taking his ease. The others had forgotten him.

'If you really want, I can get the address for you,' he said. 'I know the maid.'

Duveyrier turned round, astonished at hearing this voice that seemed to come out of the floor, and when he saw Trublot smoking all that remained of Clarisse, blowing great clouds of smoke in which he fancied he saw his twenty-five thousand francs' worth of furniture evaporating, he cried angrily:

'No; she's unworthy of me! She must beg my forgiveness on her knees!'

'Hullo! here she is, coming back!' said Gueulin, listening.

Someone, indeed, was walking in the hall; and a voice cried: 'Hullo, what's going on? Is everybody dead?' And then Octave appeared. The empty rooms and open doors astonished him. But his amazement increased when he saw the four men, in the middle of the bare drawing-room, one on the floor and the other three standing up, and lighted only by a single dim candle which the magistrate was holding like a church taper. A few words sufficed to explain to him what had occurred.

'Impossible!' he exclaimed.

'Didn't they tell you anything downstairs?' asked Gueulin.

'No, nothing at all; the concierge just watched me come upstairs. So she's gone, has she? I'm not surprised. She had such funny eyes and hair!'

He asked for details, and stood talking for a little while, forgetting the sad news of which he was the bearer. Then suddenly he turned towards Duveyrier.

'By the way, your wife sent me to fetch you. Your father-in-law's dying.'

'Oh, is he?' said Duveyrier simply.

'What, old Vabre?' muttered Bachelard. 'I'm not surprised.'

'Well, when you get to the end of the line!' remarked Gueulin philosophically.

'Yes, it's best to kick the bucket,' added Trublot, busy sticking another cigarette-paper round his cigar.

The four gentlemen decided at length to quit the deserted apartment. Octave kept saying that he had given his word of honour that he would bring Duveyrier back with him at once, no matter what state he was in. The latter carefully closed the door, as if he were leaving behind all his dead affections; but downstairs he was suddenly overcome with shame, and Trublot had to return the key to the concierge. Then, in the street, there was a silent exchange of vigorous handshakes; and, as soon as Duveyrier and Octave had driven off in a cab, Bachelard said to Gueulin and to Trublot, as they stood there in the deserted street:

'Damn it all! I must show her to you!'

He had been growing impatient, greatly excited at the despair of that idiot Duveyrier, and bursting with pleasure at his own happiness, due, so he thought, to his own deep cunning. He could no longer contain his joy.

'You know uncle,' said Gueulin, 'if you're only going to take us as far as the door again and then send us away . . .'

'No, damn it all! You shall see her! I'd like you to. It's nearly midnight, but never mind; she can get up if she's gone to bed. You know, she's the daughter of a captain—Captain Menu—and she's got a most respectable aunt, born at Villeneuve, near Lille. You can get references at Mardiennes Brothers', in the Rue Saint-Sulpice. Ah, damn it all! It'll do us good! You'll see what virtue is like!'

He took their arms, Gueulin on the right and Trublot on the left, as he hurried along in search of a cab so as to get there quicker.

Meanwhile, as they drove along Octave briefly described Monsieur Vabre's seizure to his companion, without concealing the fact that Madame Duveyrier knew the address in the Rue de la Cerisaie. After a while the magistrate asked in a doleful voice:

'Do you think she'll forgive me?'

Octave said nothing. The cab rolled along in the darkness, lit up every now and then by a ray from a gas-lamp. Just as they were reaching their destination Duveyrier, consumed with anguish, asked another question.

'The best thing I can do at present is to make it up with my wife; don't you think so?'

'Perhaps that would be wise,' said Octave, obliged to make some sort of reply.

Then Duveyrier felt that he ought to show regret for his father-in-law. A man of great intelligence, he said, with an incredible capacity for work. However, very likely they would be able to pull him through. In the Rue de Choiseul they found the street-door open and a small crowd gathered in front of Monsieur Gourd's lodge. Julie, on her way to the chemist's, was denouncing the middle classes who let one another die when ill; it was only working-folk, she said, who took each other soup or warm towels when there was sickness. The old fellow might have swallowed his tongue twenty times over, during the two hours he had spent agonizing on his bed, without his children once taking the trouble to shove a bit of sugar into his mouth. A hard-hearted lot, said Monsieur Gourd—folk that could not be stirred for anything, and who would have thought themselves disgraced if they had had to give their father an enema. Hippolyte, to cap everything, told them about madame upstairs, and how silly she looked not knowing what to do with herself, while the servants ran about doing all they could. But they all fell silent as soon as they saw Duveyrier.

'Well?' he enquired.

'The doctor's just putting some mustard-poultices on him,' said Hippolyte. 'Oh, I had such a job to find him!'

Upstairs, in the drawing-room, Madame Duveyrier came forward to meet them. She had been crying a great deal; her eyes shone beneath their reddened lids. The judge, greatly embarrassed, held out his arms and embraced her, murmuring:

'My poor Clotilde!'

Surprised at this unusual display of affection, she shrank back. Octave had kept behind; but he heard the husband say in a low voice:

'Forgive me! Let's forget our quarrels on this sad occasion. You see, I've come back to you for good. Oh, I've been well punished!'

She made no reply, but disengaged herself. Then, resuming before Octave her attitude of a woman who wishes to ignore everything, she said:

'I shouldn't have bothered you, darling: I know how urgent that report about the Rue de Provence scandal is. But I was all alone, and I felt you should come. My poor father's dying. Go in and see him; the doctor's there.'

When Duveyrier had gone into the next room she walked up to Octave who, so as to appear not to be listening, was standing by the piano. It was still open, and the air from *Zémire et Azor* lay there as they had left it on the desk. He pretended to be studying it. The soft light from the lamp still illuminated only a part of the large room.

Madame Duveyrier looked at the young man for a moment without speaking, tormented by an anxiety which led her to throw off her usual reserve.

'Was he there?' she asked briefly.

'Yes, madam.'

'Then, what is it? What's the matter with him?'

'That person has left him, madam, taking all the furniture with her. I found him in the empty apartment with only a candle!'

Clotilde made a gesture of despair. She understood. A look of disgust and discouragement appeared on her handsome face. It was not enough that she had lost her father, it seemed that this misfortune was also to serve as a pretext for a reconciliation with her husband! She knew him only too well; he would always be pestering her, now that there was nothing elsewhere to protect her, and, with her respect for all duties, she trembled at the thought that she could not refuse to submit to the abominable task. For a moment she looked at the piano. Great tears filled her eyes as she said simply:

'Thank you, sir.'

Then, in their turn, they both went into Monsieur Vabre's bedroom. Duveyrier, looking very pale, was listening to Doctor Juillerat who was explaining something in a low voice. It was a very bad attack of apoplexy. The patient might possibly linger until the next day, but there was no hope whatever. Clotilde entered just at that moment; she overheard this last statement and sank down into a chair, wiping her eyes with her tear-drenched handkerchief, which she had nervously twisted into a ball. However, she had strength enough to ask the doctor if her poor father would regain consciousness. The doctor had his doubts; and, as if he had divined the motive for the question, he expressed his hope that Monsieur Vabre had long since put his affairs in order. Duveyrier, whose mental faculties had apparently remained behind in the Rue de la Cerisaie, now seemed to wake up. He looked at his wife and then observed that Monsieur Vabre never confided in anyone; so he knew nothing, except that certain promises had been made in favour of their son Gustave, whom his grandfather often spoke of helping as a reward for their having taken him to live with them. At any rate, if there was a will it would be found.

'Does the family know what's happened?' asked Doctor Juillerat.

'No,' murmured Clotilde. 'It was so sudden. My first thought was to send Monsieur Mouret for my husband.'

Duveyrier gave her another look; now they understood each other. Slowly approaching the bed, he examined Monsieur Vabre, straight and stiff as a corpse, his rigid features covered in yellow blotches. One o'clock struck. The doctor spoke of leaving, as he had tried all the usual remedies and could do nothing more. He would call again early in the morning. He was going off with Octave when Madame Duveyrier called the latter back.

'Let's wait until tomorrow,' she said. 'You can make some excuse to send Berthe to me, I'll call Valérie, and they can break the news to my brothers. Poor things! Let them sleep in peace tonight! There's no need for any more of us to stay awake.'

She and her husband remained alone with the old man, whose death-rattle echoed through the room.

WHEN Octave went downstairs the next morning at eight o'clock, he was surprised to find that the whole building knew about Monsieur Vabre's seizure of the previous night and of the landlord's desperate condition. No one, however, was concerned about the patient; their sole interest was knowing what he was going to leave behind.

In their little dining-room the Pichons sat before their cups of chocolate. Jules called Octave in.

'I say! What a mess there'll be if he dies like that! There'll be some fun and games. Do you know if he made a will?'

Octave, without answering, asked them how they had heard the news. Marie had brought it back from the baker's; in fact it had spread from floor to floor, even to the end of the street, through the servants.

Then, after slapping Lilitte for putting her fingers in the chocolate, Marie said:

'And all that money too! If he had only thought of leaving us as many sous as there are five-franc pieces! Not much chance of that, though.'

And, as Octave was going, she added:

'I've finished your books, Monsieur Mouret. Do come and fetch them, won't you?'

He hurried downstairs, remembering that he had promised Madame Duveyrier that he would send Berthe to her before there was any gossip, when on the third floor he bumped into Campardon.

'Well,' said the latter, 'so your employer is coming into a fortune. I hear the old boy has got nearly six hundred thousand francs, besides this place. You see, he spent nothing at the Duveyriers', and he had a good bit left out of his Versailles property, without counting the twenty-odd thousand francs from the rents here. It's a big cake when there are only three to share it.'

Still chatting away, he walked downstairs behind Octave. On the second floor they met Madame Juzeur, who had come down to see what her little servant girl, Louise, could be doing all morning, taking over an hour to fetch four sous' worth of milk. She had no difficulty in joining in the conversation, being very well informed.

'Nobody seems to know how he arranged his affairs,' she said in her quiet way. 'There may be some bother about it.'

'Ah, well,' said the architect, gaily, 'I wouldn't mind being in their shoes. It shouldn't take long. Divide it all into three equal parts; each takes his share, and it's all done.'

Madame Juzeur leant over the banisters, and then looked up to make sure that no one was on the stairs. Then, lowering her voice, she said:

'And what if they don't find what they expect? There are rumours . . .'

Campardon opened his eyes wide. Then he shrugged his shoulders. Bah! That was all nonsense. Old Vabre was a miser, who hid his savings in worsted stockings. And so saying he went off, having an appointment at Saint-Roch with Father Mauduit.

'My wife was complaining about you,' he said to Octave, looking back after going down three steps. 'Call in and have a chat with her some time.'

Madame Juzeur kept the young man talking for a moment.

'And me, too! How you neglect me! I thought you liked me a little bit. When you come, I'll let you taste a liqueur from the West Indies—something quite delicious!'

He promised to call in to see her, and then hurried down into the hall. Before reaching the little shop-door under the arch he had to pass a whole group of servants. They were engaged in distributing the dying man's fortune. There was so much for Madame Clotilde, so much for Monsieur Auguste, and so much for Monsieur Théophile. Clémence stated the figures boldly; she knew well enough what they were for she had them from Hippolyte, who had seen the money in a drawer. Julie, however, disputed them. Lisa told how her first master, an old gentleman, had done her out of her wages by dying without even leaving her his dirty linen. Adèle, meanwhile, her arms dangling and mouth agape, listened to these tales of inheritance until she imagined huge piles of five-franc pieces toppling over into her lap. And in the street Monsieur Gourd, pompous as ever, was talking to the stationer over the way. For him the landlord was already dead.

'What I'm interested in', he said, 'is who'll get the house. They'll divide everything—well and good! But what about the house? They can't cut that up into three.'

Octave finally arrived at the shop. The first person he saw, sitting at the cashier's desk, was Madame Josserand, laced, combed, and carefully done up, in full battle dress. Next to her was Berthe, who had no doubt come down in a hurry. She looked very excited, and charming in her loosely fitting dressing-gown. But on seeing him they stopped talking. The mother gave him a terrible look.

'So, sir,' she said, 'this is how you show your attachment to the firm! You take part in the conspiracies of my daughter's enemies!'

He tried to defend himself, to explain the facts of the case. But she would not let him speak, accusing him of having spent the night with the Duveyriers, looking for the will so as to insert in it certain clauses. When he laughingly asked what possible interest he could have had in doing such a thing, she rejoined:

'Your own interest—your own interest! In short, sir, you should have come and told us, since God willed it that you should be a witness of the sad event. To think that, but for me, my daughter would still have been ignorant of the matter! Yes, they would have robbed her if I hadn't rushed downstairs the moment I heard the news. Eh, what? Your interest; yes, your interest, sir! Who knows? Although Madame Duveyrier has lost her looks, there are some people, not over-particular, who might find her all right!'

'Oh, mamma!' said Berthe, 'Clotilde, who is so virtuous!'

Madame Josserand shrugged her shoulders in pity. 'Pooh! you know very well that people will do anything for money!'

Octave was obliged to tell them all the particulars of the seizure. They exchanged glances. Obviously, to use the mother's phrase, there had been manoeuvres. It was really too considerate of Clotilde to wish to spare her family any distress! However, they let the young man go about his work, though they still had their doubts as to his conduct in the matter. And they continued their animated discussion.

'Who will pay the fifty thousand francs agreed in the contract?' asked Madame Josserand. 'Once he's buried, we won't see a thing.'

'Oh, the fifty thousand francs!' murmured Berthe, embarrassed. 'You know that he only agreed, as you did, to pay ten thousand francs every six months. The time isn't up yet; we'd better wait.'

'Wait? Oh, yes! Wait until he comes to life again and brings them to you personally, I suppose? You great ninny, you want to be robbed, do you? No, no! You must claim them at once from the estate. As for us, we're still alive, thank God, and we don't know whether we'll pay or not; but he's dead, and so he's got to pay.'

She made her daughter swear not to give in, for she herself was not going to be made a fool of by anybody. While working herself slowly into a frenzy, every now and again she strained her ears in an attempt to hear what was going on overhead on the first floor, at the Duveyriers'. The old man's bedroom was just above her. As soon as she told him what had happened, Auguste had gone upstairs to his father. But that did not pacify her; she wanted to be there herself, and imagined all sorts of intricate schemes.

'You go up, too!' she cried at last, in a heartfelt outburst. 'Auguste is too weak; I'm sure they'll trick him again.'

So Berthe went upstairs. Octave, who was arranging the window-display, had listened to what they had said. When he saw that he was alone with Madame Josserand and that she was moving towards the door, he asked her whether it would not be the proper thing to close the shop, hoping to get a day's holiday.

'Whatever for?' she asked. 'Wait until he's dead. It's not worth losing a day's business.'

Then, as he was folding a remnant of crimson silk, she added, in order to soften the harshness of her words:

'But I think, perhaps, you'd better not put anything red in the window.'

On the first floor Berthe found Auguste with his father. The room had not changed since the evening before: it was still damp, silent, and filled with the same noise of long, difficult breathing. The old man lay on the bed completely rigid, having lost all feeling and movement. The oak box, full of tickets, still lay on the table; none of the furniture seemed to have been moved, nor a drawer to have been opened. The Duveyriers looked more exhausted, however, worn out by a sleepless night; their eyelids twitched nervously; something was clearly troubling them. As early as seven o'clock they had sent Hippolyte to fetch their son Gustave from the Lycée Bonaparte, and the lad, a thin, precocious boy of sixteen, was there, bewildered by this unexpected holiday which was to be spent at the bedside of a dying man.

'Oh, my dear, what a terrible blow!' said Clotilde, as she went up to embrace Berthe.

'Why didn't you tell us?' replied the latter, with her mother's sour pout. 'We were there to help you to bear it.'

Auguste, with a look, begged her to be silent. The moment for quarrelling had not yet come. They could afford to wait. Doctor Juillerat, who had already been once, was to pay a second visit, but he could still give no hope: the patient would not live out the day. Auguste was explaining this to his wife when Théophile and Valérie arrived. Clotilde at once came forward, saying again, as she embraced Valérie:

'What a terrible blow, my dear!'

But Théophile could not contain his anger.

'So now', he said, without even lowering his voice, 'it seems that, when one's father is dying, one has to hear of it through the coal-merchant! I suppose you needed time to go through his pockets!'

Duveyrier stood up indignantly. But Clotilde motioned him aside while, speaking in a low voice, she answered her brother.

'You awful man! Isn't even our father's death-agony sacred to you? Look at him; look at your handiwork; it's you, yes! you who brought on the attack by refusing to pay the rent you were owing.'

Valérie burst out laughing.

'Really now, you can't be serious!' she said.

'What? Not serious?' rejoined Clotilde contemptuously. 'You know how much he liked collecting his rents. If you'd wanted to kill him you couldn't have done it better.'

Tempers ran high as they accused each other of wanting to get hold of the inheritance; Auguste, sullen and impassive as ever, called them to order.

'That's enough! There's plenty of time for that. It's not decent at a time like this!'

The others, admitting the justice of this remark, stationed themselves round the bed. There was a deep silence, broken only by the death-rattle. Berthe and Auguste stood at the foot of the bed; Valérie and Théophile, having come in last, had been obliged to remain at a distance, near the table; Clotilde sat at the head of the bed, with her husband behind her, while close up to the edge of the mattresses she had pushed her son Gustave, whom the old man adored. They now all looked at each other without uttering a word. But their shining eyes and tight lips spoke of hidden thoughts, and of all the anxiety and rancour which filled the minds of these would-be inheritors as they sat there, pale-faced and heavy-eyed. The two young couples were particularly furious at the sight of the schoolboy close to the bed, for, obviously, the Duveyriers were counting on Gustave's presence to influence his grandfather in their favour if he regained consciousness.

This manoeuvre, however, was proof that no will existed; and the Vabres furtively glanced at the old iron safe which their father had brought from Versailles and had had fixed in a corner of his room. He had a mania for keeping all kinds of things in it. No doubt the Duveyriers had wasted no time in ransacking this safe during the night. Théophile thought of setting a trap for them, to make them speak.

'I say,' he whispered at last in the judge's ear, 'suppose we send for the notary? Papa may want to make some alteration to his will.'

At first Duveyrier did not hear. As he found the waiting extremely tedious, all through the night his thoughts had gone back to Clarisse. Decidedly the wisest plan would be to make it up with his wife. And yet the other woman was so funny when she threw her chemise over her head like a little street urchin, and, as he gazed dreamily at the dying man, it was she he saw in his mind's eye, and he would have given anything just to enjoy her again, even if it were but once. Théophile had to repeat his question.

'I asked Monsieur Renaudin,' replied the judge, in bewilderment. 'There's no will.'

'Not even here?'

'Neither here nor at the notary's.'

Théophile looked at Auguste. It was clear, wasn't it? The Duveyriers must have gone through the drawers. Clotilde saw the look, and felt annoyed with her husband. What was the matter with him? Had grief robbed him of his senses? She added:

'Papa has no doubt done things properly. Heaven knows, we'll hear about it all very soon!'

She began to weep. At the sight of her grief, Valérie and Berthe started sobbing gently too. Théophile went back on tiptoe to his chair. He had found out what he wanted to know. Certainly, if his father regained consciousness he would not allow the Duveyriers to use their brat of a son to turn things to their advantage. But as he sat down he saw his brother Auguste wiping his eyes, and that affected him so much that he became tearful in his turn. The idea of death took hold of him; perhaps he would die in a similar manner; it was awful. Thus the whole family dissolved in tears. Gustave was the only one who could not weep. He was alarmed by it all and looked at the floor, breathing in time with the dying man's death-rattle in order to have something to do, just as in their gymnastic lessons he and his fellow-pupils were made to keep step.

Meanwhile the hours slipped past. At eleven o'clock they were distracted when Doctor Juillerat again appeared. The patient was sinking; it was now doubtful whether he would be able to recognize his children before he died. Then the sobbing started again, when Clémence showed in Father Mauduit. Clotilde, rising to meet him, was the first to receive his commiserations. He seemed deeply affected by this family misfortune, and gave to each a word of encouragement. Then, with much tact, he spoke of the rites of religion, hinting that this soul should not be allowed to pass away without the succour of the Church.

'I thought of that,' murmured Clotilde.

But Théophile raised objections. Their father was not at all religious; at one time he had held very advanced views, for he read Voltaire. It would be better to do nothing, as they could not consult him. In the heat of the argument he even remarked:

'It's as if you were to administer the sacrament to a piece of furniture.'

The three women compelled him to stop. They were all overcome by emotion, declared that the priest was right, and made excuses for not having sent for him because of the confusion created by this sad event. Had Monsieur Vabre been able to speak he would certainly have consented, for he always liked to oblige other people. Moreover, the entire responsibility was theirs.

'If only for the neighbours,' said Clotilde, 'it ought to be done.'

'Of course,' said Father Mauduit, who strongly approved of this remark. 'A man in your father's position should set a good example.'

Auguste had no opinion. But Duveyrier, roused from his musings about Clarisse, whose method of putting on her stockings with one leg in the air was just occupying his thoughts, strongly urged the administration of the sacraments. They were absolutely necessary, and no member of his family should die without them. Doctor Juillerat, who had discreetly stood aside, not even showing his freethinker's disdain, then went up to the priest and whispered familiarly, as to a colleague whom he often met on occasions of this kind:

'Be quick; there's no time to lose.'

The priest hurried away, saying that he would bring the sacrament and the extreme unction so as to be prepared for any emergency. Then Théophile, obstinate as ever, muttered:

'Oh, yes; so now they force the dying to take the sacrament in spite of themselves!'

Suddenly they were all greatly startled. On going back to her place Clotilde had found the dying man with his eyes wide open. She could not suppress a faint cry. They all rushed to the bedside, and the old man's gaze slowly wandered from one to the other, his head remaining motionless. Doctor Juillerat, looking very surprised, bent over his patient to watch this final crisis.

'Father, it's us. Can you recognize us?' asked Clotilde.

Monsieur Vabre stared at her; then his lips moved, but they uttered no sound. They all pushed each other aside in their eagerness to catch his last word. Valérie, at the rear, was obliged to stand on tiptoe, and said bitterly:

'You're suffocating him. Stand back! If he wanted anything no one would know what it was.'

So the others had to stand back. Monsieur Vabre's eyes were, indeed, wandering round the room.

'He wants something, that's certain,' murmured Berthe.

'Here's Gustave,' said Clotilde. 'You can see him, can't you? He's come from school to kiss you. Kiss your grandfather, my boy.'

As the lad recoiled in dismay she pushed him forward, waiting for a smile to light up the dying man's distorted features. But Auguste, following the direction of his eyes, declared that he was looking at the table. No doubt he wanted to write. This caused great excitement, and everyone hastened to bring the table close to the bedside, and to fetch some paper, an ink-stand, and a pen. Then they raised him, propping him up with three pillows. The doctor authorized all this by a simple blink of the eyes.

'Give him the pen,' said Clotilde, trembling, still holding Gustave out towards him.

Then there was a solemn silence. Crowding round the bed, the family waited anxiously. Monsieur Vabre, who did not seem to recognize anyone, had let the pen slip through his fingers. For a moment his eyes wandered across the table, on which there was the oak box full of tickets. Then, sliding off the pillows, he fell forward like a bundle of rags and, stretching out his arm in a supreme effort, he thrust his hand into the box and began dabbling about in the tickets like a baby delighted at being able to play with something dirty. He beamed, and tried to speak, but could only stammer out one syllable over and over again, one of those monosyllabic cries into which babies in swaddling-clothes can put a whole host of feelings.

'Ga-ga-ga-ga-'

It was to his life's work, his great statistical study, that he was saying goodbye. Suddenly his head rolled forward. He was dead.

'I feared as much,' murmured the doctor, who, seeing the general bewilderment, carefully straightened the dead man's limbs and closed his eyes.

Was it possible? Auguste had taken away the table, and all remained chilled and mute. Soon they broke into sobs. Well, since all hope of recovery was gone, they would soon be engaged in sharing out the inheritance. Clotilde, after hastily sending Gustave away to spare him so harrowing a spectacle, wept uncontrollably, leaning her head on Berthe's shoulder. Berthe and Valérie were also sobbing. Théophile and Auguste, at the window, kept rubbing their eyes. But Duveyrier's grief seemed the most inconsolable of all, as he stifled loud sobs with his handkerchief. No, he really could not live without Clarisse; he would rather die at once, like Vabre; and the loss of his mistress, coming in the midst of all this mourning, gave immense bitterness to his grief.

'Madam,' announced Clémence, 'the holy sacraments.'

Father Mauduit appeared on the threshold. Behind his back appeared the inquisitive face of a choirboy. Seeing them all sobbing, the priest glanced questioningly at the doctor, who held out his arms as if to say that it was not his fault. Then, after mumbling a few prayers, the priest withdrew in embarrassment, taking the sacraments with him.

'That's a bad sign,' said Clémence to the other servants, who were standing in a group by the door of the anteroom. 'The sacraments are not to be brought for nothing. You'll see if they're not back in the house within a year!'

Monsieur Vabre's funeral did not take place for two days. All the same, on the circulars announcing his death Duveyrier had inserted the words, 'Provided with the Holy Sacraments of the Church'. As the shop was closed, Octave found himself at liberty. He was delighted at getting such a holiday, since for a long while he had wanted to rearrange his room, move the furniture, and put his books together in a little bookcase he had picked up second-hand. He had risen earlier than usual, and had just finished his alterations, at about eight o'clock on the morning of the funeral, when Marie knocked at the door. She had brought back his books.

'Since you won't come and fetch them,' she said, 'I'm returning them myself.'

But, blushing, she refused to come in, shocked at the idea of being in a young man's room. Their intimacy, however, had completely ceased in the most natural manner possible, as he had stopped running after her. But she was as affectionate as ever, always greeting him with a smile when they met.

Octave was in high spirits that morning, and began to tease her.

'So Jules won't let you come to my room?' he kept saying. 'How are you getting on with Jules now? Is he nice to you? You know what I mean. Now, tell me.'

She laughed, not being the least shocked.

'Well, when you take him out you treat him to vermouth, and tell him things that make him come home half-crazy. Oh, he's much too nice to me! You know, I don't want him to be that nice! But I'd rather it happened at home than elsewhere, I'm sure of that!'

She became serious again, and added: 'Here's your Balzac; I couldn't finish it. It's too sad; he only writes about unpleasant things, that gentleman.'

She asked him to give her some stories in which there was plenty of love, adventure, and travel in foreign lands. Then she talked about the funeral. She would go to the church, and Jules would continue to the cemetery. She had never been frightened of corpses; at the age of twelve she had sat up all night with an uncle and aunt who had died of the same fever. Jules, on the other hand, hated talking about dead people, so much so that he had actually forbidden her, the day before, to mention the landlord lying on his back downstairs. But she could find no other subject for conversation, neither could he; so that, as each hour passed, they barely exchanged a dozen words, and did nothing else but think of the poor, deceased gentleman. It was becoming tiresome and, for Jules's sake, she would be glad when they took him away. Happy at being able to talk freely about it, she satisfied her urge, overwhelming Octave with questions. Had he seen him? Did he look different? Was it true that something horrible had happened as he was being put into his coffin? Were his relatives ripping up all the mattresses and ransacking everything? It wasn't surprising that there were so many rumours going around, in a house overrun by servants! Death always obsessed everyone.

'You're giving me another Balzac,' she said, looking over the fresh batch of books he was lending her. 'No, take it back; his stories are too much like real life!'*

As she held the volume out to him he caught hold of her wrist and tried to pull her into the room. She amused him with her curiosity about death; she suddenly seemed to him droll, full of life, desirable. But she understood his intention and blushed deeply. Freeing herself from his grasp she hurried away, saying:

'Thank you, Monsieur Mouret; we'll see each other, no doubt, at the funeral.'

When Octave was dressed he remembered his promise to go and see Madame Campardon. He had two whole hours to fill, as the funeral was fixed for eleven o'clock, and he thought of using the morning to make a few calls in the house. Rose received him in bed; he apologized for disturbing her, but she herself called him into her room. They saw so little of him, and she was so pleased to have someone to talk to!

'Ah, my dear boy,' she cried suddenly, 'I should be the one lying down there, nailed up between four planks!'

Yes, the landlord was very lucky; he had done with existence! Octave, surprised to find her a prey to such melancholy, asked her if she felt worse.

'No, thank you. It's always the same thing, only there are times when I feel I've had enough. Achille has had to put up a bed in his workroom, because it annoyed me when he moved about at night. And we've managed to persuade Gasparine to leave the shop. I'm so grateful to her for that, she looks after me so well! Ah, I couldn't go on living if I wasn't surrounded by so much affection and kindness!'

Just then Gasparine, with her submissive air of poor relation turned servant, brought in the coffee. Helping Rose to sit up, she propped her against some cushions and gave her the coffee on a little tray covered with a napkin. Rose, sitting in her embroidered jacket in the midst of the lace-edged linen, ate with a hearty appetite. She looked so fresh, younger than ever, and very pretty with her white skin and little blonde curls.

'Oh, my stomach's all right; there's nothing wrong with my stomach,' she kept saying, as she soaked her slices of bread and butter.

Two tears dropped into the coffee. Then Gasparine chided her:

'If you cry, I'll call Achille. Aren't you satisfied, sitting there like a queen on a throne?'

When Madame Campardon had finished and again found herself alone with Octave, she became quite consoled. Coquettishly, she again began to talk about death, but with the languid gaiety of a woman whiling away a whole morning in the warmth of her bed. Well, she would have to go too, when her turn came; but they were right, she was not unhappy, and could go on living, because they saved her from all the main worries of life. And she rambled on in her selfish, sexless-idol manner.

Then, as the young man rose to leave, she said:

'Now, do come more often, won't you? Go and enjoy yourself; don't let the funeral make you too sad. One dies a little every day. The thing is to get used to it.'

On the same floor, Louise, the little maid at Madame Juzeur's, let Octave in. She took him into the drawing-room, looked at him for a moment, laughed in her bewildered sort of way, and at last said that her mistress had nearly finished dressing. Madame Juzeur appeared almost at once; she was dressed in black, and in this mourning garb she seemed gentler and more refined than ever.

'I was sure you'd come this morning,' she sighed wearily. 'I kept dreaming about you all night long. Quite impossible to sleep, you know, with that corpse in the house!'

She confessed that she had got up three times in the night to look under the furniture.

'You should have called me,' said the young man, gallantly. 'Two in a bed are never afraid.'

She assumed a charming air of shame.

'Don't say that sort of thing; it's naughty!'

She held her hand over his lips. He was thus obliged to kiss it. Then she spread out her fingers, laughing as if she were being tickled. Excited by this game, he sought to push matters further. He caught her in his arms and pressed her to his chest, without her offering any resistance. Then he whispered:

'Come now, why won't you?'

'Oh, in any case, not today!'

'Why not today?'

'What, with that corpse downstairs? No, no, it's impossible!'

He held her tighter and she began to yield. Their warm breaths mingled.

'When will you, then? Tomorrow?'

'Never.'

'But you're quite free; your husband behaved so badly that you owe him nothing.'

He grabbed hold of her, but she, in her supple way, slipped from him. Then, putting her arms round him, she held him tightly so that he could not move, and murmured caressingly:

'Anything you like except that! Do you understand me! Not that, never, never! I'd rather die! It's the way I think, that's all. I've sworn to Heaven I wouldn't, but there's no need to know anything about that. So you're just like other men, who are never satisfied as long as they're refused anything. But I'm very fond of you. Anything you like, but not that, my sweetheart!'

She allowed him to caress her in the warmest, most intimate way, only repulsing him by a sudden nervous reaction when he attempted to perform the one forbidden act. Her obstinacy had in it a sort of Jesuitical reserve, a fear of the confessional, a conviction of pardon for petty sins, while so gross a one might cause too much trouble with her spiritual pastor. Then there were other unavowed sentiments, a blending of honour and self-esteem, the coquetry of always having an advantage over men by never satisfying them, together with a shrewd personal enjoyment of being showered with kisses without having to endure the final act of male gratification. She preferred it that way, and was quite resolute about it. No man could flatter himself that he had had her since her husband's cowardly desertion. She was a virtuous woman.

'No, sir, not one! Ah, I can hold my head up, I can! How many unfortunate women in my position would have gone wrong!'

She gently pushed him aside and rose from the sofa.

'Please leave me. That corpse downstairs really bothers me. The whole house seems to smell of it!'

Meanwhile, the time for the funeral was approaching. She wanted to get to the church before they started, so as not to see all the funeral trappings. But, as she was walking to the door with him, she suddenly remembered telling him about her liqueur from the West Indies. So she made him come back, and fetched the bottle and two glasses. It was creamy and very sweet, with a scent of flowers. When she had drunk it, a sort of girlish greediness brought a look of languid rapture to her face. She could have lived on sugar; vanilla- and rose-scented sweets troubled her senses as greatly as a lover's caress.

'That'll keep us going,' she said.

When he kissed her on the mouth in the anteroom, she shut her eyes. Their sugary lips seemed to melt like bon-bons.

It was nearly eleven o'clock. The coffin was still upstairs, for the undertaker's men, after wasting their time at a neighbouring wine-shop, were taking ages putting up the hangings. Out of curiosity, Octave went to have a look. The porch was already closed at the back by a large black curtain, but the men had still to fix the hangings over the door. On the pavement outside a group of servants were gossiping as they gazed up at the building, while Hippolyte, in deep mourning, hurried on the work with a dignified air.

'Yes, madam,' Lisa was saying to a desiccated-looking woman, a widow, who had been in Valérie's service for a week, 'it's done her no good at all. The whole neighbourhood knows all about it. To make sure of her share of the old man's money she got a butcher in the Rue Sainte-Anne to give her that child, because her husband looked as if he was going to cave in any minute. But her husband's still alive and the old boy's gone. A lot of good she's done herself with her dirty brat!'

The widow nodded in disgust.

'Serves her right!' she answered. 'Her foul tricks have done her no good. I'm not going to stay! I gave her a week's notice this morning. I found that little bugger Camille shitting in my kitchen!'

Just then Julie came downstairs to give Hippolyte an order. Lisa ran to question her and then, after a few moments' conversation, rejoined Valérie's servant.

'It's a complete mess,' she said; 'nobody knows what's going on. I reckon your mistress needn't have got herself a kid; she could have waited for her husband to kick the bucket after all, because it seems they're still hunting for the old boy's money. The cook says they've got faces like thunder in there—as if they'll come to blows before the evening's out.'

Adèle now arrived, with four sous' worth of butter under her apron, Madame Josserand having ordered her never to show any food she went to fetch. Lisa wanted to see what she was carrying, and then scolded her for being such a fool. Whoever heard of anyone being sent to fetch four sous' worth of butter! She would have made those skinflints feed her better, or else she would have fed herself before they got anything; yes, she would have eaten the butter, the sugar, the meat, everything! For some time the other servants had thus been inciting Adèle to rebel. She was gradually becoming perverted. She broke off a corner of the butter and ate it up without any bread, to show the others how little she cared.

'Shall we go up?' she said.

'No,' replied the widow, 'I want to see him brought down. I've put off doing an errand for that.'

'So have I,' added Lisa. 'They say he weighs a ton. If they drop him on their beautiful staircase it'll do it quite some damage, eh?'

'Well, I'm going up, I'd rather not see him,' said Adèle. 'I don't want to dream again, like I did last night, that he was pulling me out of bed by the heels and saying all sorts of nasty things to me about making a mess.'

She went off amid the laughter of her two companions. All night long Adèle's nightmare had been a source of merriment on the servants' floor. The maidservants, moreover, in order not to be alone, had left their doors open, which had provoked a waggish coachman into pretending to be a ghost, and little screams and stifled laughter could be heard all along the passage until daylight. Biting her lips, Lisa declared that she would never forget it. That was great fun and no mistake!

But Hippolyte's angry voice brought their attention back to the hangings. Oblivious of his dignity, he was shouting out:

'You drunken fool! You're putting it on the wrong way!'

It was true, the workman was about to hook the escutcheon bearing the deceased's monogram upside down. The black hangings, edged with silver lace, were now fixed, and only a few curtain-rests remained to be put up when a cart, laden with some poor person's possessions, appeared at the door. A young lad was pulling it along, while a tall, pale girl followed, helping to push it from behind. Monsieur Gourd, who was talking to his friend the stationer opposite, rushed forward, forgetting his grand state of mourning, and exclaimed:

'Now, then! Now, then! What's he after? Can't you see, you silly fool?'

The tall girl interrupted him.

'I'm the new lodger, sir. These are my things.'

'Impossible! Come tomorrow!' cried the concierge in a fury.

She looked at him and then at the funeral hangings, as if in a daze. The door, shrouded in black, clearly bewildered her. But, recovering herself, she explained that she could not very well leave her furniture out in the street. Then Monsieur Gourd began to bully her.

'You're the boot-stitcher, aren't you? You've taken the little room at the top? Another case of the landlord's obstinacy! Just for the sake of a hundred and thirty francs, and after all the bother we had with the carpenter! He promised me, too, that he would never let rooms to working-people any more. And now, damn it! the whole thing's going to begin again, and this time with a woman!'

Then he remembered that Monsieur Vabre was dead.

'Yes, you may look. The landlord's just died, and if it had happened a week ago you wouldn't be here; that's for sure. Come on, hurry up, before they bring him down!'

In his exasperation he gave the cart a shove, pushing it through the hangings, which opened and then slowly closed again. The tall, pale girl disappeared behind the mass of black drapery.

'She's come at a good time!' said Lisa. 'It's not much fun to do your shifting while a funeral's going on! If I'd been here I'd have let the old bugger have it!'

But she fell silent as she saw Monsieur Gourd reappear, for he was the terror of the servants. His ill-humour was due to the fact that, as people said, the house would fall to Monsieur Théophile and his wife. He would willingly have given a hundred francs out of his own pocket, he said, to have Monsieur Duveyrier as landlord; he, at least, was a judge. This was what he was explaining to the stationer. Meanwhile people were beginning to come downstairs. Madame Juzeur passed by and smiled at Octave, who had met Trublot outside on the pavement. Then Marie reappeared, and stood watching them placing the trestles for the coffin.

'The people on the second floor are really extraordinary,' remarked Monsieur Gourd as he looked up at their closed shutters. 'You'd almost think they go out of their way to avoid behaving like everybody else. Yes, they went off on a trip three days ago.'

At this moment Lisa hid behind her friend the widow, on catching sight of Gasparine, who was bringing a wreath of violets, a delicate gesture on the part of the architect who wanted to keep on good terms with the Duveyriers.

'I say!' exclaimed the stationer, 'the other Madame Campardon can doll herself up, can't she?'

He called her thus, innocently, by the name given to her by all the neighbouring tradespeople. Lisa stifled a laugh. Then suddenly the servants discovered that the coffin had been brought down, which caused great disappointment. How silly, too, to have stood all that while in the street, looking at the black curtains! They quickly went back into the house just as the coffin, carried by four men, was being brought out of the hall. The hangings darkened the porch, and at the back could be seen the pale daylight of the courtyard, which had been scrubbed that morning. Little Louise, who had followed Madame Juzeur, stood on tiptoe, wide-eyed and pale with curiosity. The coffin-bearers stopped and gasped for breath at the foot of the staircase, which, with its gilding and sham marble, wore an air of frigid pomp in the faint light that fell from the ground-glass windows.

'There he goes, without his quarter's rent!' muttered Lisa, with the spiteful wit of a landlord-hating Parisienne.

Madame Gourd, whose bad legs had kept her glued to her armchair, now rose with difficulty. As she could not get as far as the church, Monsieur Gourd had instructed her not to let the landlord go past their lodge without greeting him. It behoved her to do this. She came as far as the door in a black cap, and as the coffin passed she curtsied.

During the service at Saint-Roch Doctor Juillerat ostentatiously remained outside the church. There was, moreover, a great crowd, and several of the men preferred to stay in a group on the steps. It was very mild—a glorious June day. Since they could not smoke, they talked politics. The main door was left open, and at intervals bursts of organ music issued from the church, which was all hung with black and ablaze with tapers.

'Did you know that Monsieur Thiers is going to stand for our district next year?' asked Léon Josserand, in his grave way.

'Oh! is he?' replied the doctor. 'Of course, you, being a Republican, won't vote for him, will you?'

The young man, whose Radical opinions had become milder under Madame Dambreville's influence, drily answered:

'Why not? He's the avowed enemy of the Empire.'

A heated discussion ensued. Léon spoke of tactics, while Doctor Juillerat stuck to principles. The bourgeoisie, he maintained, had had their day; they were just an obstacle on the path of the Revolution, and now that they had become wealthy they opposed progress more stubbornly and blindly than the old nobility.

'You're afraid of everything; no sooner do you believe yourself threatened than you become totally reactionary!'

Suddenly Campardon interjected angrily:

'I, sir, was once a Jacobin and an atheist like yourself. But thank Heaven, I came to my senses. I certainly wouldn't vote for your Monsieur Thiers—he's muddle-headed, full of mad ideas!'

However, all the Liberals present—Monsieur Josserand, Octave, even Trublot, who was quite indifferent to the whole matter—declared that they would vote for Monsieur Thiers. The official candidate, Monsieur Dewinck, was a successful chocolate manufacturer from the Rue Saint-Honoré, whom they could not take at all seriously.* This same Dewinck did not even have the support of the clergy, who felt uneasy at his relations with the Tuileries. Campardon, wholly on the side of the Church, said nothing at the mention of his name. Then he suddenly exclaimed: 'Listen! The bullet that wounded your Garibaldi in the foot should have got him in the heart!'*

And to avoid being seen any longer in such company he went into the church, where Father Mauduit's harsh voice could be heard in counterpoint to the lamentations of the choir.

'He virtually lives there now,' muttered the doctor, shrugging his shoulders. 'We ought to get rid of all that nonsense!'

He felt most strongly about the Roman question.* Then, as Léon reminded them that the Cabinet Minister had told the Senate that the Empire had sprung from the Revolution precisely in order to keep the forces of revolution in check, they again began to talk about the coming elections. All agreed that it was necessary to teach the

Emperor a lesson; but they were beginning to feel anxious—divided in their opinions about the various candidates, whose very names conjured up nightmarish visions of the Terror. Close by, Monsieur Gourd, as neatly dressed as a diplomat, listened with utter contempt to what they were saying. He believed in the powers that be—pure and simple.

The service was drawing to a close. A long melancholy wail from the depths of the church silenced them.

'*Requiescat in pace.*'

'*Amen!*'

At the Père Lachaise Cemetery, as the coffin was being lowered into the grave, Trublot, still arm-in-arm with Octave, saw him exchange another smile with Madame Juzeur.

'Ah, yes!' he murmured; 'the little woman who's terribly unhappy. "Anything-you-like-except-that!"'

Octave started. What? Had Trublot tried it on too? Then, with a gesture of disdain, the latter explained that he had not, but a friend of his had. And lots of others, who went in for that sort of thing.

'Excuse me,' he added; 'now that the old boy's been stowed away I must go and tell Duveyrier about a job I had to do for him.'

The relatives, silent and doleful, were now departing. Then Trublot, detaining Duveyrier, told him that he had seen Clarisse's maid but could not find out the address, as the maid had left the day before Clarisse moved out after a terrible row. Thus the last ray of hope vanished, and Duveyrier, burying his face in his handkerchief, rejoined the other mourners.

That evening quarrelling began. The family had made a disastrous discovery. With that sceptical carelessness that notaries sometimes display, Monsieur Vabre had left no will. Cupboards and drawers were searched in vain, the worst of it being that not a sou of the hoped-for six or seven hundred thousand francs was to be found, neither in the shape of money, title-deeds, nor shares. All that they found was the sum of seven hundred and thirty-four francs, in ten-sou pieces—the hidden store of a senile old man. Moreover, there were undeniable traces—a notebook filled with figures, letters from stockbrokers—which revealed to his relatives, livid with rage, the old man's secret vice, an ungovernable passion for gambling, an inept, mad craving for stock-jobbing, which he hid behind his innocent mania for compiling his masterpiece of statistical research.

Everything had been sacrificed: his Versailles savings, his house-rents, even the money squeezed out of his children. In recent years he had even mortgaged the house for a hundred and fifty thousand francs, at three different periods. The family, dumbfounded, stood before the fabulous safe in which they believed the fortune was locked up. All that it contained, however, was a lot of odds and ends—scraps picked up about the house, bits of old iron and glass, tags of ribbon, and broken toys stolen long ago when Gustave was a baby.

Violent recriminations broke out. They called the old man a swindler; it was scandalous to fritter away his money in this way, like a sly rogue who does not care a damn for anybody and who acts out his infamous comedy so as to get people to pet and coddle him. The Duveyriers were inconsolable at having boarded him for twelve years without once asking him for the eighty thousand francs of Clotilde's dowry, of which they had only received ten thousand. But it was still ten thousand francs, Théophile angrily remarked. He had not yet had a sou of the fifty thousand francs promised at the time of his marriage. Auguste, however, complained more bitterly, reproaching his brother with having at least been able to pocket the interest on that sum for three months, whereas he would never see a centime of the fifty thousand francs specified in his contract. Then Berthe, egged on by her mother, made a number of unpleasant remarks, and appeared to be highly indignant at having become connected with a dishonest family, while Valérie, bemoaning the rent she had continued paying for so long through fear of being disinherited, could not accept the discovery at all, regretting the money as though it had been used for immoral purposes to promote debauchery.

For a whole fortnight these matters were excitedly discussed by the whole house. Finally it became clear that all that remained was the building, valued at three hundred thousand francs. When the mortgage had been paid off, there would be about half that sum to divide between Monsieur Vabre's three children. Fifty thousand francs apiece: a meagre consolation, but one with which they would have to be content. Théophile and Auguste had already decided what to do with their shares. It was agreed that the building should be sold. Duveyrier took charge, in his wife's name, of all arrangements. First of all he persuaded the two brothers not to have a public auction; if they were willing, the sale could take place at his notary's, Maître Renaudin, a man whose integrity he could vouch for. Then, acting on the notary's advice, he discreetly suggested to them that it would be best to put up the house at a low figure, only a hundred and forty thousand francs. This was a very sly move, for it would bring crowds of people to the sale; the bids would mount rapidly, and they would realize far more than they expected. Théophile and Auguste chuckled in happy anticipation. However, on the day of the sale, after five or six bids, Maître Renaudin abruptly knocked the house down to Duveyrier for a hundred and forty thousand francs. There was not even enough to pay off the mortgage! It was the final blow.

No one ever knew the details of the terrible scene which took place at the Duveyriers' that evening. The house's solemn walls muffled the shouting. Théphile undoubtedly denounced his brother-in-law as a scoundrel, openly accusing him of having bribed the notary by promising to appoint him a justice of the peace. As for Auguste, he simply talked of the assize court, where he wished to drag Maître Renaudin, whose roguery was the talk of the neighbourhood. But it never transpired how these good people, as rumour had it, finally fell to blows; their parting words on the threshold were overheard—words that had a most unpleasant ring amid the austere decorum of the staircase.

'You rotten scoundrel!' cried Auguste. 'You sentence people to penal servitude who have not done half as much!'

Théophile, who came out last, held on to the door as, half choked by fury and a fit of coughing, he yelled:

'Thief! Thief! Yes, thief! And you too Clotilde, do you hear? You're a thief!'

Then he slammed the door so violently that all the others shook. Monsieur Gourd, who was listening, grew alarmed. He stared up at the different floors, but all he could see was Madame Juzeur's delicate profile. With back bent he returned on tiptoe to his room, where he resumed his dignified demeanour. One could deny having heard anything at all. He was delighted, having decided to side with the new landlord.

A few days later there was a reconciliation between Auguste and his sister. The whole house was most surprised. Octave had been seen going to the Duveyriers'. The judge, ill at ease, had decided to charge no rent for the ground-floor shop for five years, thus shutting one of the inheritors' mouths. When Théophile heard this he went downstairs with his wife and made another scene. So he, too, had sold himself, and had joined the gang of thieves! However, Madame Josserand happened to be in the shop and she soon shut him up. She frankly advised Valérie not to sell herself any more than her daughter had done. Valérie, forced to retreat, exclaimed:

'So we're the only ones to get nothing, are we? Damned if I'll pay any more rent. I've got a lease, and that jailbird won't dare to turn us out. And as for you, my little Berthe, one day we'll see what it'll take to have you!'

Once more there was a great banging of doors. A deadly feud now existed between the two families. Octave, who had just been serving a customer, was present, just as if he were one of the family. Berthe almost swooned in his arms, while Auguste made sure that none of his customers had overheard. Even Madame Josserand put her trust in the young man. She continued, however, to judge the Duveyriers very severely.

'The rent is something,' she said, 'but I want those fifty thousand francs.'

'Of course you do, if you pay yours,' Berthe ventured to remark.

Her mother did not appear to understand.

'I want them, do you understand? That old fox Vabre must be laughing in his grave. I won't let him boast of having made a fool of me, though. What dreadful people there are in this world! Fancy promising money you haven't got! Just wait, my girl, they'll pay you, or I'll go and dig him up just to spit in his face!'

XII

ONE morning, when Berthe was at her mother's, Adèle came in looking very scared, to say that Monsieur Saturnin was there, with a man. Doctor Chassagne, the director of the Moulineaux Asylum, had told the Josserands on a number of occasions that he could not keep their son, for he was not a patient in whom the symptoms of insanity were sufficiently marked. Having heard about the papers making over the three thousand francs which Berthe had badgered her brother into signing, he feared being compromised in the matter and suddenly sent Saturnin home.

The news came as quite a shock. Madame Josserand, who was afraid she might be throttled, tried to reason with the attendant. But all he said was:

'The director asked me to tell you that when a person is sane enough to give money to his parents, he's sane enough to live with them.'

'But he's mad! He'll murder us!'

'Not so mad that he can't sign his name, though!' rejoined the man, as he departed.

Saturnin came in very quietly, with his hands in his pockets, just as if he were returning from a stroll in the Tuileries gardens. He did not say a word about his stay at the asylum. He embraced his father, who wept, and gave smacking kisses to his mother and Hortense, who both trembled with fright. Then, when he saw Berthe, he was quite delighted, and began to caress her like a little boy. She at once took advantage of his tender mood to tell him of her marriage. He showed no anger, and at first hardly seemed to understand, as if he had forgotten his former fits of rage. But when she wanted to go downstairs he began to yell; he did not care whether she was married or not, so long as she stayed where she was, always with him and close to him. Seeing her mother's frightened look as she ran and locked herself in another room, it occurred to Berthe that she could take Saturnin to live with her. They would be able to find something for him to do in the basement of their shop, even if it were only tying up parcels.

That same evening Auguste, despite his evident repugnance, consented to his wife's wish. They had hardly been married three months, but were slowly drifting apart. It was the collision of two different temperaments and types of education—a husband glum, fastidious, and devoid of passion, and a wife reared in the hothouse of false Parisian luxury, determined to enjoy life to the full, but alone, like a selfish, spoilt child. Thus he was at a loss to understand her need for constant activity, her perpetual goings-out on social calls, on walks, or to the shops, and her racing backwards and forwards to theatres, exhibitions, or other places of amusement. Two or three times a week Madame Josserand came to fetch her daughter, and kept her out till dinner-time, delighted to be seen in her company and to bask in the glory of Berthe's sumptuous clothes, for which she no longer paid. Auguste's accesses of revolt were mainly due to these showy dresses, for which he could see no use. Why dress above one's means and station? What reason was there to spend in such a way money that he so urgently needed for his business? He would often remark that when one sold silks to other women one ought to wear woollens oneself. Then Berthe, assuming her mother's ferocious demeanour, would ask if he expected her to go about stark naked; and he was disheartened still further by the doubtful cleanliness of her petticoats and her contempt for all linen that was not displayed, she having always a set of stock phrases with which to silence him if he persisted in his complaints.

'I'd rather be envied than pitied. Money's money, and when I only had twenty sous I always pretended I had forty.'

After her marriage Berthe began gradually to acquire her mother's figure. She began to fill out, and resembled Madame Josserand more and more. She was no longer the careless, lissom girl, submissive to maternal slaps; she was a woman of ever-increasing obstinacy, bent on turning everything to her pleasure. Auguste sometimes looked at her, amazed at such sudden maturity. At first she had taken a vain delight in enthroning herself at the cashier's desk in a studied costume of elegant simplicity. But she had quickly tired of the business; suffering from lack of exercise, threatening to fall ill, yet resigning herself to it all the same, assuming the attitude of a victim sacrificing her life for the good of her home. And ever since that time perpetual warfare had been going on between herself and her husband. She shrugged her shoulders behind his back, just as her mother did behind her father's; she began with him all the petty domestic bickerings of her own childhood; she treated him simply as one whose business was to pay, heaping upon him her contempt for the male sex, a contempt upon which her entire education had been based.

'Oh, mamma was right!' she would exclaim after each of their quarrels.

At first, however, Auguste had tried to please her. He liked peace, and dreamed of a quiet little home—for he was already set in his ways like an old man, having got thoroughly into the habits of a chaste and thrifty bachelor's life. As his old lodging on the entresol was too small, he had taken one of the apartments on the second floor, facing the courtyard, and thought it wildly extravagant to spend five thousand francs on furniture. Berthe, delighted at first with her room—all polished wood and sky-blue silk—had become utterly contemptuous of it later on, after visiting a friend of hers who was in the process of marrying a banker. The first quarrels, too, had arisen because of the servants. Accustomed as she was to dealing with half-witted, drudge-like maids, whose very bread was doled out to them, Berthe forced her servants to perform such awful tasks that they sat sobbing in their kitchen for whole afternoons. Auguste, not usually tender-hearted, once foolishly ventured to comfort one of them, but an hour later was forced to show her the door, amid the sobs and shouts of his wife, who furiously demanded that he choose between her and that creature. After this came a strapping girl who appeared to make up her mind to stay. Her name was Rachel—a Jewess, no doubt, although she denied it and concealed her origins. She was about twenty-five, with a hard face, a big nose, and jet-black hair. At first Berthe said that she would not put up with her for more than a couple of days, but the newcomer's mute obedience, her air of understanding all yet saying nothing, gradually won her over. It was as if the mistress, in her turn, had been subjugated, ostensibly keeping the girl for her merits, though at the same time being vaguely afraid of her. Rachel, who submitted without a murmur to the hardest tasks for dry bread alone, gradually took possession of the entire household, with her eyes open and her mouth shut, like a wily servant waiting for the fatal moment when her mistress would be able to refuse her nothing.

Meanwhile, from top to bottom, a great calm reigned throughout the house after the disturbance caused by Monsieur Vabre's sudden death. The staircase once more became as peaceful as a chapel, not a sound escaped from behind those mahogany doors which forever shut in the profound respectability of the various families. A rumour was abroad that Duveyrier and his wife had become reconciled. As for Valérie and Théophile, they spoke to no one, as they stalked by with a stiffly dignified air. Never before had the house seemed to embody so completely the strictest of moral principles. Monsieur Gourd, in cap and slippers, patrolled the building like a solemn beadle.

One evening, at about eleven o'clock, Auguste kept going to the shop door and peering up and down the street with ever-increasing impatience. Berthe, whom her mother and sister had fetched during dinner without even letting her finish her dessert, had not yet come back, though she had been gone more than three hours and had promised to return before closing time.

'Oh, goodness gracious!' he exclaimed at last, as he clasped his hands together, making his fingers crack.

Then he stopped short in front of Octave, who was ticketing some remnants of silk on the counter. At that late hour no customer ever came to this out-of-the-way corner of the Rue de Choiseul. The shop was only kept open so as to put things in order.

'I'm sure you know where the ladies have gone,' he said enquiringly.

Octave looked up with an air of innocent surprise.

'But, sir, they told you—to a lecture.'

'A lecture indeed, a lecture!' grumbled the husband. 'Their lecture was over at ten o'clock. Respectable women should be home at this time of night!'

Then he resumed his walk, giving side glances at Octave, whom he suspected of being the ladies' accomplice, or at least of wishing to make excuses for them. Octave, feeling ill at ease, watched him furtively too. He had never seen him in such a state of nervous excitement. What could have happened? Turning his head, he saw Saturnin at the other end of the shop, cleaning a mirror with a sponge soaked in spirit. By degrees, they had got the madman to do housework, so that at least he might earn his food. That evening Saturnin's eyes glittered strangely. He crept up behind Octave and said to him softly:

'Look out! He's found a piece of paper. Yes, he's got a piece of paper in his pocket. You'd better look out, if it's yours!'

Then he hurriedly continued rubbing his glass. Octave did not understand. For some time past the lunatic had shown singular affection for him, like the caress of an animal beneath whose unerring instinct lay a deeper, more subtle feeling. What made him mention a piece of paper? He had not written any letter to Berthe, but only allowed himself to look tenderly at her now and again while waiting for an opportunity to give her some little present. This was the tactic which, after mature reflection, he had resolved to adopt.

'Ten minutes past eleven—damn it all!' exclaimed Auguste, who never usually swore.

At that moment, however, the ladies came in. Berthe was wearing a charming costume of pink silk embroidered with white jet, while her sister, always in blue, and her mother, always in mauve, had kept to their gaudy, elaborate gowns, which they altered every season. Madame Josserand came first, large and imposing, to stop her son-in-law from making any complaints, which the three had foreseen when holding council together at the end of the street. She even deigned to explain their delay by saying that they had been looking in the shop-windows. Auguste, however, very pale, uttered not a word of complaint, speaking in a dry tone of voice. Evidently, he was restraining himself until later on. For a moment Madame Josserand, accustomed as she was to family quarrels, tried to intimidate him; then, being obliged to go upstairs, she merely said:

'Goodnight, my girl, and sleep well if you want to live long.'

As soon as she had gone Auguste, beside himself and oblivious of the presence of Octave and Saturnin, pulled a crumpled piece of paper out of his pocket and thrust it under Berthe's nose, as he stuttered:

'So what's this?'

Berthe had not even taken off her bonnet. She grew very red.

'That?' she replied. 'It's a bill.'

'Yes, it's a bill, and for false hair, too! For false hair, of all things; as if you hadn't got any left on your head! But that's not the point. You've paid this bill; now, tell me, what did you pay it with?'

Becoming more and more embarrassed, Berthe at last replied:

'With my own money, of course!'

'Your own money! But you haven't got any. Somebody must have given you some, or else you took it from here. Yes; and, look here, I know everything. You're in debt! I'll put up with anything, but I won't have debts, do you hear? I won't have debts—never!'

He said this with all the horror of a prudent fellow whose commercial integrity consists in owing no one a penny. He proceeded to air all his grievances, reproaching his wife for continually gadding about town, complaining of her taste for clothes and luxury items which he could not pay for. Was it right that people in their position should stay out till eleven o'clock at night, dressed up in pink silk gowns embroidered with white jet? People with such tastes ought to provide themselves with a dowry of five hundred thousand francs. However, he knew well enough who was to blame; it was that idiot of a mother, who taught her daughters how to squander fortunes without being able to give them so much as a chemise to wear on their wedding-day.

'Don't say a word against mamma!' cried Berthe, who at last became exasperated. 'She's not to blame; she did her duty. And what about your family! What a collection! People who killed their father!'

Octave had carried on ticketing the silks, pretending not to hear. But he kept an eye on the dispute, and was especially attentive to Saturnin, who had stopped polishing the mirror and, with clenched fists and flashing eyes, stood there trembling, ready to spring at Auguste's throat.

'Keep our families out of it!' rejoined the latter. 'We've got enough problems at home. You must change your ways, because I won't pay another sou for all this tomfoolery. I've made my mind up about that! Your place is here, at your desk, dressed quite simply, like a woman who has some respect for herself. And if you run up any more debts, you'll see!'

Berthe was taken aback by this marital hand so brutally laid upon her habits, her pleasures, her frocks. It was as if all that she liked, all that she had dreamed of when getting married, had been wrenched from her. But, with a woman's tactics, she hid her real wound, finding a pretext for the wrath that flushed her face as she indignantly exclaimed:

'I won't let you insult mamma!'

Auguste shrugged his shoulders.

'Your mother, indeed! You look just like her—you become quite ugly when you work yourself up like that! I can hardly tell it's you; it's your mother all over again! I tell you, it's frightening!'

Berthe immediately calmed down, and looked him straight in the face.

'Go and tell mamma what you just said, and see how she'll throw you out!'

'Would she?' cried Auguste, in a fury. 'Then I'll go up and tell her now!'

He moved towards the door and not a moment too soon, for Saturnin, with wolfish eyes, was coming up on tiptoe to strangle him from behind. Berthe sank into a chair, murmuring:

'If ever I married again, it wouldn't be to a man like that!'*

Upstairs, Monsieur Josserand opened the door in great surprise, as Adèle had gone to bed. He was just getting ready to spend the night addressing wrappers, in spite of feeling rather unwell. Thus, embarrassed and rather ashamed at having been found out, he took his son-in-law into the dining-room, alluding to some urgent work which he had to finish—a copy of the inventory of the Saint-Joseph Glassworks. But when Auguste began to accuse his daughter of running into debt, and told him of the quarrel occasioned by the incident of the false hair, the old man's hands began to tremble; deeply upset, he stammered incoherently, and tears filled his eyes. His daughter was in debt, and led a life of continual domestic bickering like his own! All the unhappiness of his life was going to be repeated in his daughter! Another fear obsessed him, and this was that, at any moment, his son-in-law would broach the subject of money, claim the dowry, and denounce him as a swindler. No doubt the young fellow knew everything, or he would never have called in like this at nearly midnight.

'My wife has gone to bed,' he stammered, his head in a whirl. 'There's no point in waking her up, is there? I'm very surprised to hear all this! Poor Berthe isn't a wicked girl, I assure you! Don't be hard on her. I'll talk to her. As for us, my dear Auguste, I don't think we've done anything to displease you.'

He looked at him enquiringly, feeling reassured; Auguste evidently knew nothing as yet. Then Madame Josserand appeared at her bedroom door. She stood there in her nightdress, white and fearsome. Angry though he was, Auguste recoiled. She must have been listening at the door, for she at once delivered a blow straight from the shoulder.

'I don't suppose you've come for your ten thousand francs, have you? The instalment isn't due for at least another two months. We'll pay you in two months, sir. We don't die to avoid keeping our promises.'

This remarkable assurance completely overwhelmed Monsieur Josserand. And she went on making the most extraordinary statements, to the utter bewilderment of Auguste, whom she would simply not allow to speak.

'You have no sense at all, sir. When you've made Berthe ill you'll have to send for the doctor, and then you'll have a chemist's bill to pay. I went away just now because I saw that you had decided to make a fool of yourself. Do what you like! Beat your wife, if you want; my conscience as a mother is clear, for God sees all and punishment is never far behind!'

At last Auguste was able to explain his grievances. He complained once more of the perpetual gadding about, the expensive dresses, and all the rest of it, and was even so bold as to condemn the way that Berthe had been brought up. Madame Josserand listened with an air of supreme contempt. Then, when he had finished, she retorted:

'Everything you've said, my dear fellow, is so absurd that it doesn't deserve an answer. My conscience is my own; that's enough for me. To think that I entrusted an angel to a man like that! I'll have nothing more to do with your quarrels, since all I get is insults. Sort them out yourselves!'

'But your daughter will end by deceiving me, madam!' cried Auguste, in a fresh burst of rage.

Madame Josserand, about to leave, turned round and looked him full in the face.

'Sir,' she said, 'you're doing all you possibly can to bring that about.'

Then she went back to her room, majestic as some colossal, triple-breasted Ceres robed in white.

The father detained Auguste a few minutes longer. He tried to humour him, pointing out that with women it is best to put up with everything; and at last he sent him away pacified and resolved to forgive Berthe. But when he found himself once more alone in the dining-room, before his little lamp, he burst into tears. It was all over; all happiness was at an end for him. He would never find time at night to address enough wrappers to help his daughter secretly. The thought that she might run into debt overwhelmed him as if with a sense of personal shame. He felt quite ill at receiving this fresh blow; one of these nights his strength would fail him. At last, straining to hold back his tears, he went on with his work.

Downstairs in the shop Berthe remained motionless for a moment, her face buried in her hands. One of the men, having put up the shutters, had gone down into the basement, and it was then that Octave thought he might approach the young woman. Ever since Auguste's departure Saturnin had been making signs over his sister's head, inviting Octave to comfort her. Beaming, he kept winking madly, and fearing that he was not making himself understood, began to blow kisses like an excited child.

'What? You want me to kiss her?' Octave asked him, by signs.

'Yes, yes,' replied the madman, nodding his head enthusiastically.

Then, as he saw Octave smilingly approach Berthe, who had noticed nothing, he sat on the floor behind a counter, out of sight, so as not to be in their way. The gas-jets were still burning—tall flames in the silent, empty shop. There was a sort of death-like peace, and a stuffy smell from the bales of silk.

'Please don't take it too much to heart, madam,' said Octave, in his caressing voice.

She started on seeing him so near her.

'I must ask you to excuse me, Monsieur Octave, but it was not my fault if you were present at this painful scene. Please make allowances for my husband; he must have been feeling unwell this evening. There are little unpleasantnesses, you know, in all families . . .'

Sobs prevented her from saying any more. The mere thought of extenuating her husband's faults to outsiders brought on a flood of tears, which completely unnerved her. Saturnin peeped anxiously over the counter, but he ducked down again as soon as he saw Octave take hold of Berthe's hand.

'Let me beg of you, madam, to be brave.'

'But I can't help it!' sobbed Berthe. 'You were there—you heard everything. All that because of ninety-five francs' worth of hair! As if all women don't wear false hair nowadays! But he knows nothing and understands nothing! He knows no more about women than the Grand Turk. He's never been near one in his life, Monsieur Octave, never! Oh, poor wretched me!'

In her furious spite, she blurted out everything. A man whom she thought had married her for love, but who soon would leave her without a chemise to her back! Didn't she do her duty by him? Could he accuse her of the least neglect? If he had not flown into a rage when she asked him to get her some false hair, she would never have had to buy some with her own pocket-money. For the least thing there was always the same fuss; she could never express a wish or say that she wanted some trivial item of clothing without meeting with her husband's sullen, ferocious opposition. Naturally she had her pride; she now asked for nothing and preferred to go without necessities, rather than humiliate herself to no purpose. Thus, for the last fortnight she had been longing for something she had seen with her mother in a jeweller's window in the Palais Royal.

'You know, three paste stars to put in my hair. An absolute trifle—a hundred francs, I think. But it was no good my talking about them from morning till night; my husband wouldn't listen!'

Octave could never have hoped for a better opportunity. He prepared to attack.

'Yes, yes, I know! I heard you mention them several times. You know, madam, your parents have always been so kind to me, and you yourself have been so obliging, that I thought I might venture to . . .'

As he spoke he drew from his pocket a long box, in which the three stars were sparkling on some cotton-wool. Berthe rose from her seat, very excited.

'But, sir, it's impossible for me to . . . I can't—you really shouldn't have . . . !'

He disingenuously invented various excuses. In the South such things were done every day. Besides, the stars were of no value at all. Blushing, she stopped sobbing and looked with sparkling eyes at the imitation gems in the box.

'Please accept them, madam, just to show me that you're satisfied with my work.'

'No, Monsieur Octave, really, you mustn't insist. I'm most touched . . .'

In the meantime Saturnin had reappeared, and was examining the jewellery with as much rapture as if they were holy relics. Soon his sharp ear detected Auguste's returning footsteps. He apprised Berthe of this with a slight click of his tongue. Just as her husband was about to enter she made up her mind.

'Well, listen,' she hurriedly whispered, thrusting the box into her pocket, 'I'll say that my sister Hortense gave them to me as a present.'

Auguste ordered the gas to be turned out, and then went upstairs with his wife to bed, without saying a word about their quarrel, secretly glad to find that Berthe had recovered her spirits as if nothing had ever taken place. The shop became wrapped in darkness, and just as Octave was also leaving he felt two hot hands squeezing his, almost crushing them, in the gloom. It was Saturnin, who slept in the basement.

'Friend, friend, friend!' repeated the lunatic, in an outburst of wild affection.

Thwarted in his designs, Octave began to conceive a passionate desire for Berthe. If at first he had followed his usual plan of seduction, and his wish to use women as a means of self-advancement, he now no longer regarded Berthe merely as his employer, to possess whom would mean gaining control of the entire establishment. What he desired above all was to enjoy in her the Parisienne, that adorable creature of luxury and grace, such as he had never tasted in Marseilles. He felt a sudden hunger for her tiny gloved hands, her tiny feet in their high-heeled boots, her soft bosom concealed by lace frippery, though perhaps some of her under-linen was of doubtful cleanliness, its shabbiness being hidden by magnificent dresses. This sudden upsurge of passion even got the better of his parsimonious temperament, to such a degree that he began to squander in presents and the like all the five thousand francs which he had brought with him from the South, and which he had already doubled by financial speculations he had not mentioned to anybody.

But what annoyed him more than anything was that he had become timid by falling in love. He had lost his usual determination, his haste to reach his goal, deriving, on the contrary, a certain languid enjoyment from not being too quick to take action. Moreover, this passing weakness, in so thoroughly practical a nature as his, led him to conclude that the conquest of Berthe would be a campaign fraught with great difficulties, needing much delay and skilful diplomacy. His two failures, with Valérie and Madame Hédouin, doubtless made him more fearful of yet another rebuff. But beneath all his uneasiness and hesitation there lurked a fear of the woman he adored, an absolute belief in Berthe's virtue, and all the blindness of a desperate love paralysed by desire.

The next day Octave, pleased that he had prevailed upon Berthe to accept his present, thought that it would be expedient to establish good relations with her husband. Accordingly, when taking his meals with him—for Auguste always boarded his assistants so as to have them close at hand—he paid him the utmost attention, listened to him during dessert, and loudly approved everything he said. In particular, he pretended to share his discontent with regard to Berthe, feigning to play the detective and report various little incidents to him from time to time. Auguste was most touched. One evening he confessed to Octave that he had been on the point of dismissing him, believing him to be in league with Madame Josserand. But when Octave immediately professed his horror for that good lady, this helped to bind them together by a community of ideas. At heart, indeed, the husband was a decent fellow; he was just bad-tempered, but easygoing enough as long as no one put him out by spending his money or shocking his morals. He vowed that he would never lose his temper again, for after the quarrel he had had a most abominable headache which had driven him crazy for three days.

'You see what I mean, don't you?' he would say to Octave. 'All I want is my peace of mind. Beyond that I don't care a damn, my honour excepted of course, and provided my wife doesn't run off with the cashbox. That's reasonable, isn't it? I don't ask anything very extraordinary of her, do I?'

Then Octave praised his sagacity, and they both extolled the joys of a dull existence such as this—each year exactly like the last, and all of them spent in measuring yards of silk. To please his employer, the young man was even content to give up all his ideas of trade on a grand scale. One evening, indeed, he had frightened Auguste by his dream of huge modern bazaars, advising him, as he had advised Madame Hédouin, to buy the adjoining house so as to enlarge his shop. Auguste, whose four counters were already enough to drive him crazy, stared at Octave with the terrified look of a shopman used to chopping centimes into four, so that the young man hastily withdrew his proposition and went into ecstasies over the soundness and integrity of small shopkeepers.

Days passed; Octave was building his nest in the house—a downy nest which he found snug and warm. The husband had a high opinion of him; and even Madame Josserand, though he avoided being too polite to her, looked encouragingly upon him. As for Berthe, she treated him with delightful familiarity. His great friend, however, was Saturnin, whose mute affection appeared to be increasing—a dog-like devotion which grew stronger as his desire for Berthe became more intense. Of everyone else the madman appeared grimly jealous; no man could go near his sister without his becoming at once uneasy, curling up his lips as if ready to bite. If, on the other hand, Octave bent over her unrestrainedly, making her laugh with the soft, tender laugh of a happy mistress, Saturnin would laugh with delight as well, while his face reflected a little of their sensual joy. The poor creature seemed to experience love through his sister's body, which instinctively he felt belonged to him, while for the chosen lover he felt nothing but ecstatic gratitude. He would stop Octave in all sorts of corners, looking about him suspiciously; and then, if they happened to be alone, he would talk about Berthe, always repeating the same stories in disjointed phrases.

'When she was little, she had such round little legs! She was so fat and rosy and happy! She used to crawl about on the floor. Then whack! whack! whack! she would kick me in the stomach. I really liked that! Oh, I liked it so much!'

In this way Octave got to know everything about Berthe's childhood, her babyish accidents, her playthings, her growth as a charming, uncontrolled creature. Saturnin's empty brain treasured up trivial details which he alone remembered, such as the day she pricked herself and he sucked the blood, and the morning he held her in his arms when she wanted to climb on to the table. But he always harked back to the great drama of the young girl's serious illness.

'Ah, if you'd only seen her! I spent the nights all alone with her. They beat me to make me go to bed. But I'd creep back barefoot. All by myself. It made me cry, she was so white. I used to touch her to see if she was getting cold. Then they left me alone, because I nursed her better than they did; I knew about her medicines, and she took whatever I gave her. Sometimes, when she complained a lot, I laid her head on my breast. It was so nice being together. Then she got well, and I wanted to go back to her, but they beat me again.'

His eyes sparkled, he laughed and cried, just as if it had all happened the day before. From these broken phrases of his the whole history of his strange attachment could be pieced together: his half-witted devotion at the little patient's bedside after all the doctors had given her up; his body and soul devoted to his beloved sister, who lay there dying, and whom he nursed in her nakedness with a mother's tenderness—all his affection and all his desires had been arrested there, checked forever by this drama of suffering from which he had never recovered. Ever since that time, despite the ingratitude which had followed the recovery, Berthe was everything to him, a mistress in whose presence he trembled; at once a daughter and a sister whom he had saved from death; his idol, whom he jealously adored. He thus pursued her husband with the wild hatred of a thwarted lover, never short of abusive remarks when unburdening himself to Octave.

'His eye's bunged up again! What a bother that headache of his is! Did you hear him shuffling about yesterday? Look! There he is, peering out of the window. The fool! Oh, you dirty brute, you dirty brute!'

Auguste could hardly move without angering him. Then he would make horrible proposals.

'If you like, we'll bleed him together like a pig!'

Octave tried to calm him. Then, on his quiet days, Saturnin would go from Octave to Berthe, delighted to repeat what one had said about the other, running errands for them, and turning himself into a perpetual bond of tenderness. He would willingly have flung himself down as a carpet at their feet.

Berthe had made no further allusion to the present. She did not seem to notice Octave's trembling attentions, treating him quite straightforwardly as a friend. Never before had he taken such pains with his dress, and he was forever gazing caressingly at her with his eyes the colour of old gold, whose velvety softness he thought irresistible. But she was only grateful to him for the lies he told on her behalf when helping her to escape from the shop. The two thus became accomplices, and he facilitated her goings-out with her mother, putting her husband off the scent if he showed the slightest suspicion. Her mania for such excursions finally made her absolutely reckless, and she relied entirely upon his guile for protection. If, on her return, she found him behind a pile of goods, she rewarded him with the hearty handshake of a comrade.

One day, however, she had a great shock. She had just come back from a dog-show when Octave beckoned her to follow him downstairs into the basement, where he gave her an invoice which had been presented during her absence—sixty-two francs for embroidered stockings. She turned quite pale, and exclaimed:

'Good heavens! Did my husband see this?'

He hastened to reassure her, telling her what trouble he had had to get hold of the bill from under Auguste's nose. Then, in an embarrassed tone, he was obliged to add discreetly:

'I paid it.'

She made a show of looking in her pockets and, finding nothing, merely said:

'I'll pay you back. I'm so obliged to you, Monsieur Octave! I really would have died if Auguste had seen that!'

This time she took hold of both his hands, and for a moment held them tightly in her own. But the sixty-two francs were never mentioned again.

She had an ever-increasing desire for freedom and pleasure—all that, as a girl, she had expected marriage to give her, all that her mother had taught her to extract from a man. She carried within her an appetite as yet unappeased, taking her revenge for her needy youth spent under the paternal roof; for all the inferior meat; for all the economy in butter, which enabled her to buy boots; for all the shabby dresses that had to be patched up a dozen times; for the falsehood of their social position, maintained at the price of squalid misery and filth. Most of all she now desired to make up for those three winters spent traipsing about in ball-slippers through all the mud of Paris, trying to catch a husband; evenings of deadly dullness during which she strove to appease her empty stomach with draughts of syrup, bored to tears by having to show off all her virginal airs and graces to stupid young men, inwardly exasperated at being obliged to affect ignorance of everything while knowing all; and all those homecomings in pouring rain without a cab, the chill discomfort of her ice-cold bed, and the maternal smacks that gave her cheeks a glow. At the age of twenty-two she had still despaired of getting married, humble as a hunchback, looking at herself in her nightgown in the evenings to see if anything was missing. But now she had at last got a husband and, like the sportsman who brutally dispatches with a blow the hare he has breathlessly pursued, so towards Auguste she showed no mercy, treating him like a fallen foe.

Thus, little by little, the breach grew ever wider between the couple, despite the efforts of the husband, who wished to lead a placid existence. He made desperate attempts to preserve the drowsy monotony of his little home, closing his eyes to small irregularities, and even tolerating grosser ones, living in constant dread of making some appalling discovery which would drive him mad with fury. Berthe's lies respecting little gifts which, as she claimed, were tokens of sisterly or motherly affection he now accepted, nor did he even grumble overmuch if she went out in the evening. Thus Octave was able to take her twice to the theatre, accompanied by Madame Josserand and Hortense—delightful jaunts, which made the ladies agree that Octave knew how to live.

Hitherto, at the slightest word, Berthe would always throw her virtue in her husband's face. He should consider himself lucky, for, in her opinion, as in that of her mother, a husband was entitled to show ill-temper only when his wife had proved herself unfaithful. Such chastity as hers, genuine enough at first when greedily indulging her appetite for frivolous amusement, cost her no great sacrifice. She was cold by nature, self-love predominating over passion; rather than being virtuous, she preferred to have her pleasures all to herself. After all her rebuffs as a marriageable young lady who thought that men had no interest in her, she was simply flattered by Octave's attentions; but she took care to profit thereby in various ways, calmly taking pecuniary advantage of it, for she had been trained to worship money. One day she allowed Octave to pay a five hours' cab fare for her; another time, when just going out, she induced him to lend her thirty francs behind her husband's back, saying that she had forgotten her purse. She never repaid anything. The young man was of no consequence, she argued; she had no designs upon him; she merely made use of him, without premeditation, just as her pleasure or circumstances required. Meanwhile she posed as a martyred wife who rigorously fulfilled all her duties.

One Saturday a frightful quarrel occurred between the young

couple, with respect to a deficit of twenty sous in Rachel's household accounts. As Berthe used to pay this account, Auguste always gave her enough money to meet the weekly household expenses. That evening the Josserands were coming to dinner, and the kitchen was full of provisions—a rabbit, a leg of mutton, and cauliflowers. Near the sink squatted Saturnin, polishing his sister's shoes and his brother-in-law's boots. The quarrel began with a long enquiry respecting the twenty-sou piece. What had become of it? How could one lose twenty sous? Auguste wanted to check the bill, to see if it had been added up correctly. Meanwhile Rachel, hard of face but supple of figure, was calmly spitting her leg of mutton, her mouth shut but her eyes on the watch. At last Auguste disbursed the sum of fifty francs, and was on the point of going downstairs when he suddenly turned back, tormented by the thought of the lost coin.

'It must be found,' he said. 'Perhaps you borrowed it from Rachel and forgot all about it.'

Berthe was greatly offended at this. 'So you think I fiddle the accounts, do you? Thank you, that's very nice.'

This was the starting-point; heated words soon followed. Auguste, despite his willingness to pay dearly for peace, became aggressive, exasperated at the sight of the rabbit, the leg of mutton, and the cauliflowers—the pile of provisions that his wife was going to thrust under her parents' noses. He looked through the account-book, exclaiming at every item. It was incredible! She must be in league with the servant to make a profit on the shopping.

'What!' cried Berthe, beside herself with anger, 'you accuse *me* of being in league with the servant? It must be you, sir, who pays her to spy on me! Yes, I can always sense her behind my back; I can't move without her looking at me. She can look through the keyhole as much as she likes when I'm changing my underclothes; I don't do anything I'm ashamed of, and I couldn't care less about all your detectives! But don't you dare accuse me of being in league with my own servant!'

For a moment this unexpected onslaught completely dumb-founded Auguste. Still holding the leg of mutton, Rachel turned round, and with hand on heart protested.

'Oh madam, how could you believe such a thing? And about me, who respects madam so much!'

'She's mad!' exclaimed Auguste, shrugging his shoulders. 'Don't trouble to defend yourself, my good girl. She's mad!'

Suddenly a noise behind his back startled him. It was Saturnin, who had hurled away one of the half-polished shoes and was coming to his sister's aid. With a terrible expression on his face and his fists clenched, he stammeringly declared that he would throttle the dirty beast if he dared once more to say that she was mad. Auguste, terrified, sought refuge behind the cistern, exclaiming:

'This is really too much! I can no longer say a word to you without this fellow interfering! It's true I took him in, but he must leave me alone. He's another wonderful present from your mother! She was terrified of him, so she saddled me with him, preferring to let me be murdered in her place. I'm so grateful to her! Look, he's got hold of a knife. For God's sake, stop him!'

Berthe disarmed her brother and pacified him with a look, while Auguste, who had turned deadly pale, continued muttering angrily. Always waving knives about! So easy to get hurt. With a madman one got no redress whatever. In short, it was not right to keep a brother like that as a bodyguard, ready to jump on one's husband at any minute, paralysing him if he sought to give vent to his just indignation, and forcing him to swallow his shame.

'Look here, sir! You have absolutely no tact!' cried Berthe scornfully. 'A gentleman doesn't discuss these things in the kitchen!'

She withdrew to her room, slamming the door behind her. Rachel had gone back to her spit as if she had heard nothing of this quarrel between her master and mistress. Like a maid who, though aware of everything that went on, knew her place, she did not look at Berthe as she left the room; and when Auguste stamped about for a while she remained utterly impassive. Very soon, however, he rushed out after his wife, whereupon Rachel, impassive as before, put the rabbit on to boil.

'Please understand, my dear,' said Auguste, on joining Berthe in her bedroom, 'I wasn't referring to you when I made that remark. It was intended for that girl who's robbing us. Those twenty sous will have to be found somehow.'

Berthe was trembling with nervous exasperation as she glared at him, pale and resolute.

'How much longer are you going to bother me with your twenty sous? It's not twenty sous I want—it's five hundred francs a month.

Yes, five hundred francs to dress on. You talk about money in the kitchen in front of the maid! All right then, I'll talk about money too! I've been holding back for a long time . . . I want five hundred francs!'

He stood aghast at this demand. Then she launched into the great tirade which her mother had directed at her father every fortnight for the last twenty years. Did he want her to go barefoot? When a man married a woman, he should at least manage to clothe and feed her properly. She would rather beg than resign herself to such a poverty-stricken existence. It wasn't her fault if he was incapable of managing his business; yes, incapable, lacking in ideas and enterprise, knowing only how to split pennies into four. A man whose ambition should have been to make a fortune as quickly as possible, so as to dress her up like a queen, and make the people at the Ladies' Paradise die of jealousy! But not a bit of it! With such a feeble brain as his, bankruptcy was certain. In this tirade one could see her veneration, her furious appetite for money, the religion of lucre, as taught to her by her own family when she saw to what base tricks they would stoop merely to appear to possess it.

'Five hundred francs?' said Auguste, at last. 'I'd rather shut up shop.'

She looked at him coldly.

'You refuse? Very well then, I'll just run up bills.'

'What? More debts, you wretched woman!'

He suddenly caught her by the arms and pushed her violently against the wall. Choking with passion, she uttered no cry but rushed forward and threw the window open as if she meant to jump into the street. But she came back, and in her turn pushed him out of the room, stammering:

'Go away, or I'll do myself an injury!'

She noisily bolted the door in his face. For a moment, hesitating, he stood and listened. Then he hurried downstairs to the shop, again seized with terror at the sight of Saturnin, whose eyes gleamed in the darkness. The noise of their brief struggle had brought him out of the kitchen.

Downstairs, Octave was selling some foulard to an old lady. He immediately noticed Auguste's agitation, and watched him out of the corner of his eye as he restlessly paced up and down in front of the counters. As soon as the customer had gone, Auguste's feelings brimmed over.

'My dear fellow, she's going mad!' he said, without naming his wife. 'She's locked herself in. Could you possibly go up and speak to her? I'm afraid something might happen, I really am!'

Octave pretended to hesitate. It was such a delicate matter! However, out of pure devotion he agreed. Upstairs, he found Saturnin keeping guard outside Berthe's door. Hearing footsteps, the madman grunted menacingly. But on recognizing Octave his face brightened.

'Oh yes, you!' he murmured. 'You're all right. She mustn't cry. Be nice to her and comfort her. And stay with her, you know. There's no fear of anybody coming. I'm here. If the servant tries to peep, I'll hit her.'

He squatted down on the floor, guarding the door. As he still had one of Auguste's boots in his hand, he began polishing it just to pass the time.

Octave knocked. No answer, not a sound. Then he called out his name. The bolt was at once drawn back. Berthe, opening the door slightly, asked him to come in. Then she nervously bolted it again.

'I don't mind *you*,' she said, 'but I won't have *him*!'

She paced up and down in a state of fury, from the bed to the window, which was still open. She muttered disjointed phrases: he could entertain her parents himself, if he wanted: yes, and explain her absence to them as well, for she wouldn't sit down to table—not she; she'd rather die first! No, she preferred to go to bed. She excitedly threw back the coverlet, tapped the pillows, and turned down the sheets, being so forgetful of Octave's presence as to begin unhooking her dress. Then she went off at a tangent about something else.

'Would you believe it? He beat me, yes, beat me! And just because I was ashamed of always going about in rags and asked him for five hundred francs.'

Octave, standing in the middle of the room, tried to find something conciliatory to say. She shouldn't let herself get upset like that. Everything would turn out all right. Then he timidly ventured to make an offer of help.

'If you're worried about a bill, why not ask your friends? I'd be very happy to help. Just a loan, you understand. You could pay me back later.'

She looked at him. After a pause, she replied:

'No, it would never do. What would people think, Monsieur Octave?'

So firm was her refusal that there was no further discussion about money. Her anger seemed to have subsided. Breathing heavily, she bathed her face and became very pale, very calm, looking quite weary with her large, resolute eyes. As he stood there before her he felt overcome by amorous bashfulness, stupid though he felt such emotion to be. Never before had he loved with such ardour; the very strength of his desire gave an awkwardness to his charms as a suave shopman. While uttering vague noises about the advisability of making it up, he was really debating in his own mind whether he should not take her in his arms. But the fear of another rebuff made him hesitate. She sat mute, watching him with her resolute air and slightly contracted brow.

'Well, you know,' he falteringly continued, 'you must be patient. Your husband's not a bad sort. If you know how to handle him he'll give you what you want.'

Beneath hollow talk such as this, they felt the same thought seize them both. They were alone, free, in no danger of being surprised, the door bolted. Such safety as this and the warm atmosphere of the room touched their senses. And yet he did not dare; the feminine side of him, his womanly instinct, was so strong in this moment of passion that it made him the woman in their encounter. Then, as if remembering one of her early lessons, she dropped her handkerchief.

'Oh, thank you!' she said to the young man as he picked it up.

Their fingers touched; this momentary contact brought them closer to each other. Now she smiled fondly; her waist grew soft and supple, for she remembered that men hate boards. One must not behave like a simpleton; one must submit to a little playfulness without appearing to do so, if one wished to make a catch.

'It's getting quite dark,' she said, as she went to close the window.

He followed, and in the shadow of the curtains she allowed him to take her hand. She began to laugh louder—a silvery laugh that almost dazed him—and enveloped him with her pretty gestures. Then, as he at length grew bold, she threw back her head, displaying her soft young neck, quivering with excitement. Distracted by this vision, he kissed her under the chin.

'Oh, Monsieur Octave!' she said, making a pretence of gracefully keeping him in his proper place.

Then, catching hold of her, he threw her backwards on to the bed, which she had just been arranging; and, his desire satisfied, all his brutal instincts returned—his ferocious disdain for women, usually hidden under his gentle air of adoration. She submitted in silence, without pleasure. When she got up, with limp wrists and her face drawn by a spasm of pain, all her contempt for men was apparent in the black look she gave him. They remained silent. The only sound to be heard was the regular beat of Saturnin's brush as he sat outside the door cleaning the husband's boots.

Meanwhile Octave, in the flush of his triumph, kept thinking of Valérie and Madame Hédouin. At any rate, he was now something more than little Madame Pichon's lover! It was as if he had rehabilitated himself in his own eyes. Then, noticing Berthe's look of pain, he felt somewhat ashamed and kissed her with great tenderness. She soon recovered her composure, however, her face resuming its expression of resolute insouciance. With a gesture she seemed to say: 'It can't be helped; it's done now.' Yet she felt the need to express the sad thoughts within her.

'Ah, if only you had married me!' she murmured.

He felt surprised, almost uneasy; but kissing her again, he answered:

'Yes, how nice that would have been!'

That evening, the dinner with the Josserands was quite delightful. Berthe had never seemed so sweet and gentle. She never said a word to her parents about the quarrel, and greeted her husband with an air of submission. Delighted, he took Octave aside to thank him, doing this with such warmth and squeezing his hands so vigorously in sign of gratitude that the young man felt quite embarrassed. In fact, they all lavished attention on him. Saturnin, who at table behaved extremely well, also looked at him with loving eyes, as if he had shared in the sweetness of his sin. Hortense even deigned to listen to him, while Madame Josserand, full of motherly devotion, kept filling his glass.

'Why, yes,' said Berthe during dessert. 'I want to take up my painting again. I've wanted for ages to decorate a cup for Auguste.'

Auguste was greatly moved by this loving thought on the part of his wife. Meanwhile, under the table, Octave had kept his foot on Berthe's ever since the soup—a gesture of possession, so to speak, at this little bourgeois gathering. Berthe, however, was not without a certain uneasiness before Rachel, whom she always caught staring at her. Was it visible then? Obviously, the girl must either be dismissed or bought off.

Monsieur Josserand, sitting next to his daughter, managed to soothe her by slipping nineteen francs, wrapped up in paper, under the tablecloth. Bending down, he whispered in her ear:

'That came from my own little work, you know. If you've got any debts, you must pay them.'

Thus, between her father, who nudged her knee, and her lover, who gently rubbed her foot, she felt perfectly happy. Life would now be wonderful. And they all became very relaxed, determined to enjoy such a pleasant family gathering, unspoiled by quarrels of any sort. It was really almost too good to be true; something must be going to bring them good luck. Auguste alone had a splitting headache which, however, he had expected after so much high emotion. At about nine o'clock he was obliged to go to bed.

XIII

FOR some time past Monsieur Gourd had gone prowling about, looking mysteriously ill at ease. One met him moving noiselessly along, his eyes peeled and his ears pricked up, forever going up and down both staircases, where the tenants had even seen him doing his rounds at dead of night. It was clear that the morality of the house troubled him; a breath of scandal had come to disturb the courtyard in its frigid nakedness, ruffling the claustral serenity of the hall and menacing the spotless virtue of the families on every floor.

One evening Octave found the concierge standing stock-still and without a light at the end of his corridor, leaning against the door opening on to the back stairs. Surprised, he asked him the reason.

'I want to find out something, Monsieur Mouret,' replied Gourd, as he shuffled off to bed.

The young man was greatly alarmed. Did the concierge have suspicions as to his relations with Berthe? Perhaps he was spying on them. There were perpetual obstacles to their relationship in a house as carefully supervised as this, whose inhabitants all professed to be so strictly moral. Thus he could only see his mistress on rare occasions; and if she went out in the afternoon without her mother, his sole joy was to leave the shop on some pretext and join her at the end of some out-of-the-way arcade, where he would walk about with her arm-in-arm for an hour. Moroever, ever since the end of July, Auguste slept away from home every Tuesday, as he went to Lyons, where he had been foolish enough to take a share in a silk factory that was in difficulties. So far, however, Berthe had refused to take advantage of this night of liberty. The thought of Rachel made her tremble, and she feared that some forgetfulness on her part might put her in the girl's power.

It was precisely on a Tuesday evening that Octave caught Monsieur Gourd on the watch near his room. This increased his anxiety. For the last week he had been vainly imploring Berthe to come upstairs to his room when everybody was asleep. Was this what Gourd suspected? Octave went back to bed discontented, tortured alike by passion and fear. His love was growing troublesome; it was turning into an insane passion, and he angrily saw himself giving way to every sort of sentimental absurdity. As it was, he could never meet Berthe in an arcade without buying her whatever took her fancy in a shop-window. For instance, only the day before in the Passage de la Madeleine, she had looked so avidly at a little bonnet that he went into the shop and bought it for her as a present—chip straw, with just a garland of roses, something delightfully simple, but costing two hundred francs! A bit much, he thought.

Towards one o'clock he fell asleep, after feverishly tossing about for a long while between the sheets. Then he was roused by a gentle tapping at his door.

'It's me,' whispered a woman's voice.

It was Berthe. Opening the door, he clasped her passionately to him in the dark. But she had not come upstairs for that. Lighting a candle, he saw that she was in a state of great agitation about something. The day before, as he had not had enough money with him, he had been unable to pay for the bonnet, while she was so delighted that she actually gave her name; accordingly they had just sent her the bill. So, terrified that they might call on her husband for the money in the morning, she had ventured to come upstairs, emboldened by the profound silence of the house and feeling certain that Rachel was asleep.

'Tomorrow morning, without fail!' she implored, trying to escape his grasp. 'It must be paid tomorrow morning!'

But he again clasped her to him.

'Stay here!'

Half awake and shivering, he whispered the words in her ear as he drew her nearer to the warm bed. Wearing only a petticoat and a dressing-jacket, she felt as if naked, with her hair already knotted up for the night and her shoulders still warm from the dressing-gown she had thrown over them on coming out.

'I promise I'll let you go in an hour. Stay!'

She stayed. Slowly the clock chimed the hours in the voluptuous warmth of the room; and at each stroke he begged her not to go, pleading so tenderly that all her strength deserted her. She succumbed. Then, at about four o'clock, just as she had finally resolved to go, they both fell asleep in each other's arms. When they opened their eyes, broad daylight was streaming in through the window. It was nine o'clock. Berthe uttered a cry of despair.

'Good heavens! I'm lost!'

Then came a moment of confusion. She leaped out of bed, her eyes half closed with sleep and weariness, groping about blindly, putting her clothes on inside out, while emitting stifled cries of terror. Octave, equally desperate, had rushed to the door to stop her from going out dressed that way at such an hour. Was she mad? People might meet her on the stairs; it was far too risky. They must think up some plan by which she could get downstairs unobserved. But she insisted that she had to leave immediately, and tried to push past him in order to get to the door. Suddenly he thought of the back staircase. Nothing could be more convenient; she could slip through the kitchen to her room. But as Marie Pichon was always in the corridor in the morning, Octave thought it prudent to go and divert her attention while Berthe made her escape. He hurriedly put on his trousers and an overcoat.

'Really! How slow you are!' muttered Berthe, to whom the bedroom had become a veritable furnace.

At last Octave went out in his usual nonchalant fashion. To his surprise, he found Saturnin in Marie's apartment, calmly watching her do her housework. The madman was glad to take refuge there as he used to, for she left him to himself; here he was sure not to be told what to do. Marie did not find him in her way but willingly tolerated his presence, though his conversational powers were not great. Still, he was company in a way; and she went on singing her song in a low, mournful voice.

'Hullo! There you are with your sweetheart!' said Octave, contriving to keep the door closed behind him.

Marie turned crimson. Poor Monsieur Saturnin! Was it likely? It seemed to hurt him if one simply touched his hand by accident! The madman grew angry as well. He would never be anyone's sweetheart, never, never! Anybody who told his sister such a lie would have him to deal with. Surprised at his sudden irritability, Octave had to pacify him.

Meanwhile Berthe slipped out by the servants' staircase. She had to go down two flights of stairs. On the very first step she stopped short at the sound of shrill laughter that came from Madame Juzeur's kitchen below; trembling, she caught hold of the railing of the open window overlooking the narrow courtyard. Then, all at once, there was a babel of voices; the morning sewage surged up in waves from this fetid drain. It was the maids, who were furiously abusing little Louise for spying on them in their rooms, through the keyhole, as they were undressing. A fine thing for a dirty brat like that, not yet fifteen, to do. Louise only laughed the louder. She did not deny it. She knew what Adèle's behind looked like. What a sight! Lisa was dreadfully skinny, while Victoire's belly was bashed in like an old cask. To make her stop, they all drenched her with disgusting language. Then, annoyed at having been stripped naked, so to speak, before each other, and longing for some method of self-defence, they began to attack their mistresses, stripping them naked in their turn. Ah yes, Lisa might be skinny, but she wasn't as skinny as the other Madame Campardon, who was like a dried shark—quite a tasty morsel for an architect. Victoire merely wished that all the Vabres, Duveyriers, and Josserands in the world might possess as well-preserved a belly as hers if ever they reached her age. As for Adèle, she certainly would not exchange her behind for such pathetic little things as those of Madame Josserand's daughters. Thus Berthe, standing motionless and amazed, received this kitchen swill full in the face. She had never dreamed of such a cesspool as this; it was her first revelation of maidservants washing their dirty linen, while their masters were busy shaving.

Suddenly a voice shouted:

'There goes the bell for master's hot water.'

At once windows were closed and doors slammed. Complete silence ensued, but Berthe did not yet dare to move. When she at last went down it occurred to her that Rachel would probably be in the kitchen waiting for her. This threw her into a fresh panic. She dreaded going in now; she would rather have gone out into the street and run off, never to return. However, she pushed the door half open and was relieved at not finding her maid there. Then, gleeful as a child at seeing herself home again and safe, she hurried to her room. But there, beside the bed, which had not even been turned down, stood Rachel. The maid looked at the bed and then at her mistress, her face impassive. In her confusion Berthe stammered out, as an excuse, something about her sister being unwell upstairs. Then, appalled at such a miserable falsehood, and aware that all was discovered, she burst into tears. Sinking into a chair, she sobbed bitterly.

This lasted a whole minute. Not a word was exchanged; sobs

alone broke the deep silence of the room. Exaggerating her discretion, maintaining the frosty manner of a girl who knows everything but says nothing, Rachel turned round and pretended to smooth the pillows, as if she had just finished making the bed. Then, as the silence only distressed Berthe even more, Rachel said respectfully, as she carried on her dusting:

'Madame shouldn't take on so, monsieur is not very nice to her.'

Berthe stopped crying. She would tip the girl; that was the best thing to do. So she at once gave her twenty francs. Then it struck her that that was rather mean, and feeling uneasy, having fancied she saw the girl's lip curl disdainfully, she followed her into the kitchen and brought her back to make her a present of a nearly new dress.

Meanwhile Octave, for his part, was again in a state of alarm on account of Monsieur Gourd. On leaving the Pichons', he found him standing silently in the same place as on the previous night, spying behind the door of the servants' staircase. He followed him, without even venturing to speak. The concierge gravely descended to the front staircase. On the floor below he took out a key, and went into the apartment which was let to the gentleman of distinction who came one night a week to work. Through the half-open door Octave got a good view of his room, which always remained as closely shut as a tomb. That morning it was in a terrible state of disorder, as, no doubt, the gentleman had been working there the night before—a large bed with the sheets stripped off it, an empty wardrobe with a glass door, the remains of a lobster and two half-empty bottles, two basins full of dirty water, one near the bed and the other on a chair. In a manner as calm as that of a retired magistrate, Monsieur Gourd proceeded to empty the basins and rinse them out.

As he hurried to the Passage de la Madeleine to pay for the bonnet, Octave's fears of discovery still haunted him. On his way back, he decided to draw out the concierge and his wife. Reclining in her commodious armchair, Madame Gourd was taking the air which came in through the open window, flanked by two flowerpots. Near the door old Mother Pérou, looking humble and abashed, stood waiting.

'Any letters for me?' asked Octave, by way of a start.

Just then Monsieur Gourd came down from the third-floor apartment. To keep this place in order was the only work in the house that he deigned to do, and he appeared flattered that the gentleman should show such confidence in him, paying him generously as well, on condition that the washbasins did not pass through other hands.

'No, Monsieur Mouret, nothing at all!' he replied.

Though perfectly aware of old Mother Pérou's presence, Gourd pretended not to see her. The day before he had sent her packing, furious with her for having spilt a pail of water in the hall. Now she had come for her money, trembling at the sight of him and cringing close to the wall.

While Octave lingered to make conversation with Madame Gourd, the concierge suddenly turned towards poor Mother Pérou.

'So you've come for your money. How much is it?'

But Madame Gourd interrupted.

'Look, dear; there's that girl again with her horrible dog.'

It was Lisa, who, a few days before, had picked up a stray spaniel in the street. Ever since there had been continual quarrels with Gourd and his wife. The landlord would not have any animals in the house. No, no animals and no women! The little thing was not even allowed to go into the courtyard; it could do its business perfectly well in the street. As it had been raining that morning the dog's paws were wet, so Monsieur Gourd, rushing forward, exclaimed:

'I won't have it running upstairs! Do you hear? Carry it in your arms!'

'So I get all dirty!' said Lisa insolently. 'Wouldn't it be a shame if he dirtied the back stairs! Go on, doggie!'

Monsieur Gourd tried to grab the animal and nearly slipped, so he vented his fury on all those filthy servants. He was forever at war with them, ill-tempered as any former servant who wishes to be waited upon in his turn. All at once Lisa turned on him, and with the strident voice of a girl reared in the gutters of Montmartre she shouted out:

'Eh! Can't you leave me alone, you dirty old flunkey? Why don't you go and empty the duke's piss-pots?'

It was the only insult that could silence Monsieur Gourd, and all the servants made ample use of it. He withdrew, fuming, muttering to himself, saying that he was proud to have been in the duke's service, and that she would not have stayed there two hours, useless bag that she was. Then he fell upon Mother Pérou, who nearly jumped out of her skin.

'Well, how much do we owe you then? Eh? Twelve francs sixty-five? That can't be. Sixty-three hours at twenty centimes an hour. Oh, you reckon the extra quarter of an hour? Not if I have anything to do with it. I told you—I never pay for extra quarters of an hour.'

And he still did not give her the money, but left her quaking and joined in the conversation between his wife and Octave. The latter was cunningly alluding to all the problems a house like that must cause them, hoping that this would make them talk about the various tenants. There must be some rare goings-on at times behind those doors! Then the concierge gravely observed:

'There are things that concern us, Monsieur Mouret, and things that don't. Now, just look over there. That, for instance, is something that quite infuriates me! Just look at that!'

He pointed to the boot-stitcher who was passing, the tall, pale girl who had arrived in the middle of old Vabre's funeral. She was walking with difficulty, for she was obviously in an advanced state of pregnancy, her belly seeming even more enormous in contrast to her narrow chest and spindly legs.

'What do you mean?' asked Octave naively.

'Can't you see? That belly of hers, that belly!'

It was the belly that so exasperated Monsieur Gourd. A single woman with a belly like that, which she had got heaven knows where, for she certainly didn't have it when she arrived! And now it had begun to swell beyond all bounds, beyond all decent proportion!

'You can well understand how annoyed I was, sir,' said the concierge, 'and the landlord too, when I first noticed the thing! She ought to have told us about it, don't you think? You don't go and lodge in a respectable house in that sort of condition! To begin with it was hardly noticeable; but I couldn't be sure, and I hoped that at any rate she would use her discretion. Well, I kept watching her, and I could see her swelling so fast that it quite alarmed me. Now look at her! She doesn't do anything to hide it; she just lets it hang out like that. She can hardly get through the entrance!'

He kept tragically pointing at her as she made for the backstairs. Her belly seemed to him to cast a shadow over the frigid cleanliness of the courtyard, and even over the imitation marble and gilded zinc decorations of the hall. It seemed to bring disgrace to the whole building, tainting the very walls and, as it swelled, undermining the placid virtue of each apartment.

'Upon my word, sir, if this sort of thing goes on we would rather retire to Mort-la-Ville; wouldn't we Madame Gourd? Fortunately we've got enough to live on; we don't depend on anybody. A house like ours made the talk of the neighbourhood by a belly like that! Because it *is* the talk of the neighbourhood! Everybody stares when she arrives!'

'She looks very ill,' said Octave, looking in her direction but afraid to show too much pity. 'She always seems so sad, so pale, so forlorn. She must have a lover, I suppose!'

At this Gourd gave a violent start.

'Exactly! Did you hear that, Madame Gourd? Monsieur Mouret also thinks she's got a lover. Such things don't happen by magic, that's for sure! Well sir, I've been watching her for a couple of months but I haven't seen any sign of a man! What a bad lot she must be! Just let me catch her man and I'll chuck him out straight away! But I can't find him; that's what worries me!'

'Perhaps nobody comes to see her,' Octave ventured to suggest.

The concierge looked at him in amazement.

'That wouldn't be natural. I'm determined to catch him! I've got another six weeks; she's had notice to quit in October. The very idea of her giving birth here! And you know, although Monsieur Duveyrier insisted that she clear out before that happens, I can hardly sleep at night for thinking that she might play a dirty trick on us and not wait. And this unfortunate business could have been avoided if it hadn't been for that old miser Vabre! Just to make an extra hundred and thirty francs, and in spite of my advice! That carpenter ought to have been a lesson to him. But no, he had to take in this boot-stitcher! All right! Fill your house with labourers and let your lodgings to a lot of dirty work-people. When you take the lower classes into your house, sir, that's what you can expect!'

And once more he pointed to the young woman's belly, as she painfully made her way up the back stairs. Madame Gourd was obliged to calm her husband; his concern for the respectability of the house might make him ill. Then, as Mother Pérou gave sign of her presence by a discreet cough, he turned his attention back to her, calmly deducting the sou she had charged for her extra quarter of an hour. Having at last got her twelve francs sixty, she was going away when he offered to take her back, but at the rate of only three sous an hour. She began to cry, and accepted.

'I can always get someone to do the work,' he said. 'You're not strong enough any more. You don't even do two sous' worth.'

Going up to his room for a moment, Octave felt reassured. On the third floor he caught up with Madame Juzeur, who was returning home. Every morning now she had to come down to look for Louise, who loafed about outside when she was sent to the shops.

'How proud you are!' she said, with her subtle smile. 'It's obvious that you're being spoilt somewhere.'

The remarks once more aroused the young man's fears. He followed her into her drawing-room, pretending to joke with her. Only one of the curtains was drawn back; the carpets and door-hangings softened the daylight; and the noise of the street was barely audible in this room as soft as eiderdown. She made him sit next to her on the low, wide sofa. But as he did not take her hand and kiss it, she asked coquettishly:

'So you don't love me any more?'

Blushing, he declared that he adored her. Then, stifling a nervous giggle, she gave him her hand of her own accord. He was obliged to raise it to his lips so as to dispel any suspicions she might have. But she at once withdrew it.

'No, no! Don't pretend you're excited. It doesn't give you any pleasure. I can feel it doesn't. Besides, it's only natural.'

What did she mean by that? He caught her by the waist and overwhelmed her with questions. But she would not answer, yielding to his embrace as she shook her head. In order to make her speak, he began tickling her.

'Well, it's because you're in love with somebody else,' she murmured.

She mentioned Valérie, and reminded him of the evening at the Josserands', when he devoured her with his eyes. Then, when he swore that he had not slept with her, she laughingly replied that she was only teasing him. But there was someone else he had slept with, and this time she named Madame Hédouin, laughing more and more at his emphatic denials. Who was it, then? Was it Marie Pichon? Well, he could not deny having slept with her. Yet he did so; but she shook her head, and assured him that her little finger never lied. And to get the names of these women from her, he had to redouble his caresses and make her whole body shiver with excitement.

However, she had not yet mentioned Berthe. He was about to let her go when she said:

'And there's one last one.'

'What last one?' he anxiously enquired.

Screwing up her mouth, she obstinately refused to say any more until he had unsealed her lips with a kiss. She really could not mention the person's name, for it was she who had first suggested her marriage. Without naming her, she related Berthe's whole history. Then, with his lips touching her soft cheek, he made a complete confession, experiencing a certain cowardly pleasure in such an avowal. How silly of him to hide anything from her! Perhaps, he thought, she would be jealous? But why should she be? She had granted him no favours, had she? Nothing but a little childish fun, as at present, but not that, oh, not that! For, after all, she was a virtuous woman, and she almost felt vexed that he should have thought that she might be jealous.

She lay back languidly in his arms, and referred to her cruel husband who, after one week of matrimony, had cruelly deserted her. A wretched woman like herself knew all too much about the affairs of the heart! For some time she had had an inkling of what she called Octave's 'little games', for not a kiss could be exchanged in the house without her hearing it. Then, ensconced in the big sofa, they had a quiet little talk, unconsciously interrupted by pattings and strokings of various parts of their persons. She called him a silly ninny, for it was entirely his fault that he had not succeeded with Valérie; she could have helped him to have her at once, if he had merely asked her advice. Then she questioned him about little Marie Pichon—hideous legs and nothing between them, eh? But she kept coming back to Berthe, whom she thought quite charming—a lovely skin and the foot of a marchioness. Eventually the game of patting and stroking reached such a pitch that she had to repulse him.

'No, no, leave me alone! Have you no shame? It wouldn't give you any pleasure either. You think it would. I know better! It's just to flatter me! It would be too dreadful if it did give you any pleasure. Keep that for her. Now, be off with you, you naughty man!'

She sent him away after making him solemnly promise to come and confess himself often to her, and to hide nothing if he wanted her to look after his love affairs.

On leaving her, Octave felt more at ease. She had restored his good humour, and her complicated notions of virtue amused him. As soon as he entered the shop downstairs, he gave Berthe a reassuring nod in answer to her enquiring look.

Thus the whole dreadful adventure of the morning was forgotten. When Auguste came back, shortly before lunch, he found them both as usual—Berthe bored to death at the pay-desk, and Octave gallantly measuring silk for a lady.

Henceforth, however, the lovers' assignations became less frequent still. He, in his ardour, grew desperate and followed her everywhere, entreating her to arrange a meeting, whenever and wherever she liked. She, on the other hand, with the indifference of a girl reared in a hothouse, took no pleasure in such guilty passion, except for the secret outings, the presents, the forbidden delights, and the hours of luxury spent in cabs, theatres, and restaurants. All her early education made itself felt again, her lust for money, for clothes, for squandering; and she soon grew tired of her lover, just as she had grown tired of her husband, thinking him too exacting for what he gave her in return, and trying, almost unconsciously, not to yield him his full, just measure of love. Thus exaggerating her fears, she kept on refusing him: she would never go back to his room; she would die of fright! And he could not possibly come to her apartment, for they might be surprised. Then, when he begged her to let him take her to a hotel for an hour, she would begin to cry, saying that he really could not have much respect for her. However, the spending continued and her whims became more extravagant. After the bonnet she conceived a desire for a fan covered with Alençon lace, not counting the many little trifles that took her fancy in shop-windows. Though as yet he did not dare refuse her anything, his sense of thrift was once more roused as he saw all his savings frittered away in this fashion. Like the practical fellow he was, in the end it seemed to him silly always to be paying when all he got in return was her foot under the table. Paris had certainly brought him bad luck; first rebuffs, and then this stupid love affair which was draining his purse. He definitely could not be accused of succeeding through women. By way of comfort, he sought to find something honourable about the whole thing, in his hidden anger at a scheme which, so far, had proved such a dismal failure.

Auguste, however, did not bother them much. Ever since the bad turn affairs had taken in Lyons he had been suffering more than ever with his headaches. Berthe had felt a thrill of delight as, on the first of the month, in the evening, she saw him put three hundred francs under the bedroom clock for her dress allowance; and despite the reduction in the sum she had demanded, as she had given up all hope of getting a penny of it, she threw herself into his arms, all warm with gratitude. On this occasion the husband had a night of endearments such as the lover never enjoyed.

September thus passed amid the great calm of the house, emptied of its occupants by the summer months. The second-floor people had gone to a watering-place in Spain, which caused Monsieur Gourd to shrug his shoulders in contempt. How absurd! As if the most genteel folk were not content to go to Trouville! Ever since the beginning of Gustave's holidays the Duveyriers had been staying at their country house at Villeneuve-Saint-Georges. Even the Josserands had gone to stay for a fortnight with a family friend near Pontoise, while letting it be rumoured that they were on the way to some fashionable seaside resort. The house being empty, the apartments deserted, and the staircase wrapped in an even drowsier silence, Octave felt that there would be less danger, and he pestered Berthe until, from sheer weariness, she agreed to let him stay with her for one night when Auguste was away in Lyons. But this meeting almost turned into a disaster. Madame Josserand (who had returned two days before) was seized with such violent indigestion after dining out that Hortense, in alarm, went downstairs to fetch her sister. Fortunately Rachel was just finishing cleaning her pots and pans, so she was able to let Octave escape by the servants' staircase. After this scare Berthe took advantage of it to refuse him everything, as before. Moreover, they were foolish enough not to bribe the servant. She waited upon them with her coldly respectful air, like a girl who sees and hears nothing. However, as madame was forever hankering after money, and as Monsieur Octave had already spent far too much on presents, she curled her lips yet more in her scorn for a dump like this where the mistress's lover did not even tip her ten sous when he slept there. If they thought that they had bought her for all eternity with twenty francs and an old gown, they were much mistaken. She was worth more than that! From this time onwards she was less obliging, no longer shutting the doors after them as before, although they were never aware of her ill-humour, for no one thinks of giving tips when he is so driven by the need to find a place to embrace in that he even quarrels about it. The silence of the house grew even deeper; and Octave, in his quest for some safe corner, was forever meeting Monsieur Gourd, on the watch for shameful things that made the very walls blush, shuffling silently along the corridors, eternally haunted by the bellies of pregnant women.

Madame Juzeur sympathized constantly with this lovesick young man who could only gaze upon his mistress from afar, giving him, as promised, the very best advice. Octave's desire reached such a pitch that he even thought of asking her to lend him her rooms for an assignation. No doubt she would not have refused, but he feared shocking Berthe by such indiscretion. He also thought of making use of Saturnin; perhaps the madman would guard them like a faithful dog in some out-of-the-way room. But recently Saturnin's mood had been somewhat strange, at one time smothering his sister's lover with affection, and at another sulking, looking at him suspiciously, giving him fiery glances full of hatred. One would almost have said he was jealous—nervously, violently jealous like a woman. He had been like this especially since, on certain mornings, he had seen Octave laughing and joking with little Marie Pichon. In fact Octave never passed Marie's door now without going in, drawn back to her by some strange fancy, some sudden, unavowed touch of passion. He adored Berthe and madly desired to possess her, and this very longing gave birth to a feeling of infinite tenderness for Marie, and a love the sweetness of which he had never tasted at the time of their first liaison. There was a perpetual charm in looking at her, in touching her, in joking with her and teasing her—all the playfulness of a man who wants to repossess a woman while secretly embarrassed by another love-affair. So, when Saturnin caught him hovering round Marie's skirts, the madman glared at him wolfishly, ready to bite; nor would he forgive him and kiss his hand like some tame animal until he saw him, loving and faithful, at Berthe's side.

As September was drawing close and the residents were about to return, Octave, in the midst of all his torment, had a mad idea. It so happened that Rachel, whose sister was to be married, had asked permission to stay away for a night, on one of the Tuesdays her master spent in Lyons. The idea was that they could sleep together in the servant's room, where no one would ever dream of looking for them. Offended by such a proposal, Berthe at first displayed the greatest repugnance, but with tears in his eyes he begged her to agree, and spoke of leaving Paris, where he suffered too much unhappiness. At last, bewildered and exhausted by all his arguments and entreaties, she consented, hardly aware of what she was doing. Everything was then arranged. On Tuesday evening, after dinner, they had tea at the Josserands' to allay any suspicion. Trublot, Gueulin and uncle Bachelard were all there. Duveyrier even came in, very late, as he occasionally slept in town now because of early business appointments, so he claimed. Octave made a show of joining the conversation and then, at the stroke of midnight, slipped away and locked himself in Rachel's room, where Berthe was to join him an hour later when everybody was asleep.

Upstairs, he was busy for the first half-hour in setting the room straight. In order to conquer Berthe's disgust he had promised that he would change the sheets and bring all the necessary linen himself. Thus he proceeded to make the bed, slowly and clumsily, fearing that someone would hear him. Then, like Trublot, he sat on a trunk and tried to wait patiently. One by one the servants came up to bed, and through the thin partitions he could hear the sounds of women undressing and relieving themselves. One o'clock struck, then a quarter past, then half past. He grew anxious; why was she so late? She must have left the Josserands' at one o'clock at the latest; and it would not take her more than ten minutes to get back to her flat and leave it again by the servants' staircase. When it struck two, he imagined all sorts of catastrophes. At last, thinking that he recognized her footstep, he heaved a sigh of relief. He opened the door to give her some light, but sheer surprise rooted him to the spot. Outside Adèle's door Trublot, bent double, was looking through the keyhole; the sudden light made him jump.

'It's you!' said Octave, in a tone of annoyance.

Trublot began to laugh, without seeming the least surprised at finding Octave there at that time of night.

'Just imagine,' he said in a whisper, 'that idiot Adèle didn't give me her key, and now she's gone down to Duveyrier's room. What's the matter? Didn't you know Duveyrier sleeps with her? Oh yes, my dear fellow. He's made it up with his wife, who lets him have it now and then; but she keeps him on strict rations so he has to fall back on Adèle. It's convenient for him, you see, when he comes up to Paris.'

Breaking off, he stooped down again to have another look, and then muttered between clenched teeth:

'No, there's nobody there! He's keeping her longer this time. What a dumbo that Adèle is! If she'd only given me the key I could've waited for her in bed and kept warm.'

Then he went back to the attic where he had been hiding, taking Octave with him. Octave was eager to ask him how the evening had ended at the Josserands'. But Trublot never gave him a chance to open his mouth, for he carried on talking about Duveyrier in the inky darkness and stuffy atmosphere of the space under the rafters. Yes, the dirty beast had wanted to have Julie at first, but she was a bit too clean for that sort of thing, and besides, in the country she had taken a fancy to little Gustave, a lad of sixteen, who seemed rather promising. So, having drawn a blank with Julie, and not daring to try it on with Clémence because of Hippolyte, Duveyrier had thought it more expedient to choose someone outside his own home. How on earth he had ever managed to get hold of Adèle nobody knew—behind some door, no doubt, in a draught; and that great slut just braced herself and took it like a slap in the face; certainly she would never have dared to be uncivil to the landlord.

'For the last month he's never missed one of the Josserands' Tuesdays,' said Trublot. 'It's very awkward. I'll have to find Clarisse again for him, so that he leaves us in peace.'

At last Octave managed to ask him how the evening had ended. Berthe had left before midnight, apparently quite composed. No doubt she was waiting for him in Rachel's bedroom. But Trublot, delighted to have bumped into him, would not let him go.

'It's stupid of her to keep me hanging about all this time,' he resumed. 'I'm half asleep as it is. My boss has put me into the liquidation department. Up all night three times a week, my dear boy! If Julie was there, I know she'd make room for me; but Duveyrier has only brought Hippolyte with him from the country. By the way, do you know Hippolyte, that great lout who sleeps with Clémence? Well, I just caught him in his nightshirt, sneaking into Louise's bedroom—that ugly young thing Madame Juzeur is so anxious to save! What a great success for Madame Anything-you-like-except-that! That lump of fifteen, a filthy bundle picked up on a

doorstep—a dainty morsel for that strapping, big-boned fellow, with
his sweaty hands and his bull neck! I don't care a damn myself, but
it's disgusting all the same!'

Bored though he was, Trublot seemed full of philosophical
insights. He went on muttering:

'Well, well, like master, like servant! When the landlords set the
example, the flunkeys become quite immoral as well. There's no
doubt about it, France is going to the dogs!'

'Goodbye, I must be off,' said Octave.

But Trublot kept him back, telling him about all the servants'
rooms in which he might have slept if the summer had not emptied
so many of them. The worst of it was that they all double-locked
their doors, even when they just went to the end of the corridor,
because they were all so frightened of being robbed by one of the
others. Lisa was a lost cause, and she seemed to him to have very odd
tastes. Victoire hardly tempted him, though ten years earlier she
might have done. What he most deplored was Valérie's mania for
changing her cook; it was becoming positively unbearable. He
counted them on his fingers—a regular string of them: one who
insisted on having chocolate in the morning; one who left because
her master made a mess of eating; one whom the police took away
just as she was roasting a piece of veal; one who was so strong that
she could not touch anything without breaking it; one who had a
maid of her own to wait on her; one who went out in her mistress's
gowns, and smacked her mistress's face when she dared to object. All
those in the space of a month! There wasn't even time to go and
pinch them in their kitchen!

'Oh! and then,' he added, 'there was Eugénie. You must have
noticed her—a tall, beautiful looking girl, a real Venus, my dear
fellow, I can tell you! People used to turn round in the street to
look at her. For ten days the whole house went mad. All the
women were furious; the men could hardly contain themselves.
Campardon licked his chops, and Duveyrier's trick was to come up
to see if there was a leak in the roof. It was pandemonium
throughout the whole bloody house. But I was careful. She was a
bit too smart. There's no doubt, my dear chap, the best ones to
choose are the ugly, stupid ones, as long as you've got plenty to
grab hold of—that's my view. And I was right about Eugénie—she
was sent packing in the end when madame saw from her sheets

that she was visited every morning by the coalman from the Place Gaillon—they were as black as soot; it must have cost a small fortune to have them washed. And do you know what happened? The coalman became very ill, while the coachman of the people on the second floor, who had left him behind, that stallion of a chap who sleeps with all of them— well, he had a dose of it too, so that he could hardly drag one leg after the other. But I haven't any sympathy for him, he's such a nuisance.'

At last Octave managed to escape, and as he was leaving Trublot there in the darkness of the attic, the latter suddenly exclaimed, in surprise:

'But what are you doing up here with the maids? You rogue! You come up too, then?'

He laughed gleefully, and promising not to tell he sent him off and wished him a very pleasant night. He was determined to wait for that slut Adèle who, when she was with a man, never wanted to go. Duveyrier would surely never keep her until the morning.

Back in Rachel's room Octave was again disappointed. Berthe had still not come. He now grew angry; she had fooled him, promising him to come simply to make him stop pestering her. While he stood there fuming she was no doubt sleeping peacefully, glad to be alone and to have the whole double bed to herself. However, instead of going back to sleep in his own room, he obstinately waited, lying down in his clothes on the bed and dreaming up plans for revenge. This bare, cold maid's room irritated him, with its dirty walls, its squalor, and its insufferable smell of an unwashed servant-girl; he could hardly bring himself to acknowledge to what depths his frenzied passion had lowered him in his craving to appease it. Far away in the distance he heard three o'clock strike. Strapping maidservants snored away to the left of him; at times bare feet made the boards creak, and then splashing as of a fountain resounded along the floor. But what most unnerved him was a continual wailing on his right, the cry of someone in pain. At last he recognized the voice—it was the boot-stitcher. Was she in labour? Poor woman, there she lay alone in her agony, close to the roof, cooped up in one of those miserable closets hardly big enough for her belly.

At about four o'clock Octave was again disturbed. It was Adèle coming to bed followed immediately by Trublot. They nearly had a quarrel. She declared that it was not her fault: the landlord had kept her, she couldn't help it. Then Trublot accused her of being vain, whereupon she began to cry. She was not vain at all. What had she done that God made men run after her like this? When one had finished another one appeared; there seemed no end to it. But she never tried to excite them, and their stupid behaviour gave her so little pleasure that she preferred to look sluttish on purpose, so as not to give them any encouragement. But they only ran after her more than ever, and her work kept increasing. It was killing her, and she had had enough of Madame Josserand bullying her to scrub the kitchen every morning.

'People like you', she stammered out between sobs, 'can sleep as long as you like afterwards. But I have to work like a slave. No, there's no justice in the world. I'm utterly sick of it.'

'There, there, don't take on so,' said Trublot, in a sudden access of fatherly pity. 'Mind you, some women would be glad to be in your place. If men like you, you silly thing, then let them.'

At daybreak Octave fell asleep. The house was now in complete silence. Even the boot-stitcher had stopped moaning, and lay half dead, clutching her belly with both hands. The sun was shining in through the narrow window when the door was suddenly opened. Octave woke up. It was Berthe, who had come up to see if he was still there, driven by an irresistible impulse. At first she had decided not to, but then had invented pretexts—the need to tidy up the room if, in his rage, he had left it in disorder. Nor had she expected to find him there. As she saw him rise from the little iron bedstead, pale and threatening, she was taken aback and, with head lowered, listened to his furious outburst. He challenged her to say something, to offer some sort of explanation. At last she murmured:

'At the last moment I couldn't do it; it was too revolting. I love you—I swear I do! But not here, not here!'

Then, as he approached her, she drew back, fearing that he might want to take advantage of the opportunity. This indeed was what he wanted. It struck eight; all the servants had gone down and Trublot had left too. Then, as he tried to catch hold of her hands, saying that when you love someone you don't mind anything, she complained of the smell of the room and went to open the window. But he again drew her to him and, bewildered by his persistence, she was about to give in when from the courtyard below there rose a turbid wave of filthy talk.

'You pig! You absolute slut! Shut up! Your dishcloth's fallen on my head again!'

Berthe, trembling, broke away from his embrace, murmuring:

'You see! Can you hear that? Oh no, not here, please! I would feel too ashamed. Can you hear those girls? They make my blood run cold. The other day they made me feel quite ill. No, leave me alone, and I promise I'll come and see you next Tuesday in your room.'

Standing there motionless, the two lovers were forced to overhear everything.

'Just let me catch sight of you,' Lisa angrily continued, 'and I'll chuck it in your face.'

Then, leaning out of her kitchen window, Adèle retorted:

'What a fuss about a little piece of rag! I only used it yesterday for washing up with, and it dropped down quite by accident.'

Thereupon a truce was declared, and Lisa asked her what they had had for dinner the night before. Another stew! What misers! If she lived in a hole like that she'd buy herself cutlets! And she kept urging Adèle to help herself to the sugar, the meat, and the candles, just to show her independence. For her part, never being hungry, she let Victoire rob the Campardons without even claiming her share.

'Oh!' cried Adèle, who by degrees was becoming corrupted, 'the other night I hid some potatoes in my pocket and they burned my thigh. It was fun! And I do like vinegar! I don't care, I drink it out of the cruet-stand now!'

Victoire then leant out in her turn, after finishing a glassful of cassis and brandy to which Lisa sometimes treated her in the morning as a reward for concealing her nocturnal and diurnal escapades. Louise, standing at the back of Madame Juzeur's kitchen, put her tongue out at them, and so Victoire started shouting at her.

'You guttersnipe, I'll shove that tongue of yours somewhere in a minute!'

'Come on, then, you old soak!' cried Louise. 'I saw you yesterday, being sick all over your plates.'

Then once more the flood of excrement surged up against the walls of the pestilential courtyard. Even Adèle, who had caught the Parisian patter, directed abuse at Louise, while Lisa cried out:

'I'll shut her up if she gives us any of her cheek! Yes, you little bitch, I'll tell Clémence. She'll soon settle you. Isn't it sickening?

Going with men at her age! But hush! Here's the man himself, and a filthy beast too!'

Hippolyte at that moment put his head out of the Duveyriers' window. He was cleaning his master's boots. In spite of everything the other servants were very civil to him, for he belonged to the aristocracy; and he despised Lisa, who in turn despised Adèle with greater haughtiness than gentry who are rich look down on gentry who are hard-up. They asked him for news of Mademoiselle Clémence and Mademoiselle Julie. Good Lord! They were bored to death down there in the country, but they were both pretty well. Then, changing the subject, he said:

'Did you hear that girl last night writhing about with her stomach-ache? Terrible nuisance, wasn't it? It's a good job she's leaving. I nearly called out to her to break her waters and have done with it!'

'Monsieur Hippolyte's right,' said Lisa. 'Nothing gets on your nerves more than a woman who's always got the belly-ache. Thank God, I don't know what it's like; but I think I'd try to put up with it so that other people can sleep.'

Then Victoire jokingly turned her attention to Adèle.

'I say, old pot-belly up there! When you had your first baby, did it come out in front or behind?'

At such coarseness all the kitchens were convulsed with merriment, while Adèle, looking scared, answered:

'A baby? No, not at all! It's not allowed; anyway, I don't want one.'

'My girl,' said Lisa, gravely, 'everybody can have a baby, and I don't suppose God made you any different from anyone else!'

Then they talked of Madame Campardon, who at least had no fears on that score; it was the only good thing about her physical state. Then all the ladies of the house were discussed in turn. Madame Juzeur, who took her own precautions; Madame Duveyrier, who felt only disgust towards her husband; Madame Valérie, who got her babies made for her out-of-doors, because her precious husband wasn't man enough to make even the tail of one. Then from the fetid hole there came bursts of crude laughter.

Berthe had again turned pale. She waited, afraid even to leave the room. She looked down in shame, as if publicly dishonoured in Octave's presence. Exasperated with the servants, he felt that their talk was becoming too filthy, and that to take her in his arms was impossible. His desire ebbed away, leaving him weary and extremely sad. Then Berthe started. Lisa had just mentioned her name.

'Talking of fun and games, I know someone who seems to be at it pretty often! Adèle, isn't it true that your Mademoiselle Berthe was up to all sorts of things when you used to wash her petticoats?'

'And now,' said Victoire, 'she gets her husband's assistant to give her what she wants.'

'Ssh!' cried Hippolyte softly.

'What for? Her pig of a cook isn't there today. Sly devil, she is; she looks as if she'd eat you the moment you mention her mistress! She's a Jewess, you know, and they say she once murdered somebody where she comes from. Perhaps that handsome Octave gets her in a quiet corner too. The governor must have taken him on just to make babies for him, the big ninny!'

Then Berthe, suffering unutterable anguish, looked at her lover imploringly, as she stammered out:

'Good God! Good God!'

Octave took her hand and squeezed it. He too was choking with impotent rage. What could they do? He could not show himself and tell them to shut up. The foul talk went on, talk such as Berthe had never heard before, like an open sewer that brimmed over every morning, close to her, though she had never suspected its existence. Their liaison, so carefully concealed, was now being trailed through all the garbage and slops of the kitchen. Though nothing had been said, the maids knew everything. Lisa related how Saturnin played the pander. Victoire laughed at the husband's headaches, and said he would do well to get himself an extra eye. And even Adèle had a go at her mistress's young lady, whose ailments, soiled underwear, and toilet secrets she did not scruple to lay bare. Thus were their kisses soiled and smeared by such filthy talk; their meetings too; in fact, all that was still sweet and tender in their love.

'Look out below!' suddenly exclaimed Victoire. 'Here's some of those stinkin' carrots from yesterday. Old Gourd can have them!'

The servants, out of sheer spite, used to throw all the rubbish they could into the courtyard, so that the concierge had to sweep it up.

'And here's a lump of rotten kidney!' cried Adèle in her turn.

All the scrapings from their saucepans, all the muck from their pots, were flung out in this fashion, while Lisa went on pulling

Berthe and Octave to pieces, commenting on all the deceptions by which they sought to hide their adultery. Hand in hand and face to face, the lovers stood there aghast. Their hands grew icy cold, their eyes acknowledged the squalor of their relationship. The servants, in their hatred, had no sympathy for the weaknesses of their masters. This was what it had come to—fornication beneath a downpour of rotten vegetables and putrid meat!

'And you know,' said Hippolyte, 'the young chap don't care a damn for his missus. He's only latched on to her to help him get on in the world. He's got no real feelings, and no scruples at all; he'd as soon hit a woman as make love to her!'

Berthe, her eyes on Octave, saw him turn pale; so changed, so upset did his face seem that it frightened her.

'Oh yes, they make a nice pair!' rejoined Lisa. 'She's not up to much either. Badly brought up, her heart as hard as stone, caring for nothing but her own pleasure, sleeping with men for their money! I know that sort of woman, and I wouldn't mind betting that she doesn't even get any pleasure with a man!'

Tears streamed down Berthe's cheeks. Octave saw how distraught she was. It was as if they had both been flayed before each other, laid utterly bare, without any possibility of protesting. Then the young woman, suffocating from the stench of this open cesspool, sought to flee. He did not attempt to make her stay; mutual self-disgust made each other's company excruciating, and they longed for the relief of no longer seeing each other.

'You promise then, next Tuesday, in my room!'

'Yes, yes!'

Extremely upset, she hurried away. Left alone, he walked about the room, his hands twitching nervously as he rolled the bed-linen up into a bundle. He no longer listened to the servants' gossip. Suddenly one phrase caught his ear.

'I tell you Monsieur Hédouin died last night. If only handsome Octave had foreseen that, he would've gone on cultivating Madame Hédouin, 'cos she'll be worth a lot now.'

To hear such news in this sewer touched him to the core. So Monsieur Hédouin was dead! He was seized by profound regret. He could not prevent himself from saying out loud:

'Yes, my God! I *was* a fool!'

When Octave at last went downstairs with his bundle, he met

Rachel coming up to her room. A few minutes earlier she would have caught them. Downstairs she had found her mistress in tears again; but this time she had got nothing out of her, neither a confession nor a sou. She was furious, convinced that they took advantage of her absence to meet and thus to cheat her of her little bonuses. She gave Octave a black, threatening scowl. A strange schoolboy timidity prevented him from giving her ten francs; then, anxious to show that he was completely at his ease, he was going into Marie Pichon's for a casual chat when a grunt from a corner made him turn round. Saturnin got up, exclaiming, in one of his jealous fits:

'Look out! You're dead!'

That very morning happened to be the 8th of October, and the boot-stitcher had to get out by noon. For a week past Monsieur Gourd had been watching her belly with ever-increasing uneasiness. That belly would surely never wait until the 8th. The poor woman had begged the landlord to let her stay a few days longer so as to get over her confinement, but had met with an indignant refusal. She now felt constant pains: the night before she was afraid she would give birth all by herself. Then, at about nine o'clock, she began to move her things out, helping the lad who had his cart in the courtyard below, leaning against the furniture or sitting down on the staircase when bent double by an excruciating pang.

Monsieur Gourd, however, had discovered nothing. No man after all! He had been tricked. All that morning he wandered about in a cold rage. When Octave met him the thought that he too knew of his secret affair filled him with dread. Perhaps he did know it, but he did not greet him any less politely, for what did not concern him did not concern him, as he had already observed. That morning, too, he had doffed his cap to the mysterious lady as she noiselessly hurried away from the gentleman's apartment on the third floor, leaving only a faint perfume of verbena behind her. He had also said good morning to Trublot, as well as the other Madame Campardon and Valérie. They were all gentry. If the young men were caught coming out of the maidservants' bedrooms, or the ladies tripping downstairs in tell-tale dressing-gowns, that was none of his business. What concerned him did concern him, and he kept his eye on the few miserable bits of furniture belonging to the boot-stitcher as if the long-sought male were escaping in one of the drawers.

At a quarter to twelve the woman appeared, her face quite waxen, and looking as sad and despondent as ever. She could hardly walk, and until she got out into the street Monsieur Gourd was all atremble. Just as she was handing in her key Duveyrier came through the hall, so excited by his night out that the red blotches on his forehead looked as if they were bleeding. He put on a haughty air, an air severely, implacably moral, as the poor thing went past him. Shameful and resigned, she bowed her head and walked out after the little cart with the same despairing gait as when she had arrived, on the day that the black funeral hangings had enveloped her.

It was only then that Monsieur Gourd felt triumphant. As though the woman's belly had removed all unhealthiness from the house, all those shameful things that caused the very walls to blush, he exclaimed to the landlord:

'That's a good riddance, sir! We can breathe freely now because, upon my word, it was getting positively disgusting! It's like a great weight off my back. In a respectable house like this, you see sir, there shouldn't be any women, least of all working women.'

XIV

THE following Tuesday Berthe did not keep her promise. This time she told Octave beforehand not to expect her, when they had a brief conversation that same evening when the shop closed. She sobbed bitterly, for she had been to confession the day before, feeling the need for religious solace, and was still greatly affected by Father Mauduit's grave counsel. Since her marriage she had given up going to church; but after the foul language with which the maids had bespattered her she had felt so sad, so forlorn, so sullied, that for an hour she went back to her childish beliefs, ardently yearning to be made pure and good. On her return, after the priest had wept with her, she grew quite horrified at her sin. Octave shrugged his shoulders, powerless and enraged.

Then, three days later, she again promised to see him the following Tuesday. Meeting him one day in the Passage des Panoramas, she had noticed some shawls of Chantilly lace and talked about them incessantly, her eyes full of desire. Thus, on the Monday morning, the young man told her laughingly, in order to temper the brutality of such a bargain, that if she really kept her word she would find a little surprise waiting for her in his room. She guessed what he meant and again began to cry. No, no, it was impossible for her to come now; he had spoilt all her pleasure in their projected meeting. She had talked about the shawl without thinking, and she did not want it now; she would throw it on the fire if he gave it to her. Nevertheless, on the following day they made all the arrangements; at half-past twelve that night she was to knock three times very gently at his door.

That day, as Auguste was leaving for Lyons, Berthe thought that he looked somewhat strange. She had caught him whispering with Rachel behind the kitchen-door; besides which, his face was all yellow, he trembled violently, and one of his eyes was closed up. But as he complained of migraine she thought he must be unwell, and assured him that the journey would do him good. No sooner had he gone than she went back to the kitchen and, feeling uneasy, tried to sound out Rachel. The young woman, however, maintained her demeanour of discreet respect, as stiff in manner as when she first came. Berthe felt that she was somehow dissatisfied, and she thought how extremely foolish she had been to give the girl twenty francs and a dress and then suddenly to stop all further gratuities, though she was obliged to do so as she was always in need of a five-franc piece herself.

'My poor girl,' she said, 'I haven't been very generous, have I? But it isn't my fault. I haven't forgotten you, and I'll reward you.'

'Madame owes me nothing,' Rachel coldly replied.

Then Berthe went to fetch two of her old chemises, just to prove her good intentions. But when the servant took them from her, she said they would do for kitchen-cloths.

'Thank you, madam, but calico gives me pimples; I only wear linen.'

However, so polite did she seem that Berthe was reassured and spoke familiarly to the girl, telling her she was going to sleep out; she even asked her to leave a lamp alight in case she came back. The front door was to be bolted, and she would go out by the back stairs and take the key with her. Rachel took her instructions as calmly as if she had been told to cook a piece of beef for the following day.

That evening, by a fine touch of diplomacy, as Berthe was dining with her parents Octave accepted an invitation from the Campardons. He thought he would stay there till ten o'clock and then go up to his room and wait as patiently as he could until half-past twelve.

The meal at the Campardons' proved quite patriarchal. Seated between his wife and her cousin, the architect lingered lovingly over the food—plain, homely fare as he termed it, wholesome and copious. That evening there was boiled chicken and rice, a joint of beef, and some fried potatoes. Ever since Gasparine had taken to managing everything the whole houshold lived in a perpetual state of indigestion, for she knew how to buy things, paying less money and getting twice as much meat as anybody else. Campardon had three helpings of chicken, while Rose stuffed herself with rice. Angèle reserved herself for the beef; she liked blood, and Lisa slyly helped her to spoonfuls of it. Gasparine was the only one who hardly touched anything; her stomach had shrunk, so she said.

'Eat up!' cried the architect to Octave. 'You never know if you might not be eaten yourself some day!'

Madame Campardon leaned over and again told Octave how delighted she was at all the happiness Gasparine had brought to the house—savings of at least a hundred per cent, the servants made respectful, and Angèle looked after properly and being set a good example.

'In short,' she murmured, 'Achille's as happy as the day is long, while I have nothing to do now—absolutely nothing. Imagine! She actually washes and dresses me now. I don't have to lift a finger; she's taken charge of the entire management of the household.'

Then the architect related how he had got the better of 'those clowns in Public Instruction'.*

'Just imagine, my dear boy, they gave me no end of trouble about my job at Evreux. Of course, my main concern was to please the bishop—only natural, eh? However, the new kitchens and heating apparatus came to more than twenty thousand francs. But they didn't vote the credit, and it's not easy to squeeze twenty thousand francs out of the small amount allowed for repairs. On top of which the pulpit, for which I had a grant of three thousand francs, came to nearly ten thousand—which meant I had to find another seven thousand from somewhere. So this morning they sent for me at the ministry, where a big lanky chap tried to give me a hard time. But I wasn't going to stand for that sort of thing! So I simply told him that I'd send for the bishop to explain the matter himself. He became very polite straight away; it was quite absurd, and it makes me laugh now when I think of it! You know they're terrified of bishops at the moment. If I had a bishop behind me, I could demolish Notre-Dame and rebuild it if I liked; I couldn't care less about the government!'

The whole table laughed at this disrespectful talk about the ministry, alluding to it disdainfully, with their mouths full of rice. Rose declared that it was best to be on the side of religion. Ever since his restoration of Saint-Roch Achille had been overwhelmed with work: the noblest families clamoured for his services; he could not attend to them all, he would have had to work all night as well as all day. God certainly was good to them, and they gave Him thanks both morning and evening.

During dessert Campardon suddenly exclaimed:

'By the way, my dear fellow, I suppose you know that Duveyrier has found . . .' He was going to say Clarisse, but he remembered that Angèle was present, so with a side glance at his daughter he added: 'He's found his . . . relative, you know.'

By biting his lip and winking, he at last made Octave understand, for the young man at first quite failed to catch his meaning.

'Yes, Trublot told me. The day before yesterday, when it was pouring down, Duveyrier stood under a doorway, when, lo and behold, there was his . . . relative, just opening her umbrella. Trublot had been on the lookout for her for a week, so as to get her back to him.'

Angèle modestly looked down at her plate, filling her mouth with food. The family was most careful that the conversation should never transgress the bounds of decency.

'Is she pretty?' asked Rose of Octave.

'That's a matter of taste,' he replied. 'Some people might think so.'

'She had the impertinence to come to the shop one day,' said Gasparine, who, thin as she was, detested skinny people. 'She was pointed out to me. She's a real beanstalk!'

'Never mind,' said the architect. 'Duveyrier's happy again. His poor wife, you know . . .'

He was going to say that the poor wife was probably much relieved and delighted. But again he remembered that Angèle was there, so he dolefully remarked:

'Relations don't always get on together. Well, well, every family has its troubles!'

Lisa, a napkin on her arm, looked across the table at Angèle who, bursting with laughter, hastened to take a long drink, concealing her face with her glass.

Shortly before ten o'clock Octave professed to be so tired that he was obliged to go up to bed. Despite Rose's tender attentions, he felt ill at ease in this worthy family, aware of Gasparine's ever-increasing hostility. He had done nothing, however, to provoke her. She merely hated him because he was a good-looking fellow who, so she suspected, had all the women in the house; and that exasperated her, although she herself had no desire for him at all. It was simply the thought of his enjoyment that instinctively roused the wrath of a woman whose beauty had faded all too soon.

As soon as he had left, the Campardons talked of going to bed. Every evening before getting into bed Rose spent a whole hour over her toilet, using face washes and scents, doing her hair, examining her eyes, mouth, and ears, even putting a little patch under her chin.

At night she replaced her sumptuous dressing-gowns with equally sumptuous nightcaps and chemises. On this particular evening she chose a nightdress and cap trimmed with Valenciennes lace. Gasparine helped her, holding basins, mopping up the water she spilt, drying her with a towel, showing her various little attentions with far greater skill than Lisa.

'Ah! Now I feel comfortable,' said Rose at last, stretched out in bed, while her cousin tucked in the sheets and raised the bolster.

She smiled contentedly as she lay there alone in the middle of the big bed. With her plump, soft body swathed in lace, she looked like some great beauty waiting to welcome her favourite lover. When she felt pretty she slept better, so she said. Besides, it was the only pleasure she had.

'Everything all right?' asked Campardon, as he came in. 'Well, goodnight, my little darling.'

He pretended that he had some work to do. He would have to sit up a little longer. Whereupon she became angry and begged him to rest; it was so foolish of him to work himself to death like that!

'Now listen to me: just go to bed! Gasparine, promise you'll make him go to bed!'

Gasparine had just put a glass of sugared water and one of Dickens's novels by the bed. She looked at Rose without replying, and then, bending over her, whispered:

'You look really nice tonight!'

Then she kissed her on both cheeks, with dry lips and a bitter mouth, with the subdued air of a poor, plain relation. Flushed, and suffering from frightful indigestion, Campardon gazed at his wife as well. His moustache quivered slightly as, in his turn, he kissed her.

'Goodnight, my poppet!'

'Goodnight, my love! And make sure you go to bed at once.'

'Don't worry,' said Gasparine. 'If he's not in bed asleep by eleven o'clock, I'll get up and put his lamp out.'

At about eleven o'clock, after yawning over some plans for a Swiss chalet that a tailor in the Rue Rameau had taken into his head to have built, Campardon slowly undressed, thinking as he did so of Rose, lying there so pretty and clean. Then, after turning down his bed because of the servants, he went and joined Gasparine in hers. It was most uncomfortable for them, as there was no elbow-room, and he in particular had to balance himself on the edge of the mattress, so that the next morning one of his thighs was quite stiff.

Just then, as Victoire, after washing up, had gone to bed, Lisa came in as she usually did to see if mademoiselle required anything else. Angèle was waiting for her in bed; and then it was that, unknown to the parents, they played interminable games of cards on the counterpane. As they played begger-my-neighbour they talked constantly of Gasparine, that dirty beast, whom the maid crudely pulled to pieces before little Angèle. In this way they made up for their humble, hypocritical demeanour during the day, and Lisa took a certain base pleasure in corrupting Angèle in this way, satisfying the girl's morbid curiosity now that she was on the verge of puberty. That night they were furious with Gasparine because for the last two days she had locked up the sugar with which the maid usually filled her pockets in order to empty them out afterwards on the child's bed. Nasty cow! They couldn't even get a lump of sugar to munch when they went to sleep!

'Your papa gives her plenty of sugar, though!' said Lisa, with a sensual laugh.

'Oh, yes!' murmured Angèle, laughing too.

'What does your papa do to her? Come on, show me.'

The child caught the maid round the neck, squeezed her in her bare arms, and kissed her very hard on the mouth, saying as she did so: 'This is what he does! This is what he does!'

Midnight struck. Campardon and Gasparine were moaning in their narrow bed, while Rose, lying contentedly in the middle of hers, stretched out her legs and read Dickens until tears filled her eyes. A profound silence followed; the chaste night cast its shadow over this eminently virtuous family.

On going upstairs, Octave found that the Pichons had company. Jules called to him and insisted that he must come in and have a glass of something with them. Monsieur and Madame Vuillaume were there, having made it up with the young couple on the occasion of Marie's churching. Her confinement had taken place in September. They had even consented to come to dinner one Tuesday to celebrate the young woman's recovery. She had only been out the day before for the first time. Anxious to appease her mother, whom the very sight of the baby, another girl, annoyed, Marie had put it out to nurse not far from Paris. Lilitte was asleep with her head on the table, overcome by a glass of wine which her parents had forced her to drink to her little sister's health.

'Well, one can just about cope with two,' said Madame Vuillaume, after clinking glasses with Octave. 'But that's enough, Jules, do you hear?'

They all began to laugh, but the old woman remained perfectly grave, saying:

'There's nothing to laugh at. We'll put up with this baby, but I swear that if another one comes along . . .'

'Oh, if there's another one,' cried Monsieur Vuillaume, finishing her sentence, 'it would prove you have neither heart nor brains. I mean, after all, it's a serious business; you've got to restrain yourself when you haven't got a fortune to spend just amusing yourself.'

Then, turning to Octave, he added:

'You see, sir. I've been decorated, you know. Well, I can assure you that, in order not to spoil too many ribbons, I never wear my decorations at home. So, if I'm prepared to deprive my wife and myself of the pleasure of being decorated at home, I'm sure our children can deprive themselves of the pleasure of having babies. No, sir, there are no half-measures.'

The Pichons declared that they would obey. It wasn't likely that they'd be up to that game any more.

'And go through what I've been through again!' cried Marie, who was still very pale.

'I'd rather have my leg cut off,' declared Jules.

The Vuillaumes gave a nod of satisfaction. Since they had promised, they would forgive them. Then, as it was just striking ten, they all embraced one another affectionately and Jules put on his hat to see them to their omnibus. So touching, indeed, was their return to their old habits that on the landing they kissed again. When they had left, Marie, who with Octave leant over the banisters to see them go, took him back with her to the parlour, saying:

'Mamma doesn't mean any harm; and after all, she's right. Children are no joke!'

She closed the door and began to remove the glasses, which were left on the table. The small room, with its smoking lamp, was still quite warm from this little family get-together. Lilitte slept on, her head resting on a corner of the oil-cloth.

'I'm going to bed,' said Octave.

But he sat down, feeling thoroughly relaxed.

'What! Already!' she replied. 'You don't often keep such respectable hours. Have you got something to do early in the morning?'

'No, I haven't,' he said. 'I'm sleepy, that's all. But I can stay another ten minutes or so.'

Then he remembered that Berthe would not be coming until half-past twelve. There was plenty of time. Although consumed for weeks by the thought of having her in his arms for one whole night, the prospect now no longer excited him. The feverish impatience of the day, his torments of desire as he counted every moment that brought him closer to his long-coveted delight—all this now vanished, dissipated by such wearisome delay.

'Will you have another glass of cognac?' asked Marie.

'Well, I don't mind if I do.'

He thought it might set him up a bit. As she took the glass from him he seized her hands and held them in his. She laughed, without becoming in the least alarmed. Pale as she was after physical suffering, he found her full of charm, and all his latent affection for her surged up again within him. As, one evening, he had given her back to her husband after placing a fatherly kiss upon her brow, so now he felt impelled to repossess her—a sudden, sharp desire which extinguished all his longing for Berthe, for whom his passion now seemed remote.

'So you're not afraid today?' he asked, as he squeezed her hands tighter.

'No, since it has now become impossible. But we shall always be good friends.'

She gave him to understand that she knew everything. Saturnin must have told her. Moreover, she always noticed on which nights Octave received a certain person in his room. Seeing him turn pale with anxiety, she immediately assured him that she would never tell anyone. She was not displeased; on the contrary, she wished him every happiness.

'Well, I'm married, you know,' she said. 'So I can hardly bear you any ill-will.'

Taking her on his knee, he exclaimed:

'But it's you I love!'

He spoke the truth, for at that moment it was her he loved, with deep, absolute passion. All his new intrigue and the two months spent in pursuit of another had vanished. Once more he saw himself in the little apartment, kissing Marie on the neck when Jules's back was turned, she as gentle and complacent as ever. That was real happiness. Why had he ever disdained it? It filled him with regret. He still desired Marie; if he no longer had her he felt that he would be eternally miserable.

'Leave me alone,' she murmured, trying to get away from him. 'You're unreasonable, and in the end you'll make me unhappy. Now that you're in love with somebody else, what's the point of teasing me?'

She tried to resist him in this gentle, languid way, feeling actual disgust for what afforded her no sort of amusement. But he was losing control and squeezed her more vigorously, kissing her breast through her coarse woollen bodice.

'It's you I love. Can't you see that? I swear by all that's sacred that I'm not telling you a lie. Open my heart, and you'll see. Oh please, be nice to me! Just this once, and then never, never again, if you don't want to. You really are too cruel; if you don't let me, I'll die!'

Marie felt powerless, paralysed by the dominating force of this man's will. In her, good nature, fear, and stupidity were equally blended. She moved away, as if anxious first of all to carry the sleeping Lilitte into the bedroom. But he held her fast, fearing that she would wake the child. Then she abandoned herself, in the same place where a year ago she had fallen into his arms like a woman who must obey. There was a sort of buzzing silence throughout the little apartment as the whole house lay in midnight peace. Suddenly the lamp faded, and they were about to find themselves in the dark when Marie rose and turned up the wick just in time.

'Are you cross with me?' asked Octave with tender gratitude, still exhausted by sensual excitement such as he had never yet experienced.

She let go of the lamp and with her cold lips gave him one last kiss, as she said:

'No, because you enjoy it. But, all the same it's not right, on account of the person I mentioned. Doing it with me doesn't mean anything now.'

Her eyes were filled with tears and, though not annoyed, she seemed sad. After leaving her he felt dissatisfied, and would have liked to go straight to bed and sleep. He had gratified his passion, but it had an unpleasant aftertaste, a touch of lechery that left him almost bitter. The other woman was now coming, and he would have to wait for her; it was a thought that weighed terribly upon him, and having spent whole nights scheming how to possess her, to keep her, if only for an hour, in his room, he now hoped that some accident might prevent her from coming. Perhaps she would again fail to keep her word. He did not dare seek comfort in such a hope.

Midnight struck. Tired as he was, Octave sat up and waited, dreading to hear the rustle of her skirts along the narrow corridor. By half-past twelve he became positively anxious, and at one o'clock he thought he was safe, though there was a kind of vague irritation mixed with his relief, the annoyance of a man made a fool of by a woman. Then, just as he was about to undress, yawning vigorously, there came three gentle taps at the door. It was Berthe. Half annoyed, half flattered, he met her with outstretched arms, but she motioned him aside, trembling, and stood listening at the door, which she had hastily closed behind her.

'What is it?' he asked in a whisper.

'I don't know,' she stammered, 'but I'm frightened. It's so dark on the stairs; I thought somebody was following me. This is all quite mad. I'm sure something awful's going to happen.'

These words had a chilling effect on them. They did not even kiss. However, she looked captivating in her white dressing-gown, with her long golden hair twisted up into a coil at the back of her head. Gazing at her, she seemed to him far prettier than Marie; but he no longer desired her; the whole thing was a bore. She sat down to get her breath back, and gave a sudden feigned start of annoyance at noticing a box on the table, which she guessed must contain the lace shawl she had been talking about for the last week.

'I'm going back,' she said, without moving from her chair.

'What, you're going?'

'Do you think I'm going to sell myself? You always manage to hurt my feelings. Tonight you've spoilt all my pleasure. Whatever did you buy it for, after I told you not to?'

However, she got up and finally consented to look at it. But so great was her disappointment on opening the box that she could not restrain an angry exclamation:

'It's not Chantilly at all, it's llama!'

Octave, becoming less liberal with his presents, had had a miserly idea. He tried to explain to her that some llama was splendid, quite as handsome as Chantilly, and he extolled the beauties of the shawl just as if he were standing behind the counter, making her feel the lace while assuring her that it would last for ever. But she shook her head disdainfully, and reduced him to silence by saying:

'The fact is, this only cost one hundred francs, while the other would have cost three hundred.'

Then, noticing that he had turned pale, she sought to mend matters by adding:

'Of course it's very kind, and I'm very grateful. It's not what a gift costs but the spirit in which it's given that makes it valuable.'

She sat down again and there was a pause. After a while he asked if she was coming to bed. Of course she was; but she still felt so upset by her silly fright on the stairs. Then she mentioned her fears about Rachel, telling how she had caught Auguste whispering with her behind the door. It would have been so easy for them to bribe the girl by giving her a five-franc piece now and again. One had to have the five-franc pieces first, though; she never had a single one herself. As she spoke her voice grew harsher; the despised llama shawl, which she no longer alluded to, exasperated her to such a pitch that at last she started with her lover the quarrel she was always picking with her husband.

'I ask you, is this a life? Never to have a penny, always to be under an obligation for the least thing! I'm sick to death of it all!'

Octave, who was pacing up and down the room, stopped short and said:

'Why are you telling me all this?'

'The point, sir? The point? Well, there are certain things which delicacy alone ought to tell you to do, without making me blush by having to explain to you. Don't you think that some time ago you should have made me feel better by bribing that girl?'

She paused, and then ironically added:

'It wouldn't have ruined you, I'm sure!'

There was another pause. Octave went on pacing up and down. At last he said:

'I'm sorry for your sake that I'm not rich.'

Then their quarrel grew more violent, developing into a real marital dispute.

'Say that I love you for your money!' she cried, with all the crudity of her mother, whose very words seemed to leap to her lips. 'I'm a mercenary woman, am I not? Well, I admit it. I'm mercenary because I'm sensible. It's no use you denying it; money's money, and when I only had twenty sous I always said I had forty, because it's better to be envied than pitied.'

At this point he interrupted her, saying wearily, like a man who only wants peace:

'Look, if you're so dissatisfied with the llama shawl, I'll get you one in Chantilly!'

'Your shawl!' she went on, in a fury. 'I'd forgotten all about the thing! It's not that that annoys me. You're just like my husband! I might walk about barefoot; you wouldn't care the least bit! But if a man loves a woman, good nature alone ought to make him feel bound to clothe and feed her. But no man will ever understand that. Between the pair of you you'd let me go about with nothing on but my chemise, if I didn't object!'

Worn out by this domestic quarrel Octave decided not to reply, having noticed that Auguste sometimes got rid of her in this way. He slowly undressed and let the storm pass, reflecting meanwhile how unlucky he had been in his love affairs. Yet for Berthe he had felt passionate desire, so passionate indeed that it had interfered with all his plans, and now that she was here in his bedroom all she did was quarrel with him and give him a sleepless night, just as if they had been married for six months.

'Let's go to bed,' he said at last. 'We thought we'd be so happy together. It's really stupid to waste our time quarrelling like this!'

Then, anxious to make it up, feeling no desire yet wanting to be polite, he tried to kiss her. But she pushed him aside and burst into tears. Seeing that reconciliation was hopeless, he began taking off his boots in a fury and decided to get into bed without her.

'That's right! Complain of my goings-out, as well!' she sobbed. 'Tell me I cost you too much! I can see it all now! It's all because of that rubbishy present! If you could shut me up in a box, you would. Going out to see my girlfriends isn't a crime. And as for mamma . . .'

'I'm going to sleep,' he said, jumping into bed. 'I wish you'd undress and stop talking about that mother of yours. She's given you a damned nasty temper, I can tell you.'

Mechanically she began undressing, growing more and more excited as she raised her voice.

'Mamma has always done her duty. It's not for you to discuss her like that. How dare you talk about her? That's really the last straw, to begin abusing my family!'

Her petticoat-string had got into a knot, and she simply snapped it. Then, sitting down on the bed to pull off her stockings, she exclaimed:

'I'm really sorry I've been so weak! If we could only see into the future, how carefully we'd think about things beforehand!'

She had now taken everything off except her chemise; her legs and arms were bare. She stood there, soft and plump. Her breasts, heaving in anger, peeped out from their lace covering. He, lying with his face to the wall, suddenly turned round and exclaimed:

'What's that? You're sorry you ever loved me?'

'Of course I am. A man like you, incapable of understanding a woman's feelings.'

As they glared at each other their faces assumed a hard, loveless expression. She was resting one knee on the edge of the mattress, her breasts tense, her thigh bent, in the pretty pose of a woman just getting into bed. But he had no eyes for her rosy flesh and the supple, fleeting outline of her back.

'Good God! If only I could relive my life!' she added.

'You mean you'd have somebody else, I suppose?' he shouted.

Lying beside him under the bedclothes, she was just about to reply in the same exasperated tone when suddenly there was a knocking at the door. They started, hardly knowing what it might mean; then they both remained motionless, as if frozen. A muffled voice was saying:

'Open the door! I can hear you, up to your filthy tricks! Open the door, or I'll smash it down!'

It was her husband's voice. Yet the lovers did not move; there was such a buzzing in their ears that they could think of nothing. They felt very cold lying next to each other—as cold as corpses. At last Berthe jumped out of bed, feeling instinctively that she must escape from her lover; while Auguste, outside, kept exclaiming:

'Open the door! Open the door, I say!'

Then there was a moment of terrible confusion, of unspeakable anguish. Berthe rushed about the room in a state of distraction, trying to find some secret exit, her face deathly pale. Octave's heart was in his mouth at each blow on the door, against which he leant mechanically as if to strengthen it. The noise grew unbearable, the idiot would soon rouse the whole house, they would have to open the door. But when she perceived his intention Berthe clung to his arms, imploring him in terror to desist. No, no, for mercy's sake! He would rush in, armed with a knife or a pistol! Growing as pale as she, for her alarm affected him too, he hurriedly slipped on his trousers, begging her in a low voice to get dressed. She sat there naked, doing nothing, unable even to find her stockings. Meanwhile Auguste grew ever more insistent.

'Ah, so you won't open and you won't answer! Right, you'll see!'

Ever since he had last paid his rent Octave had been asking the landlord to have two new screws fixed to the staple of his lock, as it had become loosened. All at once the wood cracked, the lock gave way, and Auguste, losing his balance, fell sprawling into the middle of the room.

'Damn and blast!' he cried.

He only had a key in his hand, which, grazed by his fall, was bleeding. Then he got up, livid with shame and fury at the thought of so absurd an entry. Waving his arms about wildly, he tried to spring upon Octave. But the latter, though embarrassed at being caught barefoot and with his trousers buttoned wrongly, caught him by the wrists and, being the stronger of the two, held them in a vice-like grip.

'Sir,' he cried, 'you're violating my home. It's disgraceful, it's quite ungentlemanly!'

And he very nearly struck him. During their brief scuffle Berthe rushed out through the wide-open door in her chemise. In her husband's bloody fist she thought she saw a kitchen knife, and between her shoulders she seemed to feel the cold steel. As she fled along the dark corridor she thought she heard the sound of blows, but was unable to tell by whom they were dealt or received. Voices that were unrecognizable said: 'I'm at your service whenever you want!' 'Very good, you'll be hearing from me.'

With one bound she reached the back stairs. But after rushing down two flights as if pursued by tongues of flame, she found her kitchen-door locked and remembered that she had left the key upstairs in the pocket of her dressing-gown. Besides, there was no lamp, not the slightest glimmer of light within; the maid had evidently betrayed them in his way. Without stopping to get her breath, she flew upstairs again and passed along the corridor leading to Octave's room, where the two men could be heard shouting.

They were still at it; perhaps she would have time. She ran down the front staircase, hoping that her husband had left the door of their apartment open. She would lock herself in her bedroom and open to nobody. But once more she found herself confronted by a locked door. Finding herself locked out of her own home, and virtually naked, she lost her head and rushed from floor to floor like some poor hunted animal in search of a hiding-place. She would never have the courage to knock at her parents' door. For an instant she thought of taking refuge in the concierge's lodge, but the shame of it drove her back upstairs. Then, leaning over the banisters, she stopped to listen, her ears deafened by the beating of her heart in the profound silence, and her eyes dazzled by lights that seemed to shoot out of the inky darkness. The knife, that awful knife in Auguste's bloody fist! This was what terrified her. Its icy blade was about to be buried in her flesh! Suddenly there was a noise. She fancied he was coming after her, and she shivered to the very marrow of her bones for fright. Then, since she was just outside the Campardons' door, she rang wildly, desperately, almost breaking the bell.

'Good heavens! Is the house on fire?' cried a voice anxiously from within.

The door opened at once. It was Lisa, who had only just left mademoiselle's bedroom, on tiptoe, carrying a candlestick. The furious tug at the bell had made her jump just as she was crossing the hall. The sight of Berthe in her chemise utterly amazed her.

'Whatever's the matter?' she asked.

Berthe came inside, slammed the door, and leaning, breathless, against the wall, gasped:

'Ssh! Don't make a noise! He wants to kill me!'

Lisa could get no more rational explanation from her, when Campardon, looking very anxious, appeared on the scene. This extraordinary uproar had disturbed him and Gasparine in their narrow bed. He was wearing only his underpants, his puffy face was covered in perspiration, while his yellow beard was quite out of shape, and covered with white fluff from the pillow, as he breathlessly tried to put on the bold front of a husband who always sleeps by himself.

'Is that you, Lisa?' he cried from the drawing-room. 'What on earth is this? Why aren't you upstairs?'

'I was afraid I hadn't locked the door properly, sir, and the thought of it prevented me from going to sleep, so I just came down to make sure. But here's Madame . . .'

At the sight of Berthe in her chemise, leaning against the wall, Campardon was as one petrified. A sudden sense of decency caused him to feel if his underpants were properly buttoned. Berthe, seeming to forget how scantily clad she was, repeated:

'Oh, sir, please let me stay here with you! He wants to kill me!'

'Who does?'

'My husband.'

Gasparine now made her appearance in the background. She had taken time to put on her dress, her unkempt hair was covered with fluff as well, her breasts were flaccid and pendulous, her bony shoulders stuck out under her gown as she approached, full of ill-humour at her interrupted pleasure. The sight of Berthe, soft, plump, and nude, only made her more irritable.

'Whatever have you been doing to your husband then?' she asked.

At this simple question Berthe was overcome with embarrassment. She suddenly realized that she was half-naked, and blushed from head to foot. Convulsed with shame, she crossed her arms over her bosom as if to shield herself from scrutiny and stammered out:

'He found me . . . He caught me . . .'

Campardon and Gasparine understood, and looked at each other, profoundly shocked. Lisa, whose candle lighted up the scene, affected to share in her masters' indignation. However, all explanation was cut short, for Angèle came running, pretending to have just woken up, rubbing her eyes heavy with sleep. The sight of Berthe in her chemise brought her to a sudden halt, as every muscle quivered in her slender, girlish frame.

'Oh!' she cried.

'It's nothing, go back to bed!' exclaimed her father.

Then, aware that he must invent some sort of story, he said the first thing that came into his head, and it sounded utterly ludicrous.

'Madam sprained her ankle coming downstairs, so she asked us to help her. Go back to bed, you'll catch cold.'

Lisa almost laughed as her eyes met Angèle's, and she went back to bed, flushed and rosy, delighted that she had seen such a sight. For some time Madame Campardon had been calling to them from her room. Engrossed in Dickens, she had not yet put her light out and wanted to know what was happening. Who was there? Why didn't they come and tell her?

'Come in here, madam,' said Campardon, taking Berthe by the arm. 'Just wait a moment, Lisa.'

In the bedroom Rose was still spread out in the middle of the big bed, throned luxuriously like a queen, looking as tranquil and serene as an idol. She had been greatly affected by what she had read, and had placed the book on her bosom, making it gently rise and fall as she breathed. When Gasparine briefly explained matters to her she also appeared to be most shocked. How could any woman sleep with a man who was not her husband! She was filled with disgust for something to which she had now grown unaccustomed. At this point the architect began to glance furtively at Berthe's breasts, until Gasparine began to blush.

'I can't have this!' she cried. 'Really, madam, it's shocking! Cover yourself up, please!'

She threw one of Rose's shawls over Berthe's shoulders, a large knitted shawl which was lying about. It hardly reached her thighs, and Campardon, in spite of himself, kept staring at her legs.

Berthe was still trembling from head to foot. Though safe enough where she was, she still kept glancing at the door. Her eyes filled with tears as she begged Rose, who looked so calm and comfortable, to protect her.

'Oh, madam, hide me! Save me! He's going to kill me!'

There was a pause. They all looked questioningly at each other, without attempting to conceal their disapproval of such scandalous conduct. The very idea of suddenly appearing like that after midnight in your chemise and waking people up! No, such things were not done; it showed a lack of tact, and placed them in far too embarrassing a position.

'We have a little girl here,' said Gasparine at length. 'Please consider our responsibility, madam.'

'The best thing would be for you to go back to your parents,' suggested Campardon. 'If you'll allow me to come with you, I . . .'

Berthe started back in terror.

'No, no! He's on the stairs; he'll kill me!'

She begged to be allowed to stay, on a chair, anywhere, until morning came, when she would quietly slip out. To this the architect and his wife were inclined to consent, he being fascinated by her physical charms, and she being interested in such a dramatic adventure at midnight. Gasparine, however, remained implacable. Yet her curiosity was roused, and at length she enquired:

'Wherever were you?'

'Upstairs in the room at the end of the corridor, you know.'

Campardon instantly threw up his arms, exclaiming:

'What! With Octave? Impossible!'

With Octave, that puny fellow, such a pretty, well proportioned young woman! The idea annoyed him. Rose too felt annoyed, and became very serious. As for Gasparine, her fury knew no bounds, stung to the quick by her instinctive hatred of Octave. So he had been at it again! She was absolutely convinced that he had them all; but she wasn't going to be such a fool as to keep them warm for him in her own apartment.

'Put yourself in our place,' she said sternly. 'As I said before, we've got a little girl here.'

'And there's the house to think about,' Campardon chimed in. 'There's your husband, too. I've always been on the best of terms with him. He would have a right to be surprised. We can hardly appear publicly to approve of your conduct, madam—conduct I don't presume to judge, but which is perhaps, shall I say, rather—er—thoughtless, don't you think?'

'Of course, we wouldn't be the ones to throw stones at you,' continued Rose. 'But people are so spiteful! They might say that you used to meet here. And my husband, you know, works for such strait-laced folk. The least stain on his good name, and he would lose everything. But, if I may ask you, madam, how is it that religion did not restrain you from doing such a thing? Only the other day Father Mauduit was talking to us about you in a very paternal way.'

Berthe looked first at one, then at another as they spoke, utterly dazed and bewildered. In her terror she had begun to understand, and was surprised to find herself there. Why had she rung the bell? Why had she disturbed them all at that time of night? Now she saw plainly who they were—the wife spread out in the conjugal bed, the husband in his underpants, the cousin in a thin petticoat, both covered with white feathers from the same pillow. They were right: it did not do to come bursting in on people like that. Then, as Campardon gently pushed her towards the hall, she departed without even replying to Rose's question about her religious scruples.

'Would you like me to come with you to your parents' apartment?' asked Campardon. 'Your place is with them.'

She refused, with a terrified gesture.

'Then wait a moment; I'll just see if there's anybody on the stairs, because I'd be really sorry if anything happened to you.'

Lisa had remained in the hall holding a light. He took it from her, went outside on to the landing, and came back immediately.

'There's absolutely no one there. Run up quickly.'

Then Berthe, who had not uttered another word, took off the woollen shawl and threw it on the floor, saying:

'Here! This is yours. He's going to kill me, so there's no point in keeping it.'

Then, in her chemise, she ran out into the dark, just as she had come. Campardon, furious, double-locked the door, murmuring:

'Huh! Go and get laid somewhere else!'

Then, as Lisa behind him burst out laughing, he added:

'It's true; they'd be coming here every night if we were prepared to take them in. You've got to look out for yourself. I wouldn't mind giving her a hundred francs, but I must think of my reputation!'

In the bedroom Rose and Gasparine tried to regain their composure. Had anyone ever seen such a brazen creature? Running up and down the stairs stark-naked! Really! There were some women who stopped at nothing, when the mood took them! But it was nearly two o'clock, they must get some sleep. So they all kissed again. 'Goodnight, my love.' 'Goodnight, my poppet.' How nice it was to live in perfect love and harmony when one saw what awful things happened in other people's homes! Rose picked up her Dickens, which had slipped down. He was enough for her; she would read another page or two and then fall asleep, emotionally exhausted, letting the book slide under the sheets as she did every night. Campardon followed Gasparine, making her get into bed first. Then he lay down beside her and they both grumbled, for the sheets had got cold and they felt most uncomfortable; it would take them a good half-hour to get warm again.

Meanwhile Lisa, before going upstairs, went back to Angèle's room and said to her:

'The lady sprained her ankle. Show me how she did it!'

'Like this, like this!' replied the child, as she threw her arms round the maid's neck and kissed her on the lips.

Berthe was shivering on the stairs. It was cold, as the hot-air stoves were never lighted before the beginning of November. However, her terror had subsided. She had gone down and listened at the door of her apartment: nothing, not a sound. Then she had come up again, not daring to go as far as Octave's room, but listening from a distance. It was as quiet as the grave; not a sound, not a whisper. Then she squatted down on the mat outside her parents' door, with the vague intention of waiting for Adèle. The thought of having to confess everything to her mother upset her as much as if she were still a little girl. Then gradually the solemn staircase filled her with fresh anguish; it was so black, so austere. No one could see her; and yet she was overcome with confusion at sitting there in her chemise amid such respectable gilt and stucco. The wide mahogany doors, the conjugal dignity of these hearths, seemed to load her with reproaches. Never had the house appeared to her so saturated with purity and virtue. Then, as a ray of moonlight streamed through the windows on the landing, it seemed as if she was in a church; from the hall to the attics, peace pervaded all, the fumes of bourgeois virtue floated everywhere in the gloom, while in the eerie light her naked body seemed almost to gleam. The very walls were scandalized, and she drew her chemise closer about her, covering up her feet, terrified that she might see the spectre of Monsieur Gourd emerge in velvet cap and slippers.

Suddenly a noise made her jump, and she was about to thump with both fists on her mother's door when the sound of someone calling stopped her.

It was a voice faintly whispering:

'Madam, madam!'

She looked over the banisters, but could see nothing.

'Madam, madam, it's me!'

Marie appeared, also in her chemise. She had heard the disturbance and had slipped out of bed, leaving Jules fast asleep, while she stopped to listen in her little dining-room in the dark.

'Come in. You're in distress. I'm a friend.'

Then she gently comforted her, telling her everything that had happened. The two men had not hurt each other. Octave, cursing horribly, had pushed the chest of drawers in front of his door, shutting himself in, while the other had gone downstairs with a bundle in his hand—some of the things she had left, her shoes and stockings, which probably he had rolled up in her dressing-gown when he saw them lying about. Anyhow, it was all over. It would be easy enough, the next day, to prevent them fighting a duel.

But Berthe remained standing on the threshold, still frightened and abashed at entering a stranger's apartment. Marie had to take her by the hand.

'You can sleep here, on the sofa. I'll lend you a shawl and I'll go and see your mother. Dear, dear; what a dreadful thing! But when you're in love, you never stop to think!'

'There wasn't much pleasure, though, for either of us!' said Berthe, as she heaved a sigh of regret for all the emptiness and folly of her night. 'I don't wonder he cursed and swore. If he's like me, he must have had more than enough of it!'

They were on the point of speaking about Octave, when suddenly they stopped and, groping in the darkness, fell sobbing into each other's arms. Each clasped the other's naked limbs convulsively, passionately, crushing their breasts all wet with scalding tears. It was a sort of final collapse, a great sadness, the end of everything. They did not say another word, but their tears kept falling, falling, ceaselessly in the gloom, while, lapped in decency, the chaste house slumbered on.

XV

THAT morning, as the house awoke, it wore its most majestic air of bourgeois decorum. The staircase bore not a trace of all the scandals of the night; the stucco panelling preserved no reflection of a lady scampering past in her chemise, nor did the carpet reveal the spot where the odour of her white body had evaporated. Monsieur Gourd, while doing his rounds, at about seven o'clock, sniffed vaguely as he passed the walls in question. However, what did not concern him did not concern him, and when, as he came down, he saw Lisa and Julie discussing the scandal, no doubt, for they seemed so excited, he fixed them with an icy stare, separating them at once. Then he went out, to be sure that everything was quiet in the street. There all was calm. However, the maids must already have been gossiping, for the female neighbours kept stopping, and tradesmen stood at their shopdoors looking up, agape, at the different floors, just as people stare at houses where some crime has been committed. Before so handsome a façade, however, the onlookers were silent, and soon politely passed along.

At half-past seven Madame Juzeur appeared in her dressing-gown; she was looking for Louise, so she said. Her eyes glittered; her hands were feverishly hot. She stopped Marie, who was going upstairs with her milk, and tried to make her talk. But she could get nothing out of her, and did not even learn how the mother had received her errant daughter. Then, pretending to wait a moment for the postman, she finally stopped at the Gourds' to ask why Monsieur Octave had not come down. Perhaps he was not well? The concierge said that he did not know; Monsieur Octave, however, never came down before ten minutes past eight. Just then the other Madame Campardon passed by, pale and stiff; they all bowed. Obliged to go upstairs again, Madame Juzeur at last was lucky enough, on reaching her landing, to catch Campardon just coming out, buttoning his gloves. At first they exchanged rueful glances; then he shrugged his shoulders.

'Poor things!' she murmured.

'No, no! It serves them right!' he said viciously. 'They deserve to be made an example of. A fellow I introduce into a respectable house, begging him not to bring any women, and who, to show how little he cares, sleeps with the landlord's sister-in-law! It makes me look such a fool!'

Nothing further was said. Madame Juzeur went back to her apartment while Campardon hurried downstairs in such a rage that he tore one of his gloves.

As eight o'clock was striking, Auguste, looking quite worn out, his features distorted by migraine, crossed the courtyard on his way to the shop. He had come down by the back stairs, so ashamed was he and so afraid of meeting anyone. However, he could hardly close the shop. At the sight of Berthe's empty desk in the middle of the counter his feelings almost overcame him. The porter was taking down the shutters, and Auguste was proceeding to give orders for the day when Saturnin appeared, coming up from the basement, and gave him a dreadful fright. The madman's eyes flamed; his white teeth glittered like those of some ravenous wolf. With clenched fists, he went straight up to Auguste.

'Where is she? If you touch her, I'll bleed you like a pig.' Auguste, exasperated, stepped back.

'Now there's this one,' he gasped.

'Be quiet, or I'll bleed you!' cried Saturnin once more, making a lunge at him.

Deeming discretion the better part of valour, Auguste beat a retreat. He had a horror of lunatics; there was no arguing with such people. After shouting to the porter to shut Saturnin up in the basement, he was going out into the porch when he suddenly found himself face to face with Valérie and Théophile. The latter, who had a terrible cold, was wrapped up in a thick red comforter and kept coughing and groaning. They must have heard what had happened, for they both looked sympathetically at Auguste. Since the quarrel about the inheritance the two families were no longer on speaking terms, being deadly enemies.

'You've still got a brother,' said Théophile, after a fit of coughing, as he shook Auguste by the hand. 'Don't forget that.'

'Yes,' added Valérie, 'this ought to pay her back for all the nasty things she said to me, eh? But we're very sorry for you—we're not heartless.'

Greatly touched by their kindness, Auguste took them into the back-shop, while keeping his eye on Saturnin, who was still prowling about. Here their reconciliation became complete. Berthe's name was never mentioned; Valérie merely remarked that that woman had been at the bottom of all their dissension, for there had not been a single unpleasant word in the family until she entered it and brought them dishonour. Auguste, his eyes lowered, listened and nodded. A certain cheeriness underlay Théophile's pity, for he was delighted that he was no longer the only one, and scutinized his brother to see how people looked in that predicament.

'Well, what have you decided to do?' he asked.

'Challenge him to a duel, of course!' firmly replied the husband.

Théophile's joy was spoilt. At such courage as Auguste's both he and his wife shuddered. Then their brother described the awful encounter of the previous night; how, having foolishly hesitated to buy a pistol, he had been forced to content himself with punching the gentleman's head. True, the gentleman had returned the blow; but all the same he had got a good smack in the eye. A scoundrel who for the last six months had been making a fool of him by pretending to side with him against his wife, and who actually had the impertinence to give him reports about her goings-out. As for her, the wretched creature had taken refuge with her parents; and she could stay there if she liked, as he would never take her back.

'Would you believe that last month I let her have three hundred francs for her dress allowance!' he cried. 'I've always been so good-natured, so tolerant towards her, ready to put up with anything rather than make myself ill! But this is more than anyone can stand, I can't put up with it—no!'

Théophile was thinking of death. He trembled feverishly, almost choking as he stammered:

'It's ridiculous; you'll just get spitted. I wouldn't challenge him.'

Then, as Valérie looked at him, he sheepishly added:

'If such a thing happened to me.'

'Ah, that wretched woman!' exclaimed his wife. 'To think that two men are going to kill each other on her account! If I were her I'd never sleep again.'

Auguste remained firm. He would fight. Moreover, he had already made arrangements for the duel. As he particularly wanted Duveyrier to be his second, he was now about to go up and tell him what had happened and send him to Octave forthwith. Théophile was obliged to consent; but his cold suddenly seemed to become much worse, and he put on his peevish air, like a sickly child that wants to be cosseted. However, he offered to accompany his brother to the Duveyriers'. They might well be thieves, but in certain circumstances one forgot everything. Both he and his wife seemed anxious to bring about a general reconciliation, having doubtless reflected that it did not serve their interest to sulk any longer. Valérie offered most obligingly to take charge of the pay-desk, to give him time to find a suitable person.

'Only,' she said, 'I'll have to take Camille for a walk in the Tuileries garden at about two.'

'It doesn't matter, just this once,' said her husband. 'In any case it's raining.'

'No, no; the child needs air. I must go.'

At last the two brothers went upstairs to the Duveyriers'. Théophile had to stop for a while on the first step, overcome by an appalling fit of coughing. He caught hold of the banisters and finally managed to gasp out:

'You know, I'm quite happy now; I'm perfectly sure about her. No, can't blame her for it. And she's given me proofs.'

Auguste, not understanding, stared at him and thought how yellow and jaded he looked, with the sparse bristles of his beard showing up on his flabby flesh. Théophile was annoyed at this; his brother's temerity quite disconcerted him, and he continued:

'I'm talking about my wife, you know. Poor old chap, I pity you with all my heart! You remember what a fool I made of myself on your wedding-day. But you can't have any doubts, because you saw them.'

'Bah!' cried Auguste, to show how brave he was. 'I'll soon put a bullet through him. You know, I wouldn't care a damn about the whole thing, if only I hadn't got this blasted headache!'

Just as they rang at the Duveyriers', Théophile suddenly thought that very probably the judge would not be at home, for ever since he had found Clarisse he had let himself go completely, and slept out quite regularly. Hippolyte, who opened the door, avoided giving any information as to his master's whereabouts; the gentlemen, he said, would find madame playing her scales. They went in. There sat Clotilde, tightly corseted, at her piano, her fingers running up and down the keyboard with regular precision. While indulging in this exercise for two hours daily, to preserve her lightness of touch, she used her brain at the same time by reading the *Revue des deux mondes*, which lay open on the desk before her, and her fingers lost nothing of their mechanical velocity of movement thereby.

'Ah! It's you!' she exclaimed, as her brothers rescued her from the hailstorm of notes.

She showed no surprise at seeing Théophile, who bore himself very stiffly, as one who had come on another man's business. Auguste had already thought of a story, for he was ashamed to tell his sister of his dishonour and afraid to frighten her with his duel. But she gave him no time for a falsehood and, after looking at him intently, said in her quiet way:

'What do you intend doing now?'

He started back, blushing. So everybody knew about it, apparently. He replied in the same tone of bravado he had used to silence Théophile:

'Fight, of course!'

'Oh!' she said, this time in a tone of great surprise.

However, she did not express disapproval. It would only increase the scandal, but honour must be satisfied. She was content merely to remind him of her original disapproval of the marriage. One could expect nothing from a girl who, apparently, was profoundly ignorant of all a woman's duties. Then, when Auguste asked her where her husband was:

'He's travelling,' she replied, without a moment's hesitation.

At this news he was quite distressed, for he did not wish to do anything until he had consulted Duveyrier. She listened, without mentioning the new address, as she did not wish her family to share in her domestic troubles. At last she thought of a plan, and advised him to go to see Monsieur Bachelard, in the Rue d'Enghien; he might know something. Then she went back to her piano.

'Auguste asked me to come with him,' said Théophile, who had not spoken until then. 'Shall we kiss and be friends, Clotilde? We're all in trouble.'

Holding out her cold cheek she said:

'My poor fellow, those in trouble always bring it upon themselves. I always forgive everybody. Now, you ought to take care of yourself; you seem to have got a nasty cough!' Then, calling Auguste back, she added: 'if the thing's not settled let me know, because I'll worry about it.'

The hailstorm of notes began again, lapping round her and drowning her; her fingers mechanically ran up and down, hammering out scales in every key, while she gravely resumed her reading of the *Revue des deux mondes*.

Downstairs Auguste debated for a moment whether to go to Bachelard's or not. How could he say to him: 'Your niece has cuckolded me?' Finally he decided to get Bachelard to give him Duveyrier's address without telling him the whole sad story. Everything was arranged. Valérie would mind the shop, while Théophile was to look after the house until his brother's return. Auguste sent for a cab, and was just about to leave when Saturnin, who had disappeared a moment before, suddenly rushed up from the basement brandishing a large kitchen knife and crying:

'I'll bleed him! I'll bleed him!'

This created a fresh scare. White as a sheet, Auguste hastily jumped into the cab and shut the door, exclaiming:

'He's got hold of another knife! Where on earth does he find them all, I wonder! For goodness' sake, Théophile, send him home and don't let him be here when I get back. As if I hadn't got enough to worry about as it is!'

The shop porter caught hold of the madman's shoulders. Valérie gave the address to the cabman, a hulking, dirty fellow with a face the colour of raw beef. He was recovering from the previous night's drinking-bout and did not hurry, but leisurely took up the reins after comfortably installing himself on the box.

'By distance, governor?' he asked, in a hoarse voice.

'No, by the hour, and look sharp. There'll be a good tip.'

Off went the cab, an old landau, huge and dirty, rocking alarmingly on its worn-out springs. The gaunt white skeleton of a horse walked along with a remarkable expenditure of energy as it shook its mane and threw up its hoofs. Auguste looked at his watch: it was nine o'clock. By eleven the duel might be arranged. At first the slowness of the cab annoyed him. Then drowsiness gradually overcame him; he had not had a wink of sleep all night, and this dreadful cab only heightened his depression. Rocked about in it, all by himself, and deafened by the rattling of the cracked panes, the fever which all that morning had sustained him now grew calmer. What a stupid business it was, after all! His face went grey as he put both hands to his head, which ached horribly.

In the Rue d'Enghien a new problem arose. To begin with, Bachelard's doorway was so blocked up by vans that he was almost crushed; then, in the glass-roofed courtyard, he found himself in the midst of a gang of packers lustily nailing up cases. Not one of them knew where Bachelard was; and their hammering almost split his skull. However, he had just decided to wait for the uncle when an apprentice, touched by his suffering look, whispered an address in his ear—Mademoiselle Fifi, Rue Saint-Marc, third floor. In all probability, Bachelard was there.

'Where d'ye say?' asked the cabman, who had fallen asleep.

'Rue Saint-Marc; and drive a bit quicker, if you can.'

The cab started off again at its funereal pace. On the boulevards one of the wheels caught in an omnibus. The panels cracked, the springs uttered plaintive cries, and dark melancholy further oppressed the wretched husband in search of his second. However, the Rue Saint-Marc was reached at last.

On the third floor a white, plump little old woman opened the door. She seemed very upset; and when Auguste asked for Monsieur Bachelard she at once admitted him.

'Oh sir, I'm sure you're one of his friends! Do try and calm him. The poor man, he's just been put out by something. No doubt you know who I am; he must have mentioned me to you: I'm Mademoiselle Menu.'

Auguste, quite bewildered, found himself in a small room overlooking the courtyard, a room which had the cleanliness and peace of a country cottage. There was here an atmosphere of work, of order, of the pure, contented existence of humble folk. Seated before an embroidery frame on which hung a priest's stole, a pretty fair-haired girl with an innocent air was weeping bitterly, while uncle Bachelard, his nose aflame and eyes bloodshot, stood foaming with rage and despair. So upset was he that Auguste's entrance did not seem to surprise him. He immediately appealed to him as a witness, and the scene went on.

'Now look here, Monsieur Vabre, you're an honest man; what would you say in my place? I got here this morning rather earlier than usual, went into her room with my lumps of sugar from the café, and three four-sou pieces as a surprise, and found her in bed with that pig Gueulin! Now tell me, frankly, what would you say?'

Auguste turned scarlet with embarrassment. At first he imagined that Bachelard knew of his trouble and was laughing at him. However, without waiting for a reply the uncle went on:

'My girl, you don't know what you've done, you really don't! I was growing young again, and felt so glad at having found a nice, quiet little place where I thought I'd be happy! To me you were an angel, a flower, in short, something sweet and pure, and consoled me for all those filthy women. And you go and sleep with that beast Gueulin.'

He was choked by genuine emotion; his voice quavered with the intensity of his grief. His world had collapsed; and with the hiccoughs of the previous night's drinking he bemoaned his lost ideals.

'I didn't know, uncle,' stammered Fifi, whose sobs grew louder. 'I didn't know it would grieve you so much.'

And indeed she did not look as if she knew. Her eyes, with their ingenuous look, her odour of chastity, her naivety, all seemed to belong to a little girl incapable as yet of distinguishing a gentleman from a lady. Moreover, auntie Menu declared that at heart she was innocent.

'Please don't be so upset, Monsieur Narcisse. She's very fond of you, all the same. I was sure you wouldn't like it. I told her: "If Monsieur Narcisse hears about it he'll be cross." But she don't know what life is yet, she don't, nor what pleases and what doesn't please. Don't cry any more, because it's you she really loves.'

As neither Bachelard nor Fifi listened to her, she turned to Auguste to inform him how anxious such an occurrence made her for her niece's future. It was so difficult to find a respectable home for a young girl nowadays. She, who for thirty years had worked at Messrs Mardienne Brothers' (the embroiderers in the Rue Saint-Sulpice, where any enquiries about her might be made), well knew how hard it was for a working girl in Paris to make both ends meet if she wanted to keep herself respectable. Good-natured though she was, and though she had received Fifi from the hands of her own brother, Captain Menu, on his deathbed, she could never have managed to bring the child up on her thousand-franc life annuity, which now allowed her to put aside her needle. And seeing her cared for by Monsieur Narcisse, she had hoped to die happy. Not a bit of it. Fifi had gone and made her uncle angry, just for a silly thing like that.

'I dare say you know Villeneuve, near Lille?' she said finally. 'That's my home. It's a biggish town . . .'

Auguste lost all patience. Shaking off the aunt he turned to the uncle, whose noisy grief had now become somewhat subdued.

'I came to ask you for Duveyrier's new address. I suppose you know what it is.'

'Duveyrier's address? Duveyrier's address?' stammered Bachelard. 'You mean Clarisse's address. Just wait a minute!'

He opened the door of Fifi's room. To his great surprise Auguste saw Gueulin come out; Bachelard had locked him in so as to give him time to dress, and also to keep him there until he had decided what to do with him. At the sight of the young man, looking thoroughly sheepish, with rumpled hair, Bachelard's wrath revived.

'You wretch!' he cried. 'Dishonoured by my own nephew! You besmirch your family's good name, and drag my white hairs through the mud! You'll come to a bad end; one day we'll see you in the dock!'

Gueulin listened with bowed head, half embarrassed and half furious.

'Look here, uncle,' he muttered, 'this is a bit much. There's a limit to everything. It's not much fun for me, either. Why did you bring me to see the girl? I never asked you to. You dragged me here. You drag everybody here!'

Then Bachelard, breaking into sobs again, went on:

'You've taken everything from me. She was all I had left. You'll be the death of me, and I won't leave you a sou—not a sou!'

Then Gueulin, quite beside himself, burst out:

'For God's sake shut up! I've had enough! What did I always tell you? You always pay for these things afterwards! You see what luck I've had when, just for once, I thought I'd take advantage of an opportunity. The night was very pleasant of course, but afterwards there's the devil to pay!'

Fifi had dried her tears. She felt bored at having nothing to do, so, taking up her needle, she set to work at her embroidery, raising her large, innocent eyes now and again to look at the two men, apparently dazed at their anger.

'I'm in a great hurry,' Auguste ventured to remark. 'If you could just give me the address—the street and the number, nothing else.'

'The address?' said Bachelard. 'Let me see! Oh, in a minute!'

Then, overcome by emotion, he seized Gueulin by both hands.

'You thankless fellow; I was keeping her for you, and that's the truth! I said to myself: now, if he's good, I'll give her to him, with a nice little dowry of fifty thousand francs. But, you dirty pig, you couldn't wait, you had to go and get hold of her all of a sudden like that!'

'Hands off!' cried Gueulin, touched by the old fellow's kind-heartedness. 'I can see very well that I won't get out of this mess in a hurry.'

But Bachelard led him up to the girl, and asked her:

'Now Fifi, look at him, and tell me if you would have loved him.'

'Yes uncle, if it would have pleased you,' she replied.

This answer touched him deeply. He rubbed his eyes and blew his nose, nearly choked by emotion. Well, he would see what could be done. All he had wanted was to make her happy. Then he hurriedly sent Gueulin on his way.

'Be off with you! I'll think about it!'

Meanwhile, auntie Menu had taken Auguste aside to explain how she saw things. A workman, she argued, would have beaten the little girl; a clerk would have given her babies all the time. With Monsieur Narcisse, however, there was the chance of having a dowry, which would allow her to make a decent marriage. Thank God, theirs was a respectable family, and she would never have let her niece go wrong, nor fall from the arms of one lover into those of another. No, she wanted Fifi to have a respectable position.

Just as Gueulin was about to go, Bachelard called him back.

'Kiss her on the forehead; I give you permission.'

He let Gueulin out himself, and then came back and stood in front of Auguste, holding his hand to his heart.

'I really mean it,' he said. 'I give you my word of honour that I meant to give her to him later on!'

'Well, what about that address?' asked Auguste, losing all patience.

Bachelard seemed surprised, as if he thought he had answered that question already.

'Eh? What? Clarisse's address? I don't know what it is!'

Auguste started back in anger. Everything was going wrong, and there seemed to be a sort of plot to make him look stupid! Seeing how upset he was, Bachelard made a suggestion. Trublot, no doubt,

knew the address, and they would probably find him at Desmarquay's, the stockbroker, where he worked. And the uncle, with all
the alacrity of a man accustomed to rolling about town, offered to
accompany his young friend, who accepted.

'Listen!' he said to Fifi, after kissing her in turn on the forehead,
'here's the sugar from the café all the same, and three four-sou
pieces for your money-box. Be a good girl until I tell you what to
do.'

The girl modestly plied her needle with exemplary diligence. A
ray of sunlight, falling across a neighbouring roof, brightened up the
little room, touching with its gold this innocent nook where the
noise of the traffic outside never came. It stirred all of Bachelard's
romantic instincts.

'God bless you, Monsieur Narcisse!' exclaimed aunt Menu, as she
showed him out. 'I'm more relaxed now. Listen to what your heart
tells you; that will inspire you.'

The cabman had again dropped off to sleep, and grumbled when
Bachelard gave him Monsieur Desmarquay's address in the Rue
Saint-Lazare. No doubt the horse had gone to sleep too, for it
needed quite a hail of blows to make it move. At length the cab jolted
uncomfortably along.

'It's tough, all the same,' continued Bachelard, after a pause. 'You
can't imagine how upset I was when I found Gueulin there in his
shirt. No, it's something you've got to go through before you can
understand it.'

And he went on, entering into every detail without noticing
Auguste's increasing uneasiness. At last the latter, who felt his
position becoming more and more false, told him why he was in such
a hurry to find Duveyrier.

'Berthe with that counter-jumper?' cried Bachelard. 'You
astonish me, sir!'

It seemed that his astonishment was mainly on account of his
niece's choice. But, after a little reflection, he grew indignant.
Eléonore, his sister, had a great deal for which to reproach herself. He
intended to drop the family altogether. Of course he was not going to
get mixed up with this duel; nevertheless, he deemed it essential.

'Like me, just now, when I saw Fifi with a man in his shirt, my
first impulse was to murder everybody . . . If such a thing had
happened to you . . .'

Auguste started painfully, and Bachelard stopped short.

'True, I wasn't thinking. You know only too well what it's like.'

Then there was another silence, as the cab swayed dismally from side to side. Auguste, whose valour was ebbing with each turn of the wheels, submitted resignedly to the jolting, looking more and more cadaverous and with his left eye half closed because of his headache. Whatever had made Bachelard think that the duel was essential? As the guilty woman's uncle it was not his place to insist on bloodshed. His brother's words rang in his ears: 'It's ridiculous; you'll just get spitted!' The phrase came back to him importunately, obstinately, until it actually seemed part of his headache. He was sure to be killed; he had a sort of presentiment that he would be; such mournful forebodings completely overwhelmed him. He fancied himself dead, and bewailed the sad event.

'I told you the Rue Saint-Lazare,' cried Bachelard to the cabman. 'It's not at Chaillot. Turn left.'

At last the cab stopped. Out of prudence they sent up for Trublot, who came down bare-headed to talk to them in the doorway.

'Do you know Clarisse's address?' asked Bachelard.

'Clarisse's address? Oh, the Rue d'Assas, of course.'

They thanked him, and were about to get into the cab again, when Auguste enquired:

'What's the number?'

'The number? Oh, I don't know what number!'

Whereupon, Auguste declared that he would rather give the whole thing up. Trublot tried his best to remember; he had dined there once—it was just behind the Luxembourg gardens; but he could not remember whether it was at the end of the street, or on the right or the left. But the door he knew perfectly well, and would be able to recognize it at once. Then Bachelard had another idea and begged Trublot to accompany them, despite Auguste's protestations and assurances that he would trouble no one further in the matter, but would go home. However, with a somewhat constrained air, Trublot refused. No, he wasn't going to that hole again. But he avoided giving the real reason, an astounding occurrence, a tremendous smack in the face he had got from Clarisse's new cook one evening when he had gone to give her a pinch as she stood over her fire. It was incomprehensible! A smack like that in return for a mere civility, just to get to know each other! Such a thing had never happened to him before; it amazed him.

'No, no,' he said, trying to find an excuse, 'I'll never set foot again in a house where one's bored to death. Clarisse, you know, has become quite impossible; her temper's worse than ever, and she's quite the lady now. And she's got all her family with her, ever since her father died—a whole tribe of pedlars; mother, two sisters, a big scoundrel of a brother; even an old invalid aunt, who looks like one of those hags who sell dolls in the street! You can't imagine how dirty and miserable Duveyrier looks in the middle of them all!'

Then he told how, on the rainy day when the magistrate had found Clarisse standing in a doorway, she had been the first to upbraid him, telling him with a flood of tears that he had never had any respect for her. Yes, she had left the Rue de la Cerisaie because of her resentment at a slight upon her personal dignity, though for a long time she had hidden her feelings. Why did he always take off his decoration when he came to see her? Did he think she would spoil it? She was ready to make it up with him, but he must first of all swear upon his honour that he would always wear his decoration, for she valued his esteem and was not going to be perpetually mortified in this way. Discomfited by this remonstration, Duveyrier swore that he would do as she asked. He was completely won over, and deeply touched; she was right; he deemed her a noble-spirited creature.

'Now he never takes his ribbon off,' added Trublot. 'I think she makes him sleep with it on. It impresses her family, too. What's more, since that big fellow Payan had already spent her twenty-five thousand francs' worth of furniture, this time she's got him to buy her thirty thousand francs' worth. Oh, he's had it! She's got him completely under her thumb. Some men will do anything for sex.'

'Well, I must be off if Monsieur Trublot can't come,' said Auguste, whose vexation was merely increased by all these stories.

Trublot, however, suddenly agreed to accompany them; only he would not go upstairs, but would simply show them the door. After fetching his hat and making some excuse, he joined them in the cab.

'Rue d'Assas,' he cried to the cabman. 'I'll tell you when to stop.'

The driver swore. Rue d'Assas now! Some people liked driving about! But they would just have to be patient. The big white horse, steaming, made hardly any headway, its neck arched at every step in a sort of excruciating nod.

Meanwhile Bachelard had already begun to tell Trublot about his misfortune. This sort of thing made him extremely garrulous. Yes, that pig Gueulin with a delicate young girl like that! He had caught them at it. But at this point of his story he suddenly remembered Auguste, who, glum and doleful, had collapsed in a corner of the cab.

'Of course; I beg your pardon,' he muttered. 'I keep forgetting.' Then, turning to Trublot, he added: 'Our friend has just had some trouble at home, too; that's why we're trying to find Duveyrier. Yes, you know, last night he caught his wife with . . .' With a gesture he completed his sentence, adding simply: 'Octave, you know!'

Trublot, plain-spoken as he was, was about to say that this did not surprise him. But he forbore to use this phrase, substituting another, full of angry scorn, for an explanation of which Auguste dared not ask:

'What an idiot Octave is!'

At this criticism of the adultery there was a pause. Each of the three men became lost in thought. The cab could go no further. It seemed to be dawdling along for hours on a bridge when Trublot, the first to awake from his reverie, observed judiciously:

'This cab doesn't go very fast.'

But nothing could quicken the horse's pace; by the time they got to the Rue d'Assas it was eleven o'clock. And there they wasted nearly another quarter of an hour, for, despite Trublot's boast, he did not know the door after all. First he let the cabman drive the whole length of the street without stopping him, and then made him come back again. This he did three times. Acting on his precise instructions Auguste called at ten different houses, but the concierges replied that there was 'no one of that name there'. At last a fruitseller told him the right number. He went upstairs with Bachelard, leaving Trublot in the cab.

It was the big scoundrel of a brother who opened the door. He had a cigarette between his lips, and puffed smoke in their faces as he showed them into the drawing-room. When they asked for Monsieur Duveyrier, at first he stared mockingly at them without answering, and then slouched off, presumably to fetch him. In the middle of the drawing-room, the new blue-satin furniture of which was already stained with grease, one of the sisters, the youngest, was sitting on the carpet wiping out a kitchen saucepan, while the elder girl thumped with clenched fists on a splendid piano, of which she had just found the key. On seeing the gentlemen enter they had both looked up, but did not stop; rather, they went on thumping and scrubbing with redoubled energy. Five minutes passed and nobody came. Deafened by the din, the visitors looked at each other, until shrieks from an adjoining room filled them with terror. It was the invalid aunt being washed.

At last an old woman, Madame Bocquet, Clarisse's mother, put her head round the door, not daring to show herself because of the filthy dress she had on.

'Who do the gentlemen want?' she asked.

'Monsieur Duveyrier, of course!' cried Bachelard, losing patience. 'We told the servant already! Say it's Monsieur Auguste Vabre and Monsieur Narcisse Bachelard!'

Madame Bocquet shut the door again. Meanwhile the elder sister, standing on a stool, thumped the keyboard with her elbows, while the younger sister scraped the bottom of the saucepan with a steel fork. Another five minutes elapsed. Then, in the midst of this din, which did not seem to bother her in the least, Clarisse appeared.

'Oh, it's you!' she said to Bachelard, without even looking at Auguste.

Bachelard was quite taken aback. He would never have recognized her, so fat had she grown. The big devil of a woman, who used to be as thin as a rake, and with a fluffy mop of hair like a poodle's, had been transformed into a dumpy matron, her hair neatly plastered and pomaded. She did not give him time to say a word, but at once told him with brutal frankness that she did not want a mischief-maker like him at her place, for she knew he told Alphonse all sorts of horrid stories. Yes, indeed: he had accused her of sleeping with Alphonse's friends, and of carrying on with scores of men behind his back. He could not deny it, for Alphonse had told her so himself.

'Listen, mate,' she added, 'if you've come here to booze you might as well leave now. The old days are over. From now on I intend to be respectable.'

Then she proclaimed her passion for everything that was proper and upright—a passion that had grown into an obsession. Thus, in her periodic fits of prudery she had one by one chased away all her lover's friends, not allowing them to smoke, insisting on being called Madame and on receiving formal calls. Her old superficial, second-hand drollery had vanished; all that remained was her extravagant attempt to play the fine lady, who sometimes gave way to foul language and even fouler gestures. By degrees, solitude again surrounded Duveyrier; no amusing nook for him now, but a grisly bourgeois establishment, amid whose dirt and din he encountered all the worries of his own house. As Trublot remarked, 'the Rue de Choiseul was no more boring, and it was certainly less dirty'.

'We haven't called to see you,' replied Bachelard, recovering himself, used as he was to the robust greetings of ladies such as she. 'We want to talk to Duveyrier.'

Then Clarisse glanced at his companion. She thought he was a bailiff, knowing that Alphonse's affairs had recently become rather involved.

'Oh, what do I care, after all?' she said. 'You can have him if you like. It's not much fun for me to have to look after his pimples!'

She no longer even sought to hide her disgust, feeling certain, moreover, that her rough treatment of him only made him more attached to her. Then, opening a door, she exclaimed:

'Come in here; these gentlemen insist on seeing you.'

Duveyrier, who seemed to have been waiting behind the door, came in, shook hands with them, and tried to smile. He no longer had the youthful air of former days, when he used to spend the evening with her in the Rue de la Cerisaie. He seemed overcome with weariness; he looked thin and depressed, trembling nervously now and again, as if alarmed by something behind him.

Clarisse stopped to listen. But Bachelard was not going to talk in front of her, so he invited the judge to lunch.

'Say you'll come, because Monsieur Vabre wants to see you. I'm sure that Madame will be kind enough to excuse you . . .'

At that moment Madame noticed her youngest sister thumping on the piano; giving her a hard slap, she drove her out of the room, while she boxed the other child's ears and packed her off with her saucepan. There was an infernal racket. The invalid aunt in the next room started screaming again, thinking they were going to beat her.

'Did you hear, my love?' murmured Duveyrier. 'These gentlemen have asked me to lunch.'

She was not listening, but shyly, tenderly touched the keys of the

piano. For the last month she had been learning to play. This had
been the unuttered longing of her whole life, a remote ambition
which, if attained, could alone stamp her as a woman of fashion.
After making sure that nothing was broken, she was about to stop
her lover from going merely in order to be disagreeable to him, when
Madame Bocquet once more popped her head round the door.

'Your music teacher's here,' she said.

Whereupon Clarisse instantly changed her mind, and called out to
Duveyrier:

'All right, you can clear off! I'll have lunch with Théodore. We
don't want you.'

Théodore, her music teacher, was a Belgian with a big rosy face.
She at once sat down at the piano, and he placed her fingers on the
keyboard, rubbing them, to make them less stiff. For a moment
Duveyrier hesitated; evidently he was much annoyed. But the
gentlemen were waiting for him, so he went to put on his boots.
When he came back she was playing scales in a haphazard fashion,
strumming out a perfect hailstorm of wrong notes, which made
Bachelard and his companion feel almost ill. Yet Duveyrier, driven
wild by his wife's Mozart and Beethoven, stood still for a moment
behind his mistress, apparently enjoying the sound, despite his
nervous facial twitchings. Then, turning to the other two, he
whispered:

'Her talent for music is quite amazing.'

After kissing her hair he discreetly withdrew, and left her alone
with Théodore. In the hall the big scoundrel of a brother asked him
for a franc to buy some tobacco. Then, as they went downstairs and
Bachelard expressed surprise at his conversion to the charms of the
piano, Duveyrier swore that he had never hated it, and spoke of the
ideal, saying how greatly Clarisse's simple scales stirred his soul,
thus yielding to his perpetual desire to bestrew with flowers of
innocence the rude pathway of his grosser passions.

Trublot, down below, had given the cabman a cigar and was
listening to his talk with the keenest interest. Bachelard insisted on
lunching at Foyot's;* it was just the right time for it, and they could
talk better whilst eating. Then, when the cab at last succeeded in
starting, he informed Duveyrier of all that had happened; the judge
grew very grave.

Auguste's indisposition seemed to have increased during the visit to Clarisse's, where he had not uttered a single word. Now, completely worn out by this interminable drive, his head throbbing, he collapsed in a corner. When Duveyrier asked him what he intended to do, he opened his eyes, paused for a moment as if in anguish, and then repeated his previous phrase:

'Fight, of course!' His voice, however, sounded fainter; and, closing his eyes as if asking to be left in peace, he added: 'Unless you can suggest anything else.'

Then, as the vehicle lumbered along, these good gentlemen held a grand council. Duveyrier, like Bachelard, deemed a duel indispensable. He seemed much affected by the idea of shedding blood, imagining a dark stream of it staining the staircase of his own house. But honour demanded it, and with honour no compromise was possible. Trublot took a broader view: it was stupid, he said, to stake one's honour on what, for courtesy's sake, he called a woman's frailty. With a faint movement of his eyelids Auguste expressed his approval; he was exasperated by the belligerent fury of the other two, who certainly ought to have been wholly for reconciliation. Despite his fatigue, he was obliged once more to tell the story of the night before, of the blow he had given and the blow he had received. Soon the question of adultery was forgotten; the discussion bore solely upon these two blows: they were subjected to comment and analysis in an attempt to find a satisfactory solution to the whole affair.

'Talk about hair-splitting!' contemptuously cried Trublot at last. 'If they hit each other, then they're quits.'

Duveyrier and Bachelard looked at each other aghast. But by this time they had reached the restaurant, and Bachelard declared that first of all they should have lunch. It would help them to think better. He invited them to a copious meal, ordering expensive dishes and wines, so that for three hours they sat at table in a private room. The duel was not even mentioned. Immediately after the hors-d'oeuvres the talk inevitably turned upon women—Fifi and Clarisse were perpetually explained, overhauled, and plucked. Bachelard now declared the fault to be on his side, so that Duveyrier might not think he had been grossly jilted, while the latter, to make up for having let uncle Bachelard see him weeping that night in the lonely apartment in the Rue de la Cerisaie, protested his present happiness until he actually began to believe it, becoming quite sentimental. Prevented by his migraine from eating or drinking, Auguste sat

there, apparently listening, with one elbow on the table and a doleful
look in his eyes. During dessert Trublot remembered that the
cabman, who had been forgotten, was still waiting down below. Full
of sympathy, he sent him the remains of the feast and the heeltaps of
the bottles, for, from certain remarks the fellow had made, he had an
inkling that he had once been a priest. It struck three. Duveyrier
grumbled at having to be assessor at the next assizes. Bachelard, now
very drunk, spat sideways on to Trublot's trousers, who never
noticed it, and there, amid the liqueurs, the day would have ended, if
Auguste had not roused himself with a sudden start.

'Well, what are we going to do?' he enquired.

'Well, my lad,' replied Bachelard, in familiar fashion, 'if you like
we'll settle the whole thing for you. It's stupid to fight a duel about
it.'

At this conclusion no one seemed surprised. Duveyrier nodded
approvingly. Bachelard went on:

'I'll go with Monsieur Duveyrier and see the chap, and make the
brute apologize, or my name isn't Bachelard. The mere sight of me
will make him cave in, just because I'm an outsider to all this. I don't
care a damn for anybody!'

Auguste shook him by the hand but did not seem much relieved,
for he had such a splitting headache. At length they left the private
room. Beside the kerb the driver was still having his lunch inside the
cab. He was quite drunk and had to shake all the crumbs out, while
giving Trublot a friendly poke in the stomach. But the poor horse,
which had had nothing, refused to budge, and merely gave a
despairing wag of the head. After a few slaps and pushes, however, it
reeled forward, along the Rue de Tournon.

It had struck four before they stopped in the Rue de Choiseul.
Auguste had had the cab for seven hours. Trublot, who stayed
inside, said that he would hire it himself and would wait for
Bachelard, whom he was going to invite to dinner.

'Well, you've been a long while!' said Théodore to his brother as
he ran to meet him. 'I was beginning to think you were dead!'

As soon as the others had gone into the shop, he related the day's
events. Ever since nine o'clock he had been watching the house, but
nothing had happened. At two o'clock Valérie had gone with
Camille to the Tuileries. Then, at about half-past three, he had seen
Octave go out. That was all; no sign of life, even at the Josserands',

so that Saturnin, who had been looking under all the furniture for his sister, had at last gone up to ask for her, when Madame Josserand, to get rid of him, had slammed the door in his face, saying that Berthe was not there. Since then the madman had been prowling about, grinding his teeth.

'All right!' said Bachelard, 'we'll wait for the gentleman. We'll see him come back from here.'

Auguste, his head in a whirl, was struggling to keep on his feet, until Duveyrier advised him to go to bed. It was the only cure for migraine.

'Just go upstairs; we don't need you any more. We'll let you know the result. My dear fellow, it's no good being upset about it—there's no point.'

So the husband went upstairs to bed. At five o'clock the two others were still waiting for Octave. He had gone out for no particular reason, except to get a little fresh air and forget the disagreeable adventures of the night, and had walked past the Ladies' Paradise. Madame Hédouin, in deep mourning, stood at the door, and he stopped to bid her good-day. On telling her that he had left the Vabres, she quietly asked why he did not come back to her. Without a second thought the whole thing was settled there and then, in a moment. After bidding her farewell, and promising to come the next day, he went strolling along, full of vague regrets. Chance always seemed to upset his calculations. Absorbed by various schemes, he wandered about the neighbourhood for more than an hour when, looking up, he saw that he was in the dark alley leading out of the Passage Saint-Roch. In the darkest corner, opposite him, at the door of a cheap lodging-house, Valérie was bidding farewell to a gentleman with a black beard. She blushed and tried to get away through the padded door of the church. Then, seeing that Octave smilingly followed her, she decided to wait for him in the porch, where they chatted cordially to each other.

'You're avoiding me,' he said. 'Are you angry with me?'

'Angry?' she rejoined. 'Why should I be angry with you? They can scratch each other's eyes out, if they like; I really don't care.'

She was alluding to her relations. She immediately gave vent to her old resentment towards Berthe, at first sounding the young man out by various allusions. Then, feeling that he was secretly tired of his mistress and furious still at the events of the previous night, she no longer restrained herself but poured out her heart. To think that that woman had accusd her of sellling herself, she who never accepted a sou, not even a present! Well, a few flowers sometimes, a bunch or two of violets. But now everybody knew which of them sold herself. She had prophesied that one day they would find out how much it cost to have her.

'It cost you more than a bunch of violets, didn't it?'

'Yes, it did,' he muttered.

Then, in his turn, he let out some rather disagreeable things about Berthe, saying how spiteful she was, even asserting that she was too fat, as if avenging himself for all the worry she had caused him. All day long he had been expecting her husband's seconds, and he was now going home to see if anybody had called. A stupid business altogether; she could easily have prevented a duel of this sort. And he ended by giving an account of their absurd assignation, their quarrel, and Auguste's arrival on the scene before they had so much as kissed each other.

'By all that I hold most sacred!' he said, 'I hadn't even touched her.'

Valérie laughed. She was getting quite excited, for she was being allowed to share his confidences in the most tender, intimate way, and she drew closer to him as if to some woman friend who knew all. Several times some devout worshipper coming out of the church disturbed them; then the door closed again gently and they found themselves alone, safely shrouded in the green baize hangings of the porch as if in some secure and saintly haven of refuge.

'I can't think why I live with such people,' she continued, referring to her relatives. 'Oh, I'm sure I'm not blameless! But, frankly, I don't feel at all guilty as I care so little for them. And if you only knew how boring all these love affairs are!'

'Come now, it's not as bad as all that,' cried Octave gaily. 'People aren't always as idiotic as we were yesterday. They have a good time now and then!'

Then she made a clean breast of it. It was not merely hatred for her husband, the fever that perpetually shook him to pieces, his impotence, and his eternal whimpering—it was not all this that drove her to be unfaithful six months after her marriage. No, she often did it without wanting to, simply because things came into her head for which she could give no sort of explanation. She went to pieces, and felt so ill that she could almost have killed herself. Since there was nothing to hold her back, she might as well take that plunge as any other.

'But do you really never enjoy it?' asked Octave again, who apparently was only interested in this particular point.

'Well, not as people describe,' she answered. 'I swear I don't!'

He looked at her full of sympathy and pity. All for nothing, and without getting any pleasure out of it! Surely it was not worth all the trouble she took, in her perpetual fear of being caught. He especially felt soothed in his wounded pride, for her old scorn of him still rankled. So that was why she would not let him have her one evening! He reminded her of the incident.

'Do you remember, after one of your fits of hysterics?'

'Yes, yes, I remember. I didn't dislike you, but I felt so uninterested in that sort of thing! And it was better that way, because we would have hated each other by now.'

She gave him her little gloved hand. Squeezing it, he repeated:

'You're right; it was better that way. In fact, one only has feelings for the women one has never had!'

It was quite a touching scene. Hand in hand they stood there for a moment, deeply affected. Then, without another word, they pushed open the padded church-door, as she had left her son Camille inside in the charge of the woman who let out the chairs. The child had fallen asleep. She made him kneel down, and knelt down herself for a moment, her head in her hands, as if immersed in a fervent prayer. Just as she was about to rise Father Mauduit, coming out of a confessional, greeted her with a fatherly smile.

Octave had simply passed through the church. When he got home the whole house was in a flutter. Only Trublot, asleep in the cab, did not see him. Tradespeople at their shop-doors eyed him gravely. The stationer opposite still stared at the house-front, as if to scrutinize the very stones themselves. The charcoal-dealer and the greengrocer, however, had grown calmer and the neighbourhood had relapsed into its frigidly dignified state. Lisa was gossiping with Adèle in the doorway and, as Octave passed, was obliged to be satisfied with staring at him; then they both went on complaining about the high price of poultry, while Monsieur Gourd eyed them sternly as he greeted the young man. While he was going upstairs Madame Juzeur, on the watch ever since the morning, gently opened her door and, catching hold of his hands, drew him into her hall, where she kissed him on the forehead, murmuring:

'Poor boy! There, I won't keep you now. But come back for a chat after it's all over.'

He had hardly got to his apartment when Duveyrier and Bachelard called. Astonished at seeing the latter, he sought at first to give the names of two of his friends. But, without replying, these gentlemen spoke of their age and gave him a lecture about his bad behaviour. Then, as in the course of conversation he announced his intention to leave the house as soon as possible, his two visitors both solemnly declared that this proof of his tact would suffice. There had been scandal enough; it was time for him to make a sacrifice of his passions in the interest of respectable folk. Duveyrier accepted Octave's notice to quit on the spot and departed, while Bachelard, behind his back, asked the young man to dine with him that evening.

'I'm counting on you. We're going on a spree. Trublot's waiting for us downstairs. I don't care a damn about Eléonore. But I don't want to see her, and I'll go down first so that they don't catch us together.'

He went downstairs. Five minutes later Octave joined him, delighted at the way in which the matter had been settled. He slipped into the cab, and the melancholy horse, which for seven hours had been dragging the husband about, now limped along with them to a restaurant at the Halles known for its astonishingly good tripe.

Duveyrier had gone back to Théophile in the shop. Just then Valérie came in, and they were all chatting when Clotilde herself appeared, on her return from some concert. She had gone there, however, in a perfectly calm frame of mind, for, she said, she was certain that some arrangement satisfactory to everyone would be made. Then there was a silence, a moment of embarrassment for both families. Théophile, seized with a fearful fit of coughing, almost spat out his teeth. As it was in their mutual interest to make it up, they at last took advantage of the emotion occasioned by these fresh family troubles. The two women embraced; Duveyrier declared to Théophile that the Vabre inheritance was ruining him. However, by way of indemnity he promised to remit his rent for three years.

'I must go up and pacify poor Auguste,' said Duveyrier at last.

He was climbing the stairs when he heard some hideous cries, like those of an animal about to be slaughtered, coming from the bedroom. Saturnin, armed with his kitchen-knife, had silently crept into the apartment and, with eyes like gleaming coals and frothing lips, had just leapt on Auguste.

'Tell me where you've hidden her!' he cried. 'Give her back to me, or I'll bleed you like a pig!'

Startled thus from his painful slumber, Auguste tried to flee. But the madman, with the strength of his obsession, caught him by the tail of his shirt and, throwing him backwards, placed his neck at the edge of the bed, over a basin that happened to be there, and held him in that position as if he were an animal in a slaughterhouse.

'I've got you this time. I'm going to bleed you; I'm going to bleed you like a pig!'

Fortunately the others arrived in time to release the victim. Saturnin had to be shut up, for he was raving mad. Two hours later, the superintendent of police having been summoned, they took him for the second time to the Asile des Moulineaux, with the consent of his family. Poor Auguste, still trembling, remarked to Duveyrier, who had told him of the arrangement made with Octave:

'No, I'd rather have fought a duel. You can't protect yourself from a maniac. Why on earth is he so obsessed with bleeding me, the ruffian, after his sister had made a cuckold of me? I've had enough of it all, my good fellow, upon my word I have!'

XVI

ON the Wednesday morning, when Marie took Berthe to see Madame Josserand, the latter, outraged at a scandal which touched her pride, turned very pale and said not a word. She took her daughter's hand as brutally as if she were a schoolmistress dragging some naughty pupil into a dark closet. Leading her to Hortense's bedroom, she pushed her in and exclaimed:

'Stay here, and don't show yourself. You'll be the death of your father.'

Hortense, who was washing, was taken completely by surprise. Crimson with shame, Berthe threw herself on the unmade bed, sobbing violently. She had expected a stormy reception and had prepared her defence, having resolved to shout too as soon as her mother went too far. But this mute severity, this way of treating her like a naughty little girl who had been eating jam on the sly, entirely upset her, recalling all the terrors of her childhood and the tears shed in corners when she penitently made solemn vows of obedience.

'What's the matter? What have you done?' asked her sister, whose amazement increased on seeing that she was wrapped in the old shawl lent by Marie. 'Has poor Auguste been taken ill in Lyons?'

But Berthe would not answer. No, she would tell her later; there were things she could not say, and she begged Hortense to leave her alone to weep there quietly by herself. Thus the day went by. Monsieur Josserand had gone to his office, never dreaming that anything had occurred, and when he came home that evening Berthe was still in hiding. Having refused all food, she at last avidly devoured the little dinner which Adèle secretly brought her. The maid stopped to watch her and, noticing her appetite, said:

'Don't take on so; you must keep up your strength. The house is quiet enough, and as for any one being killed or wounded, there's nobody hurt at all.'

'Oh!' said the young woman.

Then she questioned Adèle, who gave her a lengthy account of the day's proceedings, telling her of the duel that never happened and what the Duveyriers and the Vabres had done. Berthe, listening, began to feel much better, devoured everything, and asked for some more bread. It was really too silly to let the thing distress her so much when the others had apparently got over it already.

So when Hortense joined her at about ten o'clock she greeted her very cheerfully, dry-eyed. Smothering their laughter, they had great fun, especially when Berthe tried on one of her sister's dressing-gowns and found it too tight for her. Her breasts, which marriage had developed, almost split the fabric. Never mind, by moving the buttons she would be able to put it on the next day. They both seemed to have gone back to their girlhood days, there in the old room where for years they had lived together. This touched them, and drew them closer to one another in an affection that for a long while they had not felt. They were obliged to sleep together, for Madame Josserand had got rid of Berthe's old bed. As they lay there side by side, with the candle blown out, their eyes wide open in the dark, they talked on and on, for they were quite unable to sleep.

'So you won't tell me?' asked Hortense once more.

'But my dear,' replied Berthe, 'you're not married. I really can't. I had an argument with Auguste. He came back, you see, and . . .'

Then, as she hesitated, her sister broke in impatiently.

'Don't be silly! What rubbish! I'm quite old enough to know what you're talking about!'

So then Berthe confessed everything, choosing her words carefully at first, but finally telling everything about Octave and Auguste. Lying there on her back in the dark, Hortense listened, uttering a word or two every now and then to question her sister or express an opinion: 'Well, what did he say then?' 'And how did you feel?' 'That was rather odd; I wouldn't have liked that!' 'Oh, really! So that's how you do it, is it?' Midnight struck, then one o'clock, then two o'clock, and still they kept talking the thing over as their legs grew warmer under the bedclothes, though sleep did not come. In this sort of trance Berthe forgot she was with her sister and began to think aloud, relieving both mind and body of the most delicate confidences.

'As for Verdier and me,' said Hortense abruptly, 'I'll just do what he likes.'

At the mention of Verdier Berthe gave a start of surprise. She thought the engagement had been broken off, for the woman with whom he had lived for fifteen years had had a child just as he was on the point of getting rid of her.

'Do you mean you're thinking of marrying him after all?' she asked.

'Well why shouldn't I? I was a fool to wait so long. The child won't live. It's a girl, and full of scrofula.'

Then, in her disgust, she spat out the word 'mistress', revealing all her hatred, as a respectable bourgeois spinster, for a creature like that who had been living all that time with a man. It was just a manoeuvre, nothing else, her having a baby—a pretext she had invented on discovering that Verdier, after buying some nightdresses for her so that she wouldn't be sent away without a rag on her back, was trying to get her used to a separation by sleeping out more and more often. Ah, well! she would wait and see.

'Poor thing!' exclaimed Berthe.

'Poor thing, indeed!' cried Hortense bitterly. 'It's clear that you're not exactly blameless either!'

But the next moment she regretted this cruel remark and, putting her arms round her sister, kissed her and declared that she never meant to say such a thing. Then they both fell silent. Yet they did not go to sleep, but continued the story with eyes wide open in the dark.

Next morning Monsieur Josserand felt unwell. He had carried on working at his wrappers until two o'clock, although for months he had complained of depression and gradual loss of strength. However, he got up and dressed, but just as he was starting for his office he felt so exhausted that he sent a messenger-boy with a note informing Bernheim Brothers of his indisposition.

The family were just about to have breakfast. They usually breakfasted, without a tablecloth, in the dining-room, which still reeked of the previous night's dinner. The ladies appeared in dressing-gowns, wet from their basins and with their hair tied up in knots. Seeing that her husband was going to stay at home, Madame Josserand decided not to keep Berthe hidden any longer, for she was already sick at all this mystery; besides, she expected that at any moment Auguste would come up and make a scene.

'What! Have you come to have breakfast with us? What's wrong?' cried the father in surprise on seeing his daughter, her eyes puffy from lack of sleep and her bosom squeezed into Hortense's undersized dressing-gown.

'My husband wrote to say he's going to stay in Lyons,' she replied, 'so I thought I'd spend the day with you.'

The sisters had agreed on the story between them. Madame Josserand, who maintained her rigid, governess-like air, forbore to contradict. But Berthe's father eyed her uneasily, as if aware that something was wrong. As the story seemed to him somewhat unlikely, he was about to ask how the shop would manage without her when Berthe came and kissed him on both cheeks in her old carefree, coaxing way.

'Is it really true? You're not hiding anything?' he whispered.

'What an idea! Why should I hide anything from you?'

Madame Josserand merely shrugged her shoulders. What was the use of all these precautions? To gain an hour perhaps, not more. It wasn't worthwhile. Sooner or later the news would have to be broken to him. However, breakfast passed off merrily. Monsieur Josserand was delighted to find himself once more with his two girls; it seemed like old times when, scarcely awake, they used to amuse him by describing their dreams. For him they still had their fresh, sweet aroma of adolescence as, with their elbows on the table, they dipped their bread in their coffee and laughed with their mouths full. All the past came back too as, facing them, he beheld their mother's rigid countenance, her enormous body bursting through an old green silk dress, which she now wore in the mornings without a corset.

The breakfast was marred, however, by an unfortunate episode. Madame Josserand suddenly addressed the maid:

'What are you eating?'

For some time she had been watching Adèle who, wearing slippers, plodded heavily round the table.

'Nothing madam,' she replied.

'What do you mean, nothing? You're chewing something; I'm not blind. Your mouth's quite full. It's no good drawing in your cheeks! I can see anyway. You've got something in your pocket too, haven't you?'

Adèle, in her confusion, sought to withdraw; but Madame Josserand caught hold of her by the skirt.

'For the last quarter of an hour I've been watching you take something out of here and stuff it in your mouth, after hiding it in your hand. It must be something very nice. Let's see what it is.'

Thrusting her hand into the girl's pocket, she pulled out a handful of stewed prunes, with all the syrup dripping from them.

'What is this?' she cried furiously.

'Prunes, madam,' said Adèle, who, seeing that she had been found out, became insolent.

'Oh! So you like eating my prunes, do you? That's why they go so quickly. Well I never! Prunes! And in your pocket too!'

Then she accused her of drinking the vinegar. Everything disappeared in the same way; you couldn't even leave a cold potato about without being sure it would never be seen again.

'You're an absolute pig, my girl.'

'Give me something to eat then,' replied Adèle boldly; 'then I'll leave your cold potatoes alone.'

This was the climax. Madame Josserand rose, majestic, terrible.

'Hold your tongue! Don't you dare answer me like that! I know what it is: it's the other servants who've spoilt you. No sooner does one get some simpleton of a girl fresh from the country into one's house than all the other sluts in the place put her up to all sorts of tricks. You no longer go to church; and now you've begun to steal!'

Spurred on by Lisa and Julie, Adèle was not going to give in.

'If I was such a simpleton you shouldn't have taken advantage of it. It's too late now.'

'Leave the room! And leave the house!' cried Madame Josserand, pointing with a tragic gesture to the door.

She sat down, quivering, while the maid, without hurrying, shuffled about in her slippers and munched another prune before going back to her kitchen. She was dismissed in this way once a week; it no longer alarmed her in the least. At the table an awkward silence prevailed. After a while Hortense observed that it was not a bit of good dismissing her one day and keeping her on the next. Of course she stole things, and had grown insolent, but they might as well have her as anybody else, for she at least condescended to wait upon them, whereas any other maid would not put up with them for a week, even though she treated herself to the vinegar and stuffed her pockets full of prunes.

There was a charming intimacy about their breakfast, despite this episode. Monsieur Josserand, in the tenderest of moods, spoke of poor Saturnin who had had to be taken away the previous evening while he was out; he believed the tale they had told him about an attack of raving madness in the middle of the shop. Then, when he complained of never seeing Léon, Madame Josserand, who had fallen silent, curtly remarked that she was expecting him that very day. He was probably coming to lunch. A week before the young man had broken off his relations with Madame Dambreville who, to keep her promise, wanted him to marry a stale, swarthy widow. He, however, had decided to marry a niece of Monsieur Dambreville's, a creole of great wealth and beauty who had only arrived at her uncle's house the previous September, after the death of her father in the West Indies. So there had been terrible scenes between the two lovers. Consumed by jealousy, Madame Dambreville refused to give her niece to Léon, feeling it impossible to be supplanted by so fascinating a flower of youth.

'How's the marriage proceeding?' asked Monsieur Josserand discreetly.

At first the mother answered in carefully chosen phrases, because of Hortense. She now worshipped her son, a fellow who was sure to succeed; and at times she threw his triumph in the face of his father, saying that, thank God, he at least took after his mother and would never let his wife go barefoot. She slowly built up steam.

'Basically, he's just about had enough of it! But it's all right; the whole thing hasn't done him any harm. But if the aunt won't give him the niece, too bad! He'll cut off all supplies. I think he's right!'

For decency's sake, Hortense began to drink her coffee, pretending to hide behind her cup, while Berthe, who could now listen to everything, looked somewhat disgusted at her brother's success. They all rose from table, and Monsieur Josserand, feeling much better, was talking jauntily of going on to the office after all when Adèle brought in a card. The lady was waiting in the drawing-room.

'What? Is it her, at this hour of the morning?' cried Madame Josserand. 'And me without my corset on! Never mind. It's time I gave her a piece of my mind.'

It was indeed Madame Dambreville. The father and his two daughters remained chatting in the dining-room, while the mother made for the drawing-room. Before pushing the door open she uneasily surveyed her old green silk dress, tried to button it, removed stray threads that had got on to it from the floor, and with a tap drove her immense bosom back into place.

'You'll excuse me, dear lady,' said the visitor with a smile, 'I was passing and thought I'd call to see how you were.'

Corseted and coiffed, her toilet was perfect in every detail, and her easy manner suggested the amiable lady of fashion who had just dropped in to wish a friend good morning. Her smile, however, was tremulous, and lurking beneath her worldly suavity one could feel the deep anguish that shook her whole being. At first she talked of a thousand trivial matters, avoiding any mention of Léon's name, but at last she furtively drew from her pocket a letter of his which she had just received.

'A terrible letter, quite terrible!' she murmured, as her voice, changing, became choked with tears. 'Why is he so angry with me, dear madam? He won't even come near us now.'

She held out the missive with a shaking hand. Madame Josserand coolly took it and read it.

It was to break matters off; three lines, most cruelly concise.

'Well,' she said, handing back the note. 'I dare say it isn't Léon's fault.'

Madame Dambreville began forthwith to sound the praises of this widow, a woman not yet thirty-five, a most worthy person, fairly well-off, and of such energy that she would not rest until she had got her husband a place in the Ministry. She had kept her promise, she said, after all; she had found a good match for Léon; so why should he be angry with her? Then, without waiting for an answer, in a sudden nervous impulse she mentioned Raymonde, her niece. Could it really be possible? A little thing of sixteen, a raw creature who knew nothing of the world.

'Why not?' Madame Josserand kept repeating in reply to each question. 'Why not, if he's fond of her?'

'No, no! He's not fond of her, he can't be fond of her!' Madame Dambreville cried, losing all self-control. 'Listen to me!' she exclaimed; 'all I ask from him is a little gratitude. I made him; it's thanks to me that he got his position in the High Court, and as a wedding present he'll get a promotion. Madam, I implore you, tell him to come back, ask him to do me that pleasure. I appeal to his heart, to your heart as a mother, to all that is noble in you.'

She clasped her hands and her voice faltered. There was a pause, as they both sat facing each other. Then all at once she burst into tears, sobbing hysterically:

'Not with Raymonde; oh, no, not with Raymonde!'

It was the fury of passion, the cry of a woman who refuses to grow old, who clings to her last lover at that burning moment before old age arrives. She seized hold of Madame Josserand's hands, bathed them in tears, confessing all to her, the mother, humiliating herself before her, repeatedly saying that she, and she alone, could influence her son, declaring that she would serve her devotedly if only she would restore Léon to her. Doubtless she had not come there to say all this; on the contrary, she had resolved to reveal nothing; but her heart was breaking, she could not help it.

'Please, my dear! You make me feel quite ashamed,' replied Madame Josserand rather angrily. 'My girls might hear you. I know nothing, and I don't want to know anything. If you've had any differences with my son, well, you'd better make it up between you. I'll never interfere.'

However, she overwhelmed her with advice. At her time of life she ought to be resigned. In God she would find great succour. But she must give up her niece, if she wished to offer an expiatory sacrifice to Heaven. Besides, this widow would not suit Léon at all; he required a pleasant-looking wife to preside at his dinner-table. And she spoke admiringly of her son, full of maternal pride, enumerating his good qualities and showing him to be worthy of the loveliest of brides.

'Just think, my dear friend, he's not yet thirty. I'd hate to seem unkind, but you could be his mother, you know. Oh! he knows what he owes you, and I'm deeply grateful myself. You'll always be his guardian angel. But, you know, when it's over, it's over. Surely you didn't think you could keep him for ever, did you?'

Then, as the unhappy woman refused to listen to reason, wishing simply to get her lover back at once, the mother lost her temper.

'That's quite enough, madam, you'd better be off! I really can't help you. The boy wants an end to it and that's all there is to it! Look after yourself! I'd be obliged to remind him of his duty if he again yielded to your importunities, because, I ask you, what point would there be for either of you now? He'll be here very soon; and if you counted on my . . .'

Of all these words Madame Dambreville only heard the last phrase. She had been pursuing Léon for a whole week without ever getting to see him. Her face brightened as she uttered the heartfelt cry:

'If he's coming, I'll stay!'

She sank into an armchair, gazed vacantly into space, and fell completely silent, stubborn as an animal that even blows cannot force to budge. Regretful at having said too much, and exasperated at the presence of this great millstone in her drawing-room which she dared not try to remove, Madame Josserand at last withdrew, leaving her visitor to herself. Moreover, a noise in the dining-room made her uneasy; she fancied she heard Auguste's voice.

'Upon my word, madam, such behaviour is unheard of!' she exclaimed, as she slammed the door violently. 'It shows an appalling lack of tact!'

As it happened, it was indeed Auguste, who had come upstairs to make some arrangements with his wife's parents on terms which he had been planning the evening before. Monsieur Josserand, growing more and more chirpy, had given up all idea of the office; he was bent on fun, and just as he was proposing to take his daughters out for a walk Adèle announced Madame Berthe's husband. This sent a tremor round the room; the young wife turned pale.

'What! Your husband?' said the father. 'I thought he was in Lyons. So you didn't tell me the truth? I knew there was something wrong. I've felt it for the last two days!'

Then, as she rose to go, he stopped her.

'Tell me: have you been quarrelling again? About money, eh? Perhaps about the dowry of ten thousand francs we haven't paid him yet?'

'Yes, yes, that's right!' stammered Berthe, as she shook him aside and escaped.

Hortense got up too and ran after her sister, whom she joined in her bedroom. The rustle of their skirts left behind a sort of shiver of fear for their father, who suddenly found himself seated alone at table in the middle of the silent dining-room. All the signs of illness came back, his ghastly pallor, his desperate weariness of life. The hour he dreaded, which he awaited with shame and anguish, had come: his son-in-law was going to mention the insurance, and he would have to admit the dishonesty of the scheme to which he had consented.

'Come in, come in, my dear Auguste,' he said in a choked voice.

'Berthe has just told me all about your quarrel. I'm not very well, so they're spoiling me. I'm terribly sorry I can't give you that money. I should never have promised, I know.'

He faltered on, like some guilty person making a clean breast of it. Auguste listened to him in surprise. He had already been informed about the bogus insurance but had never dared claim the payment of the ten thousand francs for fear that that terrible Madame Josserand might first of all send him to old Vabre's tomb to get his own paternal inheritance of ten thousand francs. But since the subject had been raised, he took it up and began to air his grievances.

'Yes, yes, sir,' he said, 'I know everything; you completely took me in with all your fine tales and promises. As to not getting the money, that wouldn't matter so much; it's the hypocrisy of the whole thing that enrages me! Why all that nonsense about an insurance that never existed! Why pretend to be so tender-hearted and sympathetic, offering to advance sums which, as you said, would only come to you three years afterwards, when all the while you hadn't got a sou! There's only one word for such behaviour!'

Monsieur Josserand was on the point of retorting, 'It wasn't me; they did it!' But a sense of family shame restrained him, and he hung his head in acknowledgment of the dirty trick, while Auguste went on:

'Besides, everybody was against me; Duveyrier, with that crooked notary, behaved shamefully as well, because I asked them to insert a clause in the contract guaranteeing the payment of the insurance money, but they told me to shut up. If I had insisted on that you would have been guilty of forgery sir, yes, forgery!'

At this accusation the father, white as a sheet, rose and was about to reply, offering to work hard for the rest of his life if only he might purchase thereby his daughter's happiness, when Madame Josserand rushed in like a whirlwind, lashed to fury by Madame Dambreville's stubbornness. She no longer paid any attention to her old green silk dress, the bodice of which was split by her heaving bosom.

'Eh? What's that?' she cried. 'What's that about forgery? You, sir? You'd better go to Père-Lachaise first, sir, and see if your father's cash-box is open yet!'

Auguste was expecting this, but nevertheless he was dreadfully annoyed. However, with head erect, she went on with amazing self-possession:

'We've got your ten thousand francs. Yes, they're quite safe, in that drawer over there. But we're not going to let you have them until Monsieur Vabre comes back to give you your inheritance. What a family! The father a gambler who swindles us all, and the brother-in-law a thief who steals the inheritance!'

'Thief? Thief?' spluttered Auguste, beside himself with rage. 'The thieves are here, madam!'

With burning cheeks they stood facing each other, and Monsieur Josserand, extremely upset by turbulent scenes of this sort, strove to separate them. He begged them to be calm. His whole frame quivered, and he was obliged to sit down.

'At any rate,' said Auguste, after a pause, 'I won't have a tramp in my house. You can keep your money and your daughter, too. That's what I came to tell you.'

'You're changing the subject,' coolly remarked Madame Josserand. 'Very well, we'll talk about that presently.'

But the father, powerless to rise, looked at them aghast. He no longer understood what they meant. What were they saying? Tramp! Who was the tramp? Then, as, listening to them, he learned that it was his daughter, his heart was torn as by a gaping wound through which all that remained to him of existence ebbed away. Good God! So his daughter would be his death! For all his weaknesses she was to serve as punishment, she whom he had never known how to educate! Already the thought that she was living in debt and always quarrelling with her husband saddened him in his old age, and revived within him all the petty worries of his own life. And now she was an adulteress, having sunk to that lowest grade of infamy for a woman. The idea was revolting to his simple, honest soul. He grew cold as ice, listening, mute, while the others wrangled.

'I told you she would be unfaithful!' cried Auguste with an air of indignant triumph.

'And I told you you were doing your best to make her unfaithful!' screamed Madame Josserand exultantly. 'I'm not saying Berthe was right; in fact, she's behaved like an idiot, and I'm going to tell her what I think, too; but since she's not here, I repeat, you, and you alone, are to blame!'

'What do you mean? I'm to blame?'

'Of course you are! You don't know how to treat women. For example, did you ever condescend to come to one of my Tuesday receptions? No; and if you did you only stayed half-an-hour at the most, and then you only came three times during the whole season. It's all very well to say you've always got a headache. Manners are manners, that's all. I'm not saying it's a great crime; but you just don't know how to behave!'

She hissed out the words with a venom that had gradually accumulated, for when her daughter had married she had especially counted on her son-in-law to fill her drawing-room with desirable guests. But he had brought no one, and never even came himself; thus another of her dreams had vanished as she saw that she could never hope to rival the Duveyrier choruses.

'However,' she added, with a touch of irony, 'I don't force anybody to come and enjoy themselves at my house.'

'The fact is, nobody ever enjoys it,' he retorted petulantly.

This threw her into an absolute rage.

'That's right, let's hear your insults! I'd have you know, sir, that if I wanted I could get the best society in Paris to come to my parties, and I certainly never depended on you for my social position.'

It was no longer a question of Berthe's misconduct; in this personal quarrel the adultery had disappeared. As though the victim of some hideous nightmare, Monsieur Josserand sat there listening to them. It was not possible; his daughter could never have caused him such grief as this. At last, rising with difficulty, he went out, without saying a word, to find Berthe. As soon as she came, he thought, she would fling her arms round Auguste's neck; everything would be explained, everything would be forgotten. He found her arguing with Hortense, who kept urging her to ask forgiveness of her husband, for she was already tired of her and feared that she might have to share a room with her for some time to come. At first Berthe refused, but finally followed her father. As they came back to the dining-room where the dirty breakfast-cups still stood, Madame Josserand was shouting:

'No, absolutely not, I don't pity you in the least!'

Then, at the sight of Berthe, she fell silent, relapsing into her severely majestic mood, while Auguste, when his wife appeared, made a grand gesture of protest as if to sweep her from his path.

'Now look here,' said Monsieur Josserand, in his gentle, tremulous voice, 'what's the matter with all of you? You're driving me mad with all this quarrelling; I don't know where I am. Tell me, my child, your husband's mistaken isn't he? You explain it to him, please. You ought to have some consideration for your poor old parents. Now, kiss and make up, for my sake.'

Berthe, who was quite willing to kiss Auguste, stood there half-throttled in her dressing-gown, looking very awkward as she saw him recoil from her with an air of tragic repugnance.

'What? You won't kiss him my darling?' continued the father. 'You're the one who should take the first step. And you, my dear fellow, you should encourage her, and be indulgent.'

Then, finally, Auguste burst out:

'Encourage her! I like that! I caught her in her nightdress, sir, with that fellow! Do you take me for a fool to think that I'd kiss her? She was in her nightdress, do you hear sir?'

Monsieur Josserand was thunderstruck. Then, seizing Berthe's arm, he exclaimed:

'You're not saying anything? So it's true? Down on your knees, then!'

But Auguste had already reached the door.

'That's no good. Don't give me that nonsense, or try to saddle me with her again. Once was enough. I've had enough, do you hear? I'd rather get a divorce. Give her to somebody else if you find her a nuisance. And anyway, you're just as bad as she is.'

He waited until he had got into the hall before delivering himself of this final taunt:

'Yes, when you've turned your daughter into a slut, you don't force her down an honest man's throat.'

The front door slammed, and profound silence reigned. Berthe mechanically sat down at the table, her eyes downcast, examining the dregs in her coffee-cup, while her mother strode up and down, swept away by the tempest of her emotions. Her father, white-faced and utterly worn out, sat aloof in the far corner of the room, leaning against the wall. The room reeked of rancid butter, of the cheap kind you could buy at the Halles.

'Now that that insolent fellow has gone,' said Madame Josserand, 'we might be able to hear ourselves speak. All this, sir, is the result of your incapacity. Can you at last see how much at fault you've been? Do you think that quarrels like this would ever have occurred in the house of one of the Bernheim Brothers, the owners of the Saint-Joseph Glassworks? No, I think not! If you'd listened to me, if you'd got your employers on your side, that insolent person would now be grovelling at our feet, because obviously all he wants is money. If you've got money people will respect you, sir. It's much better to be envied than pitied. If I only had twenty sous, I always pretended I had forty. But you sir, you don't care if I go barefoot or not; you've deceived your wife and daughters in a most disgraceful fashion by letting them drag out their existence in this hand-to-mouth way. Oh, it's no good denying it! All our misfortunes are due to that.'

Monsieur Josserand stared blankly into space, without moving. His wife stood in front of him, full of mad desire for a scene. Then, seeing that he would not react, she continued to pace up and down.

'Yes, yes, play at being disdainful. It doesn't affect me in the slightest, you know that. Just you dare say anything about my family after what's happened in your own! Uncle Bachelard is a saint, and my sister too! Do you want to know what I think? Well, if my father hadn't died you would have killed him. As for your father . . .'

Monsieur Josserand's face became whiter still as he gasped:

'Eléonore, I beg of you—say what you want about my father, about my whole family; but I beg of you, leave me in peace; I don't feel well!'

Berthe, taking pity on him, looked up.

'Mamma, do leave him alone,' she said.

Then, turning on her daughter, Madame Josserand went on with even greater fury:

'I was keeping you till last. I've been holding it in since yesterday. But I can't any longer. With that counter-jumper, of all people! You must have lost all pride! I thought you were only making use of him, showing him just enough friendliness to keep him on his toes in the shop. And I helped you. I encouraged him! Now tell me, what did you hope to gain in all this?'

'Nothing whatever!' stammered Berthe.

'Then why did you carry on with him? It's even more mad than scandalous!'

'How funny you are, mamma! One never thinks about that sort of thing in advance!'

Madame Josserand continued to pace up and down.

' "One never thinks . . ."! Oh really. But yes, you *have* to think! Misbehaving like that! There's absolutely no sense in it—that's what annoys me! Did I ever tell you to deceive your husband? Did I ever deceive your father? He's sitting there; ask him. He can tell you if he ever caught me with another man.'

Her pace slackened; her gait grew majestic and she lustily slapped the green bodice of her dress.

'No, never; not a slip, not one indiscretion, not even the thought of one! My life has been quite chaste, yet God knows what I've had to put up with from your father! I had every excuse, and lots of women would have taken their revenge. But I was sensible; that's what saved me. You see, he's got nothing to say! He just sits there, unable to make a single complaint. I've got every right to call myself a virtuous woman! Oh, you great ninny, you surely see what a fool you've made of yourself!'

Then she delivered a lecture on domestic morality with regard to adultery. Was not Auguste now entitled to lord it over her? She had given him a terrible weapon. Even if they made it up, she could never have the least argument with him without being told to shut up at once. A nice state of affairs, eh? How delightful it would be for her always to eat humble pie! It was all over, and she could never hope to enjoy any of the little privileges she might have obtained from a compliant husband, little kindnesses, attentions, and the like. No, it was better to live a virtuous life than not to have the upper hand in one's own house!

'I swear before God,' she cried, 'I would always keep myself decent, even if the Emperor himself had pestered me! The loss is too great!'

She strode on, silent for a while, as if lost in thought, and then added:

'Besides, it's the most shameful thing of all.'

Monsieur Josserand looked at her, and then at his daughter, moving his lips without speaking, his whole dejected frame protesting against such harrowing explanations. Berthe, however, daunted by violence, felt hurt at her mother's moral lecture. And at last she rebelled, for, true to her old training as a marriageable daughter, she failed to recognize the gravity of her sin.

'Well!' she cried, planting both elbows on the table, 'you shouldn't have made me marry a man I didn't care for. Now I hate him, and I've taken up with somebody else.'

So she went on. The whole story of her marriage was rehearsed in short phrases, pronounced in bursts: the three winters devoted to man-hunting, the various youths at whom she was thrown, the failure of this offer of her body in the market of bourgeois drawing-rooms. Then she spoke of everything that mothers taught their dowryless daughters. A complete series of lessons in polite prostitution: the touch of fingers in the dance, the relinquishing of hands behind a door, the indecency of innocence speculating on the prurient appetites of the foolish; then, one fine evening, the full-blown husband, landed just as a common prostitute lands a man; the husband trapped behind a curtain, falling for the bait in the fever of his desire.

'Well, he bores me and I bore him!' she exclaimed. 'It's not my fault that we don't understand each other. The very next day after our wedding he seemed to think we'd swindled him; yes, and he looked as glum and unpleasant as he does now when things go badly in the shop. I was never taken with him. If that's all the fun you get out of marriage! That's certainly how it all began! Never mind, it was bound to happen and it's not all my fault.'

She stopped, and then, with an air of profound conviction, added:

'Ah, mamma, how well I understand you now! You remember when you told us you'd had more than enough of it?'

Standing before her, Madame Josserand listened, indignant and aghast.

'*I* said that?' she screamed.

But Berthe was unstoppable.

'Yes you did, lots of times. And I'd like to see how you'd have behaved in my place. Auguste isn't easygoing like papa. You'd have had a fight about money before the week was out. Auguste is the sort of man who would've made you say that all men are good for is what you can get out of them!'

'*I* said that?' repeated her mother, beside herself with rage.

So threateningly did she advance towards her daughter that the father held out both hands, as if begging for mercy. The raised voices of the two women struck him to the core; each fresh outburst seemed to widen the wound. Tears filled his eyes as he stammered out:

'Do stop; spare me all this!'

'No, it's dreadful!' continued Madame Josserand, raising her voice. 'The wretched girl is telling me I'm responsible for her shameful behaviour! The next thing she'll say is that I was the one who was unfaithful to her husband! So it's my fault, is it? That's what it seems to come down to. My fault, eh?'

Berthe continued to sit with her elbows on the table, pale but resolute.

'It's absolutely certain that if you'd brought me up differently . . .'

She never finished the sentence. Her mother gave her such a huge clout that it banged her head down on the oilcloth table-cover. Madame Josserand's hand had been itching to do this since the night before; it had been making her fingers tingle, as in the far-off days when her little girl used to oversleep.

'There, take that for your education!' she cried. 'Your husband should've killed you!'

Without lifting her head Berthe burst into tears, holding her cheek to her arm. She forgot that she was twenty-four; this slap reminded her of slaps received when she was younger, and of all the timorous hypocrisy of her girlhood. Her resolution, as an emancipated, grown-up person, was lost as she felt the sharp pain of a little girl.

Hearing her sobs, her father was nearly overcome with emotion. Stumbling forward, he pushed his wife aside, saying:

'Listen, do you both want to be the death of me? Must I go down on my knees to you?'

Having relieved her feelings, and having nothing more to say, Madame Josserand withdrew in regal silence. Opening the door suddenly, she caught Hortense listening behind it. This caused a fresh outburst.

'So you were listening to all this filth, were you? One of you does shocking things, and the other gloats over them! A pretty pair! Goodness gracious! Whoever could have brought you up?'

Hortense came calmly in, and said:

'There was no need to listen; you can be heard from the far end of the kitchen. The maid's in fits. Besides, I'm old enough to get married now so there's no reason why I shouldn't know.'

'Verdier, I suppose!' was the mother's biting reply. 'That's the sort of satisfaction you give me. Now you're waiting for that brat to die; but you'll have to wait, because she's big and fat, so they say. A good job, too!'

A rush of bile turned the girl's gaunt face yellow, as she replied through clenched teeth:

'If it's a big, fat baby Verdier can get rid of it. And I'll make him get rid of it quicker than you think, just to show you all. Yes, yes, I can find a husband without your help; the matches you make are too healthy!'

Then, as her mother advanced towards her, she said:

'Don't think you can slap me! Just look out!'

They glared at each other, and Madame Josserand was the first to yield, masking her retreat with an air of disdainful superiority. The father, however, thought that hostilities were about to recommence. Watching these three women, the mother and her daughters, beings he had loved and who now were ready to murder one another, he felt as if the whole world was giving way under his feet; and he, too, escaped to his room as if he had received his death-blow and wished to die alone. And in the midst of his sobs, he kept repeating:

'I can't bear it, I can't bear it!'

Silence reigned once more in the dining-room. Berthe, heaving huge sighs, her cheek on her arm, had calmed down somewhat. Hortense sat at the other end of the table, buttering a piece of toast by way of recovering her equanimity. Then, with various gloomy remarks, she brought her sister to a pitch of desperation: life at home, she said, had become unbearable; if she were in her place she would prefer to be slapped by her husband rather than by her mother, as that was a far more natural thing. Moreover, once she had married Verdier she would simply send her mother packing, as she was not going to have rows of this sort in her home. Just then Adèle came in to clear away; but Hortense went on, saying that if there was any more of this she would give warning; and the maid was of this opinion too—she had been obliged to shut the kitchen-window because Lisa and Julie had both been peeping out to see what was going on. The whole thing, however, had amused her greatly, and she was still chuckling about it. What a smack Madame Berthe had got! She was the worst off, after all. And as she waddled about, Adèle uttered a phrase full of profound philosophy. After all, she said, what did the other people in the house care? Life went on, and before the week was out nobody would even remember madam's affair with the two gentlemen. Hortense, who nodded approval, broke in with a complaint about the butter; her mouth was tainted by the filth. Goodness Gracious! Butter at twenty-two sous! It must be poison! And since it left a nauseous deposit in the saucepans, the maid proceeded to explain that it was not even economical to buy the stuff. At this moment a dull thud, like something falling on the floor, set them all listening.

Berthe at last looked up in alarm. 'What's that?' she asked.

'Perhaps it's madam and the other lady in the drawing-room,' suggested Adèle.

On going through the drawing-room, Madame Josserand had started back in surprise. A lady sat there, all by herself.

'What? Are you still here?' she exclaimed, on recognizing Madame Dambreville, whose presence she had entirely forgotten.

The latter did not stir. The family quarrels, the raised voices, the banging of doors, all this had passed over her; she seemed oblivious of it all. There she sat, motionless, gazing into space, absorbed in passionate despair.

But something was at work within her; the advice of Léon's mother had shaken her, persuading her to pay dearly for a few final fragments of happiness.

'Come on,' cried Madame Josserand brutally, 'you can't sleep here, you know. I had a note from my son, he's not coming.'

Then, with a dry mouth, as if she were just waking up, Madame Dambreville spoke.

'I'm going now; please excuse me. Tell him from me that I've thought it over and I give my consent. I'll think about it further, and perhaps I'll arrange for him to marry that girl, since he really must. But it's I who am giving her to him, and I want him to come and ask me for her; ask me, me only, do you see? Oh, make him come back to me, make him come back!'

Her ardent voice pleaded, and then, lowering her tone, like a woman who, after sacrificing everything, obstinately clings to one last consolation, she added:

'He'll marry her, but he must live with us. Otherwise, nothing can be done. I'd rather lose him altogether.'

Then she prepared to take her leave. Madame Josserand grew quite gushing and said all sorts of consoling things in the hall. She promised to send Léon that very evening in a contrite, affectionate frame of mind, declaring that he would be delighted to live with his new aunt. Then, having shut the door after Madame Dambreville, full of pity and tenderness, she thought to herself:

'Poor boy! She'll make him pay a high price!'

But at that moment she too heard the dull thud which shook the flooring. What on earth could it be? Was the maid smashing all the crockery? She rushed back to the dining-room and asked her daughters what had happened.

'What's the matter? Did the sugar-basin fall over?'

'No, mamma, we don't know what it was.'

Turning round to look for Adèle, she caught her listening at the bedroom door.

'What are you doing?' she cried. 'Everything's being smashed to bits in your kitchen while you stand there spying on your master. Yes, yes, you start with prunes and you end with something else. For some time past, my girl, I haven't liked the look of you: you smell of men . . .'

Wide-eyed, Adèle looked at her. Then she observed:

'That's not it. I think it's master who's fallen down in there.'

'Good gracious, I think she's right!' said Berthe, turning pale. 'It was just like someone falling.'

They entered the room. On the floor, near the bed, lay Monsieur Josserand. He had fainted; his head had knocked against a chair and a trickle of blood was coming from his right ear. Mother, daughters, and maidservant gathered round to examine him. Only Berthe burst into tears, sobbing convulsively as if still smarting from the blow she had received. And as the four of them were trying to lift him and place him on the bed, they heard him murmur:

'It's all over. They've killed me.'

XVII

Months passed, and spring came. In the house in the Rue de Choiseul everybody was talking of the likelihood of a marriage between Octave and Madame Hédouin.

Things, however, had not yet reached that stage. Octave had resumed his old post at the Ladies' Paradise, and every day his responsibilities increased. Since her husband's death Madame Hédouin had not been able to take sole charge of the ever-expanding business. Old Deleuze, her uncle, was bound to his chair by rheumatism and could attend to nothing; so naturally Octave, young, active, and full of new ideas about doing business on a large scale, quickly assumed a position of great influence in the shop. Still sore about his ridiculous love affair with Berthe, he now no longer thought of making use of women; he even fought shy of them. The best thing, he thought, would be for him quietly to become Madame Hédouin's partner and then to pile up money. Remembering, too, the absurd snub she had given him, he treated her as if she were a man, which was exactly what she wanted.

Henceforth their relations became most intimate. They would shut themselves up for hours in the little back room. When he had set out to seduce her he had followed a complete set of tactics, trying to exploit her excitement about business, breathing on the back of her neck as he mentioned certain figures to her, waiting for a time when takings were heavy in order to take advantage of her enthusiasm. Now he was simply good-natured, with no end in view except business. He no longer even desired her, though he still remembered her little thrill of excitement as she leaned against his chest when they waltzed together on the evening of Berthe's wedding. Perhaps she had been fond of him, after all? Anyhow, it was best to remain as they were; for, as she rightly observed, perfect order was necessary in the business of the shop, and it was foolish to want things which would only upset them from morning to night.

Seated together at the narrow desk, they often forgot themselves after going through the books and settling the orders. Then it was that he reverted to his dreams of aggrandizement. He had sounded out the owner of the neighbouring shop, who was quite ready to sell.

The second-hand dealer and the umbrella-maker must be given notice to quit, and a special silk department must be opened. To this she listened gravely, not daring as yet to commit herself. But her liking for Octave's business capacity grew ever greater, for in his ideas she recognized her own; her aptitude for commerce and the serious, practical side of her character showed, as it were, beneath his urbane exterior as a polite shopman. And he displayed such passion and audacity—qualities lacking in herself, and which filled her with enthusiasm. It was imagination applied to business, the only sort of imagination that had ever troubled her. He was becoming her master.

At length, one evening as they sat side by side looking over some invoices under the hot flame of the gas, she said slowly:

'I've spoken to my uncle, Monsieur Octave. He's given his consent, so we'll buy the shop. But . . .'

Merrily interrupting her, he cried:

'Then the Vabres are done for!'

She smiled, and murmured reproachfully:

'So you hate them, do you? It's not right; you're the last person who should wish them any ill.'

She had never once made any reference to his relationship with Berthe, so that this sudden allusion greatly embarrassed him, without his exactly knowing why. He blushed and stammered some excuse.

'No, no! That doesn't concern me,' she continued, still smiling and very calm. 'Forgive me, I didn't mean to say that; I never meant to say anything about that subject. You're young. So much the worse for those who want it, eh? Husbands ought to look after their wives if their wives can't look after themselves.'

He felt relieved to see that she was not angry. He had often feared that if she found out about his old liaison she might grow cold.

'You interrupted me, Monsieur Octave,' she went on gravely. 'I was about to add that if I buy the shop next door, and so double the value of my present business, I can't possibly remain a widow. I'll have to remarry.'

Octave was astonished. So she already had a husband in view and he knew nothing about it. He suddenly felt that his position was compromised.

'My uncle', she continued, 'told me as much himself. Oh, there's no hurry just yet! I've been in mourning for eight months, so I'll wait until the autumn. But in business all affairs of the heart must be put on one side, so that one may consider the necessities of the situation. A man is absolutely necessary here.'

She calmly discussed all this as if it were a business matter, while he watched her, with her beautiful regular features, clear healthy complexion, and neat, wavy black hair. And he felt regretful that since her widowhood he had not again sought to become her lover.

'It's always a very serious thing,' he faltered. 'You need to think about it very carefully.'

Of course she thought so too. And she mentioned her age.

'I'm getting on, you know. I'm five years older than you, Monsieur Octave.'

Then, overcome, he interrupted her, thinking he understood. Seizing her hands he exclaimed:

'Oh, madam! Oh, madam!'

But she rose from her seat and freed herself. Then she turned down the gas.

'Well, that'll do for today. You have excellent ideas, and it's only natural that I should think of you as the best person to carry them out. But it won't be easy, and we must think the whole thing through. I know that you're really very serious about it. Think about it, and so will I. That's why I mentioned it to you. We can discuss it some other time, later on.'

Things remained like this for weeks. Business went on as usual. As Madame Hédouin always maintained her calm, smiling demeanour towards him, never once hinting at any tenderer feeling, Octave at first affected a similar serenity and soon, like her, grew healthfully happy, trusting implicitly in the logic of things. Her favourite remark was that reasonable things always happened of their own accord. So she was never in a hurry about anything. None of the gossip respecting her intimacy with the young man had the slightest effect on her. All they had to do was wait.

Everyone in the house in the Rue de Choiseul declared that the match was made. Octave had given up his room there and had moved into lodgings in the Rue Neuve-Saint-Augustin, close to the Ladies' Paradise. He no longer visited anyone, and never went to the Campardons' nor the Duveyriers', who were shocked at his scandalous behaviour. Even Monsieur Gourd, when he met him, pretended not to recognize him to avoid having to bow. Only Marie and Madame Juzeur, on the mornings when they met him in the neighbourhood, stopped and chatted for a few moments in a doorway. Madame Juzeur, who eagerly questioned him as to his reported liaison with Madame Hédouin, wanted him to promise that he would come and see her and have a nice chat about it all. Marie was in despair at being pregnant again, and told him of Jules's amazement and her parents' wrath. However, when the rumour of his marriage was confirmed Octave was surprised to get a very low bow from Monsieur Gourd. Campardon, though he did not yet offer to make it up, nodded cordially to him across the street, while Duveyrier, when looking in one evening to buy some gloves, appeared very friendly. By degrees the whole house seemed ready to forgive and forget.

Moreover, they had all returned to the beaten track of bourgeois respectability. Behind the great mahogany doors fresh founts of virtue played; the third-floor gentleman came to work one night a week as usual; the other Madame Campardon passed by, inflexible in her integrity; the maids sported aprons of dazzling whiteness, while, in the tepid silence of the staircase, all the pianos on all the floors flung out the self-same waltzes, making music at once mystic and remote.

Yet the taint of adultery still lingered, imperceptible to common folk but disagreeable to those of fine moral sense. Auguste obstinately refused to take back his wife, and so long as Berthe lived with her parents the scandal would not be erased; the material trace of it must remain. Yet not one of the tenants openly told the exact story, as it would have been so embarrassing for everybody. By common and, as it were, involuntary consent, they agreed that the quarrel between Berthe and Auguste had arisen because of the ten thousand francs—a mere squabble about money. It was so much more decent to say this; and one could allude to the matter before young ladies. Would the parents pay up or would they not? The whole farce became so perfectly simple, for not a soul in the neighbourhood was either amazed or indignant at the idea that money matters could bring a family to blows. It was true, of course, that this polite arrangement did not affect the actual situation, and though calm in the presence of misfortune, the whole house had suffered a cruel shock to its dignity.

It was Duveyrier in particular who, as landlord, bore the brunt of this persistent and undeserved misfortune. For some time Clarisse had been worrying him so much that he often returned to his wife in tears. The scandal of the adultery too distressed him greatly, for as he said, he saw the passers-by looking scornfully at his house, the house that his father had sought to adorn with all the domestic virtues. Such a state of affairs could not be allowed to go on. He talked of purifying the whole place, to satisfy his own personal honour. And for the sake of public decency he urged Auguste to effect a reconciliation, but unfortunately the latter refused, backed up by Théophile and Valérie, who had fully installed themselves at the pay-desk, delighted by the domestic quarrel. Then, as the Lyons business was in a bad way and the silk warehouse likely to come to grief for want of capital, Duveyrier had a brainwave. The Josserands were doubtless most anxious to get rid of their daughter and Auguste should offer to take her back, but only on condition that they pay the dowry of fifty thousand francs. Perhaps uncle Bachelard would yield to their entreaties and consent to give them the money. At first Auguste vehemently refused to be a party to any such arrangement; even if the sum were a hundred thousand francs it would still not be enough. However, feeling very uneasy about his April disbursements, he at last yielded to Duveyrier's arguments, for the latter spoke in the name of morality, his sole aim being, as he said, to perform a righteous act.

When they were agreed, Clotilde chose Father Mauduit to negotiate matters. It was rather delicate; only a priest could intervene without compromising himself. As it happened, the priest had been much grieved by all the shocking things that had occurred in one of the most interesting households of his parish. Indeed, he had already offered to use all his wisdom, experience, and authority to put an end to a scandal over which enemies of the Church would only gloat. However, when Clotilde mentioned the dowry and asked him to inform the Josserands of Auguste's conditions, he bowed his head and maintained a painful silence.

'The money my brother claims is money due to him, you understand,' said Clotilde. 'It's not a bargain. He absolutely insists on it, too.'

'It must be done, so I'll go,' said the priest at last.

The Josserands had been expecting a proposal for days. Valérie must have said something, for everyone in the house was talking about it. Were they so hard-up that they would have to keep their daughter? Would they manage to find the fifty thousand francs in order to get rid of her? Ever since the subject had been raised Madame Josserand had been in a state of fury. What! after all the trouble they had had to get Berthe married a first time, they were now obliged to get her married again? Nothing had been settled, the dowry had again been asked for, and all the money worries had begun afresh. No mother had ever had to go through such a thing twice over. And all because of that silly fool whose stupidity was such that she forgot her duty! The house became a sort of hell on earth; Berthe suffered perpetual torture, for even her sister Hortense, furious at not having the bedroom to herself, never spoke now without making some cutting remark. Even meals became a source of reproach. It seemed rather odd, when one had a husband somewhere, to come and sponge on one's parents for a meal, for they had little enough to eat themselves! Then, in despair, poor Berthe slunk away sobbing, calling herself a coward, afraid to go downstairs and throw herself at Auguste's feet, and say:

'Here I am. Beat me, do; for I can't be more wretched than I am now!'

Monsieur Josserand alone treated his daughter with kindness. But her sins and tears were killing him; the cruelty of his family had dealt him his death-blow, and, having taken unlimited leave of absence, he hardly ever rose from his bed. Doctor Juillerat, who attended him, said it was blood-poisoning; it was actually a breakdown of his whole system, each organ being affected in turn.

'When you've made your father die of grief, you'll be happy, won't you?' cried Madame Josserand.

Berthe, indeed, was afraid to go into her father's room, for when they were together they both wept and only made each other feel worse. At length Madame Josserand decided to make a decisive move. She invited uncle Bachelard to dinner, having resolved to humiliate herself once more. She would gladly have paid the fifty thousand francs out of her own pocket, had she got them, so as not to have to keep this married daughter of hers, whose presence cast a shadow over her Tuesday receptions. Moreover, she had heard some shocking things about her brother, and if he did not do as she wanted she fully intended to give him a piece of her mind.

Bachelard behaved in a particularly disgusting way at dinner. He had arrived half-drunk; since the loss of Fifi he had sunk to the lowest depths. Fortunately Madame Josserand had not invited anyone else, for fear of disgrace. He fell asleep during dessert while telling certain rakish and ribald anecdotes, and they were obliged to wake him up before taking him into Monsieur Josserand's room. Here, signs of skilful stage-management were evident: with a view to working on the old drunkard's feelings, two chairs had been placed beside the bed, one for the mother, the other for the uncle, while Berthe and Hortense were to remain standing. They would see if the uncle would again dare to deny his promises when confronted with a dying man in such a mournful room, half-lighted by a smoky lamp.

'Narcisse,' said Madame Josserand, 'the situation is very serious.'

Then, in low, solemn tones, she explained what the situation was, telling of her daughter's deplorable misfortune, of Auguste's revolting greed, and of their painful obligation to pay the fifty thousand francs so as to put an end to the scandal that was covering their family with shame. Then she said severely:

'Remember your promise, Narcisse. The night the contract was signed you slapped your chest and swore that Berthe could rely on her uncle's kindness of heart. Well, where is that kindness? The time has come for you to show it! Monsieur Josserand, please join me in showing him what his duty is, if your physical state will allow you to do so!'

Deeply repugnant though it was to him, Monsieur Josserand, from sheer love of his daughter, murmured:

'It's true; you promised, Bachelard. So, before I'm gone, do me the pleasure of acting like an honourable man.'

Berthe and Hortense, however, hoping to soften their uncle, had filled his glass somewhat too frequently. So dulled were his senses that they could no longer take advantage of his inebriated state.

'Eh? what?' he stuttered, without needing to exaggerate his drunken air. 'Never promise . . . don't understand! Just tell me that again, Eléonore.'

Accordingly Madame Josserand began anew, and made Berthe, sobbing, embrace him, begging him to keep his word for the sake of her sick husband and proving to him that in giving the fifty thousand francs he was fulfilling a sacred duty. Then, as he dropped off to sleep again without apparently being affected in the least by the sight of the sick man or the mournful bedchamber, she suddenly burst out:

'Look here Narcisse, this has gone on far too long; you're an absolute scoundrel! I've heard all about your swinish behaviour. You've married your mistress to Gueulin, and given them fifty thousand francs—the very sum you promised us. Nice, isn't it? And that little wretch Gueulin cuts a fine figure, doesn't he? As for you, you're far worse, because you take the bread out of our mouths and squander your fortune; yes, you squander it, you rob us of money that was really ours for the sake of that bitch!'

Never before had she vented her feelings to such an extent as this. Hortense had to busy herself with her father's medicine so as not to show her embarrassment, while Monsieur Josserand, brought to fever-pitch by the whole scene, tossed about restlessly on his pillows and murmured in a trembling voice:

'Eléonore, be quiet, please! He won't give us anything. If you want to say all that to him take him away, so that I can't hear you!'

Berthe began to sob even louder as she joined in her father's entreaties.

'That'll do, mamma; for father's sake, do stop! Goodness gracious! How miserable I am at being the cause of all these quarrels! I'd much rather go away somewhere and die quietly!'

Then Madame Josserand bluntly put the question to Bachelard:

'Now, will you or will you not give us the fifty thousand francs, so that your niece can hold her head up?'

In his bewilderment he sought to explain.

'Listen to me for a moment. I caught Gueulin and Fifi together. What could I do? I had to marry them. It wasn't my fault!'

'Will you or will you not give us the dowry you promised us?' she furiously repeated.

His speech faltered; he seemed so befuddled now that words failed him.

'Can't do it, I swear, can't! Utterly ruined! Else I would, straightaway! Honest I would!'

She cut him short with a terrible gesture.

'Very well!' she exclaimed, 'I'll call a family council and declare you incapable of managing your affairs. When uncles become doddering idiots, it's time to send them to an asylum.'

Whereupon Bachelard was at once greatly overcome. He looked

round the room, which seemed to him very gloomy with its one flickering lamp; his gaze turned to the sick man who, supported by his daughters, was about to swallow a spoonful of some black liquid, and he immediately burst into tears, accusing his sister of never having understood him. Gueulin's treachery had been quite grievous enough for him, he said. They knew how sensitive he was, and it was not right of them to ask him to dinner and then play on his feelings directly afterwards. Instead of the fifty thousand francs they could have every drop of blood in his veins!

Utterly worn out, Madame Josserand had decided to leave him alone when the maid announced Doctor Juillerat and Father Mauduit. They had met on the stairs and came in together. The doctor found Monsieur Josserand much worse, for he was still upset by the scene in which he had had to play a part. As the priest sought to take Madame Josserand into the drawing-room, having, as he said, a communication to make, she instinctively guessed where he had been and majestically replied that she was in the bosom of her family and could bear to hear everything. The doctor himself would not be in the way, for a physician was a confessor as well.

'Madam,' said the priest, with somewhat awkward gentleness, 'what I'm doing is, as you'll see, motivated by an ardent desire to reconcile two families.'

He spoke of God's pardon, and of his great delight at being able to reassure honest hearts by putting a stop to so intolerable a state of affairs. He alluded to Berthe as a wretched child, which drew from her fresh tears, and there was such fatherly tenderness in all he said, and his expressions were so carefully chosen, that Hortense was not obliged to leave the room. However, he was obliged at last to touch on the subject of the fifty thousand francs. Husband and wife had, seemingly, only to kiss and make up, when he mentioned the formal condition of the payment of the dowry.

'Father, forgive me for interrupting you,' said Madame Josserand, 'we're deeply touched by your efforts. But we can never traffic in our daughter's honour. Some people, too, have already made it up behind the child's back! Oh! I know all about it; they were at daggers drawn and now they're inseparable and abuse us from morning to night. No Father, such a bargain would be a disgrace.'

'But madam,' the priest ventured to observe, 'it seems to me . . .'

She cut him short, as she went on with glorious assurance:

'Listen! Here's my brother, ask him what he thinks. Only a moment ago he said to me: "Here, Eléonore, I've brought you the fifty thousand francs. Do settle this wretched business." Well, just ask him what my answer was. Get up, Narcisse! Get up, and tell the truth!'

Bachelard had gone to sleep again in an armchair at the end of the room. He stirred slightly and uttered a few incoherent words. Then, as his sister continued to address him, he placed his hand on his heart and stammered:

'When duty calls we must obey. Family before everything!'

'There, you hear what he says!' cried Madame Josserand, triumphantly. 'No money! It's a disgrace! Just tell those people that we're not in the habit of dying to avoid having to pay. The dowry's here, and we would have paid it; but now that it's being exacted as the price of our daughter the whole thing really has become too disgusting. Let Auguste take Berthe back first; then we'll see what can be done.'

She had raised her voice to such a pitch that the doctor, who was examining his patient, had to tell her to be quiet.

'Softly, please, madam,' he said. 'Your husband is in pain.'

Then, growing more embarrassed, Father Mauduit approached the bed and made a few sympathetic remarks. Then he withdrew without further allusion to the matter, hiding the confusion of his failure beneath a good-humoured smile, while his lip curled with vexation and disgust. As the doctor was leaving in his turn, he bluntly informed Madame Josserand that there was no hope; they ought to take the greatest possible care, as the least emotion might prove fatal. She was thunderstruck and went into the dining-room, to which Bachelard and the girls had already withdrawn, so as to leave Monsieur Josserand in peace as he seemed inclined to go to sleep.

'Berthe,' she murmured, 'you've killed your father this time. The doctor has just told me.'

Then the three of them, seated round the table, began to cry, while Bachelard, also in tears, mixed himself some grog.

When Auguste was told of the Josserands' answer he grew more furious than ever with his wife, and swore that he would send her packing with a few good kicks if she ever came and asked for forgiveness. But the fact was that he missed her greatly. There was a void in his life, and in his solitude and with all his new worries he seemed lost, for his present troubles were quite as serious as those of his married life. Rachel, whom he had kept on in order to annoy Berthe, robbed him and showed her bad temper now, being as coolly impudent as if she were his wife. He began to miss the many little pleasures of their life together, the evenings of mutual boredom, followed by costly reconciliations beneath warm sheets. Above all, he was heartily tired of Théophile and Valérie, who had made themselves at home downstairs and filled the whole shop with their importance. He even suspected them of taking money from the till without the least compunction. Valérie was not like Berthe; her delight was to sit enthroned at the pay-desk, but as it seemed to him, she had a way of attracting men openly, under the very eyes of her imbecilic husband, whose perpetual catarrh forever made his eyes dim with tears. So he preferred Berthe. At least she did not turn the shop into a thoroughfare for oglers. But besides this, another thing worried him. The Ladies' Paradise was prospering, and threatened to rival his own business, where the takings grew daily less. True, he did not regret the loss of that wretched Octave; yet he was fair-minded enough to recognize his excellent business capabilities. How smoothly things would have gone if only there had been a better sort of understanding! Moods of tenderness and regret assailed him, and there were moments when, sick of solitude and finding life quite empty, he felt as though he must go upstairs to the Josserands and take Berthe back from them for nothing.

Duveyrier, however, did not despair, but constantly urged Auguste to make up with his wife, being more and more grieved at the moral pall which the whole affair had cast over his property. He even affected to believe what Madame Josserand had told the priest—that if Auguste would take his wife back unconditionally, her dowry money would be paid the very next day. Then, since Auguste flew into a rage at such a proposal, the judge appealed to his heart. He would walk with him along the banks of the Seine, on his way to the Palais de Justice, preaching the doctrine of pardon for injuries in a voice half-choked with tears, trying to imbue him with the philosophy, at once dismal and cowardly, which sees the only possible happiness in tolerating the wife, since one could not do without her.

Duveyrier was visibly in decline. The whole of the Rue de

Choiseul was depressed and uneasy at the sight of his lugubrious gait and pale face, on which the red blotches were getting larger and more inflamed. Some hidden grief seemed to be weighing him down. It was Clarisse, who was growing ever fatter, more insolent, and more presuming. As her bourgeois plumpness increased, he found her genteel airs and affected good-breeding more and more insupportable. She now forbade him to address her familiarly when members of her family were present, though in his presence she flirted in a most outrageous fashion with her piano-teacher, to his great distress. Twice he had caught her with Théodore; after losing his temper he had begged her, on his knees, to forgive him, accepting whatever terms she chose to make. Also, with a view to keeping him docile and submissive, she would constantly express her disgust at his blotchy face; and she had even thought of handing him on to one of her cooks, a buxom girl accustomed to rough work of all sorts. However, the cook declined to have anything to do with her master. Thus, each day life grew more and more difficult for Duveyrier at his mistress's house, which had become a veritable hell. It was worse than his own home. The tribe of parasites—the mother, the big blackguard of a brother, the two little sisters, and even the invalid aunt—robbed him right and left, sponging on him mercilessly, and even emptying his pockets at night when he was asleep. Other things helped to aggravate the situation: he was running out of money, and trembled at the thought of being compromised in his professional capacity. True, he could not be dismissed from his post; but young barristers looked at him cheekily, which embarrassed him when administering justice. And when, driven away by the dirt and the noise, he fled in self-disgust from the Rue d'Assas and took refuge in the Rue de Choiseul, the hateful coldness of his wife plunged him into total despair. It was then that he would lose his head, glancing at the Seine on his way to the court, thinking that he might drown himself one night when emboldened to do so by some supreme feeling of anguish.

Clotilde had noticed her husband's nervous state with some anxiety, and she felt incensed at this mistress of his who, despite her immoral conduct, still failed to make him happy. She, for her part, was much annoyed by a deplorable incident, the consequences of which revolutionized the whole house. On going upstairs one morning for a handkerchief, Clémence had caught Hippolyte and that little wretch Louise on her own bed; since then she had taken to boxing his ears in the kitchen at the least provocation, which had had a disastrous effect on the other domestics. The worst of it was that madame could no longer shut her eyes to the illicit relations that existed between her parlourmaid and her footman. The other servants laughed; gossip about the scandal spread among the tradespeople, and if she wished to keep the guilty couple it was absolutely necessary to make them marry. Thus, as she still found Clémence a most satisfactory maidservant, she thought of nothing but securing this marriage. To negotiate matters, however, seemed a somewhat delicate task, especially with lovers who were always scratching each other's eyes out; so she determined to entrust the task to Father Mauduit, for in the circumstances he seemed to be marked out for the part of moral mediator. For some time past, indeed, Clotilde's servants had caused her great anxiety. When in the country, she had become aware of the liaison between her big lout of a son Gustave and Julie. At first she thought of dismissing the latter—with regret, for she liked her cooking. Then, after much sage reflection, she kept her on, preferring that the young cub should have a mistress in her own house—a decent girl, who would never make a nuisance of herself. Elsewhere, one never could tell what sort of woman a lad got hold of, especially when, as in this instance, he started all too early. So she kept her eye on them without saying anything, and now the other two had begun to plague her with their wretched affair.

One morning it so happened that, as Madame Duveyrier was about to go and see Father Mauduit, Clémence informed her that the priest was just on his way to administer the last rites to Monsieur Josserand. The maid, being on the staircase, had crossed paths with the Holy Ghost, and had hurried back to the kitchen, exclaiming:

'I knew He'd come back again this year!'

Then, alluding to the various misfortunes which had befallen the house, she added:

'It has brought us all bad luck!'

This time the Holy Ghost had not come too late—an excellent portent for the future. Madame Duveyrier hurried to Saint-Roch, where she awaited the priest's return. He listened to her, sadly and in silence, and then could not refuse to enlighten the footman and the chambermaid as to the immorality of their position. Besides, he would have to get back to the Rue de Choiseul very soon, as poor Monsieur Josserand would certainly not last through the night; and he hinted that in this circumstance, distressing though it was, he saw the possibility of a reconciliation between Auguste and Berthe. He would endeavour to arrange both matters at the same time. It was high time that the Almighty gave their efforts His blessing.

'I have prayed, madam,' said the priest. 'The Lord God will prevail.'

That evening, indeed, at seven o'clock, Monsieur Josserand's death-agony began. The whole family had assembled, except uncle Bachelard (whom they had sought vainly in all the cafés) and Saturnin, who was still in the Asile des Moulineaux. Léon, whose marriage, owing to his father's illness, had unfortunately been postponed, showed dignity in his grief, while Madame Josserand and Hortense bore up bravely. Berthe, however, sobbed so loudly that, out of consideration to the sufferer, she escaped to the kitchen where Adèle, taking advantage of the general confusion, was drinking mulled claret. Monsieur Josserand died very quietly—a victim of his own honesty. He had lived a useless life, and he went off, worthy to the last, weary of all the petty things in life, done to death by the heartless conduct of the only human beings he had ever loved. At eight o'clock he stammered out Saturnin's name; then, turning his face to the wall, he expired.

No one thought that he was dead, for they had all feared a long and dreadful death-agony. They waited for a while, letting him sleep. But, on finding that he was already cold, Madame Josserand, amid the general sobbing, began to scold Hortense, whom she had instructed to fetch Auguste with the aim of giving Berthe back to him just as her husband was about to breathe his last breath.

'You never think of anything!' she exclaimed, wiping her eyes.

'But, mamma,' said the girl, in tears, 'none of us thought papa was going to die so soon! You told me not to go down and fetch Auguste before nine o'clock, so as to make sure he was there at the end!'

This quarrel helped to distract the family from their grief. Another thing that had gone wrong! They never managed to get anything right! Fortunately, though, there was the funeral, which might serve to reconcile husband and wife.

The funeral was a pretty decent one, but not as grand as Monsieur Vabre's. Nor did it create nearly as much interest either in the house or in the neighbourhood, for Monsieur Josserand was not a landlord, but merely an easygoing soul whose death had not even troubled the slumber of Madame Juzeur. Marie, who the day before had been expecting her confinement by the hour, was the only one who said how sorry she was not to be able to help the ladies in laying the poor old gentleman out. Downstairs Madame Gourd thought it sufficient to stand up and raise her hand as the coffin passed, without going to the door. Everybody, however, went to the cemetery: Duveyrier, Campardon, the Vabres, and Monsieur Gourd. They talked about the spring and how the crops had been affected by the recent heavy rains. Campardon was surprised to see Duveyrier looking so ill; and noticing his ghastly pallor as the coffin was lowered into the grave, the architect whispered:

'Now he's smelt churchyard mould. God save the house from more bereavements!'

Madame Josserand and her daughters had to be helped to their carriage. Léon, with uncle Bachelard's help, was most attentive, while Auguste walked sheepishly in the rear and got into another carriage with Duveyrier and Théophile. Clotilde went with Father Mauduit, who had not officiated but put in an appearance at the cemetery so as to give the mourners a proof of his sympathy. The horses set off homewards more gaily; and Madame Duveyrier at once begged the priest to come back to the house with them, deeming the moment a favourable one. So he consented.

The three mourning coaches silently deposited the sorrowing relatives at the Rue de Choiseul. Théophile at once went back to Valérie, who, as the shop was shut, had remained behind to superintend a general cleaning.

'You can pack up your things,' he furiously exclaimed. 'They're all egging him on. I bet he'll end by begging her forgiveness!'

They all felt the urgent need to put an end to this deplorable business. At least something should come out of all this misfortune. Auguste could easily see what they wanted. He sat alone, defenceless and confused. One by one the mourners slowly passed in under the porch, which was hung with black. No one spoke. On the staircase the silence was unbroken, a silence full of deep thought, as the crape petticoats sadly and softly ascended. In a last attempt at revolt Auguste hurried on ahead, intending to shut himself up in his own rooms, but Clotilde and the priest, who had followed, stopped him just as he was opening the door. Behind them on the landing stood Berthe, in deep mourning, accompanied by her mother and sister. All three had red eyes; Madame Josserand's condition was, indeed, painful to behold.

'Come now, my friend,' said the priest simply, with tears in his eyes.

That was enough. Auguste gave in at once, aware that there was no better moment than this in which to make his peace. His wife wept, and he wept also as he stammered:

'Come along. We'll try not to do this again.'

Then there was general kissing, while Clotilde congratulated her brother, saying that she had been relying on his kindness of heart. Madame Josserand displayed a sort of disconsolate satisfaction, as that of a widow whom unlooked-for joys could no longer touch. And with their happiness she linked her poor dead husband's name.

'You're doing your duty, my son-in-law. My dear departed husband thanks you for this.'

'Come along!' repeated Auguste, quite unnerved.

Hearing a noise, Rachel came out into the hall and, noticing the maid's mute look of rage, Berthe hesitated for a moment. Then she sternly entered the apartment, and her black mourning dress disappeared in the gloom. Auguste followed her, and the door closed behind them.

A deep sigh of relief floated along the staircase and filled the house with joy. The ladies shook the priest by the hand; God had answered his prayers. Just as Clotilde was taking him off to settle the other matter, Duveyrier, who had stayed behind with Léon and Bachelard, came wearily up. They had to explain the good news to him, yet he hardly seemed to understand, though for months past he had been wishing for it. His face had a strange expression, as if he were in the grip of some obsession. As the Josserands went back to their apartment, he followed his wife and the priest. They were still in the hall when the sound of stifled screams made them tremble.

'Don't be alarmed, madam,' explained Hippolyte complacently. 'The little lady upstairs is in labour. I saw Doctor Juillerat run up just now.' Then, when alone, he philosophically added: 'One goes, another comes.'

Clotilde took the priest into the drawing-room and, offering him a seat, said that she would send Clémence to him first. To help him while away the time she gave him a copy of the *Revue des Deux Mondes*, in which there were some really charming verses. She wanted to prepare her maid for the interview. But in the dressing-room she found her husband seated on a chair.

Ever since the morning Duveyrier had been in a state of agony. For the third time he had caught Clarisse with Théodore, and when he protested all her parasitic relatives—mother, brother, and little sisters—had fallen upon him, driving him downstairs with kicks and blows, while Clarisse called him all sorts of names, threatening in her fury to send for the police if he ever dared set foot in her place again. It was all over; the concierge had told him downstairs that for the past week a rich old fellow had been offering to provide a comfortable home for madame. Thus driven away, and no longer having a snug corner to call his own, Duveyrier, after wandering about the streets, had entered an out-of-the-way shop and bought a small revolver. Life for him had become too sad; he had better end it at the earliest opportunity, once he had found a suitable place. It was the search for some quiet spot which was preoccupying him as he trudged back to the Rue de Choiseul to attend Monsieur Josserand's funeral. On the way to the grave he conceived the notion of suicide in the cemetery; he would withdraw to a secluded spot behind a tombstone. This appealed to his sense of the romantic, to his yearning for a tender ideal—a yearning that made his rigid, matter-of-fact existence appear utterly dreary. But as the coffin was lowered into the grave he began to quake in every limb, shuddering at the chill churchyard mould. This was certainly not the right place; he must find somewhere else. Then, returning home more distressed than ever, haunted by this one idea, he sat meditating on a chair in the dressing-room, trying to choose the best place in the house—the bedroom perhaps, near the bed, or here in the dressing-room, just where he was.

'Would you be good enough to leave me alone?' said Clotilde to him.

He already had his hand on the revolver in his pocket.

'Why?' he asked, with a great effort.

'Because I want to be alone.'

He thought she wanted to change her dress and would no longer even let him see her bare arms, so great was her disgust for him. For a moment, blear-eyed, he looked at her, standing there so tall and beautiful, her complexion the hue of marble and her hair bound up in burnished coils. Ah, if she would only consent everything would be all right! Staggering forward, he stretched out his arms and tried to embrace her.

'What is it?' she murmured, in surprise. 'What's got into you now? Not here, surely? Haven't you got that other woman any more? So you're going to start with that beastly behaviour again, are you?'

Her disgust seemed so great that he stepped back. Without another word he went out into the hall, where he stopped for a moment. A door faced him—the door of the water-closet. He pushed it open, and slowly sat down on the seat. This was a quiet place, where nobody would come and disturb him. Putting the barrel of the revolver into his mouth, he pulled the trigger.

Meanwhile Clotilde, who all the morning had felt uneasy at her husband's strange manner, had listened to see if he was going to do her the favour of going back to Clarisse. As the creak of the door told her where he had gone she paid no further attention to him, but was ringing for Clémence when the dull report of the pistol startled her. What could it be? It was just like the report of a revolver. She ran out into the hall, not daring at first to ask him what was the matter. Then, as a strange sound of breathing came from the closet, she called out to him and, getting no answer, pulled the door open. It was not even bolted. Duveyrier, stunned by fright more than by actual pain, was huddled up on the seat in a very sad posture, his eyes wide open and his face streaming with blood. The bullet had missed its mark and, after grazing his jaw, had passed through the left cheek. He had not had the courage to fire a second shot.

'So that's what you've been doing in there, is it?' cried Clotilde, beside herself with rage. 'Why can't you go outside to shoot yourself?'

She was indignant. Instead of softening her heart, the whole scene utterly exasperated her. Grabbing hold, she roughly pulled him, anxious to get him out before anybody saw him in such a place. In the water-closet! And to miss the mark too. That really was too much!

Then, holding him up, she led him back to the bedroom; Duveyrier, half choked with blood, kept spitting out teeth as he gurgled:

'You never loved me!'

And he burst into tears, bewailing his lost ideals and the little blue flower of romance that it had never been his lot to pluck. When Clotilde had got him to bed she at last broke down too, as her anger gave way to hysterics. The worst of it was that both Clémence and Hippolyte came to answer the bell. At first she told them it was an accident, that their master had fallen down on his chin; but this fantastic account she was soon obliged to abandon, for when the manservant went to wipe up the blood on the seat, he found the revolver, which had fallen behind the little broom. Meanwhile the wounded man was losing a great deal of blood, and the maid suddenly remembered that Doctor Juillerat was upstairs attending to Madame Pichon, so she ran out and caught him on the stairs as he was coming down after a most successful delivery. The doctor instantly reassured Clotilde; possibly there might be some disfigurement of the jaw, but there was no danger whatever. He hastily proceeded to dress the wound, amid basins of water and blood-stained rags, when Father Mauduit, alarmed at all the commotion, ventured to enter the room.

'Whatever has happened?' he asked.

This question was enough to upset Madame Duveyrier. At the first words of explanation she burst into tears. The priest, indeed, had guessed everything, knowing as he did all the secret troubles of his flock. Already, in the drawing-room, despondency had seized him, and he felt half sorry at his success in having once more joined that wretched young woman to her husband without her showing the least sign of contrition. Awful doubts assailed him; perhaps God was not with him after all. His anguish only increased as he saw Duveyrier's fractured jaw. Approaching him, he was about to denounce suicide in the most fervent terms when the doctor, busy with his bandaging, pushed him aside.

'Wait a minute, Father! Can't you see that he's fainted?'

Indeed, no sooner had the doctor touched him than Duveyrier lost consciousness. Then Clotilde, to get rid of the servants, who were no longer of any use and whose staring disconcerted her greatly, murmured, as she dried her eyes:

'Go into the drawing-room. Father Mauduit has something to say to you.'

The priest was obliged to take them there—another unpleasant task. Hippolyte and Clémence, extremely surprised, followed him.

When they were alone he began with a series of vague exhortations: heaven rewarded good conduct, while one sin alone was enough to cast one into hell. Besides, it was high time to put a stop to the scandal and think of saving their souls. While he harangued them thus their surprise changed to utter bewilderment. Arms dangling, she with her slight figure and screwed-up mouth, and he with his flat face and hulking limbs, they exchanged glances of alarm. Had madame found some of her napkins upstairs in a trunk? Or was it because of the bottle of wine they took upstairs every night?

'My children,' said the priest in conclusion, 'you're setting a bad example. The greatest sin of all is to corrupt others—to bring one's own household into disrepute. Yes, you're living in a disorderly way which, alas! is no secret to anyone, because you've been fighting with each other for a whole week.'

He blushed; a certain prudish hesitation made him choose his words carefully. The two servants heaved sighs of relief. They drew themselves up, smiling gleefully. So that was all! They needn't have been so alarmed.

'But it's all over sir,' declared Clémence, glancing at Hippolyte most fondly. 'We've made it up. Yes, he has explained everything.'

The priest, in his turn, seemed amazed and grieved.

'You don't understand, my children. You can't go on living together like this; it's an offence against God and man. You must get married.'

At once their look of astonishment returned. Get married? Whatever for?

'I don't want to,' said Clémence. 'I don't see why.'

Then the priest tried to convince Hippolyte.

'Look here my good fellow, you're a good man; persuade her; talk to her about her reputation. It won't alter your life in any way. You must get married.'

The servant laughed a waggish, awkward laugh. At length, looking down at the tips of his boots, he blurted out:

'That's right; I dare say we should; but I'm married already.'

This reply cut the cleric's moralizing short. Without another word he stowed away his arguments, and put God back again, as useless, into his pocket, distressed at having sought to invoke divine aid in such a futile task. Clotilde, who now joined him, had over-heard everything and, with one gesture, terminated the interview. In obedience to her orders the footman and the maid left the room one after the other, chuckling inwardly though apparently very grave. After a pause, the priest bitterly complained. Why expose him in this fashion? Why stir up things that were best left alone? Now the situation was absolutely scandalous. But Clotilde repeated her gesture. So much the worse; she had other worries now. However, she certainly could not dismiss the servants, for if she did the whole neighbourhood would know about the suicide attempt that very evening. Later on they must see what could be done.

'You won't forget, will you? He must have complete rest,' enjoined the doctor, as he left the room. 'He'll soon be all right again, but you mustn't tire him in any way. Don't lose heart, madam.' Then, turning to the priest, he added: 'You can preach him a sermon later on, Father, I can't give him up to you just yet. If you're going back to Saint-Roch I'll come with you; we can walk together.'

They both went downstairs.

Gradually the whole house regained its calm. Madame Juzeur had lingered in the cemetery, trying to make Trublot flirt with her as they read the inscriptions on the gravestones, and though he had no taste for fruitless philandering of this sort, he had to take her back in a cab to the Rue de Choiseul. The sad business of Louise deeply grieved the good lady. At their journey's end she was still talking about the wretched girl, whom the day before she had sent back to the home for destitute children. It was a bitter experience for her, a final loss of illusions which left her bereft of all hope that she would ever get a respectable maidservant. Then, at the door, she asked Trublot to come and see her sometime and have a chat. But his excuse was that he was always so busy.

At this moment the other Madame Campardon went by. They duly greeted her. Monsieur Gourd informed them of Madame Pichon's happy deliverance. They all shared the opinion of Monsieur and Madame Vuillaume—three children for a mere clerk was sheer madness; and the concierge hinted, moreover, that if there were a fourth baby the landlord would give them notice, as too many children in a house did not look well. At this they were silent, when a lady, wearing a veil and leaving behind her a faint scent of verbena, glided through the hall without speaking to Monsieur Gourd, who pretended not to see her. That morning he had got everything ready in the distinguished gentleman's apartment on the third floor in preparation for a night's work.

He hardly had time, however, to call out to the other two:

'Look out! They'll run over us like dogs!'

It was the second-floor people driving past in their carriage. The horses pranced under the vaulted gateway, and, leaning back in the landau, the father and mother smiled at their two pretty, fair-haired children, who were struggling with each other over a large bunch of roses.

'What strange people, to be sure!' muttered the concierge indignantly.

'They never even went to the funeral, for fear of seeming as polite as anybody else. They splash you from head to foot, yet there's plenty we could say . . .'

'What?' asked Madame Juzeur, greatly interested.

Then Monsieur Gourd told how they had had a visit from the police—yes, the police! The second-floor tenant had written such a filthy novel that they were going to imprison him at Mazas.*

'Horrible stuff!' he went on in a tone of disgust. 'It's full of filth about the most respectable people. They even say our landlord's described in it—yes, Monsieur Duveyrier himself! What a nerve, eh? It's good for them that they keep themselves to themselves; we know now what they get up to, in spite of their stand-offishness. You see, they can afford to keep their carriage, because their filth is worth its weight in gold!'

It was this reflection above all that exasperated Monsieur Gourd. Madame Juzeur only read poetry, while Trublot admitted that he was not well versed in literature. Yet, as both censured the novelist for besmirching with his books the very house in which he and his family dwelt, they suddenly heard someone shrieking from the far end of the courtyard.

'You cow! You were glad enough to have me when you wanted me to hide your lovers! You know exactly what I mean, you awful cow.'

It was Rachel, to whom Berthe had just given notice and who was now giving vent to her feelings on the servants' staircase. All of a sudden this quiet, respectful girl, whom the other servants could never get to gossip, had broken into a fit of fury. It was like the bursting of a sewer. Already incensed at madame's return to monsieur, whom since the estrangement she had quietly plundered,

Rachel became quite beside herself when told to fetch a porter to remove her box. Berthe, aghast, stood listening in the kitchen, while Auguste, with an air of authority, remained at the door and received all this revolting abuse full in the face.

'Yes, yes!' the infuriated maidservant went on, 'you didn't kick me out when I hid your chemises so that your cuckold of a husband wouldn't see them! Nor that night when your lover had to put his socks on in my kitchen while I prevented your cuckold of a husband from coming in. You bitch!'

Berthe ran off in disgust. But Auguste was obliged to show a bold front as, pale and trembling, he heard all these nauseous revelations bawled out on the back stairs. He could only exclaim:

'Wretched woman! Wretched woman!'

It was all he could say to express his pain at learning all these crude details of his wife's adultery, at the very moment that he had condoned it. Meanwhile all the servants had come out of their kitchens and, leaning over the window-ledges, listened to every word. Even they were amazed at Rachel's fury. Gradually they withdrew, appalled by the whole scene, which they thought really too much. Lisa expressed the general feeling when she remarked:

'Well, well! Talking's one thing, but you shouldn't speak to your masters like that.'

Everyone slipped away, leaving Rachel to vent her wrath by herself, for it became unpleasant to have to listen to all these awful things which made everybody uncomfortable, the more so as she now began to abuse the whole house. Monsieur Gourd was the first to withdraw to his room, observing that nothing could be done with a woman when she was in a temper. Madame Juzeur, shocked beyond measure at these ruthless disclosures, seemed so upset that Trublot, against his wish, was obliged to see her safely to her own apartment lest she might faint. Wasn't it unfortunate? Matters had been nicely arranged; there was no longer the least ground for scandal; the house was relapsing into its former dreamy respectability; and now this horrid person had to go and rake up things that had been forgotten and about which nobody cared any more!

'I'm only a servant, it's true, but I'm respectable,' Rachel screamed at the top of her voice, 'and there's not one of you bloody genteel bitches as can say the same in this goddamned house. Don't you worry; I'm going, because you all make me sick!'

The priest and Doctor Juillerat were slowly descending the stairs. They had heard all this too. Then came a great calm; the courtyard was empty, the staircase deserted. The doors seemed hermetically sealed; not a window-blind stirred, each apartment was shrouded in majestic silence.

In the doorway the priest stopped, as if exhausted.

'What miseries!' he murmured sadly.

The doctor, nodding, answered:

'Such is life!'

They were wont to make remarks of this sort as they came away together from the chamber of birth or of death. Despite their opposed beliefs, they occasionally agreed upon the subject of human frailty. Both shared the same secrets; if the priest heard the ladies' confessions, the doctor, for the last thirty years, had attended the mothers in their confinements while prescribing for the daughters.

'God has forsaken them,' said the priest.

'No,' replied the doctor; 'don't drag God into it. It's a question of bad health or bad upbringing, that's all.'

Then, going off at a tangent, he began violently to abuse the Empire; under a republic things would surely be better. And amid all this rambling talk, the vague generalizations of a man of mediocre intelligence, there came a few acute remarks of the experienced physician thoroughly familiar with all his patients' foibles. He did not spare the women, some of whom were brought up as dolls and were made either corrupt or crazy thereby, while others had their feelings and passions perverted by hereditary neurosis; if they sinned, they sinned vulgarly, foolishly, without desire as without pleasure. Nor was he more merciful to the men—fellows who merely ruined their constitutions while hypocritically pretending to lead virtuous and godly lives. And in all this Jacobin frenzy one heard, as it were, the inexorable death-knell of a whole class, the collapse and putrefaction of the bourgeoisie, whose rotten props were cracking beneath them. Then, getting out of his depth again, he spoke of the barbarous age, and foretold an era of univeral bliss.

'I'm really far more religious than you are,' he declared in conclusion.

The priest seemed to have been listening silently. But he had heard nothing, being completely absorbed in his own mournful meditations. After a pause, he murmured:

'If they are unconscious of their sin, may Heaven have mercy upon them!'

Then, leaving the house, they walked slowly along the Rue Neuve-Saint-Augustin. Fear that they had said too much kept them silent, for they both needed to be discreet in their positions. At the end of the street they spotted Madame Hédouin, who smiled at them from the door of the Ladies' Paradise. Octave stood close behind her and smiled too. That very morning, after a serious discussion, they had decided to get married. They were going to wait until the autumn. And they were both very glad that the matter had at last been settled.

'Good day, Father,' said Madame Hédouin gaily. 'Always on the go, eh, doctor?'

And as he told her how well she was looking, she added:

'Ah, if you only had me as a patient, you wouldn't do much business!'

They stood chatting for a moment. When the doctor mentioned Marie's confinement, Octave seemed glad to know that his former neighbour had got over it safely. And when he heard that number three was a girl too, he exclaimed:

'So her husband can't manage a boy, can he? She was hoping to get Monsieur and Madame Vuillaume to put up with a boy; but they'll never stand another girl.'

'I shouldn't think so,' said the doctor. 'They've both taken to their bed; the news upset them so much. And they've sent for a solicitor, so that their son-in-law won't inherit a stick of their furniture even.'

Then there was more joking. But the priest remained silent and kept his eyes on the pavement. Madame Hédouin asked if he was unwell. Yes, he was very tired; he was going to rest for a little while. Then, after a cordial exchange of good wishes, he walked down the Rue Saint-Roch, still accompanied by the doctor. At the church-door the latter abruptly said: 'Bad sort of patient, that, eh?'

'Who?' asked the priest in some surprise.

'The lady who sells the calico. She doesn't care a damn for either of us. No religion wanted there, nor medicine either. There's not much to be got out of folk like that, who are always well!'

With that he went off, while the priest entered the church.

A bright light fell through the broad windows, their white panes edged with yellow and pale blue. There was no sound, no movement in the deserted nave; marble facings, crystal chandeliers, and gilded pulpit, all slumbered in the peaceful light. In its drowsy tranquillity it might have been some bourgeois drawing-room, with the furniture covers removed for a grand evening party. A solitary woman, in front of the chapel of Our Lady of the Seven Dolours, stood watching the guttering tapers, which emitted a smell of melted wax.

The priest thought of going straight up to his room. Yet, so great was his agitation that he felt impelled to enter the church and remain there. It was as if God was calling to him, vaguely and in a far-off voice, so that he could not clearly hear the summons. He slowly crossed the church, striving to read the thoughts that arose within him and allay his fears, when suddenly, as he passed behind the choir, an unearthly sight made his whole being tremble.

Behind the lily-white marble of the Lady chapel and the chapel of the Adoration, with its seven golden lamps, golden candelabra, and golden altar glittering in the aureate light from some gold-stained windows, there in this mystic gloom, beyond this tabernacle, he saw a tragic apparition, the enactment of a drama, harrowing yet simple. It was Christ nailed to the cross between the Virgin and Mary Magdalene, who wept at His feet. The white statues, lighted from above and set in sharp relief against the bare wall, seemed to be moving forward and growing larger, making this human tragedy in its blood and tears the divine symbol of eternal sorrow.

The priest, utterly overcome, fell to his knees. It was he who had whitened that plaster, contrived that method of lighting, and prepared so appalling a scene. Now that the hoarding was removed and the architect and workmen gone, it was he who was the first to be thunderstruck at the sight. From that austere, terrible Calvary there came an overpowering breath. It seemed as if God was passing over him, and he bowed beneath the breath of His nostrils, tortured by doubts, by the terrible thought that perhaps he was a bad priest.

Oh, Lord! Had the hour come when the sores of this festering world would no longer be hidden by the mantle of religion? Was he no longer to help the hypocrisy of his flock, nor always be there, like some master of ceremonies, to regulate its vices and follies? Should he let it all collapse, even at the risk of burying the Church itself in the ruins? Yes, such was his command, no doubt, for the strength to probe human misery yet deeper was forsaking him, and he felt consumed by utter impotence and disgust. All the abominations he had witnessed during the day seemed to choke him, and with outstretched hands he craved forgiveness—forgiveness for his lies, his base complacency and time-serving. Dread of God's wrath seized hold of him; he seemed to see God disowning him, forbidding him to take His name in vain, a jealous God bent on the destruction of the guilty. All his worldly airs of tolerance vanished before such searing stabs of conscience. All that remained to him was the faith of the believer—a faith shaken, terror-struck, struggling in the uncertainty of salvation. Oh, Lord God! what road should he take? What should he do amid this festering society, which brought infection even to its priests?

Then Father Mauduit, as he gazed up at the Calvary, burst into tears. He wept, just as the Virgin and Mary Magdalene wept; he wept for truth which was dead, for Heaven which was void. Beyond the marble walls and gleaming jewelled altars, the huge plaster Christ had no longer a single drop of blood in its veins.

XVIII

IT was in December, after she had been in mourning for eight months, that Madame Josserand consented for the first time to dine out. The Duveyriers had invited her, so it was almost a family dinner, to celebrate the resumption of Clotilde's Saturday receptions. The day before Adèle had been told that she would have to go down and help Julie with the washing-up. When giving parties these good ladies were in the habit of lending each other their servants in this way.

'And above all, try and put some go into it,' was Madame Josserand's advice to her maid. 'I don't know what's got into you lately. You're as limp as a rag. Yet you're plump enough.'

The fact was, Adèle was nine months pregnant. For a long time she had thought she was getting fat, and this had surprised her somewhat. Famished as she always was, it enraged her when madame triumphantly pointed to her in front of all her guests, saying that if anyone accused her of rationing her servant's food they could come and see what a great glutton she was; her belly hadn't got as round as that by licking the walls, had it? When the dull-witted girl finally became aware of her misfortune, she was often within an ace of telling her mistress the truth, for the latter took every advantage of her condition to make all the neighbours think that at last she was feeding her up.

From that moment, however, she became mad with fear. Within her dull brain surged up all the crude fancies of her native village. She believed herself lost, that the gendarmes would come and carry her off, if she confessed that she was pregnant. Then all her low cunning was employed to hide her condition. She concealed her feelings of sickness, her intolerable headaches, and her terrible constipation, though more than once, when mixing sauces by the kitchen fire, she thought she was about to drop down dead. Fortunately it was her hips that grew big, and her belly, though widening, did not stick out too much, so that madame never suspected anything when exultant at her astounding plumpness. Moreover, the wretched wench squeezed in her waist until she could scarcely breathe. Her belly seemed to her fairly well-proportioned, though it felt awfully heavy when she was scrubbing the kitchen. The last two months had been months of dreadful pain, borne in stubborn and heroic silence.

That night Adèle went up to bed at about eleven o'clock. The thought of the reception terrified her. More slavery and more bullying from Julie! And she could hardly stand; her limbs were like jelly! Yet her confinement seemed to her vague and remote as yet; she preferred not to think about it, hoping that, somehow, it would all go away. She had therefore not made the slightest preparation, being ignorant of any symptoms, incapable of recollecting or calculating a date, devoid of any idea, any plan. She was only comfortable when she was in bed, lying on her back. As it had been freezing since the previous day, she kept her stockings on, blew out her candle, and waited until she could get warm. At length she fell asleep, but almost immediately slight pains caused her to open her eyes—faint twinges, as if a gnat were biting her close to her navel. Then the pricking pains ceased and she quickly forgot them, used as she was to all the strange, unaccountable things that went on inside her. Yet suddenly, after half-an-hour's uneasy sleep, a dull throb woke her again. This time she grew quite angry. Was she going to have a stomach-ache? How fresh she would feel the next day if she kept running to the potty all night long! She had been thinking that evening that what she needed was a good clear-out; her stomach was so tense and heavy. Yet she attempted to stave it off by rubbing her belly, and believed that she had soothed the pains. But within a quarter of an hour they returned with greater violence.

'Blast it all!' she muttered under her breath, deciding to get up this time.

Groping about in the darkness for the pot, she squatted down, and exhausted herself in fruitless effort. The room was icy cold; her teeth chattered. After ten minutes the pains ceased and she got back into bed. But soon they returned. Again she rose, and again she tried, without success, going back to bed chilled through. She enjoyed a few moments' rest. Then so violent was the pain that she stifled a cry. How dreadful! Did she want to do something or did she not? Now the pains became persistent, almost continuous, and more excruciating—as if some hand had roughly gripped her belly from within. Then she understood; and shivering beneath the coverlet, she muttered:

'Good God! Good God! That's what it is!'

Birth-pangs tortured her; she felt a need to get up and walk about in her agony. She could no longer stay in bed; so she lighted a candle and began to pace up and down the room. Her mouth became dry, a burning thirst overcame her, while her cheeks grew red as fire. When a sudden spasm bent her double she leant against the wall and caught hold of the back of a chair. Hours passed in this pitiless shuffling up and down. She dared not put on her boots for fear of making a noise. Her only protection from the cold was an old shawl, which she wrapped round her shoulders. Two o'clock struck, then three o'clock.

'There's no such thing as God!' she muttered, as if impelled to talk to herself in order to hear the sound of her own voice. 'It's too long; it'll never be over!'

The process of parturition continued, however; the weight lay now in her hips and thighs. And, when her belly gave her a moment's respite, she felt there a perpetual gnawing pain. In order to get relief she grasped her hips with both hands, and supported them thus while she swayed about barelegged, with only coarse stockings on up to her knees. No, there was no such thing as God! Religion disgusted her; her patience, her brute submission, which hitherto had made her bear her pregnancy as merely one more misery, forsook her. So it wasn't enough to be starved to death, and the dirty drudge whom everyone bullied: her masters had to get her pregnant as well! Filthy brutes! She could not say if it was the young one or the old one that had done it. In any case, neither of them cared a damn; they had had their pleasure, while she had to suffer for it! If she went and had her baby on their doormat, that would make them take notice! Then her old fears came back; she would be put in prison; it was best to say nothing. And between two spasms she kept repeating in a choked voice:

'Dirty beasts! How could they do this to me! Oh, my God! I'm going to die!'

And, with hands clenched, she pressed her hips with greater vigour, her poor aching hips, stifling her cries of pain as she rocked from side to side. Next door no one stirred; everybody was snoring; she could hear Julie's sonorous organ sound, while Lisa's breathing sounded shrill and sibilant as a fife.

Four o'clock struck, when suddenly she thought that her belly had burst. During one of the spasms there had been a rupture of some kind, followed by a flow of liquid, which trickled down, soaking her stockings. For a moment she remained motionless, terror-struck, stupefied, thinking that perhaps in this way she would get rid of her burden. Perhaps she had never been pregnant after all. Then, fearing that she had some other malady, she looked at herself to see if all the blood in her body were not running away. Feeling somewhat relieved, she sat down for a few moments on her trunk. The mess on the floor worried her; and the flickering candle was on the point of going out. Then, unable to walk, and aware that the crisis was near, she had just enough strength left to spread out on the bed an old piece of oilcloth that Madame Josserand had given her as a toilet-cover. Hardly had she lain down than the process of expulsion began.

For nearly an hour and a half the pains assailed her continually and with increasing violence. The internal spasms had ceased; with all the muscular force of her loins and belly, she kept straining to free her frame from this intolerable weight. Twice more, she thought she should use the potty and her hand stretched out for it feverishly; the second time she could hardly stand up again. Each fresh effort was accompanied by shivering, her face grew burning hot, perspiration broke out on her neck, while she bit the bedclothes to stifle her groaning, which sounded like the grim, involuntary gasp of a woodcutter felling an oak. After each effort to expel, she murmured, as if addressing someone:

'It's not possible! It won't come out. It's too big.'

With tumbled breasts and legs wide apart, she clutched hold of the iron bedstead, which shook with every spasm. Fortunately it was a splendid birth, a cranial presentation of the normal sort. The head as it emerged kept slipping back again, sucked in by the elasticity of the surrounding tissues that were stretched to breaking point while, as her labour continued, excruciating cramps held her in a grip of iron. Her bones cracked; everything seemed to be breaking. An awful feeling came over her that her bottom and belly had burst, forming one hole through which her life was ebbing away; and then between her thighs the child rolled out on to the bed in a pool of viscous bloody evacuations.

She uttered a loud cry, the wild triumphant cry of a mother. At once the maidservants in the adjoining rooms began to stir, while drowsy voices asked: 'Hullo?—What's the matter?—Someone being murdered or raped?—Don't shout out in your sleep like that!' Alarmed, she bit the bedclothes again, squeezed her thighs together, and pulled the coverlet over the baby, which cried plaintively like a little kitten. Soon she could hear Julie snoring again after turning over in bed; Lisa was asleep once more; her high-pitched breathing had ceased. Then for about a quarter of an hour she felt indescribable relief, a sense of infinite calm and repose. She lay there as one dead, as one glad to give up life.

All at once colic seized her again. She woke up in a panic. Was she going to have another? On opening her eyes she found herself in pitch darkness. Not even a tiny bit of candle! There she lay, all by herself, in a pool, with something slimy between her legs that she did not know what to do with. There were doctors for dogs, but not for such as she. She and her brat might die, for all anyone cared. She remembered having lent a hand when Madame Pichon, the lady opposite, was confined. How carefully she was looked after! The child was not crying now. She stretched out her hand and caught hold of a cord that hung out of her belly. She vaguely remembered having seen this cut and tied in a knot. Her eyes had got used to the gloom; the garret was now dimly lighted by the rising moon. Then, groping about blindly, acting by instinct, without rising, she performed a tedious and painful operation. Pulling down an apron from a hook behind her, she tore off one of its strings, tied the cord in a knot, and cut it with a pair of scissors she had in the pocket of her skirt. The effort exhausted her and she lay down again. Poor little thing! She didn't want to kill it, of course!

Her stomach pains continued. Something uncomfortable was still there which, with straining, might be expelled. She tugged at the cord, first gently, then with all her strength. Something was coming away; it fell out in a great lump, and she got rid of it by throwing it into the potty. Thank goodness, this time it was over and she would suffer no more! Warm blood trickled down her legs.

She must have dozed like that for nearly an hour. It was striking six when, conscious of her state, she awoke. There was no time to lose. Rising with difficulty, she began to do whatever came into her head. A pale moon shone directly into the room. After dressing herself, she wrapped the child in some rags and rolled it up in two sheets of newspaper. It was quiet now, but its little heart was still beating. As she had forgotten to look if it were a boy or a girl, she undid the parcel. It was a girl! One more unfortunate girl! A tit-bit for some brawny groom or footman, like that Louise, whom they had found in a doorway! The servants were still in bed, and after getting the sleepy Monsieur Gourd to pull back the front-door latch, she managed to go out and deposit her bundle in the Passage Choiseul just as the gates were being opened. Then she crept upstairs again, without meeting a soul. For once in her life, luck was on her side!

She immediately began to tidy her room. She rolled up the oilcloth under the bed, emptied the potty, and sponged the floor. Then, utterly worn-out, as white as a sheet, and with blood still streaming down her thighs, she lay down again after wiping herself with a towel. Here Madame Josserand found her when, at about nine o'clock, she decided to go upstairs, being amazed that Adèle had not come down. The maid complained of a violent attack of diarrhoea which had kept her awake all night, when her mistress exclaimed:

'I expect you've over-eaten again! All you can think about is stuffing yourself!'

Alarmed at the girl's pallor, however, she talked of sending for a doctor, but was glad enough to save the three francs when Adèle declared that all she wanted was rest. Since her husband's death Madame Josserand had been living with Hortense, on a pension arranged for her by the Bernheim brothers. This did not prevent her from vilifying them as cheats and crooks, and she now lived in a stingier style than ever, rather than lose her social standing by leaving her apartments and giving up her Tuesdays.

'Yes, that's what you want, sleep,' she said. 'There's some cold beef left, which will do for lunch, and tonight we're dining out. If you can't come down and help Julie, she'll have to do without you.'

That evening the Duveyriers' dinner passed off very pleasantly. The whole family was there—the two Vabres and their wives, Madame Josserand, Hortense, Léon, and even uncle Bachelard, who was on his best behaviour. They had also invited Trublot to make up numbers, and Madame Dambreville, so as not to separate her from Léon who, after wedding the niece, had fallen back into the aunt's arms as she was still most useful to him. They went about everywhere together as before, making excuses for the young bride. She had a cold, or was tired, and could not come, so they declared. Everyone at table expressed regret at not seeing her more often, for they were all so fond of her; she was so charming! They talked of the chorus which Clotilde was going to have at the end of the evening. It was the 'Benediction of the Poniards' again, but with five tenors this time—something very grand. For the last two months Duveyrier, who had grown quite agreeable, had gone about buttonholing all his friends, addressing to each the same stereotyped phrase: 'You're quite a stranger; do come and see us; my wife's going to begin her choruses again.' Thus, by the time dessert was on the table they were talking of nothing but music. Perfect harmony and light-hearted gaiety prevailed from start to finish.

Then, after coffee was served, while the ladies sat round the drawing-room fire, the gentlemen, grouped in the dining-room, engaged in grave debate. Meanwhile other guests arrived. Soon there were Campardon, Father Mauduit, Doctor Juillerat, besides those who had dined, with the exception of Trublot, who, on leaving the table, had disappeared. They immediately began to talk politics, for these gentlemen were deeply interested in the parliamentary debates, and were eager to discuss the success of the Opposition candidates, who had all been returned to Paris at the May elections. This triumph of the disaffected elements of the bourgeoisie alarmed them, despite their apparent satisfaction.

'Well,' said Léon, 'Monsieur Thiers has great talent, certainly. But his speeches about the Mexican Expedition are so acrimonious that they lose all their force.'

Léon had just got his promotion, through Madame Dambreville's influence, and had at once joined the government party. There was now nothing of the starving demagogue about him, except a total intolerance of all doctrine.

'You used to say it was all the government's fault,' remarked the doctor, smiling. 'I hope that you, at least, voted for Monsieur Thiers.'

The young man avoided making a reply. Théophile, a martyr to indigestion and to fresh doubts as to his wife's fidelity, chimed in:

'Yes, I voted for him. As soon as men refuse to live together as brothers, so much the worse for them!'

'Exactly, and so much the worse for you, eh?' said Duveyrier, who, though he said little, uttered words of deep wisdom.

Théophile stared at him, aghast. Auguste no longer dared admit that he also had voted for Monsieur Thiers. Then, to their surprise,

Bachelard professed to be a Legitimist; there was something uncommon about that, he thought. Campardon warmly approved; he himself had refrained from voting, as the official candidate, Monsieur Dewinck, did not offer sufficient guarantees with regard to religion. Then he launched into a violent diatribe against *The Life of Jesus*,* which had just appeared.

'It's not the book that ought to be burnt, it's the author,' he repeated.

'Perhaps you are too radical, my friend,' interjected the priest, in a conciliatory tone. 'But certainly the signs of the times are becoming dreadful. There's talk of deposing the Pope; Parliament is in revolt. We're on the edge of a precipice.'

'So much the better,' said Doctor Juillerat drily.

At this they were all scandalized. Once more he attacked the bourgeoisie, declaring that if the masses ever got the upper hand they would be swept away; but the others, interrupting, loudly protested that in the bourgeoisie lay the virtue, energy, and thrift of the nation. Duveyrier at last made himself heard above the general din. He confessed that he had voted for Monsieur Dewinck, not because the senator represented exactly his own opinions, but because he stood for the maintenance of order. Yes, it might be that they would see a new Reign of Terror. Monsieur Rouher,* that very remarkable statesman, who had just replaced Monsieur Billaut, had formally prophesied as much in a recent speech. Then, with this image, he ended:

'The triumph of the Opposition is simply the first shock to the whole edifice. Be careful that it doesn't crush you to death as it falls!'

The others fell silent, vaguely afraid that they had let themselves be carried away so far that now their own personal safety was in jeopardy. Visions floated before them of workmen, caked in dust and soaked in blood, breaking into their houses, raping their maidservants, and drinking their wine. The Emperor deserved a lesson, but they began to be sorry for having given him such a severe one.

'Don't worry,' added the doctor, mockingly, 'you'll be rescued by force of arms.'

However, he always exaggerated, and they said how eccentric he was. It was precisely this reputation for eccentricity that kept him from losing his practice. Then he proceeded to pick his eternal quarrel with Father Mauduit about the imminent collapse of the

Church. Léon was now on the side of the priest; he talked of Divine Providence, and on Sundays went with Madame Dambreville to nine o'clock mass.

Meanwhile guests kept arriving, and the large drawing-room was filled with ladies. Valérie and Berthe, like old friends, were exchanging confidences. The architect had brought with him the other Madame Campardon, doubtless in place of poor Rose, who lay in bed upstairs reading Dickens. She was giving Madame Josserand an economical recipe for bleaching linen without soap, while Hortense, sitting apart, waited for Verdier and kept her eyes fixed on the door. Suddenly Clotilde, while chatting to Madame Dambreville, rose and held out both her hands. Her friend Madame Octave Mouret had just arrived. The marriage had taken place in early November, as soon as her term of mourning had ended.

'And where's your husband?' asked the hostess. 'He's not going to disappoint me, I hope.'

'No, no,' replied Caroline, smiling. 'He'll be here directly; something detained him at the last moment.'

There was a great deal of whispering, and everyone surveyed her curiously, so calm, so lovely was she, always the same, with the bland assurance of a woman who succeeds in everything. Madame Josserand shook hands with her as if delighted to see her again. Berthe and Valérie stopped talking to examine the details of her dress, which was straw-coloured and covered in lace. But just as the past seemed to have been quietly forgotten, Auguste, whom the political discussion had left quite cold, began to show signs of wrathful amazement as he stood at the dining-room door. What! His sister was going to receive the wife of Berthe's former lover? And to his marital rancour was added the bitter jealousy of the tradesman ruined by a successful rival; for the Ladies' Paradise, now that it was enlarged and had opened a special department for silks, had so drained his resources that he had been obliged to find a partner. While everyone was congratulating Madame Mouret, he approached Clotilde and whispered:

'I say, I'm not going to stand for that!'

'For what?' she asked, in surprise.

'I don't mind the wife; she's done me no harm. But if the husband comes, I'll take Berthe by the arm and leave the room in front of everybody.'

Clotilde stared at him, and then shrugged her shoulders. Caroline was her oldest friend, and she certainly wasn't going to give up seeing her simply to satisfy one of his fads. As if anybody ever remembered the matter now! Far better not to rake up things that everyone but him had forgotten. Then, as he excitedly turned to Berthe to back him up, expecting her to get up and leave with him there and then, she tried to pacify him with a frown. Was he crazy? Did he want to look a bigger fool than ever?

'But it's just because I don't want to look a fool!' he exclaimed in despair.

Then Madame Josserand, leaning forward, said severely:

'This is quite indecent; people are looking at you. Do behave yourself for once!'

He fell silent but still looked resentful. At once a certain uneasiness was perceptible among the ladies. Only Madame Mouret, sitting opposite Berthe and next to Clotilde, preserved her calm, smiling manner. They watched Auguste, who had retreated to the bay window where, not so long ago, his marriage had been decided. Anger had triggered off his migraine, and every now and then he pressed his forehead against the icy windowpanes.

Octave did not arrive until very late. He met Madame Juzeur on the landing. She was coming downstairs, wrapped in a shawl. She complained of a cold in her chest, but she had got up on purpose so as not to disappoint the Duveyriers. Her feeble state did not prevent her from throwing herself into the young man's arms as she congratulated him on his marriage.

'I'm very pleased, my friend! I'd really begun to despair about you; I never thought you'd do it. Tell me, you naughty boy, how did you manage to get round her, eh?'

Octave smiled, and kissed her fingertips. Just then someone bounding upstairs with the agility of a mountain-goat disturbed them. To Octave's astonishment it was Saturnin. He had left the Asile des Moulineaux the week before, as Doctor Chassagne had again declined to keep him there any longer, for his mania, he still thought, was not sufficiently marked. No doubt he was going to spend the evening with Marie Pichon, just as he used to do when his parents had a party. All of a sudden all those bygone days came back. Octave seemed to catch the sound of Marie's voice upstairs, as she faintly crooned some old song to while away the hours. And he saw her once more sitting by Lilitte's cot waiting for Jules's return, complacent, useless, gentle as ever.

'I wish you every happiness in your married life,' said Madame Juzeur, as she tenderly squeezed Octave's hands.

In order not to enter the room with her he took his time removing his overcoat, when Trublot, in evening clothes, bareheaded and looking rather agitated, emerged from the kitchen passage.

'She's not at all well, you know!' he whispered, while Hippolyte was announcing Madame Juzeur.

'Who's that?' asked Octave.

'Adèle, the maid upstairs.'

On hearing that there was something wrong with her, he had gone up in a fatherly fashion as soon as dinner was over. Probably it was a violent attack of colic. What she wanted was a good glass of mulled wine; but she did not even have a lump of sugar. Then, observing Octave's smile of indifference, he added:

'Of, I forgot! You're married now, you humbug! This sort of thing doesn't interest you any more, I suppose? I never thought of that when I saw you in the corner with Madame Anything-you-like-except-that.'

They went into the drawing-room together. The ladies were talking about servants and, in their excitement, did not notice them at first. They all affably accepted Madame Duveyrier's faltering explanation as to why she still kept Clémence and Hippolyte. He was a brute, it was true; but she was such an excellent lady's-maid that she willingly forgot her other failings. Valérie and Berthe both declared that they could not find a decent girl. They had given it up as a bad job after all the agencies had sent them an endless stream of disreputable sluts. Madame Josserand violently abused Adèle, recounting fresh and amazing instances of her filthiness and stupidity. However, she had not discharged her, she said. The other Madame Campardon praised Lisa to the skies. She was a pearl; there was no fault whatever to be found with her; she was one of those rare servants that are worth their weight in gold.

'She's one of the family,' said Gasparine. 'Our little Angèle attends lectures now at the Hôtel de Ville, and Lisa always goes with her. Oh! they might be out for days, but we would never feel the least anxious.'

Just then they caught sight of Octave. He stepped forward to shake hands with Clotilde. Berthe looked at him and coolly went on talking to Valérie, who gave him a friendly glance. The others, Madame Josserand and Madame Dambreville, without being too gushing, surveyed him with kindly interest.

'So you've come at last!' said Clotilde, in her most gracious voice. 'I was beginning to be very concerned about the chorus.'

When Madame Mouret gently scolded her husband for being so late, he proffered his excuses.

'But my love, I couldn't get away. Madame, I'm sorry. I'm entirely at your disposal now.'

Meanwhile the ladies glanced uneasily at the bay window, where Auguste had taken refuge. For a moment they were frightened when they saw him turn round on hearing Octave's voice. His migraine was obviously worse; his eyes were dim after gazing out into the gloomy streets. But, making up his mind, he went up close to his sister and said:

'Get rid of them, or we'll leave.'

Clotilde again shrugged her shoulders. Then Auguste seemed to give her time to consider the matter. He would wait a few minutes longer, particularly as Trublot had taken Octave into the other room. The ladies were still uneasy, for they heard the husband whisper to his wife:

'If he comes back here you must get up and follow me. If you don't, you can just go back to your mother's.'

Octave's reception by the gentlemen in the parlour was equally cordial. If Léon's manner was somewhat cool, uncle Bachelard and even Théophile seemed willing to show, as they shook hands, that the family was ready to forgive and forget. Octave congratulated Campardon, who for the last two days had been wearing his new decoration, a broad red ribbon. The architect, beaming, scolded him for never coming to see them and spend an hour or two with his wife. It was fine to get married; but it really wasn't nice of him to forget his old friends. At the sight of Duveyrier, however, Octave appeared quite startled. He had not seen him since his recovery, and was alarmed to see his distorted jaw, which gave a lopsided look to his whole face. His voice, too, gave him another surprise; deeper by a couple of tones, it sounded quite sepulchral.

'Don't you think he looks much better now?' said Trublot, as he led Octave back to the drawing-room door. 'It makes him positively majestic. I heard him the day before yesterday at the Assizes. Listen! they're talking about it.'

The gentlemen had indeed passed from politics to morals. They were listening to Duveyrier, who was giving details of a case in which his attitude had attracted much comment. There was even talk of appointing him to a most senior position and making him an officer of the Legion of Honour. The case was one of infanticide which had happened more than a year ago. The unnatural mother, a regular savage as he called her, was none other than the boot-stitcher, his former tenant, the tall, pale, sad-looking girl whose enormous belly had so enraged Monsieur Gourd. What a stupid fool, besides! For, not even reflecting that a belly like that would betray her, she actually cut the child in two and then hid it in a hat-box! Of course, she told the jury a cock-and-bull story: how her seducer had deserted her, and how hunger and wretched, mad despair had overcome her at the sight of the baby she could not feed. In a word, the usual story. But an example must be made of such people. Duveyrier congratulated himself on having summed up with such striking clarity that the verdict was a foregone conclusion.

'What was the sentence?' asked the doctor.

'Five years,' replied the judge, in his new voice, which sounded cavernous and hoarse. 'It's high time that we raise a barrier to check the tide of debauchery which threatens to engulf the whole of Paris.'

Trublot nudged Octave, for they both knew about the unsuccessful attempt at suicide.

'There, you hear what he says?' he whispered. 'Joking apart, it really does improve his voice. It's more stirring, isn't it? It goes straight to the heart now. And if you'd only seen him standing there in his long red robes, with his face all crooked! He quite frightened me, he looked so odd, so strangely majestic that he really gave me the shivers.'

At this point he stopped to listen to what the ladies were saying in the drawing-room. They were again on the subject of servants. That very day Madame Duveyrier had given Julie a week's notice. Certainly she had nothing to say against the girl's cooking; in her eyes, however, good conduct was the first thing. The real fact was that, acting on the advice of Doctor Juillerat, and anxious about the health of her son, whose goings-on at home she tolerated so as to control them better, she had cross-examined Julie, who for some time past had been unwell. Julie, as behoved a first-class cook, of the sort that never quarrel with her employers, had accepted her dismissal without even condescending to retort that perhaps she had misbehaved, but all the same, she would not have fallen ill if it had not been for the unclean state of Master Gustave, her son. Madame Josserand immediately expressed her agreement with Clotilde. Yes, one had to be very strict on the question of morality. For instance, she kept on that slut Adèle, with all her filthy, stupid ways, simply because the fool was so thoroughly honest. Oh! on that score she had nothing whatever to reproach her with!

'Poor Adèle! When one thinks of it,' muttered Trublot, touched at the thought of the poor wretch lying half-frozen upstairs under her thin counterpane.

Then in Octave's ear he whispered, sniggeringly:

'I say, Duveyrier might at least send her up a bottle of claret.'

'Yes, gentlemen,' continued the judge, 'statistics show that infanticide is assuming alarming proportions. Sentimental reasons nowadays carry far too much weight; people put too much trust in science, in your so-called psychology, which before long will prevent us from distinguishing good from evil. There's no cure for debauchery; we must destroy it at its root.'

This retort was directed mainly at Doctor Juillerat, who had sought to give a medical explanation of the boot-stitcher's case. All the other gentlemen, however, displayed great severity and disgust. Campardon failed to understand vice; uncle Bachelard spoke in defence of children; Théophile demanded an enquiry; Léon discussed prostitution in its relation to the state; and Trublot, in reply to Octave, told him all about Duveyrier's new mistress, who this time was quite a presentable person, decidedly mature, but of a romantic disposition, able to understand that ideal which her keeper declared was so necessary to the perfect purification of love—in short, a worthy woman who would give him a well-ordered home, imposing upon him and sleeping with his friends, but never being too much bother. The priest alone remained silent as, with downcast eyes, he listened, sad at heart and deeply troubled.

They were about to sing the 'Benediction of the Poniards'. The drawing-room soon became full; there was a crush of bright dresses under the light of the chandeliers and lamps, and laughter rippled along the rows of chairs. Amid the general murmur, Clotilde chided

Auguste in a low voice as he caught hold of Berthe's arm and tried to make her leave the room when he saw Octave and the other chorus-singers enter. But his resolution wavered as migraine now completely overcame him, while the mute disapproval of the ladies served to increase his confusion. Madame Dambreville's austere gaze utterly disconcerted him; even the other Madame Campardon sided against him. It was Madame Josserand, however, who finished him off. She abruptly interfered, threatening to take back her daughter and never to pay him the dowry of fifty thousand francs, for she was always promising this dowry in the most unblushing manner. Then, turning to Bachelard, who was sitting behind her and next to Madame Juzeur, she made him renew his promises. Hand on heart, the uncle declared that he would do his duty: family before everything. Auguste, baffled, was obliged to beat a retreat; he fled to the bay window, where he pressed his burning brow against the ice-cold panes.

Then Octave had the strange feeling that it was all beginning anew. His two years in the Rue de Choiseul were like a blank. There sat his wife, smiling at him, yet no change had come into his life; today was the same as yesterday, with neither pause nor stop. Trublot pointed out the new partner, a fair, dapper little fellow, sitting next to Berthe. He was said to give her heaps of presents. Uncle Bachelard, grown poetical, was disclosing his sentimental side to Madame Juzeur, who was quite touched at certain confidential details concerning Fifi and Gueulin. Théophile, a prey to doubts and doubled up by violent fits of coughing, took Doctor Juillerat aside and begged him to give his wife something to soothe her nerves. Campardon, his eyes fixed on cousin Gasparine, talked about the Evreux diocese, and then of the big alterations in the new Rue du Dix-Décembre. God and art were all that mattered; the rest could go hang, for all he cared; he was an artist! Behind a flower-stand could be seen a gentleman's back, which all the young ladies contemplated with the utmost curiosity. It was Verdier, who was talking to Hortense. They were having a somewhat acrimonious discussion about the wedding, which they again postponed until the spring so as not to turn the woman and her brat into the street in midwinter.

Then the chorus burst forth. The architect, with his mouth wide open, declaimed the opening phrase. Clotilde struck a chord, and uttered her usual cry. Then the voices broke forth into ever-increasing uproar; so great was the din that the candles flickered and the ladies grew pale. Trublot, found wanting as a bass, was again being tried as a baritone. The five tenors, however, made the greatest effect, especially Octave; Clotilde was sorry that she had not entrusted him with a solo. As the voices fell and, with the aid of the soft pedal, she imitated the footfall of a patrol departing in the distance, there was loud applause and both she and the gentlemen were showered with compliments. Meanwhile, in the adjoining room, behind a triple row of black coats, Duveyrier could be seen clenching his teeth so as not to shout out in anguish, while his jaw was all askew and his blotches inflamed and bleeding.

Then, when the tea was served, the same set filed past, with the same teacups, the same sandwiches. For a moment Father Mauduit stood alone in the middle of the empty drawing-room. Through the wide-open door he watched the throng of guests and, as though vanquished, smiled as once more he threw the cloak of religion over this corrupt bourgeois society, as if he were some master of ceremonies, veiling the canker in an attempt to delay the final moment of decomposition. Then, as usual on Saturdays, when it struck twelve the guests departed one by one. Campardon was one of the first to leave, accompanied by the other Madame Campardon; Léon and Madame Dambreville were not long in following, quite like husband and wife. Verdier had long since disappeared, when Madame Josserand took Hortense off with her, scolding her for what she called her sentimental obstinacy. Uncle Bachelard, who had got very drunk on punch, kept Madame Juzeur talking at the door for a moment. Her advice, based on wide experience, he found quite refreshing. Trublot, who had pocketed some sugar to take to Adèle, was going to make a getaway by the back stairs but, seeing Berthe and Auguste in the hall, he became embarrassed and pretended to be looking for his hat.

Just at this moment Octave and his wife, accompanied by Clotilde, also came out and asked for their wraps. There was an awkward pause. The hall was not large; Berthe and Madame Mouret were squeezed against each other, while Hippolyte was turning everything upside-down. They smiled at each other. Then, when the door was opened, the two men, Octave and Auguste, brought face to face, stepped aside and bowed politely. At last Berthe consented to pass first, while slight bows were exchanged. Then

Valérie, who was leaving with Théophile, gave Octave another glance, the glance of an affectionate, disinterested friend, as much as to say that they two alone were able to tell each other everything.

'Goodbye!' said Clotilde graciously to the two couples before going back to the drawing-room.

Octave suddenly stopped short. Downstairs he caught sight of Auguste's new partner going away, the dapper little fair man. Saturnin, who had come down from Marie's, was squeezing his hands in a wild outburst of affection, as he stammered, 'Friend, friend, friend!' At first he felt a strange twinge of jealousy; then he smiled. The past came back, with visions of his bygone affairs and reminiscences of his whole Parisian campaign—the complaisance of that good little Marie Pichon; Valérie's rebuff, of which he had a fond recollection; his stupid intrigue with Berthe, which he regretted as so much lost time. Now he had achieved what he had come to do. Paris was conquered; and he gallantly followed her whom in his heart he still styled Madame Hédouin, stooping at times to prevent her train from catching in the stair-rods.

Once again the house had resumed its grand air of bourgeois dignity. He fancied he could hear the faint echo of Marie's plaintive ballad. In the hall he met Jules coming home; Madame Vuillaume was dangerously ill, and refused to see her daughter. Everybody had gone; the doctor and the priest were the last to leave, still arguing. Trublot had slyly crept up to see Adèle, and the deserted staircase slumbered in its warm atmosphere, with its chaste portals shut close upon so many righteous hearths. One o'clock was striking when Monsieur Gourd, whom Madame Gourd was snugly awaiting in bed, turned out the gas. Then the whole house was plunged into solemn darkness, lulled by chaste and virtuous dreams. Not a trace of indecency remained; life fell back to its usual level of apathy and boredom.

The next morning, when Trublot had gone after watching over her like a tender parent, Adèle dragged herself down to her kitchen to allay suspicion. During the night it had thawed, and she was opening the window, feeling stifled, when Hippolyte shouted up furiously from the bottom of the narrow courtyard:

'Eh, you sluts! Who's been emptying the slops out of the window again? Madame's dress is totally messed up!'

He had hung one of Madame Duveyrier's gowns out to dry after getting the mud off it, and had found it splashed with greasy slops. Then all the maids from the top of the house to the bottom looked out of their windows and violently denied the charge. The sluice was opened, and filthy language surged up out of this stinking sewer. When it thawed the walls dripped with damp, and a stench arose from the dark little courtyard. All the secret corruptions of each floor seemed to fuse into each other in this stinking drain.

'It wasn't me,' said Adèle, leaning over. 'I've only just come down.'

Lisa looked up sharply.

'Hullo! So you're on your legs again? What was the matter then? Did you nearly kick the bucket?'

'Yes, I had stomach-ache real bad, I can tell you.'

This interruption put a stop to the quarrel. The new maidservants of Berthe and Valérie, christened 'The Big Camel' and 'The Little Donkey' respectively, stared at Adèle's pale face. Victoire and Julie both wanted to have a look at her, and craned their necks in the attempt. They both suspected something, for it was not normal for someone to writhe about and groan in that way.

'Perhaps you ate something that didn't agree with you,' said Lisa.

The others burst out laughing, and there was another flood of filthy talk, while the unfortunate girl stammered out in her fright:

'Just shut up with your foul jokes. I'm bad enough as it is. Do you want to finish me off?'

Of course not. They didn't want to go that far. She was the biggest fool going, and dirty enough to make the whole neighbourhood sick, but they were too clannish to want to do her any harm. So, naturally, they vented their spite on their employers, and discussed the previous night's party with an air of profound disgust.

'So it seems they've all made it up again, eh?' asked Victoire as she sipped her syrup and brandy.

Hippolyte, sponging madame's gown, replied:

'None of 'em 'ave got any more feelings than my old boots! When they spit in each other's faces they wash themselves with it, to make you believe they're clean.'

'It's better that they've made up, though,' said Lisa, ' 'cos otherwise it would soon be our turn.'

Suddenly there was a panic. A door opened and the maids rushed back to their kitchens. Then Lisa said it was only little Angèle.

There was nothing to fear with the child; she was all right. And from
the black hole all the resentment of the domestics arose once more
amid the stale, poisonous smell of the thaw. All the dirty linen of the
previous two years was now being washed. How glad they were not
to belong to the bourgeoisie when they saw their masters living in
this filthy state, and liking it too, for they were always getting up to
their tricks all over again.

'Eh! you up there!' suddenly shouted Victoire, 'was it old
Twisted-face who gave you that stomach-ache?'

Crude laughter echoed round the stinking cesspool. Hippolyte
actually tore madame's dress; but he didn't care, it was far too good
for her as it was. 'The Big Camel!' and 'The Little Donkey' split
their sides laughing as they looked out over their windowsills.
Meanwhile Adèle, terrified and dizzy with weakness, reeled backwards. Above the coarse shouting came her answer:

'You're all heartless! When you're dying I'll come and dance
round your beds!'

'Ah, mademoiselle,' continued Lisa, leaning over to address Julie,
'you must be really pleased to be leaving this rotten house next week!
My word! It makes you bad in spite of yourself. I hope you'll find
something better.'

Julie, with bare arms all bloody from cleaning a turbot for dinner,
leant out again by the side of the footman. She shrugged her
shoulders and, in conclusion, delivered herself of the following
philosophic declaration:

'Dear me, mademoiselle, if it's this hole or that hole it doesn't
matter. They're all pretty much alike. If you've been in one of 'em
you've been in 'em all. They're just pig-sties.'

EXPLANATORY NOTES

3 *November afternoon*: the action of the novel takes place between November 1861 and December 1863.

Plassans: Plassans, the origin of the Rougon-Macquart family, is Zola's fictional name for Aix-en-Provence. Octave Mouret is the son of François and Marthe Mouret, the protagonists of *The Conquest of Plassans* (1873) and grandchildren of Tante Dide, the ancestor of the whole family (*The Fortune of the Rougons*).

4 *Le Moniteur*: the quasi-official organ of the Imperial regime.

9 *every day*: rents increased very rapidly during the Second Empire, chiefly because of Baron Haussmann's spectacular redevelopment of Paris, which caused land and property values to skyrocket.

opera house: Charles Garnier's grandiose opera house (the one we know today) was built between 1862 and 1874. The 'big thoroughfare' between the Bourse (France's Stock Exchange) and the Opéra was to be called the Avenue du Dix-Décembre, renamed the Rue du Quatre-Septembre after the fall of the Empire on 3 September 1870. Its construction was officially announced in August 1864, but work on it did not begin until late 1868 (and was completed in 1869).

10 *Gazette de France*: the oldest newspaper in France, founded by Théophraste Renaudot in 1631. During the Second Empire it was the organ of the Legitimist (monarchist) party.

11 *left it*: Octave Mouret is only tenuously connected to the genealogical tree of the Rougon-Macquart. The action of *The Conquest of Plassans* extends from 1858 to 1864—in other words, it overlaps substantially with the action of *Pot Luck*, yet there is no reference in *Pot Luck* (or *The Ladies' Paradise*) to the tragic fate of Octave's parents as described in *The Conquest of Plassans*: it is as if Octave is disconnected from his own family.

16 *gas*: the gradual displacement of oil lighting by gas lighting represented a major change in the nineteenth-century urban environment. Gaslight spread throughout Paris during the 1840s; by the 1850s 3,000 new gas lamps had been installed on the streets, along with the practice of all-night lighting, and the main boulevards were fully equipped with gas lamps in 1857. During the Second Empire gaslight, like the railway, reigned supreme as a symbol of human and industrial progress. See Wolfgang Schivelbusch, *Disenchanted Night: The Industrialization of Light in the Nineteenth Century* (Berkeley: University of California Press, 1988).

22 '*. . . like that!*': see note to p. 226.

24 *Le Temps*: the newspaper of the moderate liberals.

27 *Jocelyn*: a long lyrical poem by the Romantic poet Alphonse de Lamartine (1790–1869).

saint's day: or 'name day' is, according to Catholic custom, the feast day of the saint after whom a person is named.

43 *Béranger*: Pierre-Jean de Béranger (1780–1857) was an extremely popular songwriter.

50 *throat*: a lump in the throat was considered at the time to be a hysterical symptom.

52 *Dame Blanche*: a comic opera (1825) by François Adrien Boieldieu, some of whose tunes were highly popular thoughout the nineteenth century.

54 *'Girl with a Broken Pitcher'*: Jean-Baptiste Greuze (1725–1805) was a painter of sentimental genre subjects. This painting, considered to be his masterpiece, was reproduced many times throughout the nineteenth century.

66 *uplifting*: Monsieur Vuillaume's eulogistic remarks about George Sand's novel (1834) indicate, through ironic inversion, Zola's views on the noxious effects of this type of romantic literature on girls whose upbringing was as cloistered as that of Marie Pichon. Campardon, it is noted, owns Sand's complete works.

sacrifices: the piano was a supreme emblem of bourgeois culture: it is the focal point of Clotilde Duveyrier's social activity, one of Berthe Josserand's vital weapons in her quest for a husband, and a telling symbol of Clarisse's social rise.

69 *chlorotic*: chlorosis (also called green-sickness) is a benign type of iron-deficiency anaemia in adolescent girls, marked by a pale yellow-green complexion.

83 *Salon*: the annual exhibition of contemporary art in Paris sponsored by the Académie des Beaux-Arts.

84 *Pope*: since November 1860 the Chamber of Deputies and the Senate had debated the Emperor's speech opening each parliamentary session. The reference here is to the debate in February 1862 on the Roman question, which opposed the partisans of Italian unification, with Rome as capital, and their Catholic adversaries, who defended the temporal power of the Pope (the policy of the party in the Catholic Church that favoured enhancing the Pope's power and authority being called 'ultramontanism'). Napoleon III, anxious to secure the Catholic vote, had despatched a French force to Rome in April 1849. The French troops fought their way into the city and ejected the Republicans. A French garrison remained there to guarantee the territorial rights of the restored Pope. When the Kingdom of Italy was proclaimed in 1861, Rome remained outside it and became a magnet for patriotic Italians, led by Garibaldi (see note to p. 215).

85 *Orleanist*: supporter of the Orléans branch of the former French royal family and of its claim to the throne of France through descent from the younger brother of Louis XIV.

Mexican Expedition: French troops fought in Mexico from 1862 to 1865 in support of the Archduke Maximilian as emperor of that country. In 1867 Maximilian was captured and executed and a republic was set up in Mexico.

88 *Benediction of the Poniards*: this is a famous scene from Giacomo Meyerbeer's opera *The Huguenots*, with a libretto by Eugène Scribe and Émile Deschamps (1836).

93 *Revue des Deux Mondes*: a generally conservative intellectual review, founded in 1829.

131 *red ribbon*: the emblem of the Legion of Honour.

143 *. . . benedicimus*: 'Bless, O Lord our God, this wedding-ring which we bless in Thy name . . .'

155 *modern society*: an allusion to Émile Augier's *Le Fils de Giboyer*, first performed at the Comédie Française on 1 December 1862.

162 *streets of Paris*: this passage anticipates the themes of *The Ladies' Paradise*, which describes Octave's creation of the first great Parisian department store.

176 *Mignon yearning for Heaven*: an engraving based on a famous painting of 1839 by Ary Scheffer (1795–1858).

Fountain of Vaucluse: a famous spring 28 kilometres from Avignon.

181 *Zémire et Azor*: a comic opera by André Grétry, with a libretto by Jean-François Marmontel, first performed in 1771.

208 *'. . . real life'*: Zola's veneration for Balzac (whom he saw as a forerunner of Naturalism) contrasts with his contempt for the escapist literature represented, so he thought, by George Sand.

215 *seriously*: the parliamentary elections under discussion took place on 31 May 1863. The candidates for the second constituency of Paris, which encompassed the Palais-Royal and the Place Gaillon districts (in which the action of *Pot Luck* takes place), included Thiers and Dewinck. Dewinck, the sitting member, was the government's candidate; but in the event the prominent veteran politician Adolphe Thiers was elected. Thiers became a forceful critic of Napoleon III's handling of European problems, and after the fall of the Empire became President (1871–3) of the Third Republic.

'. . . heart!': Garibaldi attempted to seize Rome in August 1862 but was wounded in the foot and captured by Italian troops at Aspromonte before making contact with the French. See note to p. 215.

Roman question: see note to p. 84.

226 *'. . . like that!'*: a precise echo of the phrase used by Madame Josserand: see p. 22.

269 *Public Instruction*: as a diocesan architect, Campardon is responsible to the Ministry of Public Instruction and Religion—an amalgamation of Public Instruction and Ecclesiastical Affairs.

304 *Foyot's*: one of the most famous restaurants in Paris—in the Rue de Tournon, on the corner of the Rue de Vaugirard.

353 *Mazas*: a prison in Paris, built in 1850.

366 *The Life of Jesus*: Ernest Renan's rationalistic study of the life of Jesus, published in 1863, created a scandal by denying miracle or mystery of any kind; Jesus himself was treated as a historical figure personifying resistance to state authority.

Rouher: Eugène Rouher replaced Billault as leader of the government in the Chamber of Deputies on 18 October 1863. He was the model for Eugène Rougon, the protagonist of Zola's novel about the political system of the Second Empire, *His Excellency Eugène Rougon*.

A SELECTION OF   **OXFORD WORLD'S CLASSICS**

ÉMILE ZOLA

L'Assommoir
The Attack on the Mill
La Bête humaine
La Débâcle
Germinal
The Kill
The Ladies' Paradise
The Masterpiece
Nana
Pot Luck
Thérèse Raquin

*The
Oxford
World's
Classics
Website*

www.worldsclassics.co.uk

- Information about new titles
- Explore the full range of Oxford World's Classics
- Links to other literary sites and the main OUP webpage
- Imaginative competitions, with bookish prizes
- Peruse the Oxford World's Classics Magazine
- Articles by editors
- Extracts from Introductions
- A forum for discussion and feedback on the series
- Special information for teachers and lecturers

www.worldsclassics.co.uk

American Literature

British and Irish Literature

Children's Literature

Classics and Ancient Literature

Colonial Literature

Eastern Literature

European Literature

History

Medieval Literature

Oxford English Drama

Poetry

Philosophy

Politics

Religion

The Oxford Shakespeare

A complete list of Oxford Paperbacks, including Oxford World's Classics, Oxford Shakespeare, Oxford Drama, and Oxford Paperback Reference, is available in the UK from the Academic Division Publicity Department, Oxford University Press, Great Clarendon Street, Oxford OX2 6DP.

In the USA, complete lists are available from the Paperbacks Marketing Manager, Oxford University Press, 198 Madison Avenue, New York, NY 10016.

Oxford Paperbacks are available from all good bookshops. In case of difficulty, customers in the UK can order direct from Oxford University Press Bookshop, Freepost, 116 High Street, Oxford OX1 4BR, enclosing full payment. Please add 10 per cent of published price for postage and packing.